TATTERED BODIES

THE BROKEN SERIES

BOOK 3

SHAE RUBY

Tattered Bodies Copyright © 2023 by Shae Ruby

All rights reserved.

No portion of this book may be reproduced in any form, or stored in a retrieval system, or transmitted in any form or by any means, electronic, mechanical, photocopying, recording or otherwise, without written permission from the publisher. It is illegal to copy this book, post it to a website, or distribute it by any others means without permission, except for the use of brief quotations in a book review.

This novel is entirely a work of fiction. The names, characters, and incidents portrayed in it are the work of the author's imagination. Any resemblance to people, living or dead, and events is entirely coincidental.

ISBN: 979-8-9860000-5-3

Cover Design by: Quirky Circe
Edited by: Lunar Rose Editing Services
Formatted by: Champagne Book Design at champagnebookdesign.com
Published by: Shae Ruby

Now we heal.

PLAYLIST

Eat Your Young—Arankai
Never Know—Bad Omens
Limits—Bad Omens
Digging My Own Grave—Five Finger Death Punch
Popular Monster—Falling in Reverse
Panic Room—Au/Ra
Love Chained—Cannons
Side Effects—Carlie Hanson
Make Hate to Me—Citizen Soldier
Numb—Envy on the Coast
Relate—FJ Outlaw
Blackout—Freya Ridings
Serotonin—girl in red
Pill—Heuse & Zeus x Chrona ft Emma Sameth
Upperdrugs—Highly Suspect
The Loneliest—Maneskin
Dial Tone—Catch Your Breath
Can You Feel My Heart—Bring Me The Horizon
Mine—Sleep Token
Disease—Bear Tooth
F**K About It—Waterparks ft blackbear
Heartless—The Weekend
Drowned in Emotion—Caskets
Home—Cavetown
The End of Heartache—Killswitch Engage
Sabotage—Thousand Below

You can find the complete playlist on Spotify.

TRIGGER WARNINGS

Hello reader,

I write dark stories that can be disturbing to some. My books are not for the faint of heart, and my characters, many times, are not redeemable. This book contains dark themes to include graphic sex scenes, sharing the FMC, obsession, choking/breath play, blood play, dubious consent, mentions of sexual abuse, physical abuse, **graphic rape**, **graphic murder**, **torture**, drug use and abuse, mental health disorders, self-harm, suicidal thoughts with a plan, suicide attempt, and captivity.

I trust you know your triggers before proceeding, and always remember to take care of your mental health.

For more things Shae Ruby, visit authorshaeruby.com

National Suicide Prevention

If You Know Someone in Crisis:

Call the National Suicide Prevention Lifeline (Lifeline) at **1-800-273-TALK (8255),** or text the Crisis Text Line (**text HELLO to 741741**). Both services are free and available 24 hours a day, seven days a week. All calls are confidential. Contact social media outlets directly if you are concerned about a friend's social media updates or dial 911 in an emergency.

Is there no way out of the mind?
-Sylvia Plath-

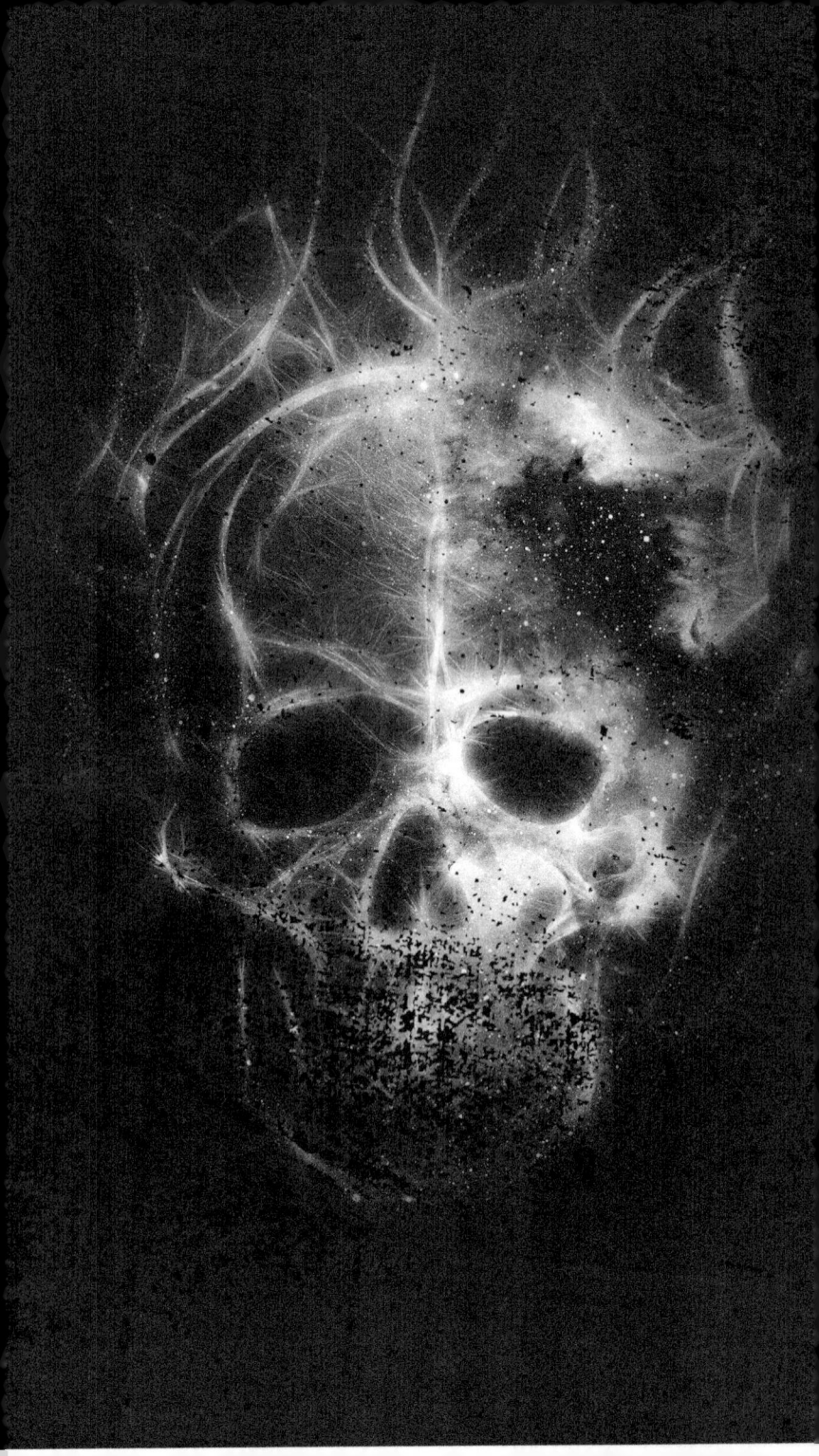

THE CAPTIVE

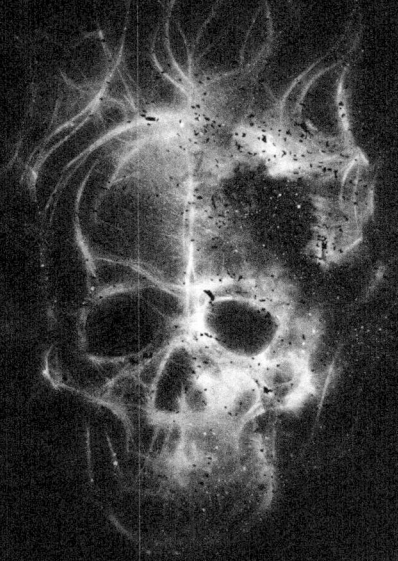

CHAPTER 1

Damien

The sting of betrayal cuts deep when inflicted by the one person you love most in the world. I'm not saying I don't deserve it. In fact, I know I do. For some deluded reason though, I never imagined it would be Hallie giving me a taste of my own medicine. I thought I knew pain before now, but nothing compares to this helpless feeling coursing through my body as I watch her run up the stairs and out the door. To her fate. Her fucking undoing.

I grab the bedsheets and bring them to my side, trying to stop the bleeding as much as possible, but it just keeps pouring out of the gaping wound. It's as open as the hole in my weak fucking heart and soaking the sheets faster than I can replace them. The phone sits on the bed right next to my knee, mocking me, and I pick it up and attempt to get off the bed.

Hot, searing, soul-crushing pain invades my body, stealing my breath as I clutch my side and lean into it. My feet must weigh at least a thousand pounds each, and my small shuffles toward the stairs won't get me anywhere any time soon. Somehow, I still have a small glimmer of hope that Hallie didn't get far. Maybe I could still find her if she ran on foot. My truck keys are too far from me, but what she probably didn't remember from the airport is that I keep a spare hidden behind my front license plate.

It takes insane effort to put one foot in front of the other and climb the stairs, more like crawl up them, on all fours. After what feels like hours, and at least seven pauses, I finally reach the top. The basement door is wide open. She didn't give me much of a chance here.

Does she even fucking care?

Did she lie about loving me?

She threw me to the fucking wolves. I'm actually lucky no one is in this house finishing what they started.

Hallie didn't just stab my side, she also stabbed me in the back and the heart. I can't even believe she did it. I didn't see that shit coming at all. Not in a million years. Yet here I am, remembering her sweaty hand on my knife, plunging it deep between my ribs. The look in her eyes when she did it, the way she apologized before pulling it out, will haunt my nightmares until I find her again. The way she cried, looking at me like a deer in headlights, will be tattooed into my broken heart forever. I will, however, never accept her goodbye, like I was nothing to her. 'I was never meant to stay,' she said to me. Well, fuck that, I'm getting her back. And she's fucking staying.

Rage pulses through me, directing my steps to the garage with newfound energy, even through the pain. I'm going to find her, probably in the fucking woods somewhere, and drag her to the truck by the fucking hair. I might be all fucked up right now, but she's not stronger than me.

The spare keys are exactly where I left them last, and even though the truck is freezing, I definitely don't have time to warm it up. My shirt is completely soaked in blood, and I shiver as I close the door, turn the key in the ignition, and attempt to blast the heat. Fuck me, because that shit is blowing colder air than outside.

I peel out of the garage, not giving a fuck about the pile of snow behind the truck, and pause to look around. I don't expect to see her. She's probably deep in the woods, knowing her. But she just won't stop making stupid fucking choices. She didn't even have snow boots on, for fuck's sake. I lower my window a few inches, just in case I can hear her, and scan the snow for any signs of her. Just a few seconds later, I spot her tiny little fucking footprints leading toward a tree line, and I start driving toward it. As I get closer, though, I hear a scream, and suddenly everything is silent again.

Fuck.

What the fuck have you done, Hallie?

I drive toward the sound, but by the time I get there, all that is left is her black running shoe and spattered blood on the snow.

No. *No.*

Sharp pain shoots up my side as my fists repeatedly land on the steering wheel, making my wound feel like it's on fire and opening even more. I try to take deep breaths, but it's getting more challenging and even more painful by the minute. I hate to say it, but maybe now is the time to go to a hospital. I'm in no shape to go after her. I only have two weapons in this vehicle, and knowing what I know, they will be driving straight to wherever the fuck they're headed. Mexico, I assume. They will not be making any stops unless absolutely necessary, and they sure as fuck will not be staying anywhere for me to catch up to. As far as I'm concerned though, I will not make it very far with broken ribs and a stab wound, so there's no way I can save her right now.

I take the next right turn and head into town on the main road. Right about now, I'm grateful for my off-road tires and the traction they provide, because I need to speed to the hospital at this point.

A violent cough takes over me, making me double over onto the steering wheel as I finally make it into town. Bile rises to the back of my throat, and it tastes like I'm sucking on pennies. When I attempt to swallow it down, it starts to pour out of my mouth. I bring my hand to my chin to wipe it off, just to realize it's fucking blood. Goddamnit, I better not die from internal bleeding because someone has to go after this little bitch.

Yeah, I think I kind of fucking hate her right now, but can I really blame her for wanting to leave? Even though it was for the best, I did keep her prisoner. She already didn't want to be with me, but I can imagine it pissed her off even more when I did that. But whatever, she needs to get over herself and realize I was trying to help her. Now she's well and truly fucked.

I manage to park the truck—like fucking shit, by the way, but I'm injured, so they need to give me a break—and wobble across the parking lot and into the emergency department's lobby. I don't make it very far, though. In fact, just a few feet from the receptionist's desk, I collapse.

My body feels cold, heavy, numb. Something is fucking wrong. Probably due to the fact I've lost half my body weight in blood, but hey, no big deal.

Thanks, Hallie.

There's a commotion, and I don't have to turn my head to know that every nurse available is rushing to me right about now. My eyes become unfocused on the ceiling lights, and floating, little, white orbs take over my vision. I barely register myself moving. I'm assuming they're carrying me somewhere, but my eyes can't stay open anymore, either.

I'm aware that I should hate Hallie right about now. Maybe I do hate her a little, at least, but not for the reasons I should. Somehow, I don't hate her for stabbing me. No. I fucking hate her because she made me love her, risk everything for her, then she rejected me. I gave her all of me, and she shit on it. She fucked me over, when all I've ever done is protect her and try to get us to a safe place. Fucking dramatic for her to leave me behind just to get captured.

The problem is, no matter how much I hate her, or tell myself that I do, I can't abandon her. She wouldn't survive what she just got herself into—no. The cartel isn't going to play games with her, and she's too stubborn to give in to what they want. If she doesn't fold, they will break her. Which is why I have to fucking find her, and I really, *really* need to hurry.

My anxiety grows the more days that pass me by without being able to locate her. I've been in the hospital for a week, life-flighted to Denver due to head trauma and a stab injury. I've been told I'm almost done here and need to take it easy for at least six weeks. Anything could pop my stitches, according to them. Sudden movements, exercise, killing people. The usual. It's a good thing I know how to stitch myself up. Either way, the real hindrance is the broken ribs. At least they are healing. They're not exactly where they need to be, so I do need to take it easy for a few more days until they feel back to normal.

I hate to think about what got me here. How I barely made it to the hospital before I became unconscious, and for a split second before I faded, I didn't think I'd ever wake up again. The feeling of panic that gripped my chest was unlike any I'd ever felt before, but then I woke up. I woke up, and she wasn't there. It wasn't a nightmare. *I didn't protect her.*

That feeling still has me by the throat, the white walls of this hospital room choking me, closing in on me, driving me fucking insane. I don't care what it takes, I'm going to find her and get her back. Just so I can kill her, then fuck her. She deserves that much for stabbing me.

There must be a reason why the cartel let me live. They're not careless enough to leave me behind by accident. Why did they leave me in that house? Did they know she stabbed me? Or maybe they want me to live in fear, looking over my shoulder constantly until one of them decides to show up and make me pay for my transgressions. I want to say I have no regrets, that I wouldn't change anything, but that's simply not true. There's so much I would do differently, starting with running away with

Hallie instead of going back to Texas in the first place. But it's too late now to think about what I should've done. Now I need to come up with a plan on how I'm getting her out of this.

I ask myself every day why the hell I want to look for her in the first place. She stabbed me, almost killed me. It's possible she may have felt it was the only way to save herself, and I can relate to that. Sometimes when you're cornered, forced to do something you don't want to, you do things you don't mean to do. I'm choosing to believe she didn't actually want to kill me, that she meant what she said when she told me she loved me. I know her heart is split in half, but I know there's also no fucking way I'm letting her choose anyone but me.

I think I owe it to her to get her out of this mess. She wouldn't be in it if I didn't bring her to Breck. Or maybe I just want her back. I want to get on my knees and beg her to take me back, plead with her to forgive me. I don't think I'll ever forgive myself for what I've done to her, but she's a better person than me. She's always been.

Somehow, in a moment of weakness, I thought it would be a good idea to call my father and tell him what happened. He more than likely feels relieved that she's finally been handed over, but what he doesn't understand is that I will not be giving up. I will not rest until I've found her, and right now, they're hiding her under fucking rocks. There's no trace of her at all, which is why I'm risking my life by having my father visit me at the hospital. I'm surprised he showed up at all. I thought he didn't give a shit whether I lived or died, but I guess I can be wrong sometimes. Or he just wants to find me in a vulnerable state and finally turn me in, put us all out of our misery.

If it wasn't for Hallie and the fate that awaits her—the new life she's living while my hands have been tied and I haven't been able to look for her—I would've surrendered myself and let them kill me. This entire situation is just exhausting.

Who wants to live on the run for the rest of their lives? Maybe the nurse's hand will slip the next time she gives me morphine, and I will overdose. I don't think it would be so easy though, so I guess fuck me.

Although maybe it's a good thing death hasn't opened its gates for me yet, because then I wouldn't have gotten to experience my father in all of his glory, with a look of despair on his face. Even now, it's a bit jarring as he stands in front of me. I once thought that if something like this happened, it would bring me happiness to know he gives a damn about me, but as it stands, all I feel is confusion. Why has he treated me like shit for years on end if he cares about me? Why does he want to see me now? What are his real intentions? Can I trust him? *You can't trust anyone.*

Victor stands at the foot of the hospital bed, gently holding my leg over the blankets. He doesn't move, barely even breathes as he watches me. I may have been pretending to be asleep for the past twenty minutes, or so it feels like, but I still feel his stare burning right through me.

"Are you going to stand there and stare all day?" I ask him, finally opening my eyes. He's clad in a suit, which of course he is. He probably doesn't own anything else. Victor lets go of my leg to adjust his cufflinks. "Or are you going to turn me in so I can finally die?"

"Neither," he replies gruffly. His blue eyes, just like my own, are cold and dead. There's no kindness in them. Maybe a tinge of sadness and regret, if I look close enough. Who knows though, everything is an act when it comes to him. He only cares about what benefits him. "I wanted to make sure you're in one piece, before I never see you again." I don't even know how to feel about that. There are too many things going through my mind. Does he actually care enough about me to want to see me one last time, or is this him trying to turn me in to the cartel and save his own ass?

I chuckle as I look at his dark hair, hating him even more. I can't be sure if I'm glad I look more like my mother than him. "How very fatherly of you. But of course, you wouldn't know anything about parenting if it slapped you in the face. Where was this attitude when we were with Mom? Where were you then? She could've died and instead—"

Victor sighs, the way he always does when I'm in his presence, like he couldn't be more annoyed with me. "Aren't you tired of the bullshit, Damien?" Yes. No. I don't know. I don't care enough to think about it right now. Or maybe I do, but it doesn't matter anymore. "Anyway, I've gone back to the safe house and collected your suitcase with money, weapons, and some belongings. I wouldn't recommend going back there. They've probably sent more men to hunt you down at this point."

My face must show my surprise, since my father chuckles and goes to sit in the chair near my bed, pulling it closer to talk to me. "You didn't think I wasn't keeping tabs on you, did you?"

I don't know what to think. However my father keeping tabs on me, following me, tracking me in general, did not readily cross my mind. That was clearly a stupid mistake. Now I wonder how long he's known about my safe house in Breckenridge. Suppose he's had people watching me, Hallie, or even both of us. I'd rather not think about all the implications that accompany that reality. Instead, I lean my head back on the pillow and look at the ceiling for a brief moment before letting my eyes flutter closed.

"Do they have her?" I know there was no way for her to escape. So why am I hurting myself by asking the obvious? Why do I need to hear it? Will it make it more real if someone says it out loud?

"You can't be serious," my father replies. "You know the cartel took her, and before you tell me not to assume, I know this for a fact."

"What about Zayne?" I fist my hands on the bed, grabbing the rough waffle blanket they put over me. For some reason, something is fishy. I didn't see him die. In fact, once the car flipped, I didn't see much of anything at all.

"What about him?" To someone else, my father may appear serious, the picture of calm. To me, he looks like a goddamn fucking liar. He's the kind of man who uses questions to answer questions to distract you from the true answer, just so he can divulge all your secrets, your deepest darkest thoughts. "Oh, wait, don't tell me you care about him too?"

I breathe in slowly, and he smiles at my annoyance. One of these days, I'm going to make him pay for everything he's done to me, with interest. "Is he dead like I wanted him to be?"

"You see, the problem with you is that you believe I care about what you want when it comes to this job." I tense, and the veins in my neck feel like they're bulging. I don't want to show my true feelings about the matter. In fact, I want to look outraged, absolutely pissed off that he didn't go through with it. When in reality, all I feel is relief. If Hallie ever found out I was responsible for his death, it wouldn't matter how many times I rescued her. She'd fucking hate me forever. "But I'm the boss here, and you best remember that."

My eyes almost roll in annoyance, but I force myself to remain calm and collected. "So what did you do then?"

His smile makes the hairs on my arms stand on end, a very disturbing feeling coursing through me. "What I do best," The way his footsteps sound as they get closer to my side of the bed makes me want to throttle him. "I sold him."

My stomach drops, and I'd probably throw up if I didn't have an empty stomach. It might be easier to get my father to give me information about Zayne's buyer than Hallie's, but I'll have to take what I get.

I will say, however, of all the things I thought I'd be doing after Hallie stabbed me and left me to die—looking for Zayne wasn't one of them. I have a theory though, and I think he will be close to wherever Hallie is. Maybe that's a long shot, except I'm fucking desperate. I have to have faith that it'll be easier to find her once I get to him.

I force myself to chuckle, even though I'm scared for him deep down. "About fucking time someone made him suffer." The smirk on my face makes my father smile, and I know I'm snaring him in my trap. He just doesn't know it. "You're doing me a bigger favor than you think, *Dad*. Prolonging his pain brings me more joy than a quick death."

Do I hate Zayne? Hell yes, I fucking do. Did I want him dead? Also yes. However, now that he might lead me to her, I don't care about my feelings.

"You should've seen Carl's face when I told him I had a male in his early twenties." Victor adjusts his tie with a proud look on his face. God, my father is truly fucking sick. The things that disgust me make him the happiest, and I'm not disgusted by much. I know I've been involved in this for a decade, yet it has never brought me an ounce of joy. On the other hand, Victor would kill someone every day and bathe in their blood if he could. Instead, he has to run the business. "That man does depraved things to his slaves."

I want to snap at him not to call anyone that. It's fucking degrading and revolting. But I have to be quiet for once, hold my damn tongue so his can become looser.

I have no fucking clue who that man is, but I sure plan to find out. "Good." I nod, "I want him to be in pain."

My father looks curious for a moment, "Why do you hate him, Damien?"

My eyes narrow of their own accord, and I force myself to relax. Why the fuck does he care now, anyway? This conversation is getting tedious, and even though I could be discharged today, I still have had many surgeries to repair my insides from this stupid stab wound between my ribs. There's an incessant throbbing at my side, much like my incessant father, who won't shut the fuck up.

"He was getting in my way, and you know how I usually take care of that." The hospital room makes me shiver, and now that I'm in a lower level of care, it's a smaller space so it feels even colder here than in the ICU. "I hope they hang him for everyone to see when they're done with him."

Even if I don't mean that, my father hears the hatred in my voice. The feelings are not forced, in fact, they come naturally. I do hate him. I just also need him.

"Juarez is the perfect place for that to happen." Victor shrugs, then smooths down the front of his suit like it got a crease from the small movement. "So, nothing to worry about on that front."

Bingo motherfucker.

Victor's eyes widen, and his mouth sets in a thin line at his own revelation. It was too easy to get him to run his mouth. Maybe I should pretend to like him more often. It's like one entire conversation made him soft. I'd hate to see what he'd divulge over some pussy, and yet he was the one giving me shit about that same damn thing.

"Indeed it is." The smile on my face is of pure contentment now, and I hope he believes it's over Zayne's suffering and doesn't see right through me. He must know I'm not giving up on her. "Thank you for dropping my belongings off. I really appreciate it." Saves me a trip and probably a beating at the very least. He's doing me a solid before I disappear for good. Actually, he's doing me more of a favor than he knows by giving me my fake identities and passports.

Victor's face falls, and I can't tell if it's from the realization of what he just divulged or if he's sad that I just hinted at him to leave the room. That's what people do to politely kick someone out, right? Tell them thanks for whatever it may be. This might be the last time I see my father, but it's not hitting me as hard as I expected.

"Son." He fidgets, shifting his weight from one foot to the other. There's no way in hell I'm seeing correctly, because there are tears in Victor Carlisle's eyes. He reaches for my leg again and squeezes it softly. "I'm sorry." A knot gets lodged in my throat, making breathing difficult. One lone tear trails down my right cheek, and I look away from him. "I should've done more, been better... I'm sorry I took you away from your brothers."

I don't reply.

"I'm sorry I wasn't a better father, Damien." At my name, I do stare at him. My blue eyes clash with his, and he grabs my hands. "I know there's nothing I can do to improve it, and that's why I'm here. There's double the money in your suitcase and a burner phone. Anything you need, you call me from that, and I will help you. It doesn't matter what it is."

"You'd risk your life to help me?" My hoarse voice breaks, and tears fall down Victor's cheeks now too.

"I've always loved you, son." A slow squeeze to my hand, "I'm just terrible at showing it."

With that, he lets go, turns around, and walks toward the door. My chest squeezes as he reaches for the doorknob, "I love you too, Dad." I sniffle, "Thank you."

Victor walks back swiftly toward the bed and embraces me, and I can tell he's holding back in order to spare my injuries. My ribs scream in pain at the sudden movement, but my inner child feels strangely… at peace.

As I watch him walk down the hallway, I feel a new book has just begun. Twenty years of trauma will never be erased, but it's a step in the right direction. The lost little boy in me has finally found a map and a compass, and I'm ready to embark on a new journey. One where my past doesn't haunt me. Only for that, I need to set my future up for success, and I can't do that until all my unfinished business is resolved.

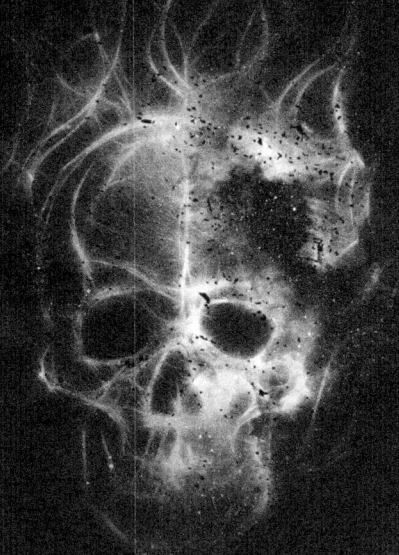

CHAPTER 2

Hallie

My wrists burn from the zip ties they've been using on me, the skin shredded where the plastic assaults it. I probably did it to myself, and even though it hurts like a bitch I still don't regret it. Let's just say I haven't been the easiest captive. I won't go down without a fight, not this time. And I still have a lot of fight in me.

After two weeks in this hell hole, I can feel my mind slipping a little. It's been the same every single day. Wake up, eat bland ass food, learn from Marcela or Penelope on how to act for Michael, and go back to the room to stare at the damn walls.

Marcela and Penelope teach us how to be submissive. Always on our knees, hands clasped on our laps, eyes down. It's the only acceptable way to act here. I've been living in an old t-shirt that looks like a man's. The fit isn't that big either, so almost everything is showing. It's…different from the other girls who have to be naked at all times. I definitely get more privileges, and they clearly resent me for it. I can't blame them for it, they live even shittier than me, and that's saying a lot. However, when I go into the dungeon room where we train, I do so naked.

We practice with the guards on how to pleasure a man, and when we don't follow Marcela and Penelope's instructions, each man shows us what they like. After all, everyone has different tastes. They're allowed to do whatever they want to our bodies, except maim or kill us. With me, it's a little different. I can't be marked or hurt while they do filthy things to me. No, that's only for Michael's pleasure; he wants to be the only one who inflicts suffering upon me.

Michael still hasn't fucked me, *yet*. I think he wants to save it for when I'm at my breaking point, so emotionally exhausted that I'll do anything to make him stop treating me like shit. It's not going to happen; only he doesn't know that. However, the guards, along with Marcela and Penelope, can hurt me if I'm not obedient in other ways. Withdrawing food, continuing to drug me out of my mind, or if I'm very unlucky, they give me lashings or beat my ass into unconsciousness. That's only if I do something particularly out of character.

Even with this knowledge, I'm still not cooperating. Which is precisely why I'm covered in bruises from head to toe. Everything I do digs a deeper hole for me. When they tell me to kneel, I don't. When they force me down, I hold my head high. When they tell me to keep my hands on my lap, I refuse. I'm purposely defiant every chance I get. I even bit one of the guard's dicks. It brought me so much joy and possibly a life-threatening illness, but I don't care.

Maybe I'll be buried in the yard by the end of the month. It's not like anyone is coming for me. No, I fucked that up royally when I literally stabbed Damien and ran out of the house. There are only two possible outcomes from that choice. The first one is that he's dead and obviously can't come for me. The second being that he hates my fucking guts for betraying him and no longer cares about what happens to me. I bet he wishes me dead right about now. If it wasn't for the fact that I wish death upon myself too, I'd probably be sad.

Turning off my emotions and dissociating myself has proven to be more difficult than usual. In the past, I've been able to put my mind to it and ignore the trauma. Stay distracted by any means necessary, usually drugs, sex, or cutting. Except at the moment I don't have access to two of those options, and willingly giving a part of my body to these fucking monsters is out of the question.

Only memories of Zayne and Damien keep me going at this point, and the same images of both of them keep replaying in my mind like a broken record. Zayne running after me, his car flipping. Him telling me to hang up so I wouldn't hear them kill him. I'm sure he believed he was doing me a favor, probably thought I wouldn't survive that trauma, and maybe in a way he was right. But now I can't stop wondering what they did to him. Did they kill him? My gut churns just thinking about it, a stabbing pain to my chest, my heart. I live in despair every fucking day, crying myself to sleep every night over it.

On the other hand, when I think of Damien, I feel a pang of guilt that eats me alive from the inside out every second of the day. My heart is torn, and half of it has his name on it. I did it to myself, though. It's my fault everything ended the way it did. That's what hurts the most. The worst part? I told him I loved him, then did that shit. I've never felt lower in my life, fucking worthless. I do love him however, so at least that wasn't a lie. I love him more than life itself… so why did I do that to him?

Now that I'm here, I wish I had believed him when he said he wanted to protect me. I know in my bones he loves me. He didn't have a reason to say that to me if he didn't mean it. He also risked everything to save me, including his life. Even if the stab wound didn't kill him, the cartel probably will.

Stabbing him was the ultimate form of betrayal, yet my shaky hands, sweaty palms, and racing heart didn't stop me. I still can't believe I did it. The deep despair that I felt as I walked out of the house—more like ran—I don't think I'll ever feel that way again in my life.

Now fucking look at me, on my knees and sucking dick because I have no choice but to. I miss Damien so fucking much. It's not even about being here—it's that he completed me and knew me from the inside out. Sometimes I think even better than Zayne. He knew things about me that I couldn't share with another person, like our love for books. I regret so much how it ended, how I didn't believe him, how I should have. If I could go back, I would change everything. I would take him up on leaving the country and building a life together. Except I can't go back, and this damsel doesn't get the Prince. No, I get a fucking monster instead. I know what's coming, and Michael's mind games always work in the end.

The door to what is now my room, I fucking hate even calling it that, opens slowly, and the bright light from the hallway hurts my eyes. It's been dark for what feels like forever. I don't have a clock, no way to tell the time, and the only thing keeping me sane for now are the tally marks I've been scratching on the wall. Hopefully, no one cares about the paint, although my fingernails don't appreciate it.

Tomás comes into my room, his steps light until his boot hits the edge of my mattress. I squint up at him and see his tall, dark form, but I still can't see his face. As if he understands, he kneels beside the bed and gives me a pitying look. "I'm sorry, Hallie, but you must come with me."

"W-what?" I ask him, confused. This man is the same one who brought me here initially. He was kind to me, telling me not to fight Michael. Although he doesn't know, I have already done that for a very long time.

"Where am I going?" Images of being fucked in the ass in a dark room while Michael yanked my hair back, fill my mind. Blood running down my legs. My sliding down the bathroom wall after cleaning myself up the best I could.

He grimaces, then wipes a hand down his tan face. "Trust me

when I say you don't want to piss him off today. He's in a chaotic mood already."

"What the fuck does that even mean?"

His hand shoots out, grabs my jaw and squeezes my cheeks together. "It means you're going to hate your fucking life tonight, and there's nothing you can do about it. If you fight him, he will make me do things I don't want to do to you. Keep that in mind."

Fear crawls slowly down my spine, and it feels like all my reactions and responses are happening in slow motion. I forcefully turn my head away from him as one tear escapes, and he lets my face go. I don't want him to see more weakness than I've already shown. I'm dirty and probably smell. My wrists and ankles feel freshly shredded from the tight zip ties, and I just want to curl up into a ball and fucking die.

I have nothing left to live for either way.

I'm tired of the mind games; I know how he works. Michael wants me to be pliable, compliant, and quiet. He will punish me until he weakens me, fucking me up so much, until ultimately I have no choice and give in.

Tomás cuts the zip ties from my ankles and wrists, and I feel instant relief. Although I also feel the throbbing pain more intensely now. I should be grateful I can at least move them. If he's cutting these, it means I'm expected to participate somehow, and that's the last thing I will do. It doesn't matter what they expect of me, I will fucking fight until my last breath. I don't even care that I've been tied up for two weeks unless I'm 'serving my master'. No amount of pain from the zip ties will push me to complete madness, yet. Not when they keep numbing me to make me more compliant.

His brown eyes lock on me and his brow furrows. His black hair falling over his eyes slightly reminds me of Zayne a little, and my heart squeezes in my chest at the mere thought. They're not even that similar, except I just keep trying to find ways to find comfort in the familiar.

"Let's go," he barks at me, grabbing my upper arm roughly. Usually, he doesn't treat me like this when we're in my room, but he has to act a certain way around the other guys. Especially since all of them are loyal to Michael. I don't understand why the hell that is, but I also know I'm not in a position to ask questions. All I know is that I'm confused.

I keep my arms at my sides as he yanks me around, guiding me through the house until we go to what they call the dungeon. It's where we are taught how to serve our master. I don't feel relief though, because when we enter, Michael is standing in the middle of the room with two girls kneeling submissively at his feet, their heads bowed and hands clasped on their laps. His blond hair shines under the bright white lights that keep flickering, threatening to make me go insane, which is probably the purpose of them. His hazel eyes crinkle in the corners when he looks at me. If he weren't such a vile creature, I'd think he's handsome with his tall muscular form, but he's a piece of shit, therefore making him seem ugly in my eyes.

We go down the rough concrete steps into the open room. Metal chains with wrist clasps hang from the ceiling at the far end of the space. It's just an open room, no furniture, just a blank slate of a disgusting place with dark gray walls. It's depressing.

"There you are, baby girl." Michael and I make eye contact, and I'm suddenly swatted on the back with something sharp. I cry out from the sting, my back bowing uncomfortably, and the man beside me tightens his grip around my arm in warning. "Take off your clothes." I do as I'm told, reluctantly, and drop my shirt to the ground.

"Eyes down, you stupid girl," an older woman, Penelope, growls. "*La insolencia se castiga en esta casa.*" *Insolence is punished in this house.* She says that every fucking time she sees me. Well, she better get used to it, because they can beat me to death, but I'm standing my ground either way.

"Now, now, Penelope." Michael chuckles, knowing damn well that my back is probably bleeding right about now. "I want her to look at what I'm about to do anyway. She can be punished later for not waiting to acquire my permission."

Penelope narrows her black eyes on me, they match her hair perfectly, and I look around frantically at everyone who is scared as fuck. She wants me to be submissive, all of us, willing to do whatever he says because he wants to feel wanted, like no one is being raped. He has some deep-rooted fucking issues, and he acts like, after everything he's done to me, I still love him. I may have at one point, but I've grown up a lot since then. Now all I feel for him is a hatred from so far within my soul it may never see the light. He sure as fuck won't see any light from me, that's for sure.

My body stiffens involuntarily, and Tomás lets go of me, taking a few steps back until Michael seems satisfied. No one speaks, and the hairs on the back of my neck stand on end as he stares at me with a malicious glint in his eyes. This behavior will probably cost me later, but I can't bring myself to give a shit. I don't care about any of it. I'm numb to everything around me except maybe my mind.

Okay, not really, that's a lie. It's hard to keep being numb. Maybe I was good at it a week ago, but now I feel myself slipping.

"Come." Michael points at the free spot next to one of the girls kneeling at his feet. She can't be much older than me. How long have they been here? Then again, I'm not surprised since I'm walking proof that he likes young girls, and he's sick in the fucking head. "Get on your knees for me."

"No."

He walks around the girls kneeling before him until he reaches me, and I close my eyes and try to take a deep breath. My entire body trembles like a leaf in the wind. I silently pray to whomever the fuck is up there that he doesn't notice, but I highly doubt that will be the case.

"Hallie," Michael tsks, "I know you don't give a fuck about these girls. However your actions have consequences. Come here and save them some pain."

Maybe this argument would've swayed me a few weeks ago, but no one prepared me for this bullshit. Now that I know he's the one who took me, bought me, I will do everything in my power to be left alone. I don't care if that's naive, I need to believe that shit to survive my brain fucking with me. At this point, I don't care who is collateral damage. Yes, it sucks for those girls. I hate that this is happening to all of us, but at the end of the day, I will save my damn self. He's right, I don't give a shit about anyone else.

I shake my head, tears stinging my eyes. I'm not entirely heartless, "I will not, Michael."

"I'm your fucking Daddy," his voice booms. "And that's what you will call me." Over my dead fucking body. Literally.

There's a blonde girl kneeling at his feet, her blue eyes making her look angelic. She has a small nose and full lips that make her absolutely gorgeous, and as sick as it is, I guess I can see why he picked her. Michael grabs her by the hair and yanks her up, turning her around and pushing her back down onto the ground until she's on all fours. His eyes find mine, and he holds my gaze. I refuse to show weakness and look away first. That only makes him smile though, and it feels like a thousand spiders are crawling down my back when he removes the leather belt from his slacks. The metal buckle makes a jingling sound as he folds the leather belt in half, and it lands on the naked girl's ass.

She doesn't make a sound.

That seems to piss him off. So this time, he hits her with the buckle instead of hitting her with the belt. On her back. The skin instantly splits open and dark blood starts to pour out of the open wound.

Her shrill screams increase in volume when he hits her again, and he finally looks satisfied when my face betrays me, a horrified expression painting my features.

"Such a good girl, Amy."

I cringe so hard I'm sure I just pulled a muscle. The other girl, who is still kneeling with her head down, keeps whimpering softly. He doesn't pay her any attention though, instead he unbuttons the trousers and pushes them down his legs then steps out of them.

The kneeling girl looks back at me, her dark hair shifting with the movement, and under her eyes are deep purple-black circles.

Her thin lower lip wobbles, and tears stream down her face, darkening her eyes. I know what that's from. It used to happen to me when he fucked me in the ass too roughly. When someone doesn't care about you or your pain, they can sometimes hurt you. But when someone wants to hurt you, they will make you suffer until you wish you were dead. I know my turn will come, and I think this time I will lose my fucking mind. There's no way I'm surviving this. I can't even help myself as tears stream down my face, but I still watch. It's like a train wreck you can't tear your eyes away from.

Amy's knees squeak on the tile as he drags her back toward him, fingers digging into her wounds because he's a fucking asshole. Her sobs are loud as his cock settles against her back entrance, and she braces herself. Michael is a fucking sadist. I already knew that from my time with him, but this just proves to me he's a different kind of monster. It makes what he did to me as a teenager look like fucking child's play, which I suppose, in a way, it was.

I think of another time, a different day, when he fucked me relentlessly until I couldn't walk the next day. Literally could not physically do it, and I had to feign illness so my mom would let me stay home. Except I was genuinely sick. Sick to my stomach.

He makes eye contact with me once more, and with a brutal thrust, he shoves himself all the way inside her. He didn't even fucking spit on her to lube her up a bit.

More screams. More sobs. More struggle.

She tries to get away from him, clawing at the ground until two of her fingernails break clean off. He doesn't go easy on her at all, his grip on her hips brutal as he pounds into her. For some twisted reason, I glance at where they're joined, and he grins at me and raises an eyebrow. As if I like what I see. No, I'm fucking disgusted, but also shocked.

There's blood covering his cock, the color bright red, and when he looks down at it, his grin deepens even more. He slaps Amy's ass so loud it echoes, then throws his head back in pure ecstasy. His eyes close, his mouth opens, and he pulls her forcefully back and forth onto him. At this point she's wailing, loud, shrill sounds escaping her throat.

"STOP!" She screams, "*S-stop!*"

My eyes water without my permission, more tears spilling out of me, and when I look at the other girl, her shoulders are shaking as she cries. She doesn't dare make a sound, in any case. She knows she's probably next.

"Shut the fuck up," Michael growls and pushes Amy onto the ground until she's completely flat on her belly with her arms extended forward.

His body envelops hers like a blanket, his front to her back, except he's literally crushing her with the weight of his body. His knees are on the ground, spread apart, and he has her legs spread wide to accommodate him and probably let him hit even deeper. All the while she continues to scream, telling him to stop. I can't even imagine the kind of damage he has done already; damage she probably won't recover from physically or mentally. Fuck, I don't even think I'll ever recover from this, and it's not happening to me.

"I told you to shut up." Michael laughs maniacally, then clamps his teeth onto her shoulder. When he lets go, he has blood dripping down his chin. "But you don't fucking listen."

Meaty hands wrap around Amy's throat, as he continues to ram into her savagely. Except she's gone from red to purple to blue at this point. And he still doesn't let go, doesn't even loosen his grip at all.

She struggles, thrashes, hits, claws, and tries to crawl away. It's impossible. When her fight wanes, I know she's well and truly fucked. Her body goes completely limp in less than two minutes, and he still doesn't let go. He comes with a roar, making all of us jump, and I'm pretty sure he did that shit on purpose. It's now apparent he enjoys these mind games, and I refuse to play.

I focus on Amy as he lets go of her neck and pulls out, and the sight before me makes me want to scream. Maybe then I'll release an ounce of the fucking rage and guilt I'm feeling. Her back, ass, and legs are covered in blood, and there's a puddle of it between her legs. Michael didn't hold back at all. I look at her back, her ribs. There's no rise and fall, no breathing. She's *gone*.

"What have you fucking done?!" I scream, running to him and hitting him, unable to contain myself. I hate him. I fucking hate him so much I want to claw his eyes out and shove them down his filthy throat.

Michael wastes no time grabbing me by the neck and crushing my windpipe single-handedly. I remain still. This is not my first time being choked, and I won't waste energy attempting to get free. He's not going to kill me.

"That's just a taste of what will happen if you keep acting this way." He chuckles, bringing his lips to mine and biting down gently on my bottom one, making me taste blood. Bile rises in my throat, and I close my eyes, feeling like I might pass out. "Everyone will be fucking punished until I fuck that tight little pussy again. No one can save you, Hallie. No one is coming for you, except me."

My chest heaves with the sobs that can't make their way up my throat, and I silently cry as his hand loosens from around my neck, my shoulders shaking. I can't believe this is happening. If I continue to disobey and refuse him, there are a few options, and none of them will end well for me. They can always hold me down until he gets his way. He could tie me up. Or he could torture me mentally until I'm well and truly unhinged enough to want to make everything stop. Then I will willingly give myself over to him. At least if it's the latter, I know I fought it as long as I could.

"That's it, baby girl. I'll have you shaking for me in no time."

I spit in his face, which only makes him smile. Then again, I also should've known pain was coming. The slap makes my head whip to the side so quickly that it hurts my neck. Pretty sure my lip is split and bleeding too. I don't dare move though. I keep my face to the side, my eyes on the ground. I'm so tired of the violence tonight and just want to go back to bed and be left alone. I want to forget this night ever happened. If someone could take pity on me and make me stop breathing permanently, that would be a welcomed mercy.

Michael nods at the guys behind me, and they come forward with their hands wrapped around…stuff. I can't see what they're holding as someone yanks my head back. One of the bald men who took me two weeks ago grips my jaw into some kind of pressure point until it hurts so bad I have no choice but to open up. When I do, he puts a pill on my tongue and closes it back up. The same kind they've been giving me because it tastes the same.

The bitter taste of it makes me gag, and it's fucking chalky. They're obviously not going to give me the courtesy of water, so I guess I'm swallowing this bitch dry. It's not the first time I've done it, yet I also don't want them to think I'll willingly take their drugs whenever they want to shove them down my throat. Although, if I'm being honest, I'm okay with forgetting everything for a little while.

So I do it.

I fucking swallow.

The bald motherfucker lets go of my face, and Michael and I stare at each other. With a smile, he nods at the guys once more, and they each take one of my arms and drag me out. I close my eyes as they do, not caring to see the stupid house that they've turned into my prison. I already know the hallways like the back of my hand, as well as the dungeon. I'd rather not keep discovering any more places.

I land on my mattress and rub my jaw, which is surprisingly not aching as much. My body is relaxing into the bed, and my limbs feel a thousand pounds heavier by the second. I can barely move, but the feeling of euphoria wrapping itself around me is unlike anything I've ever felt before. My fingers tingle, and even though I know it's not happening, it feels like I'm floating outside my body.

"Hallie," Tomás whispers, slapping my face, except I can barely feel it. My eyes open back up, and I stare at the ceiling. Everything looks distorted. "Are you okay?"

"Never better," I reply with a smile on my face, my body sinking into the mattress. The tingles spread from my fingers all the way to my limbs, then the rest of my body. I've never been so relaxed in my life. Even my Xanax wasn't this damn good. Fuck, maybe I've always craved the wrong drugs, the wrong things, the wrong men.

"I told you to do as you were told…" He sighs as he kneels beside the mattress and brushes my hair away from my face. "If you want to survive, you need to figure out how to be obedient."

"Why do you care?" I snort, suddenly feeling like this is funny. It's fucking not, even as my body says otherwise. "You helped him."

"He's my boss!" he whisper-yells. "I'll die if I don't do it."

Even as I force myself to respond with barely intelligible speech, I actually don't know if what I'm saying is true. Knowing how long it's been since I was taken away from my mother and him, and yet he's still fucking obsessed with me, I don't know that he'd ever kill me. More than likely, this would be life in prison, and I'm way too young for that shit.

"He wants you too much to do that." My eyes are heavy, and even as I struggle to open them, I can't. I feel myself drifting, everything moving in slow motion. "So give him what he wants. Be smart about it."

"Over my d-d-ead," I breathe in deeply, trying to stay awake, "fucking body."

"Everyone but you will die, *linda*." Tomás puts the blankets over me, and I'm grateful someone in here gives a fuck about me. I have no one else left in this world. I have to hold on to him. Maybe if I do what he says, he will love me. I need someone to. *Anyone*. "Make sure you can live with that."

"By the time he's done with me," I force myself to continue to talk even as the drug keeps pulling me under. "I won't be able to live with anything, not even myself."

If Michael gets his way with me, which I believe is just a matter of time, I know I won't survive. Not this time. My mind is already a fucked up place to be. This will finish breaking me until all my pieces are pulverized, and I have no chance of putting them back together.

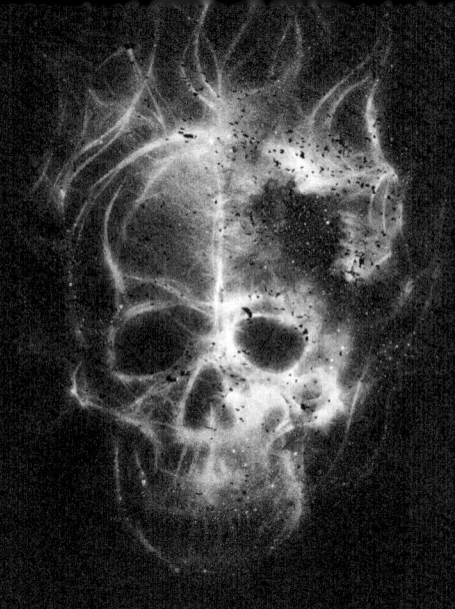

CHAPTER 3

Zayne

I don't know how long it's been since I got here, but just when I thought I would die, the fucking cartel one-upped me. I guess death wasn't punishment enough. Instead, they took me to Mexico and sold me to a man named Carl. One moment I had these fuckers pressing something to my nose that knocked me the fuck out, and the next, I was here. My memory is hazy. I can't recall anything about the trip. The only reason I know I'm in Mexico is because a maid told me. In Spanish, by the way. Guess I should've paid attention in high school.

After Hallie ran off on me and I chased her, my car crashed and flipped, resulting in a few injuries. The most painful one was the hit to my head, which seemingly resulted in a concussion and some stitches. Nothing major other than that, but it doesn't make me ache any less. My neck is still fucked from the whiplash, and these fuckers aren't making my body feel better. Just worse.

My arms are sore from how they're positioned above my head,

joined at the wrists. The chain restraints are cutting off my circulation even more, and my entire upper body screams in agony at every minor shift in position. I'm trapped in some sort of basement, except I don't know if it's the lower level of the house since I haven't been out of here. There are six more women with me, and they look like their ages range from twenty-one to twenty-five years old. I could be wrong, though, for all I fucking know. My brain isn't working properly either way. These women are actually caged like animals, but not me. I've been in this position all day. I'd rather be lying on the cold, dirty floor right now. I'd trade places with any one of them.

It's been so awful here that I think it's ironic that even though all of us are naked, we don't even look at each other with any level of attraction. Actually, we don't look at each other at all, or at least they pay no attention to me. I feel nothing when I see these girls with no clothes on, which I think is a testament to the bullshit we've been through here already, considering how attractive they are. I think our fear keeps us in line, though. We know that if we step out of line, we will be fucked up. Not in the 'hanging with my arms above my head' way. No, that's child's play for Carl.

Carl has done unspeakable things to me in the last two weeks of being in this room, and I'm sure he will continue. I don't expect this to get better, either. No one is coming for me. Hallie probably thinks I'm dead, and she went on to live her life in Canada or Alaska or wherever the fuck she went. I can't lie; I'm fucking pissed at her. I wouldn't be in this situation if she didn't make me chase her. Hallie told me she was leaving without me, leaving me behind to keep me safe. The little fucking liar eventually agreed to let me come, just to ask me to get her stuff from the hotel room and leave me behind. Of course I chased her. Did she really expect less from me? Yeah, I chased her right to my death.

Images of us flash through my mind like a shutter, making me scrunch my lids tighter. The way I fucked her tight little pussy and ass, shoving her under the water because she likes that shit. When I asked her why she called me, she said she wanted to tell me goodbye… I couldn't think straight anymore. I had to go with her. However, Hallie lied and chose herself. She still tugs at my heartstrings though, even when she fucks me over.

I don't want to think of her right now, of what could've been. We could be well on our way to another country *together* had she not lied to me.

I wouldn't fucking be *here*.

This place is a living hell, and I'm close to losing my mind already. Carl's been alternating between tying me up in uncomfortable positions and coming in here with toys and other gadgets to fuck me with until I'm bleeding. When he finally grows bored, he leaves me alone long enough to make me believe I'm safe. Then does it again, repeating the process until I feel like I'm on the brink of insanity.

To top it off, the motherfucker records everything. Whatever he does to me, to the girls, it's all on his camera. Sometimes he will record us, and I can see we are part of a live feed on his computer. Sick fucks like him are watching and getting off on it.

My eyes scan the room, the basement, and it's just white walls and white floors. The kind where if you scrape your knee, you're fucked because the concrete isn't smooth. There are over ten cages here, and they look like oversized kennels—something where you'd put a pet but human-sized. The girls, and I'm assuming me as well, eventually sleep on the concrete without trying to move. It looks uncomfortable as fuck, but it can't be worse than hanging with your arms suspended above your head. I'd trade them right now.

I try to reposition myself so I'm not putting so much stress on my arms and shoulders, which not only hurt like a bitch but at this point also feel like they're going to fall right off, but it's useless. My body is not functioning as it should, and I can't even be surprised about it because the amount of time I've been hanging like this would incapacitate anyone.

When I look down at the ground, there's a small puddle and splatters of blood on the concrete floor. I follow the trail up my leg, until I can't see it anymore. My asshole is raw, abused, and probably torn from Carl's assault. I don't want to think about what he's going to do next. The worst part is he wants me to like it, like *him*, and when I refuse to show any enjoyment he punishes me. My mind can't take the games it will play on me if I do give in to him though. So I take the abuse, the torture, the pure fucking agonizing pain because it's all I have now. Sadly, I'll have to embrace it for the moment.

Sweat trails down my back as I look between the girls, and none of them make eye contact with me. I'm hanging from the ceiling between all the cages, and not one of them gives a fuck. It pisses me off. I know it's probably weird having me here. They definitely don't trust me, but I don't need them to. All I want is some information. Like how long they've been here, if there's ever been any men besides me, and where in Mexico we are. Surely they can tell me something. Fucking anything at all.

All I know about my situation is that Carl wants to fuck me, and since I've been resisting, he's been taking other measures. He's thought about this thoroughly, and no matter how much I fight him, deep down, I know I don't stand a chance. So far, I've been tied up while he does what he wants to me in the room he uses, and when I fight I get chained the way I am now.

One of the girls repositions herself on the concrete floor, probably moaning from pain since we're all in a shitty situation. Just because I'm being punished right now doesn't mean they're ignored. No, I've watched him fuck every single one of them in the span of a few hours. Sometimes he takes them somewhere private and none of us are able to see what he does to them. I'm thankful for those times, yet the look in their eyes when they return always haunts me. I think it comes from knowing what he's capable of behind closed doors, and I'm more afraid of what else he has in store for me than I care to admit.

"Hey," I whisper-yell. They never talk to me, never even attempt to. It's as if I don't exist, and I fucking hate it. "I need your help." I don't even know if they speak English. They could've come from anywhere. In fact, some of them do look Hispanic. It's possible they're also from Mexico and don't speak my language.

One of the Hispanic girls looks from me to the door and back over again until I'm afraid something is wrong with her eyes. Hazel orbs, long dark hair, and a delicate little nose face me; she even reminds me of Hallie a bit. Fuck my life.

She sits with her back against the bars of the enclosure, arms wrapped around her legs as her knees rest against her chest. Dirt covers her cheeks, her arms, and even some of her legs. Our living conditions are fucking disgusting, and honestly, we're pretty filthy. I've only been able to shower three times in two weeks. I can't imagine what they feel like. Thank whomever the fuck is supposed to be watching over me that I don't have a pussy. But also, fuck whoever it is because this shit should've never happened to me.

"Shut up!" The girl whispers loudly, "You're gonna get us all in trouble…"

"I just have some questions…" I reply, whimpering softly when I move my body to avoid hurting so much. "Please."

"One."

I think hard about this one. What's the one question I need answered, and why is it so important? If I only get one, then are my questions even good enough? Why do I even want to know anything? There's no saving me from this nightmare.

Inhale. Exhale. Pull the trigger. "Where in Mexico are we?"

We hear footsteps approaching us, but she looks at me and replies softly, "Juarez."

A chill runs down my spine, and my body stiffens. I know how close that is to the border. If I could get out of here, I bet I could tell them all about how I've been kidnapped, and they'd let me back into the country. There's no fucking way I'm staying. I know the fate that awaits me if I do.

I close my eyes as I hear the footsteps getting closer to me and prepare myself for another beating. As if my body knows, my vision and right temple start throbbing all over again.

A rough hand grips my face until my teeth bite down on my

cheeks, and I breathe in loudly through my nose. Reluctantly, I open my eyes. When I do, an ugly face stares back at me. Amber eyes, white hair, and a beer gut are the most noticeable attributes. Bile rises in my throat from thinking of what he will make me do, but I need to keep it together. There has to be a way to escape from here, and I'm going to find it.

I refuse to die here, at his hand, in these conditions.

"Mornin' sunshine." Carl smiles, and I suppress the urge to head-butt him yet again. Last time didn't end well for me, just a rougher round of getting fucked by a dildo, so I guess you could say I'm learning from my mistakes and exhibiting more self-control. I look down at his right hand, which is currently holding a camera. Here we go again. "It's your time to shine."

I grimace, which makes him narrow his eyes at me.

"I'm doing you a favor, you know." A shit-eating grin appears on his face, and I know I'm going to hate my fucking life. "It's not every day I let one of my girls pleasure someone else. You've been quite the star with that pretty face so they want to see more of you. And I'm going to give it to them."

They.

Them.

Everyone watching me on the fucking live feeds when I'm being raped, crying on the inside. I've never found pleasure in what they've witnessed, and yet they have. Sick fucking bastards. I wonder if they know that we're here against our will. Who the fuck watches this shit? Men? Women?

"Adriana!" he barks, and a guard goes to the cage of the woman who just spoke to me. Maybe he heard us, and this is her punishment for giving me any information I shouldn't know. "Come."

I look around, and sure enough, cameras are everywhere in the room. More than likely I didn't notice before now for the simple reason that I've been too focused on the pain I'm experiencing. Maybe if I don't fight him now, he will be merciful and put me in a cage. I never in my life would've thought that would be merciful. Look at me now, adapting to my situation.

In a way, it's amusing because I never would've imagined that I'd die here. No, I've always thought meth would kill me. That my last breath would be blissful while riding on the monster's back, the poison filling my veins until my heart stops beating. It used to scare me that I didn't know when my last day would be. My addiction was controlling my life. I'd take that death any day now.

The cravings haven't disappeared. Rehab was just slapping a Band-Aid over a gaping wound that needed surgery, not a long-term fix. My skin still crawls with the need to use, my hands fucking itch to plunge myself into oblivion. I bet if I spoke up about it, Carl would use it against me and force me to get high. As if that would be the worst thing in the world for me. Unfortunately, I need to stay sober so I can plot my escape. If I accept drugs from him, I will accept my fate and let him feed me meth until I die. That would make everything better. I'd forget all the fucked up things happening to me and let him have his way with me, as long as I get another fix.

Adriana stands in front of me, eyes on the ground, and waits for instructions from her 'master' as she calls him. It's the name he makes *all* of us call him. Fuck that shit. You won't catch me saying those goddamn words to that piece of shit.

"Get on your knees and do what you do best." I stiffen, peering down at her. Of all the things I thought would happen here, getting my dick sucked by someone who isn't Hallie was not one of them. *At least they look alike.* "And make sure it's good." Carl winks. "We need to keep them watching."

Hazel eyes look up at me, begging me to keep my shit together and not fuck this up. Her tan skin is riddled with small freckles under her eyes, cheekbones, and small nose. I focus on the features that remind me of Hallie, but it's not exactly her. The eyes aren't right. Adriana's are almond-shaped, while Hallie's are not. Her lips aren't full enough, and her hair is not long enough. Her tits not big enough. Fuck—I really need to stop thinking of Hallie in moments like these. I'm never seeing her again, so why the fuck torture myself?

I want to push her away, not let her touch me, except I can't. Even still, I know it's not her intention to do this to me. He's forcing her to. Although, it still doesn't make it better.

I'm betraying *her*. Hallie.

Only why do I give a shit after what she did to me back at the hotel? She fucking left me behind. Didn't want me at all. If it weren't for my crash, she would've never stopped her car for me.

Adriana's fingers trail up my leg, and her light touch makes my skin light up. It's been a while since someone has touched me like this. Yeah, I fucked Hallie not too long ago, but I was in control. I don't want to enjoy this, but I also know if I don't come, it's going to piss him off. That won't be good for any of us, but especially not for me. And I'll be honest, I'm fucking tired of my arms hanging above my head. I can't even feel my fingers anymore.

I look around her to see Carl setting up the camera and suppress a moan when Adriana bites the inside of my thigh lightly. She's not looking at me like someone is forcing her to suck me off, and a twisted part of me is glad since I wouldn't be able to finish if she did.

When the tip of her tongue licks the head of my cock my head falls back instantly, and I breathe in deeply as I attempt not to groan. I have no control over it when she takes me into her mouth, her pouty, full lips wrapping around my dick. My eyes meet hers as she takes me all the way to the back of her throat, creating a seal so tight it feels like a pussy. *Fuck.*

My body jerks, the chains digging into my wrists once again, and I flinch. The pain is short-lived in any case, because Adriana is fucking good at what she's doing. I refuse to think of all the men she must have done this to, probably because she was forced to. The guilt hits me again, but I ignore it. This will probably be the only blow job I will get for the remainder of my time in this shit hole, and who knows how long I'll even be here.

My arms begin to shake when her head bobs up and down, mainly because it's taking a lot of effort to keep myself upright. Now that pleasure is coursing through my body, I have a renewed sense of energy, but my body is still fucked up. Adriana makes me forget about all of that as her tongue circles me, and the way she keeps making eye contact is fucking with my head. Why does it feel like she's enjoying this? Does she actually want to suck my cock?

I refuse to look at the camera after I quickly glance up and see Carl beating his dick to the sight of us. I scrub the image out of my brain because the longer I take to come, the longer the sick people on the other side of the camera get to see us.

Either way, I don't think it'll be hard to finish. Not with the way she keeps staring into my eyes, her hazel ones slightly widen when I moan while looking right at her. Tingles spread throughout my body as she deepthroats me again, tears filling her eyes as she gags on me, then spilling down her cheeks. I wish I didn't have restraints so I could grab onto her head, even fuck her mouth. I need to forget about everything else that's happened in this fucking place. Maybe this is the fastest way to achieve that.

Adriana fists my cock with one hand and jerks it while sucking me, and her other hand cups my balls and gently massages them. At this point, my eyes roll to the back of my head, and hers seem different when I look back down. Almost like she's smiling about this, even though her mouth is clearly too busy to achieve that.

I close my eyes as I get closer, for the sake of feeling it even more intensely. When my moans get closer together and I begin to bite my lip, Adriana switches her attention and grabs onto my ass. Her fingernails dig into my ass cheeks and her pace picks up on my cock until she's red and more tears stream down her face. She gags multiple times, but that doesn't deter her. In fact, she goes even faster.

Maybe I'm a masochist, but the pain of her fingernails digging into me is actually fueling my pleasure. I can feel it mounting, and my body begins to shake as I feel my balls tighten. I groan loudly when I spill into her mouth, unable to contain myself. My eyes automatically close as I ride the post-orgasm high, but like every high, it comes with a crash.

Within a minute, my body feels heavy. The way my legs give

out on me is not reassuring, and I do end up hanging by just my arms. Intense pain shoots through my arms all the way up to my shoulders, and Adriana attempts to help me up. When I look up, I see Carl smirking at the scene before him. He doesn't attempt to help or even say anything at all. Thankfully, he does snap his fingers, and two of his goons come forward and begin to open the metal restraints from my wrists.

Eyes low and body tense, Adriana retreats all the way back into her cage, acting like nothing ever happened. Not once does she look at me. It's like I don't exist all over again.

When my wrists are finally free though, I don't have the time or energy to worry about her. All I can focus on honestly, is the open cuts on them and the blood trailing down my fingertips. How the fuck did I not notice that? Was I so focused on her that I forgot all about my pain? Or maybe I just couldn't see it? Either way, I can't keep going like this. I need to figure out how the hell to make it all stop.

The two men lead me to an empty cage I thought belonged to someone else, but I guess everything is temporary. Somehow, I'm happy I get to have this instead of being hung by my arms. Then again, it shouldn't be that surprising with how shitty the alternative is. The cage is right next to Adriana's, just big enough that a person can stand in it. Maybe a few inches above six feet tall since I have about three inches of space above my head. There's nowhere to lie down, nowhere to use the bathroom, but somehow I never noticed that last part before.

I stumble in, my feet dragging like they weigh a thousand pounds each, and fall to my knees. The concrete makes my bones scream in pain, my skinned knees now stinging, but it's nothing compared to the rest of my body. So I let myself fall to my side and curl up in the fetal position, ready to sleep before it's taken away again. Maybe he's giving me a taste of what it's like to be comfortable, just to end it for me and drive me insane.

"I hope you enjoyed yourself," Carl drawls, and I open my

eyes to look at him. Hatred flows through my veins until it feels like I'll have an aneurysm, and he smiles at me.

"Fuck. You. Bitch," I reply, my eyes shooting daggers at him. If I could kill him with my gaze, I would've by now.

He chuckles, standing right at the entrance of my cage, then shuts and locks it while I watch. "Oh, I will. It'll be my turn to play with you again soon."

"The fuck it will," I say under my breath.

Carl turns around and stares at me with malice in his eyes. You can just see the evil that takes residence in his soul. After all, the eyes are the windows to it, or however the fuck it goes. Maybe this is a bad idea because I'm getting his attention more than usual, and I really don't want to go back to the chains.

Holding my breath, I try not to make a sound. I don't want him to know how scared I am of him, of this entire fucked up situation. Unfortunately, it's hard to hide that all day every day. I want to turn this all off. My feelings. My cravings. My memories.

That's why I turn my face back to the ground and rest my cheek on the concrete floor, closing my eyes once more and trying to summon thoughts of Hallie to my brain. Her eyes, her smile, her laugh. But they don't come. Instead all I get is a black image in my brain with hints of her. She's slowly fading, giving way to the darkness creeping in on my mind to survive. It's taking over, this darkness, and it wants to drag me into it until I reach a new level of insanity that I know has no escape.

My only goal in life at this point is to get to see her one more time.

Just one.

Then I can tell her how much I hate her for making me love her.

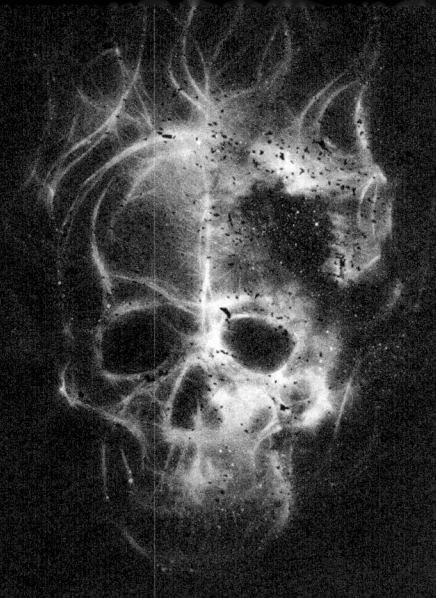

CHAPTER 4

Damien

My chances of finding Zayne under a rock are higher than in Juarez. When my father mentioned the city, I thought he was dumb as fuck for letting it slip and that I was going to be the genius who figured everything out quickly. What I didn't realize was how fucking difficult it would be to find a person who doesn't involve himself with the cartel except to purchase girls here and there. I swear to fucking God, it feels like I'm searching for a needle in a haystack. I've even consulted my tech guy, Sean, to see if he's noticed anything. See if he could check on the men that came to my cabin with face recognition. Thankfully, I know them since I worked with them before. I just need a fucking breadcrumb. Not even a trail. Even still, lately, it feels like maybe that is asking for too much. If one of them could just turn their head toward the camera in any gas station from Breckenridge to El Paso, then I'd have a shot. Anywhere, truly. They do have to fuel up eventually.

I still can't return to San Antonio, it's too risky. Not only do people know me from my father's business and wouldn't hesitate to open their fucking mouths, but the cartel is also probably waiting for me to fuck up and return to my apartment with my tail tucked between my legs.

First of all, I'm not capable of *tucking* my tail. It's not in my genetic composition to be a fucking pussy. No, that's Zayne's specialty. I bet if he hadn't been captured already, he'd still suffer the same fate. Fucking dumbass. Never mind the fact that, technically, I gave the order to kill him.

Yet, I didn't expect to be played in the process as well, and now I'm being forced to save him. No matter how much I hate him and can't even stand to look at his face without wanting to gouge his eyes out, my main concern is figuring out where the fuck Hallie is. I need this asshole to help me find her. I think the motherfuckers who have him will know precisely the ones dealing in sex trafficking. Then, hopefully, I'll be able to find Hallie from there; I know I will. I have to have faith that I'll find her, or this feeling that's eating me alive on the inside will consume me.

Yeah, she fucking stabbed me and almost killed me. And I may hate her a little right now, but I love her a hell of a lot more. I have to get her back. Then once she's safe, I'll take care of the rest. Like punishing her for putting me through this shit.

The people keeping Zayne better talk too, because they do not want to play with me and my torture tactics. I've been doing it for way too long. No matter how long waterboarding, ripping nails, or slowly stabbing them to death takes; I won't rest. Without batting an eyelash, I'll make them wish they were dead within the first five minutes. Honestly, I rather enjoy the screams. They bring me a sense of peace and calm when I'm going insane. That's exactly what I'm looking forward to as soon as I figure out where they are.

Out of all the searching, the only information I've gathered from Sean is that the man who purchased Zayne is named Carl Hewitt. Of course, there's no fucking trace of him in Juarez. This brings me to the conclusion that he is operating with an alias, or the house is under someone else's name. A wife, possibly.

I've been hiding in El Paso, Texas, mainly in little rundown motels where they accept cash and customers never have to show identification. It's been easier this way since I'm primarily carrying cash, identification for myself and Hallie, and a few sets of clothes. My father gave me more money in my suitcase, but I suspect I'll have to use the new duffel bag I bought , although a suitcase may be a little suspicious.

As for where I'm staying, no one has questioned my use of cash or lack of identification thus far, which is a huge fucking red flag. Any fine establishment would require it, and that's how I know something is off.

The motel must be involved in the skin trade somehow; that much is obvious by the lack of tracking of who comes and goes. My instinct tells me it won't be long until I see someone looking for me, so I only leave the room when necessary. I've been ordering food via delivery and paying cash. I'm untraceable so far, and it needs to stay that way.

There's a chance, hopefully a low one, that I'll get arrested at the border. If they figure out that my identification and passport are fake, then I'm well and truly fucked. Not only will I be banned from entering the country forever, more than likely, but I will also spend some time in jail, if not prison. I'm not even sure at this point. But I need to get Hallie. That is the only thing that matters to me.

I'm not living large by any means right now. The full-sized bed and rough sheets prove that. Not even the pillows are comfortable. When I first arrived, I was disgusted by the dirt on the tub and the bathroom, but then I figured I couldn't be too demanding and draw attention to myself. In the past week, I've only had one motel employee knock on my door to offer to clean. There was a very high chance the bathroom was not going to be part of the job, and it wasn't.

A knock sounds at the door, and I get up from the bed quickly, peeking out through the curtains to make sure it's not a team of men about to take me the fuck down. If it is, then I'm dead for sure. These rooms were definitely built to prevent escape. There's no bathroom window, no alternate entrances, and only one window facing the front. I think the chances of me surviving an ambush are close to zero, and I can only hope that my baseball cap and fake mustache conceal my identity until I can get through the border. Then I'll really have to lay low either way. I don't know who might recognize me.

I can't see anyone out the window, and there's also no peephole. Again red flags everywhere. Still, I open the door just wide enough to look out, but it's just another one of the ladies who works here.

"Towels?" She smiles, though it doesn't reach her eyes. She looks older, possibly in her fifties. It's subtle, but she glances to her right. There's a black SUV running idle in the parking spot right next to my door.

"No," I reply, looking at the SUV, making it obvious I see it. "Thanks, though."

I'm about to shut the door, but she sticks her hand in the frame, stopping me. "Those men are looking for you," she whispers, fear evident on her face. "They asked about a tall blond man with blue eyes. Been here for three hours in front of your door. I think they know you're here."

Fuck.

I need some kind of diversion so I can gather my shit. I was smart enough not to park my vehicle in front of the door, since I didn't want to give myself away.

"Can you go back to the office, wait ten minutes, and then come back to tell them you found the guy?"

Her face looks horrified, "You want me to tell them you're here?"

"I want you to tell them," I pause, making sure I'm not visible to the men out there, "I'm on the other side of the motel. The back of the building. Once they drive that way, I'll get in my car and leave."

Maria, according to the name tag, nods frantically. "Yes, yes."

"Thank you."

The towels are rough when I take them from her hands and close the door quickly. Promising myself to never come back to this shit hole. I gather all my belongings, putting them in my new, spacious duffel bag.

Something has been nagging me at the back of my mind for the last week. The Sinaloa Cartel was involved in Hallie's trade, yet I still can't find out the name of the person who bought her. All I know is that he works for the cartel in some capacity. If he has this much anonymity, I assume he's important somehow.

After ten minutes, I watch Maria go to the black SUV and point to the other side of the building. I keep the curtains drawn, only looking through the thinnest slit, and I wait until they pull out of the parking spot and disappear before grabbing my bag and sprinting to the car. I don't bother putting anything in the trunk, instead I just throw it from the driver's side to the passenger side and slam my door shut.

I manage to reverse out of my parking spot and get on the main road before spotting the black SUV in my rearview mirror. They're coming back around the building, and one bald man makes his way into the front office. My new beat-up Kia, which I purchased for the sake of not drawing attention to myself, makes a loud sound when I accelerate and flinch. For fuck's sake. This shit better not die on me before I make it to where I need to go.

My phone begins to ring, except this piece of shit car doesn't have Bluetooth, so I glance down and slide it with my finger. "This is not a good time, Sean," I bark out, taking a left so fast that my tires squeal. I need to chill the fuck out. Then I need to know if the men trailing after me somehow figured out it was me all along and Maria lied to them. She won't make it very long once they realize she did, and whatever they do, I know it won't be pretty. I can't even feel guilty, though. I only have one goal right now, and don't give a fuck who it hurts or who I fuck over on this journey, so long as it takes me back to her.

"Well, make it a good one, because I have news for you." I hold my breath and clear my throat, waiting for him to continue. "Carl frequents a bar called the Kentucky Club. He goes every Friday and every weekend night."

"What about Hallie?" I ask him impatiently, hoping he knows something. Anything. My hope is dwindling by the second. But I have to make it to Juarez today. I'm not spending one more fucking day in this country hiding out in a motel.

"She's a ghost, man," he says with pity in his voice, and I slam my hand against the steering wheel with enough force that it starts to throb. "However I'm not giving up. You, on the other hand, need to go after this Carl motherfucker. I have a feeling everything is connected."

I've had that feeling since my dad opened his big ass fucking mouth, yet there's not much I can do without more information. I'm lucky as fuck I have Sean, my tech guy, in the first place. If I didn't, this process would be so much longer. Hallie is going through the inevitable at this point. There's literally nothing I can do about it, at least not until I know where she is.

"I'm on the way to the border right now." Which may or may not work. This might just send me to prison, and I won't have any way of getting her back. "Any places I should stay at?"

"Komfort Motel is the cheapest around if you don't want to draw attention to yourself." He laughs, "And for the love of God, please wear a fucking hat, *güero*."

I laugh right along with him, "*Cállate cabrón*." It's not my damn fault I was born with golden hair.

"Call me when you settle in, then we can talk about how to keep you safe. You'll need weapons if you want to get anything done over there, and you won't be able to get them through the border."

"I have a way to make sure they will get through."

"Oh?" Sean questions, "And how do you plan to do that?"

"Let's just say that someone owes me a favor." I drive up to the line at the checkpoint, about twenty cars away from the front. There's this guy, Eric, who owes me a favor. I saved his life a time or two; now it's time to collect. He usually works in this lane, so I cross my fingers and hope he's working right now. The last thing I need is for it to be someone else, and then I'll have to turn around and figure out what to do.

"Let me know if you need me. If you don't call me by tomorrow morning, I will call you to check in."

I scoff, trying not to be offended at the lack of faith on his end. "I'll be alive, chill."

"I hope so," Sean replies, cutting the line.

About ten minutes later, I'm two cars away from it being my turn. I take out my identification and passport in advance, ready to get this over with. I see that it is Eric is guarding this lane, and once he sees me, he does a double-take. I'm almost entirely positive that he knows about my situation, as he leans over and talks in a low voice so no one else can hear him.

"Damien," Eric nods, "I'm going to let this one time slide since I owe you for saving my life. However, I have to report this to the cartel if I see you again."

"You won't," I reply, but even I know that's impossible. Someone will see us when we return from Mexico, and I bet it will be him all over again. My life is one big fucking joke in that regard.

Eric doesn't inspect my vehicle or even check my identification or passport. All I can gather from this is that if you're the right person or work for the right people, you can be waved through without any issues. Be the wrong person to them in any capacity, and they will fuck you until you never want to cross a border again, much less Mexico's.

We smile at each other, even though it's tense. I hope he keeps his word and his mouth shut, because if he doesn't, and I survive this shit, I'll be back to slit his throat while he sleeps on shift. Either way, I don't wait for him to change his mind, and I ease my foot off the brake and begin to drive across the bridge.

It's a good thing I have a GPS on my phone right now, that way I don't have to use a map. The downside is possible tracking, and I have to double and triple-check every day to ensure they haven't figured out how to do it. Or if they even know this phone exists. Maybe not, if I'm lucky.

I enter the address to the motel into my GPS and make my way to it, keeping my eyes on the road and not fiddling with my mustache—which is itchy as fuck—so I'm not recognized. I haven't even told my dad that I'm here, though I'm sure he expects it, but I will contact him if I need his help. He fucking told me to anyway, so I will be holding him to it. There's a very big possibility that I'll need him, whether I want his help or not. Although when it comes to my girl, I won't waste any time or take any chances.

A few minutes go by, and I make it to the motel. It's a small place, looks about as run-down as the one I was staying at in El Paso, and the parking lot is deserted as fuck. Not a great first impression; still, I guess beggars can't be choosers. I park right in front of the front office, at least until they give me a room. I refuse to be caught vulnerable this time, and my car won't be far from me anymore. If there comes a time when I need to get the fuck out of here, I need to be able to make it to my car within seconds. Or I'm going to die. It's that simple.

I make sure my gun is tucked in the back of my jeans and lock the car behind me. Thankfully, the parking lot is paved, but there are potholes on almost every other step, and I have to dodge each of them. They're so damn deep, they could be a ditch.

A small bell rings as I enter the office, and I cringe. Every sudden noise is triggering me. I'm jumpy as fuck lately, and I've realized life on the run is not for me. Once I get her back, we're going far away from North America. I refuse to keep doing this shit.

The front desk is empty, not a damn soul in sight, which is not very reassuring. Look, I just need a fucking room, and I'll be out of your hair. *Please*. There's a sign on the desk that talks about reporting human trafficking to the Mexican police if you believe something suspicious is going on, and I snort. These fuckers are probably involved as well. I know for a damn fact there are plenty of crooked cops on their payroll. Can't believe that shit.

I adjust the baseball cap on my head—a new tic—making sure the blond is not apparent. Just as I do, a young woman who looks around twenty comes to the desk. She does a double-take when she sees me, and I plaster a bright smile on my face. Hopefully, they have at least one room vacant. It would be just my luck if there wasn't.

"Buenas tardes, Monserrat." Good afternoon, Monserrat.

I call her by the name on the tag attached to her shirt. People usually feel at ease when they're given that courtesy. It makes them feel safe, like they can trust you. People can be really stupid. *"Me gustaría reservar una habitación, por favor." I would like to book a room, please.*

"Por supuesto." Of course, Monserrat replies with a smile. She begins to swipe cards and work on her computer while I remove my wallet from my back pocket and retrieve my identification card. *"No se preocupe, no necesito su tarjeta de identificación." Don't worry about it, I don't need your identification card.*

While I'm not surprised, it still pisses me off because now I know exactly what kind of establishment this is. Which means I have a lot more to worry about than just being spotted by someone who used to work with me, or for me. Theft, kidnapping, and the skin trade, among other problems, are at the forefront of my mind as I ask her, *"¿Acepta dólares americanos?"* Do you take American dollars?

"Sí, aceptamos dólares americanos."

I hand her the money for the room, she gives me the key card, and just as I'm heading out the door to move parking spots, she speaks again.

"Si tienes tiempo, puedo mostrarte los alrededores." If you have time, I can show you around. Monserrat winks, and I bet that gets her whatever she wants often. She's pretty enough, though I don't consider that a good thing around here. Especially if you're involved in anything illegal.

"Gracias."

With that, I return to my car and pull out of the parking spot, looking for the one right in front of my room. I can't be too careful here. If I get too comfortable, my car might just disappear. My luggage is going to be the major dilemma. It can't stay in my car while I'm in the hotel room, and it can't stay in the hotel while I'm not in the room. Which is why I grab it now as I exit my car. It's no wonder I have fucking trust issues.

The place is run down as fuck. My door is red and beat up, and I just hope it closes properly and has multiple locks. When I enter the room, it smells like cigarettes, but at least the queen bed is neatly made. The door does have three locks, which is a little scary, so I use all three the moment I shut it. A small desk takes up half of the room. There's a card on it with the WiFi information, but I don't trust it enough to use it. Then there's the bathroom with a tiny tub. At least it's clean though, surprisingly, due to how shitty the place looks.

I'm grateful it's Thursday because that means I don't have anywhere to go tonight except to get some fast food, plot my next move and get some rest.

What will I do once I find Carl?

Will I attack right away? Or will I learn more about his house and come back after scoping it out? Those are the questions riddling my brain as I try to figure out what's best for everyone.

Trying to look inconspicuous and keep a low profile is a challenge with my fair skin and blue eyes, so I put on dark brown contact lenses to help out a little, along with my baseball cap. I don't want to draw too much attention to myself, especially when sitting in a crowded bar in a sketchy city.

I take a bite of the *chiles rellenos* as I watch Carl from a few stools away. Two young women are perched on his lap and a few men are clearly with him. Must be fucking nice not to have a conscience and be able to live your life as if you don't have any people chained up at your house.

My margarita is sweating because I've only taken two sips in the past twenty minutes. It would look odd if I didn't drink at a bar, yet I also can't be risking myself by following a very dangerous man when I'm not sober. So I sit here and try to enjoy my food as much as I can, though I can't deny it really is fucking delicious. I'm just nervous as fuck.

"*¿Quieres otra bebida?*" *Do you want a different drink?* a woman asks as she wipes the bar top.

I smile and shake my head, taking a sip through the straw. *"No, gracias."*

When I'm satisfied that she's no longer watching me like a fucking hawk, I return to observing the men again. Two of them look younger than him by at least a decade, except Carl looks to be in his fifties. I knew right away who he was; no one else fit that name in the first place. What really gave him away was the women. Once he caught my attention, I started listening in on their conversations and found out he was, for sure, the person I was looking for.

A message dings on my phone, and I lower the volume as I unlock it. It's an encrypted email from Sean; when I open it, I regret doing it in public. It's a little too late for that though, and all I can do is shield my phone with my hands to prevent the people on either side of me from peering at the screen.

Zayne is tied up with chains, his body suspended by his wrists, his arms weak. But right at his feet is a girl that can't be more than twenty-one, and she's sucking his cock. He looks conflicted, as if he's fighting whatever he's feeling, but then he throws his head back and his mouth opens. I know he's moaning even though I can't hear it, and it kind of pisses me off for a small moment that he's doing this to Hallie. Then I remember he doesn't have a choice in the matter and neither does she. I also don't know why I give a fuck, especially since she's *mine*. There's no fucking way I'm letting him have her.

Two more men walk up to the group, and I put my head down right away when I realize I know them. I'm just hoping they haven't noticed or recognized me—contact lenses, ball cap, mustache, or not. I've done enough recon to know there's not much more I can find out from this distance. I hand the bartender some money and walk out of the bar. Luckily, the walk to my car is short. If I want to follow him home, I need to stay in my parking spot until Carl decides to leave. With any luck, he doesn't make any stops, for there's only so much I can do before he realizes I'm following him.

Thankfully, he only takes thirty more minutes before getting in his vehicle. Except, seconds later, a woman comes around and gets in the passenger side. Fuck. I really hope she's clueless and doesn't notice they're being tailed, or I'm definitely not going to be able to do it again. This is a one-time shot. No second chances.

Carl pulls out of the parking lot and drives away from the bar. I go after him, waiting a few seconds before I drive up to his car, staying a little further back so he doesn't realize what I'm doing. The key to this is not looking suspicious, and I have a lot of experience with following people around. I see him glance in the rearview mirror a few times once I've been tailing him for a few minutes, and I can tell he's getting suspicious. Goddamnit.

I don't make eye contact with him. Instead, I raise the volume on the radio and act like I'm jamming out. We drive until we're not in the city anymore. In fact, I have no fucking idea where I am right now, which isn't good. I can only guess it's on the outskirts of Juarez at this point.

I try to stay a few car spaces behind him, slowing down at least ten miles an hour to look less noticeable. There's a sign that says we're on Highway forty-five, and I know where it leads, fortunately. He turns right quickly, and now I'm too far to see where he's going. I speed up significantly, hoping there are no police around, and when I make it to yet another highway, forty-five D, his car is nowhere to be fucking seen.

He lost me.

"Fuck!!" I scream, a fire starting in my chest and spreading through my veins to the rest of my body. "I'm sorry, Hallie."

Tears sting my eyes as I turn around, going back the way I came and hoping for better luck next time. Maybe he will go back to the bar again tomorrow, and if he does, I swear on my fucking life he will not get away from me this time. I'm not failing her. I *will* get her back, even if it's the last thing I ever do.

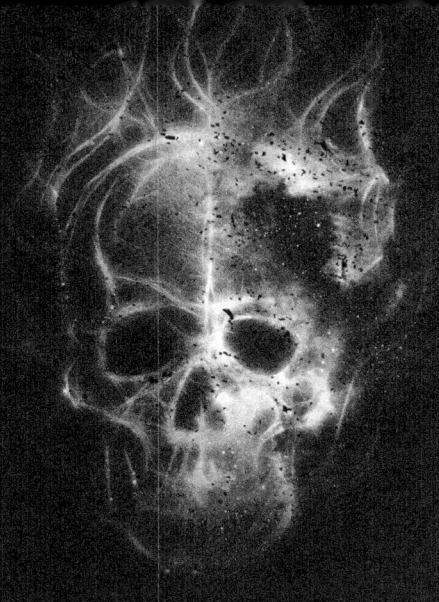

CHAPTER 5

```
Hallie
```

The warm tile hurts my knees, and I shift my weight to alleviate the pain. Ximena, the girl who watched Amy die with me five days ago, kneels to my right, and a new girl, Nicole, to my left. We all look down at the ground, and I try to clear my mind. I don't want to think about what's happening here tonight, who I have to watch get killed now. One time was enough. I'm waiting for the nightmares to return, but so far they haven't. Whether that's a good or bad thing, I'm not sure, I'm just relieved either way.

Penelope calls this the dungeon, and I will say this part of the enormous mansion is not nice. You would think everything would follow the same decor as the main area. When the bag slipped off my head as we entered the house, I saw the shiny tiles, a grand staircase, and very expensive-looking furniture. Of course, our side of the house is a fucking dump. They treat us worse than animals.

"It's okay," Ximena whispers to me, not moving her head to

glance at me, as her hand briefly comes closer to me then returns to her lap. "I'll do it. You're still new." I turn my head to glimpse at her profile. Tan skin, hooked nose, full lips. She looks like a Mexican princess with her brown eyes and dark hair. She's absolutely gorgeous, but then again, I'd say all of us are. That's why we're here.

"Please don't do that for me." I choke out. While I will put myself first, I can't survive with the guilt of yet another death on my shoulders.

"Be quiet," Nicole whispers from my left side, and I see her shifting her weight as well. The floor fucking hurts. "He's coming."

We keep our heads down, but it's not one set of footsteps coming into the large area, it's multiple. I discreetly look up through my lashes and promptly regret it when I make eye contact with Michael. He has a smirk on his face as he stops a few feet away from me. I keep my eyes up, trying not to show too much fear. Their shoes are close enough to count them, so I do. Seven pairs. I can't even imagine what task would take seven men, and the only one that comes to mind makes a shiver run down my spine and takes over my body.

"That's right, baby girl." Michael says with a sneer, but I refuse to look up at him. Maybe that's the right thing to do either way. Last time I looked at him without permission, someone died. "You *should* be scared." Michael laughs at me when I shiver.

"Well I'm not," I say through gritted teeth. "So shove your words up your ass."

Michael chuckles, then it turns into a full belly laugh, echoing off the walls of the empty dungeon.

Nicole whimpers at my side, and I remember she's the new one here right along with me. Not that it matters, she and I have a lot in common. Neither of us has been broken in yet, and I sense something big's going to happen tonight. According to Tomás, I've been here for three weeks. I don't think I'll get much more time. In fact, I don't even know how he's had mercy on me for this long. I'm starting to get suspicious.

Footsteps echo in the room as Michael steps forward and

stops right in front of me. The only sound in the room is heavy breathing, I'm assuming from us girls, and the buckle of his belt being undone. Black slacks drop to his ankles, and my eyes follow a trail up his leg to see him jerking his big dick. I quickly drop my gaze, regretting that choice. But my curiosity got the best of me. I hate the unexpected. Not knowing what comes next gives me anxiety, and the worst part is that he knows me like I'm his daughter because he raised me my entire life. He's clearly playing mind games with me, trying to drive me insane with crippling and paralyzing fear. I squeeze my eyes shut, scrunching them tightly. I don't want to watch whatever the fuck he's about to do.

"José," Michael says, "Help me with her."

More footsteps.

These are from behind however, since they sound different. My body tenses further when I feel heat pressed up against my back. Suddenly my hair is painfully yanked back until my neck is straining, and my body is forced up to face Michael's thick erection, the veins on the shaft straining from his tight grip. I don't know what the fuck is so arousing about this situation, yet he seems to be enjoying it.

I close my eyes and try to go to another place, picturing when Zayne was between my legs, or the first time Damien and I had sex. Even with those thoughts, my fear still doesn't go away. Then I mentally slap myself for being stupid enough to think that memories of them would help me right now.

My fear is palpable as the man behind me touches my face, pressing his fingers into the small space under my ear, right between my neck and jaw, forcing my mouth wide open. I cry out from the pain, tears springing to my eyes, and Michael takes advantage of that opportunity to shove himself into my mouth, hitting deep into my throat until I'm gagging. He doesn't let up, not even so I can breathe, and even though I try to close my mouth and bite him I'm unable to with my mouth being forced open.

I begin to choke on him, my throat contracting from the need to throw up, and I taste the bile rising. "Yessss," Michael hisses, "That's it."

My sobs are inaudible with his cock shoved down my throat, and I don't have to put any work in as he fucks my mouth until I can feel my lips splitting. The cuts burn when my tears touch them, making trails down my face until they fall from my chin and onto my chest. If I had a shirt, it'd be soaked. Only my decency is not preserved here. It holds no value. I'm just another piece of shit on the bottom of his shoe, and he wants to remind me more than ever. In fact, he makes it a point to remind me every single day that I'm his favorite, and that will always make me feel worse than shit. Disgusting doesn't begin to cover it anymore. I'm tainted forever now, and I'll never be able to erase his touch from my skin.

When he spills down my throat, I gag, sputter, choke, refusing to swallow it. Michael removes himself from my mouth roughly, and I instantly throw up on the black and white speckled tile. My body contracts with the force of my heaves, and I keep gagging even after there's nothing left to expel. I crawl away from the puke, not wanting to touch it, and they let me go a few feet before Michael laughs.

A heavy boot comes to my back, pushing me down onto the tile until I'm flat on my stomach, and then a body restrains me so I can't move. Once I stay still, I feel a bare erection against my ass, and all of the fight returns to my body as if my heart was restarted. Except I still feel dead.

I kick and flail my arms, "No!" I scream, trying to rock my body to get him off, but he's too heavy. José keeps me in place by pushing me down, putting all his weight into my back, and opening my legs with his knee, shoving them apart. "Get the fuck off me," I cry out, but it's weak.

Is there even a point to this?

Why the fuck do I keep fighting this hard?

I know I will suffer the same fate regardless of what I do, and this is just making them want to hurt me even more. Maybe if I stay still and let this guy fuck me, Michael will finally leave me the fuck alone.

After a lot of convincing myself, I let my body go slack. I can't describe it as allowing myself to relax, for there's no way that could ever happen. But I am limp, a puppet for them to play with. The man at my back definitely controls me as he shoves himself deep inside me without thinking about how dry I am. I hope it feels like he's fucking sandpaper because that's exactly what it feels like to me.

He grabs my hips and pulls me up toward him until I'm on my knees, my ass angled up, and fucks me roughly. I try not to make a sound even though it hurts, but a small whimper escapes me.

"Fuck her harder," Michael taunts, "I want to hear her screams."

"Get the fuck off me!" I scream, a shrill sound, a desperate plea that goes unheard.

The man does as Michael tells him. My face is forced onto the tile, my cheek throbbing from how it rocks, and the bone feels like it's breaking with every thrust. I cry in earnest when he hits my cervix, and my eyes search the men in the room for Tomás. I don't even know why the fuck I do, it's not like he can save me. In fact, he's probably in line to get a piece of my ass.

I'm grateful this asshole finishes fast, probably because of how hard he just fucked me, and he lets go of my body. His cum drips out of me, and silent tears stream down my face, trailing over my nose and the side of my face until they land on the tiles. My body is spent already, fucking weak, and I sag onto the floor, letting myself close my eyes. I don't want to do this anymore. My limbs are heavy, but moving is futile—I can't do it. I open my eyes just to see Michael kneeling at my side. He wipes my face with the back of his fingers, being gentle. The hate I feel seeps from my pores, and the same hazel eyes that have haunted my nightmares for over a decade look into mine.

His face reflects pity, but it feels condescending. His hazel eyes turn down, and he tsks, his bottom lip drawing into his teeth. There's not one genuine bone in his rotten body, so I shouldn't be surprised. "Are you going to let me fuck you yet?" Michael whispers, "I don't want you to fight me."

"Fuck no," I reply through gritted teeth.

"I'll be gentle, baby girl." This time he smiles, and it chills my bones. It's more disturbing than pity. His eyes promise violence if I don't get my ass in line. I have a feeling he's going to force me to toe said line. "I can't promise the rest of them will be."

Before I can think about what I'm doing, my hand shoots out and grabs his neck, my fingers gripping the front of it as hard as I can, and I dig my nails in. The look of unrestrained rage is scary as fuck, but it's too late to back out now. What's done is done. "I said no."

Over my dead fucking body, will I ever give him a piece of myself willingly.

Michael's hand comes to my wrist, gripping it tightly and forcing me to let go of him. Surprisingly, he doesn't hurt me, not personally. Instead, he nods to the next man who has been standing around, and with a solemn expression, he steps forward. I've never seen him before, maybe he's new, and if he has a conscience he will leave here and never come back. I don't think that's how it works, sadly. Once you're in, it's for life.

I know what it's like to sell your soul to the devil.

Or devils.

I'm flipped over onto my back, and the man doesn't make eye contact with me as he spreads my legs apart and looks at my pussy. I can't blame him for the way his eyes light up. Pussy is pussy, I fucking guess. My back makes a squeaking sound as he drags my body toward him, and he spreads my pussy lips, rubbing the last guy's cum all over my labia and clit. He plays with it, with me, like he's trying to turn me on. How fucking delusional of him to think I give a fuck about whatever he's doing to me. When he realizes my expression stays neutral, he seems to snap out of it and shoves his way inside me.

Dissociation has always been my specialty; for once, it's not failing me. I try to keep my mind blank, but the images that come to mind are of Damien and Zayne. I never seem to think of the bad ones, no, of course not. I only ever remember the good times. That's why I keep going back like nothing ever happened. And so I see them clear as day, Zayne kissing the inside of my wrist, Damien yanking my head back roughly. Their eyes flash through my mind repeatedly, alternating between blue and green until I feel dizzy. Even when I scrunch my eyes I can't get them out of my head, and it might just be worse than living in this moment.

It's pure fucking torture because I'll never see them again. Never get to kiss them, talk to them, fight with them. And I did it to my fucking self. This is all my fault, and now I'm paying for my mistakes.

I snap out of my trance enough to feel my body rocking with the speed of this man's thrusts, and I make eye contact with Tomás across from me, watching intently. There's a crease between his eyebrows that looks a lot like worry, but that can't be right. His body looks tense, and he doesn't take his eyes off me, doesn't break eye contact even for a second. It's a bit unnerving, albeit comforting.

For some stupid reason I thought the man fucking me was trying to be nice when he wanted to make me come. Only that foolish thought is instantly wiped from my brain when he slaps me across the face. Hard. My head snaps back toward him, and he seems angry. "Look at me when I fuck you, bitch." My lip stings, and I feel a trickle of blood down my chin.

I nod frantically, keeping my eyes on his face while also unfocusing my gaze until he's blurry. Just because I can't look away doesn't mean I will give him the satisfaction of actually watching him. He takes longer than the last guy though, and my vision can only un-focus for so long before I have to try again. I think he's trying to draw out the torture, but I guess I should be grateful no one is beating my ass. Or fucking it.

Finally, he roars his release, then slumps over me. I cry when his sweat rubs against my bare skin, and he laughs at me. I want to burn my skin off, singe it until there's nothing left, and the remnants of these men are incinerated forever. Tears stream down my face as he gets up and pulls his zipper back up, effectively tucking himself away.

"How about now, pretty girl?" Michael walks over to me, halting right in front of my face and crouching down to my level. "You ready to make it all stop? I can make it nice for you."

"Please," I sob, "Don't do this to me."

Michael tsks, his face morphing into the most sinister smile I've ever seen. "I already have, baby girl."

I shake my head once more. "No."

Maybe I'm the masochist to his sadist, and that's why he torments me so much. However I can't give him what he wants. Not willingly. I need to know without a shadow of a doubt that I at least tried my damn hardest to keep my sanity this time around. I just feel like it's costing me way more than I bargained for, and my sanity is less intact than it has ever been, even though he hasn't even gotten started with me.

He stands and gives me his back, his dress shirt and black slacks, a contrast to how he used to dress. How the fuck did he get here? Whose dick did he suck to afford this house? How does he even have enough money to buy people?

"Tomás," Michael barks, "You're up."

Not him.

I don't want his image tainted in my eyes. I can't handle him treating me like shit too. Chewing me up and spitting me back out, not when he's helped pick up some of the pieces that were trying to fall apart.

My eyes plead with Tomás, but his eyes stay hard, and I sweep mine over his body, trying to find his jeans and boots attractive, the way his fitted shirt clings to lean muscle. I try not to hate him, I know he has no choice either way. It's not like he can tell Michael. No, he'd probably be killed on the spot. I don't want that fate for him; I also don't want to hate him.

Not even the girls who are here for the same purpose have shown any kind of caring. I can't blame them. Everyone is on their own here. We have to watch our own backs, not each other's.

"Be gentle with her. Maybe then she'll start to listen."

Tomás kneels on the ground, and I willingly part my legs for him, giving him what I haven't given the others—unspoken consent. We share a look, and he seems to understand as he unbuttons his pants and shoves them down as far as he can while kneeling. His tan skin is exposed to me, and he fists his cock in one hand and works himself slowly while he looks at my face. It almost reminds me of Zayne.

I notice Tomás is not looking at my pussy, probably because it's got other men's nasty shit leaking out of it. No reason to be offended though, I'd be grossed out too.

I *am*.

He grabs my thighs gently and spreads them further apart, then positions himself between them. His body is warm when he puts his elbows on either side of me as his mouth comes to my ear, and he kisses it gently. "You have to come, *linda*, or he won't stop," he whispers, and I still for a moment. "I'll make you feel good; you can forget about this place for a minute."

Tomás reaches between us and gently enters me. It's almost worse than how the others treated me. I knew it didn't mean anything to them, and I tried to ignore their hands on me, their bodies on top of mine. But this feels different. Intimate.

Guilt claws its way up my throat, making it hard to breathe as he begins to move inside me slowly, dragging out his thrusts, turning me on. Zayne is dead though, and Damien fucking hates me. There aren't any other chances for us in this lifetime, especially with me being trapped here. I need to stop thinking about them.

Stop.

I look into his eyes and nod, and he comes to my ear and whispers, "You're so pretty," My legs wrap around his waist, and his pelvis grinds against my clit expertly. He knows what he's doing, thankfully. "I want to see your face when you come." His teeth sink into my earlobe softly, and I moan, unable to contain it.

Suddenly, there's no one else except him in this room. I don't want to look at Michael or the other men who got a turn with me like I'm some kind of amusement ride. The only thing that matters to me right now is forgetting about everything, just like Tomás said. It doesn't even matter if it only lasts one minute. I'd gladly take it.

Tomás goes back to his knees, pulling me up off the ground until only my upper back rests on the tile, my shoulder blades hurting from the hardness of it. But when he pulls out and slams back in, making me see black, I don't even feel it anymore. My fingernails dig into his legs as he repeats the motion, this time running his hand down my belly and resting his palm on it. His thumb brushes against my clit softly, and I clench, making him tighten his hold on me. I plant my feet on the ground and fuck him back. He stares at my pussy like it's his salvation. When his thumb circles my clit and he rocks us back and forth, I close my eyes to savor the feeling.

This is the closest I've felt to being cared for since I arrived. Yes, he has been nice to me, sweet even, yet this is different. I realize maybe I do have a problem, after all. Needing sex as a form of reassurance that someone fucking loves me.

Only it is what it is. Maybe Tomás will be that for me. The one who saves me from going batshit crazy. He can't stop anything Michael wants to do, but he can tape me back up after everything is said and done.

Tomás increases his pace, his thumb also speeding up to match his thrusts. I moan again when he hits the spot inside of me that makes me want to pull him closer, so I do. I wrap my legs around his ass and pull him further into me, and his mouth opens on a moan. I'd never let myself notice how handsome he is with his tan skin and dark brown eyes, black hair that falls over his forehead and hides him from my view, depending on what angle I'm seeing him from.

My spine tingles the longer he rubs my clit, and my legs begin to tremble where I have them locked at the ankles. I let them fall and just ride out the wave. He doesn't speak but mouths the words instead, and I read his lips perfectly.

"Come for me." I nod, closing my eyes and biting my lip to keep myself from making a sound, but as he goes faster and faster, it feels like I'm going to fucking explode. Then he pinches my clit hard, and all sense of self disappears. I come so hard it feels like I'm pulling a fucking muscle, and he waits until I'm finished to cover me like a blanket all over again.

"Beautiful." Tomás breathes against my ear, moaning as he gets closer to his release, pounding me harder right before he comes.

We catch our breaths for half a second before my stepfather begins to clap, and I cringe. "That's how I've wanted to see you this whole time, Hallie." Michael chuckles, "Good job, Tomás. Finally, someone who can do the job right."

We breathe a sigh of relief and then he pulls out of me, putting his pants back on and zipping them up before walking away without a second glance. Leaving me on the ground spread wide open, empty. Discarded like the fucking trash that I am.

Maybe this has been my fate all along because I deserve it.

I deserve this.

All the pain I'm feeling is for a reason: I'm worthless.

I don't deserve anything good in this fucking lifetime. I need to come to terms with that already and stop being fucking delusional that this is temporary.

Michael nods at the two men who fucking tainted my body and mind, and they come to either side of me, holding me down. My fight-or-flight instincts kick in, and the violence returns, possessing my body like a demon. I do end up clawing someone's face in my fit of rage, but when a fist lands on my temple I don't have it in me to fight anymore.

When Penelope comes to me with a needle at the ready, I freak out all over again. She doesn't even try very hard to do it correctly. I'm sure she could've done a better job at looking for a vein. At least, all she did just now was put her finger on one and jab the needle in. I don't know what the fuck is in there, but I know it can't be good.

"Stop, stop!" I yell, not wanting to be given drugs that could ruin my life forever. "Don't do this!"

"It's too late for you, girl," Penelope replies, then pushes the plunger.

A warmth spreads throughout my body, as if I'm going to pee myself from how hot it feels down there. It feels like I'm tripping, tumbling, falling, soaring over a precipice. It's indescribable, except it's also clear that this euphoric feeling can't be good for me.

Except nothing has ever felt more right.

I smile at the feeling of pure bliss enveloping my body, and I decide I don't give a fuck about anything anymore. Nothing but pocketing this feeling to remember it forever. And that's the last thought that passes through my mind before I black out.

My body feels like shit today. I'm sore all over, probably due to all the abuse I suffered yesterday. Whatever they gave me is also making me feel like I have a massive hangover, and even though I have a pretty good idea about what it was due to the needle, I'm trying my best not to think about it. I don't need to become addicted to yet another drug. I *can't*. Xanax and alcohol have been my vices for a long time, but I sense I could be best friends with just about any downer. I don't want Michael to figure that out, so no matter how much I enjoyed that little stint, I won't act willing about them drugging me.

Thankfully I'm not getting zip tied in bed anymore, so I can finally use the bathroom on my own. Not that I want to get out of bed anyway; however, they'll probably come get me soon. I better take care of business while I can.

The pedestal sink is super small, and the wall has no mirror. At least they provide me with toothpaste and a toothbrush, and I can shower every morning now. The meals are pretty crappy, however. I bet prisoners get fed better than us, but I'd rather starve to death than be kept here for longer.

I brush my teeth, making sure to be thorough to hopefully get the taste of him out of my fucked up mind, and use a water bottle to swish and spit. No way am I putting the nasty water in my mouth. I've heard horror stories about getting the bubble guts here, and I'm unwilling to put myself in that position.

My door opens, and I cover myself, but it's pointless. I'll always be naked here, no matter what I do. It's not like they haven't seen all of it anyway, and I guess some of them have already sampled me, so why do I give a fuck anyway. When I glance over my shoulder though, I see it's just Tomás coming in, and the sound of the door shutting behind him makes me cringe. I need to stop being so fucking scared of everything. It gives Michael ammunition to manipulate and take advantage of me. Although I'm sure he'd still do it, regardless.

"Are you okay?" Tomás asks me, and I turn around all the way as tears spring to my eyes. Fucking pathetic. All I do lately is cry. He takes a few steps toward me, and I take one back. He halts, holding his hands up in surrender.

"What do you think?" I ask him.

The memory of his hands on me last night is burned into my mind, him calling me pretty, making me feel special. I'm anything but, and I'm not delusional. This man could care less about me. In fact, he'd still do whatever Michael says. Only I don't really want to think about it. I want to forget I'm here in this shit hole, being used and abused, wholly forgotten by the only people who have ever mattered to me.

"I think," Tomás starts as he walks toward me, stopping directly in front of me until he's almost flush with me. "You need someone to make this all better."

"And what makes you think that?"

He looks into my eyes without touching me, his hands still by his side. Except his body against mine feels warm, inviting, like a safe harbor. "Because everything is about to get so much worse."

I know he's not wrong. I can only be given a little leeway for so long, and I can tell Michael's patience is wearing thin. After what happened last night, I'd go as far as saying it vanished, and I'm in for a world of pain. Way more than he's already inflicted. I guess I better prepare myself for when he decides it's his turn to take me for a spin.

"Make it better then," I counter, "But just a little. I don't need to start seeing you as an escape." Even though that's exactly what he will be if I don't put a stop to it.

Tomás grabs my ass and pulls me against him then kisses me. He doesn't hold my face, and I don't hold his. It's almost impersonal, like we're just taking what we need from each other, that is, until his hand makes it between my legs from behind and he cups me. His tongue glides between my lips, and I part for him, letting him take even more than I've already given him. Red flags wave in my mind, but I ignore them. Something is causing me to feel like I'm making a huge mistake, like I'll regret this later. Only I can't put my finger on it. Why should I feel guilty? I have enough guilt to live with.

No one gives a fuck about me anymore.

I palm his cock over his jeans, and he's straining against them. He groans when I rub him down his length and over the head as I suck his tongue harder. His fingers thrust inside me softly, hooking into me, and he begins to fuck me with them slowly, as if he cares that I'm in pain. Soon enough, I'm panting against his mouth, so close and almost there. I bite the inside of my cheek when my eyes start rolling to the back of my head as I come.

He releases me almost as quickly as he made me come and washes his hands in the sink. I take toilet paper and wipe myself, not wanting wetness dripping down my legs. Tomás goes to stand by the door, as if waiting for me, then motions for me to come to him.

"Penelope is expecting you."

My back goes ramrod straight, dread seeping through my bones. What if she can smell me? Will she know Tomás made me come?

I clear my throat and nod. "Okay." My voice breaks regardless.

I need to stop being such a fucking coward. I know what my stepfather is capable of, and he might hurt me to an extent, but not permanently. He will not kill me; I know that for a damn fact. Michael didn't go through all this trouble, jump through so many hoops, just to let me go. No, I'm stuck with him for life now.

My worst nightmare has become my reality.

"I'm sorry," Tomás tells me as he roughly grabs my upper left arm and drags me out of the room. "I have to play the part."

I don't reply. There's nothing to say. What happened a few minutes ago was nice while it lasted, but I know I can't trust him. I don't trust anyone and never will again after this. The last time I trusted someone…it didn't end well. Regardless of what Damien said, he did lie to me, did take me against my will, did keep me in a basement. Regardless of intentions, he still did those things. So excuse me if I have fucking trust issues now.

Once we're in what they call the dungeon, Tomás releases me. There's an older man, maybe in his forties, who has a small cart set up with items I don't recognize. They're all wrapped anyway, so I can't tell until he gets them out of the packaging, which only makes me more nervous.

Did I do something?

Are they going to punish me for what just happened?

How did they find out?

It smells like antiseptic and sex in this place, and it makes me wonder even more what the fuck he's brought to me.

"Come here, girl." Penelope's voice booms out. She thinks she has authority here, but the fact remains that Marcela is the top bitch. Penelope just wishes she was. "Sit." She motions to a long chair next to the strange man, and I don't miss the restraints attached to the chair. It looks like something you'd lie on at the doctor's office.

Fear seems to be the primary emotion I experience nowadays, but even still, it's stronger in some situations than in others. And right now, I feel like I may need a fucking Xanax. My mouth dries up the longer I look at the chair, and I shake my head. "What are you doing to me?" I gesture at the man and the chair.

Penelope laughs, "You need to learn to shut your fucking mouth, *pendeja*." Her accent is strong, but she speaks English very well. It's a shame, really. I'd rather not understand a word coming out of her mouth. "Here, you bow your head and do as you're told."

"Listen bitch," I say through gritted teeth, "There's no way in hell I'm getting on that fucking chair, especially if you don't tell me what it's for."

"Get on that chair," Penelope grins, "Or get doped up and end up on the chair anyway."

Chills erupt over my body, spreading like wildfire. So it was heroin, what they gave me last night. My suspicions are right; I can't let them do that again. "You're not doping me up."

Penelope nods her head once, and José steps up to me, a needle in his hand. "Have you changed your mind yet?" She asks me, head cocked to the side.

I look up at José, now only two feet away, feet shoulder-width apart. He's a big man with a broad back and clearly fit. I thought he was going to break me last night. There's no fucking way I can fight him and win. That much is already evident. So when I see the punch coming, I turn my face to the side, effectively avoiding the blow to the center of my face. Instead, he hits my cheekbone, and I hear a loud crack.

I fall to my knees, holding the side of my face as I sob, and when I take one hand off, it's covered in blood. I hold it up to him, "Stop, please." José halts, looking down at me with a smile. "I'll get on the chair."

Penelope walks over to the chair as I struggle to get up from the ground, and José leads me to it from behind. I willingly sit down, lying back on it all the way and closing my eyes. I try to ignore the feeling of hands on my limbs as my ankles and forearms are restrained. It's weird that it's not at the wrists, especially since that's how they have usually secured me.

"Leave us," the man now sitting beside me tells them. Penelope looks fucking pissed but, surprisingly, turns around and walks out of the room.

"What's your name?" I ask him as he turns his back to me and returns to the cart, beginning to unwrap something. I hope he's not planning on torturing me, I haven't prepared myself for that mentally just yet. "Or what should I call you?"

I realize I'm just trying to fill the silence, yet it's giving me anxiety. A name to a face would ease it a little bit, I think, though I can't be sure. It all depends on what he's planning on doing to me, I guess.

"Tony." The man replies. He looks around forty, with tanned skin and almond-shaped eyes. He's wearing a loose white t-shirt and black slacks, like he just took off a suit jacket and button-up shirt. "But I doubt you will want to talk anyway." He may be right in about five minutes, but at this time, I do. The vibe I get from him is off, creepy.

"Have you been doing this a long time?"

Maybe there is something wrong with me after all. Why would I ask that? I shouldn't care how long he has been doing whatever he's about to do. The one thing that's bothering me currently is my state of undress. I know everyone here has seen me naked, and I probably shouldn't care at this point, but this man hasn't. For some reason, that makes me nervous. Not to mention the fact that I'm spread wide open for him with these restraints on.

"Yes, I have." Tony replies, "At least half of my life."

All thoughts die a short death in my brain when he turns around with a buzzing needle in his hand and ink in the other. He sits on a stool with wheels and glides around to the side of the bed, then sets the ink next to me and clamps a hand around my arm.

"W-what are you doing?" My voice shakes, and I can almost taste my fear. Fuck, I can smell it emanating from my damn pores like alcohol poisoning.

"Stay very still, Hallie," Tony warns me. "Or this will be more painful than it needs to be."

More painful.

So this is going to be a painful ordeal as it is. The vibrating needle goes into the ink pot, and he presses it to the inside of my wrist that Zayne loved to kiss so damn much. I scream as the needle meets the sensitive skin, and my hips buck reflexively. The restraints are secured better than I thought though, and no matter how much I yank, move, or thrash, they won't fucking budge.

Tony's grip is bruising, and he doesn't let go. No matter how much I fight, he expertly holds my arm down, probably because he's had a lot of practice with this. He's giving me a fucking tattoo, and quite frankly, I don't want to know what it is. I know I won't like it, and that's why I close my eyes tightly and try to ignore the pain in my wrist. But the pain in my heart is much harder to disregard. I can't believe this is happening to me. I wish I was dead. I need to find a way to make that happen. I'm too weak to live with these memories.

After what feels like forever, the buzzing turns off. My skin is on fire. Tony, however, wipes it down with some kind of lotion and then slaps a bandage on it.

Just like that. I'm fucking ruined.

He rolls around to the end of the chair with his stool and rests his hands on the edge of it, staring right at my pussy with appreciation. I close my eyes so I don't have to see what happens next. I'm sure he's been given permission to fuck me, just like everyone else in this disgusting place. Anything to make me suffer and give in to what Michael wants. I will endure; I'd rather give myself to countless men than be snared in the one trap that ensures my death.

Fingers part me, pry me, grope me. I still refuse to look. Except a door suddenly opens, and Tony's hands disappear. When Michael's voice booms through the ample space, all my muscles lock up. I'm like a deer in the headlights, frozen, useless.

"Are you putting your hands on my property?" Michael questions Tony, and at that word, I flinch. Fucking *property*. That's all I am now—the same as a car or a house. I'm nothing.

"No, sir," Tony lies, beginning to pack up quickly.

Before I know it, he's gone and all that's left in the room is me and the motherfucker who has ruined my entire life. I hate him so much I could fucking kill him right now. He better hope I never get the chance, because I won't think twice before taking it.

"Did you see it yet, baby girl?" Michael asks me with a grin, his eyes appreciative of the bandage like he already knows what it looks like. I shake my head no. "Let's take a peek, yes?" I nod, not because I want to, but because I'm fucking exhausted.

My shitty fucking mattress sounds good right about now, and so does the dope they gave me last night. Anything to put me in a deep slumber and make me forget what's happening.

Michael gently pulls the bandage back, carefully peeling the tape back like he cares about my pain. I want to laugh and slap him all at the same time. If he gave a shit, he wouldn't be letting everyone touch me, fuck me, inflict pain on me. He can take all this fake concern and shove it up his ass. Or maybe it's all an act, yet another way to fuck with my head. Yeah, that's probably it.

"Look, baby girl," Michael purrs, and this time I do turn my head at the awe in his voice. I don't know what I was expecting, but my eyes fill with tears when I take in the sight before me. Swollen, angry red skin stares back at me, but on top of that… a barcode with his name below it. "Now you can see every day that you belong to me."

A tear slides down my cheek, betraying me. Only there's no way I can keep holding myself together. My tattered body is not strong enough to hold all the pieces falling apart. Breaking away from me. I'm tired, torn apart. I can feel the fight draining from me ever so slowly.

It all makes sense now, why they haven't zip-tied me anymore. Michael has been planning to brand me all along, like I'm fucking cattle. But it makes sense, I basically am. He can't be letting me get away from him, someone else stealing me from under his nose. I wonder what he has planned for me if he needs this on my wrist. Is he taking me to other places? Showing me off? Letting people sample me? The thought of more men touching me makes me sick to my fucking stomach. Just not as sick as him touching me.

Michael wipes my tears away, his fingers brushing against the cut on my cheek. I cry out from the pain, and he shushes me. "It's okay. If you're a good girl, I'll give you a break. No one will touch you anymore."

"What does being a good girl mean?" I blurt out in a moment of weakness.

Michael's eyes glimmer with interest, and I probably unleashed the beast within him unknowingly. "Letting me have you without a fight." His hand trails from my face all the way to my breast, squeezing gently, pinching my nipple. "Going back to how it used to be."

"Never."

"Are you sure?" His hand goes to my pussy, and he cups it, parting me with his fingers and rubbing my clit in slow circles. My body responds, my hips buck to meet the touch, and I fucking hate myself. "I don't have much patience left, Hallie."

With a look of pure lust in his eyes, he continues to rub me, this time faster, and I begin to rock my hips without noticing. More tears stream down my face as he brings me pleasure that I don't want but also can't control. There's a smirk on his lips when my body begins to shake. I fight the restraints, but his hand disappears from between my legs.

"See?" He taunts, "I can make it good for you too." With that, he walks away from me, going to the door. Before he exits, he turns around and peers over his shoulder at me. "Oh, and, Hallie?"

"Yes?" I whisper, barely audible, and I don't know if he hears me.

"There's a surprise in your room." I freeze, not sure I want more surprises anyway. "Either you accept my terms, or I will start taking more from you than you can imagine."

Michael walks out of the dungeon, leaving me wondering about what the fuck he's talking about, yet also managing to scare me shitless. It doesn't take long before José comes back for me, however. When he drops me off in my room and I find a second bed right next to mine, I understand what he means. This is how he gets me to comply, how he forces my hand and leaves me no choice.

Brittany's eyes meet mine from across the room, her body naked and tears streaming down her face, just like me. My best friend is perched on her bed completely naked, with a bloodied lip and sobs racking her body. Just when I thought my heart can't break any more than it already has, I feel it shattering in my chest all over again.

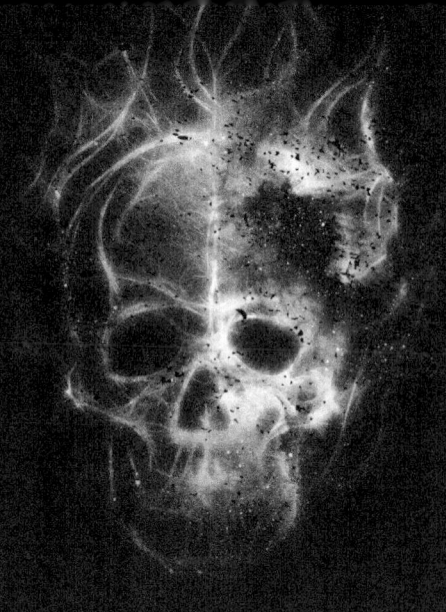

CHAPTER 6

Damien

The Kentucky Club is busy as fuck tonight, being Saturday, and I'm hoping to have better luck tonight. If everything goes my way, I won't even have to go inside the bar tonight. It's possible Carl may already be looking for me here, wondering why I followed him last night and if maybe I'm watching him. He may have even brought back up tonight, for all I fucking know, and I could be walking right into a trap. I'd rather not give him the satisfaction of letting that happen. That's why I brought a trusty little friend with me, a tracker.

My plan is to attach it to his vehicle somewhere not visible to him. It's a tie between the inside of a wheel or behind the license plate. Under his car might be the first place he looks, especially if he's paranoid. As he should be, the fucker must know he's not getting away with this shit forever. Or maybe he's delusional and deems himself untouchable. It's laughable how people make things up in their heads to make themselves feel better or even continue making the same mistakes over and over again. The lines are blurred, their boundaries nonexistent, and that's why they always get caught.

He will be no different. I will snare him in my trap sooner or later, but I won't make him a clean kill. I'm taking my time with him. It's not even for Zayne's sake, it's for my damn self. I need to inflict pain, to channel this fucking rage that seems to be consuming me from the inside out. There's no better way for me than torturing someone for hours on end. It's therapeutic.

I choose the back of the license plate, for the simple reason that it's easier for me to stay concealed from everyone else's view if I stand behind the car. Carl's black vehicle faces the bar entrance, and if I crouch and start looking suspicious by one of his tires, someone is bound to come asking questions. I can't have that, not tonight. The only thing I currently have on me is the tracker. The rest of my belongings are in my locked car on the other side of the parking lot. The plan is to attach the tracker to the car and get the fuck out of here.

My eyes scan the area, looking in all directions before discreetly walking behind Carl's vehicle and planting the tracking device behind the license plate. It's very subtle, and if someone didn't know exactly what I was doing, they would just think I accidentally grazed the back of the car with my hand as I walked by.

Once I walk away from the car, I head straight for my own. I'm waiting until he's gone and then I'll follow him using the app on my phone that shows me where he is. All I have to do is click on the directions so the GPS takes me there, and voilà, I get to his hiding spot.

Except when I begin digging in my back pocket for my key, a white van skids across the parking lot and stops behind my car. Two men get out and grab me, not even bothering to put anything over my head or conceal their identities. They want me to know who they are. I'd like to say I have no idea who they are or what they want, but that would be a lie. Sadly, I've pissed off too many people lately, and a lot of them want me dead. Like the Cartel. The problem with that is that they have friends here too, and so did I and my father. Now, they're not as friendly. Clearly.

I recognize both men as soon as they close the van's door behind them, and someone begins to drive. I'm glad I don't have my phone and that I didn't get my keys out. I can't imagine losing those; it would mean all of my belongings would also be gone. Everything I own is in that small car, and I need it all in order to find Hallie. Maybe I'm being stupid by thinking I'll get out of this and back to looking for the love of my fucking life, but if I'm not able to do that, I might just manifest it. The universe loves to play cruel fucking games.

"*¿Sabes quién soy?*" *Do you know who I am?* This guy has always been one of the top picks for enforcement regarding the skin trade. He's efficient and has no conscience—a little like I used to be prior to getting to know Hallie. "*Estoy hablando contigo güero.*"

I nod my head, "*Sí.*" There's not much I can say to keep them from doing whatever they want with me. I'll take it like the fucking man I am while hoping they don't kill me. I don't beg. Not for anyone.

"*Entonces, ¿por qué estás tan tranquilo?*" *Then, why are you so calm?* The man looks puzzled, but what he doesn't know is that I no longer fear death. I only fear what will happen to the person I leave behind. Only I won't make that obvious.

I shrug, "*No te tengo miedo.*" *I'm not scared of you.*

He lifts one eyebrow then grins like we're going to have so much fun together. I know the look; I've given the exact same one before. He's about to fuck up my world, and I'm going to let him. However, if I see an opportunity, I will tell him my plans. If I have nothing to lose, I might as well take a blind shot.

"*No te preocupes pronto lo tendrás.*" *Don't worry, you will be soon.*

I'm sure I will be at some point. I'll probably even wish death upon myself, but the chances that I'll give in to that weakness are low. Mind over matter, and I've trained myself for this countless times. There's a lot they can do to me to try to break me. They might even succeed to a certain extent, but I'll never give them the most valuable parts of me. If I don't want them to know a piece of information, then they won't.

After a while of driving, the van stops. It's hard to know exactly how long we were on the road since I don't have a watch. Yeah, I know, stupid fucking mistake. I don't know what I was thinking, but here I am.

For some reason, the second man in the back of the van hasn't directed a word to me the entire time. It's only been this other fuck face, and honestly, I'm more afraid of the quiet one. He's a little more like me. There's more chaotic energy hidden under layers of silence than the people who talk shit, and that's why you don't fuck with the silent ones. We're fucking unpredictable.

The driver gets out of the van, slamming the door, and everything goes quiet except for the sound of our breathing. Thankfully, I don't embarrass myself by breathing too hard or too fast. I act like I'm the picture of calm, like none of this shit affects me. There's truth in it to a certain extent, but I can't deny I'm afraid for Hallie if I don't make it out of here tonight. I can't bear the thought of her having to live this way until her last breath. She's my fucking weakness, one that is proving to be my undoing. If there's one thing I've learned from this entire ordeal is to not fall in love.

Love will get you killed.

The door in front of me opens, and I'm dragged out of the van by the two men who captured me. My feet trail across tiny little rocks scattered on a dirt road, and a warehouse comes into view after a minute or so of walking. I want to drag my feet, plant them, and resist, but I won't for the simple reason that I need to preserve my energy. Fighting won't get me anywhere, and I refuse to tire myself before they've even gotten started.

The warehouse is made out of steel, and the door is loud as fuck when they open it. I'm shoved into the building roughly, and if it weren't for the fact that they're holding on to me, I would've fallen face-first onto the concrete floor. It's dark here, with only one dim light on in the back. Chains are hanging from the ceiling, which I'll probably be tied up with soon enough, and one lone metal chair right below.

"Let's go, *puto*," the quiet guy tells me, and it's the first time he even looks at me. I willingly walk to the chair, quickening my steps so I'm not dragged, and then he shoves me down, not bothering to tie me up. He's either very stupid, or confident. I'm not sure which one is worse. "We have some talking to do."

I want to make a joke about how silent he's been, but I refrain. Reading the room is essential in this line of work, and right now, everything tells me to shut the fuck up. My time will come. "What's your name?" I ask him, not able to remember since I've only seen them a few times.

"I'm Diego," the quiet guy replies, his almond-shaped dark eyes sparkling even in the darkness. Oh, he gets off on this shit. Great. He points at the other guy, "And this is Armando. That's the last question you get to ask motherfucker."

Diego is a short, brown-skinned man with dark hair and stubble. His face looks like he wants to grow a beard but is in the early stages of it, and his almost black eyes are void of life, except for when he just threatened to inflict violence.

Armando whispers in his ear and laughs, but Diego's face remains emotionless. Not one indication as to what he was told, what he's feeling or planning. This is probably why he's one of the best in the game. His poker face is flawless.

I don't say anything to that, mainly because there is nothing to say. They know who I am, my name, and probably a lot more than I can imagine. It's possible they know why I'm here too, who I'm looking for. I might have nothing to lose if they're aware of all of that.

"Here's how it's gonna go," Diego says with a thick accent. "Armando is going to tie you to the chair, and you're not going to fight him. Then you're gonna sing for us real fucking pretty."

Sure.

I nod, staying still while Armando yanks my hands behind

my back and ties my wrists together with rope. I'm not exactly immobile, but I'd prefer not to make this harder than it needs to be.

"We're gonna start simple, *güero*." Diego flicks a knife open at his side, and I tense. I do not feel like getting stabbed again this soon. He couldn't just go for fingernails? Goddamn. "I'm going to ask you some questions, and you're going to answer them."

The fuck I am.

I don't reply, and they're not expecting me to.

"Why are you in Mexico?" Diego asks. Guess we're getting right into it, then. I'm assessing the situation in any case. Why do they want to know? Are they going to hurt Hallie if I talk? Are they going to ruin my chances of finding Carl's hiding spot? No fucking way am I wasting any of my plans over a bit of pain.

So I don't talk.

Armando rips my shirt down the front of it until it's just two scraps, then tosses it on the ground. He tsks, "*Alguien lo apuñaló.*" *Someone stabbed him.* They both laugh, and I can't lie, I would join them if I wasn't in this situation. Yeah, my love is a little fucking traitor.

I look into Armando's green eyes. He has lighter skin than Diego but not quite as light as mine. He would pass for American if he were in the United States, except here, maybe he doesn't because his hair is dark as well.

Diego sobers up quickly, his laugh dying in his throat faster than it came out. "I asked you a question, motherfucker. You like getting stabbed?" Fuck. Not again…

I shake my head and keep my eyes down on the ground. The knife comes under my chin, the tip against my skin until I feel the sting. It's meant to be a warning, but I couldn't care less about the pain. I welcome it at this point. I'll trade the pain in my heart for this one any fucking day.

Diego points at the chains hanging from the ceiling, and Armando smirks. "*Átalo allí.*" *Tie him up there.* Fuck, Diego, chill out man.

Of course, Armando does as he's told. I've noticed in the short time I've been here that the man seems to want to please Diego. Not only is he willing to do whatever he's told, but he's also enthusiastic about it. So accommodating. It's clear who's in charge here.

I willingly follow him to the chains while he acts like he's dragging me there. He's not fooling anyone. Even Diego can tell he doesn't have to make any effort for me to get there. It doesn't matter though, as long as I go where I'm supposed to.

Armando cuts the rope restraining my wrists just to replace it with chains. It's a good thing I've stayed calm. The last thing I need is to have my skin rubbed raw or have no energy left to deal with what's coming. They're clearly itching to let out some pent-up anger. I'd even go as far as saying they're a little bored and haven't seen any action in a while. At least Armando. The other guy doesn't look like he gives a shit about anything at all, except for the little twinkle in his eyes earlier. I'd say that's me too, but it's not true anymore. He, on the other hand, seems to have lost interest already.

When my arms are suspended above me, the chains pulling them so far up it feels like they're about to pop out of their sockets, Diego begins to circle me. "Are you ready to sing, little bird?"

I chuckle under my breath. Can't help myself. The fact that this is happening to me, that this is my life right now, is fucking ironic. Years and years of doing this shit to other people. I guess Karma does exist, and she's a fucking bitch. She really wants to fuck me right about now. In the ass. With no lube.

"The fuck is so funny, *pendejo*?" Diego asks me, and Armando hands him a whip. "You won't be laughing much longer."

Well, looks like we're having fun soon, after all.

"I'm going to ask you one more time, Damien." I look up at him at the mention of my name, meeting his eyes with my own narrowed ones. It only makes him smile. "What the fuck are you doing in Mexico?"

"Why do you want to know?"

Diego flexes his hand and the whip lashes across my back, forcing my body to straighten as much as it can. My back goes from warm to hot as my skin splits fucking open. I breathe in slowly through my nose, letting it out even slower.

"This ain't twenty questions, *puto*." Diego walks around to my front, crossing his arms across his chest with the whip hanging from a hand. Armando laughs in the background, and the sound irritates me to no end. "Only *I* ask the questions here."

I nod, keeping my eyes on the floor. "Understood."

"So you gonna talk or what?"

I look up at him, "Not until you tell me why you want to know."

Armando laughs again, "*Tiene cojones el cabrón.*" *The asshole has balls.* Not once have I heard him speak English, only Diego has. He's probably low ranking because of it.

Diego nods and uncrosses his arms, and I steel myself for the next lashing, which happens to be right on my stab wound. Soul-crushing pain floods my abdomen, and when the skin splits back open, it feels like it's on fire. I groan, and Diego smiles.

"We're getting somewhere now, yeah?"

Wrong.

Try again, asshole.

I'm not going to let this shit break me. Does it hurt? Fuck, yes, it does. The only difference is that I've done this for a living. I've done it so many times I know what to expect because they think like me. Now that they know I'm in pain, they'll try to break me even more. It's up to me to let it happen or not.

"Let's try something different, D," he says, and I sigh when he uses my nickname. I'm so fucking tired of this life, I have been for a long time. But this right here just reinforces that feeling. I want out. Living my own life away from this bullshit is my goal. "What were you doing at the Kentucky Club?"

"Drinking."

Another lashing, this time across my chest. Another groan past my lips. I hate myself more and more with every lashing, mainly for making noise and showing my pain. I refuse to scream, though. "Have you had enough yet? Are you going to tell me what I want to know?"

I grin a crooked smile even through the pain, which seems to piss him off even more. "*No, cabrón.*"

This time he walks around and whips me five times across my back. I hold my breath through it all, and the pain makes me dizzy. When I sway on my feet, it causes my arms to give out on me, effectively making me hang by them even further. I swear on my life, my shoulders will pop out of their sockets soon if they don't stop. I'd rather have my toenails ripped off.

"Were you following someone?"

I look up at that question, and he smiles. Something must be showing on my face because he raises one eyebrow while waiting for my answer. I hate that he read me; it must have been fucking evident for that to happen.

"Who?"

My eyes don't deviate from the ground even as I shake my head no, and Diego sighs impatiently. He's getting bored, which means soon enough he will switch tactics, and nothing he comes up with will be pleasant. Armando is a few feet behind Diego, which I can tell by the position of their shoes, and I let my eyes focus on him. He seems to find it amusing. Well, that makes one of us.

"*A mi no me mires, güero.*" *Don't look at me, white boy.* Armando comes to stand in front of me, "*No te voy a salvar.*" *I'm not going to save you.*

"You like acid baths, D?" No fucking way. What do I say to appease them without divulging too much? How *do* I appease them? I don't need to be set back even more, and there's no way I'm recovering from that quickly. Think. *Fucking think.* "I bet you've done that to someone else once or twice. Maybe now it's your turn?"

"I'll talk," I tell him, my voice hoarse. I cough to clear it and school my features into fear as much as possible, making Armando laugh again. It's all a fucking act, dumbass. "I *am* looking for someone."

"Who?"

"A man who has something I want back," I speak slowly, weighing my words, thinking about my exact words before saying them. "I wanted to follow him to wherever the fuck he hides."

Diego nods, and I know I'm saying the right thing because he drops the whip and begins to pace. "And who is he?"

"Do you know the line of work I usually deal in?"

He narrows his eyes at me, "I'm not fucking stupid, Damien." I narrow mine right back at him. "*Everyone* knows what you do."

"So then you must know the kind of client he is."

"Let me guess," He taps his chin with his forefinger in an exaggerated show of thinking, only serving to piss me off. I hate being mocked, and this fucker is going to die when I get out of these chains. "He took your woman?"

She left me, then they took her, but that's beside the point. "Something like that." Heat flares down my back all over again, and I stand straighter, trying to make it stop. One moment it feels like ants are crawling down it, and the next, it feels like it's on fire. It's driving me fucking nuts.

"Who is the man?"

I clench my fists and readjust myself yet again. "Some *gringo*."

"Name?"

Silence.

Diego walks right up to me and grips my cheeks in one hand, squeezing until it feels like he's going to break my jaw. That probably will still hurt less than if he fucked up my plans. "You might want to start talking, fucker."

I don't think it matters anymore. They're going to kill me anyway. No one makes it out of this shit, especially if they're targeted. I clearly have been. The best outcome I can hope for at this point is being shot in the head, and even then, they will more than likely hang me under a bridge once I'm dead. It's a warning not to fuck with them. "Carl."

They exchange looks, and Armando comes to stand next to Diego. Maybe I'm imagining things, possibly delusional, but it looks like they know who I'm talking about. It's not a comforting thought, mainly since I don't know who they work for. What if they work for him and take me to him? I'm not trying to end up like Zayne, that's for fucking sure.

"Last name?"

Fuck.

I'm out of options. Do I talk and die? Or do I shut the fuck up and die?

"Why?"

"Stick to answering the questions," Diego growls, "I hate sounding like a broken fucking record." Still, I don't answer him. "We might know who he is."

"Hewitt."

Armando asks, "*¿Es él quien compró a Adriana?*" *Is he the one who bought Adriana?* They seem to know who the guy is, possibly even want to take something from him. A girl?

Diego nods but doesn't say anything to Armando. "Is your woman there?"

"No, but he knows who took her."

He walks away, yelling over his shoulder, "*Bájalo.*" *Take him down.*

Armando does as he's told, just like when Diego gives him instructions. I immediately fall to my knees, my aching arms trembling and weak as fuck. The concrete does nothing to make me feel cooler, and as sweat runs down my spine, it stings my cuts. Pretty sure I need fucking stitches. Even still, I lower my body until I'm lying flat on my stomach, and rest my cheek against the floor. It hurts to fucking breathe at this point, but I'm still in better shape than three weeks ago. My ribs are not healed though, not all the way at least.

I don't know how long I've been here, lying on the nasty concrete that has dried bloodstains on it, but I can't find the will to get up. It's as if all the energy has been sucked from my body, and I'm just an empty shell. Armando and Diego went inside a different room, and who knows what the fuck they're plotting now and how I'll play a part in it.

Who the fuck is Adriana? Does Carl have her? And why does she matter to them?

Even though I can barely move right now, I'm very uncomfortable, so I slightly shift my weight only to have my arm slip while trying to do so. There's a puddle of blood under me, more like a river. I don't want to see what the fuck my cuts look like if I'm bleeding this much. Also, pretty sure my stab wound is wide open again. It feels like someone gutted me, which is extremely inconvenient because it was just now getting better after weeks of recovery. Fuck my life.

A door creaks in the distance, but I don't have the energy to care. "It's your lucky day, *güero*." Diego's voice booms even though it's a large space. "We're not going to kill you."

Not yet, at least.

"What do you want?"

Diego comes up to me and squats about a foot away, getting closer to face level and grimacing when he looks at the state I'm in. "You're a smart man." He stands back up and turns around, beginning to pace again. "If you're going after Carl, we want in."

"And why should I let you?"

"Other than not dying?" He laughs. Diego has a point, but whatever, I don't want to seem too eager to be alive. I nod anyway, even though I know it's going to piss him off. "We can help you get rid of any kind of security there when we tag along." Not *if*, but when. He really believes he has the right to insert himself into my operation just because he can cause me pain.

Maybe I need to set my ego aside. If they help me, it might get some people out of the way quicker than it would if I went on my own. There's a chance that they have better weapons than me, also a better vehicle to leave with more than one person and still keep them concealed. There are a lot of pros. Except what guarantee do I have that they won't leave me there after they get what they want?

"I need to know why you want to go in the first place." I don't even know if he can understand me. I feel like I'm drunk, my voice slightly slurring, and my stomach queasy.

"He took my sister," Diego replies, "and we're getting her back."

I sure as fuck won't be doing shit any time soon, thanks to the little stunt they just pulled on me. This was so fucking pointless, to fuck me up just to have me work with them. "Help me then."

I make eye contact with Diego, and he nods. "I'll get a doctor to fix you up, and as soon as you can walk, we'll go."

Even as everything else has gone to shit, I haven't made progress with my operation and just got fucked up, yet there is a bright side. I didn't think it was possible to have anything positive come out of this, however I was wrong. Because having two allies to help me out is about as close to a great thing as I'm going to get.

Let's just hope they don't betray me.

CHAPTER 7

Zayne

I must be doing something right, because I've been able to sleep in my cage for the past few days. The fact that I see that as something positive, that it even brings me happiness, fucking sickens me. Only here I am, doing things I never thought possible.

Adriana and I are still being forced to film live videos almost every day, and Carl hasn't stopped being a disgusting motherfucker. Not only does he show us to a bunch of pedophiles, but he's clearly one himself. Most of these girls are in their teens. He has no fucking business being around them in the first place. I think he has much more cash than these living conditions show, especially considering how many of us are in here.

Carl hasn't even been trying to ease me into his depravity. He's not exactly the patient type, anyway. I'm sore in places I shouldn't be, and I'm sure he hasn't even gotten started. I have a feeling all the fucked up shit he's been doing to me is just a warm-up, and the endless pain I've been experiencing is a small taste of what awaits me here.

The only thing that has kept me going is my growing friendship with Adriana. Obviously, we're not supposed to talk, and we rarely do. I barely know shit about her, but she's always there when I'm brought back to the cage. Even though she can't hug me or do much from the other side, sometimes she slips her hand through the bars and holds mine for a little while. Like right now. She's lying on her side, her pretty face against the ground, with her eyes closed. Her hand reaches through the bars holding mine, and when I squeeze it she opens her eyes and smiles at me.

A sharp pain explodes in my chest, taking my breath away, and I close my eyes once more. It feels wrong to do this, to betray Hallie in every single way. Only I know I'll never see her again.

The thought of never seeing Hallie again is fucking incapacitating, and I wish I could physically pluck these thoughts away from my mind. It's hard enough that I have to endure what's happening to me, but dealing with her loss is too much. So I try not to think about her at all, and every time I do, I ignore it. Whatever need, obsession, love I have for her… I need to bury it. I'm never going to get out of here, that's for fucking sure. Carl will never willingly let me go. I'm the lone man here, so he clearly saw something in me when he purchased me. Not to mention, Hallie is probably in Alaska or Canada or wherever the fuck is farthest from Texas. I'm the last thing on her pretty little mind. She doesn't care about me. That much was evident when she left me behind.

So why am I still crying over her? Feeling debilitating chest pain over her? Why is there constantly a knot in my throat when I think of her? And why the fuck should I not let someone else nurse my fucking wounds? Bring me back to life?

Maybe it's wrong of me to be using someone else to escape my intrusive thoughts of Hallie, but it's fucking depressing to sit here and think about her all day. My brain is playing tricks on me, and the cravings, the raw need I feel for the girl who is my entire fucking world, are even stronger than my addiction to meth. I never thought I'd see the damn day when she would matter more, except here we are. Either way, I'm suffering because neither of my vices is available.

"Zayne," Adriana whispers, and my eyes flutter open. "What do you want to do when we film again?" A smile takes over her face, and I force myself to return it.

"I—" The door opening cuts off my words, and she quickly lets go of my hand, withdrawing back into her cell.

A tall white man enters the room, his footsteps loud as fuck as all of us cower and avert our gazes. One thing I have noticed is that Carl primarily employs Americans, which makes sense since he is one too. I think it's possible he doesn't know much Spanish and doesn't want to hire anyone who does. Out of all the staff, I believe only two or three speak the native language here. They're women, and all of them are maids. You can tell they don't like what's happening here, that they're against it, but they can't say or do anything about it without risking their deaths. Or even be one more woman who doesn't make it out of this house and ends up in a cage, just like the rest of us.

There's a woman in the opposite corner of the room from where I am. She's more secluded than the rest of us and looks older. Her body is frail, her limbs bony and emaciated. Her dirty blonde hair is splayed on the floor, and she lies on her side. She doesn't even move when the guard opens the cell and grabs her arm. Instead, she stays very still when he takes out a—

Needle.

Fuck.

My body suddenly feels hot, tingles spreading through my limbs, spiders crawling on my face. I watch in awe and jealousy as the man uses a tourniquet on her arm and injects her with a drug. She still hasn't moved. Her expression hasn't changed.

Is she even alive? What the fuck? Is she constantly high? Do they even give her a moment of sobriety? Something tells me they're keeping her this way on purpose. Maybe revenge on someone? Or, possibly, she pissed him off too much for too long. I wouldn't put it past Carl to be that fucking petty.

The guard cleans up, putting the needle away and closing the cage back up. When he turns around, we make eye contact, and he smirks like he knows my deepest darkest secrets. I avert my gaze quickly, hoping I haven't given myself away. The last thing I need is for them to take advantage of my addiction as a form of manipulation, though I wouldn't expect any less from him.

Yeah, there's no fucking way in hell I'm admitting to shit.

"You," the man says, coming up to my cage and opening it. "Carl wants you." I cringe at the wording, although it's probably on purpose. He wants me to make another video with Adriana, which I don't mind anymore.

Speaking of, she kneels in the cage with her hands on her lap, her gaze on the ground in a submissive gesture. Adriana is always ready to do her job. Not because she wants to, but because she knows he won't be upset with her if she does it well and without complaints. Which, in turn, means he won't pick on her because she gives him what he needs.

"No," the guard tells her. "He won't be needing you for this."

Panic must show on my face, as when Adriana and I make eye contact, her eyes widen and her lips part. She's as surprised as I am, except I'm much more than that. I'm fucking scared shitless.

I'm led out of the room and into a dark hallway, one where I've never been before. I can't see much as my eyes are not used to this lighting, and I basically just go wherever this guy is dragging me. A chill runs down my spine when he stops and knocks on a door, and my instincts tell me that this is about to ruin my entire fucking life.

The door is opened, and on the other side stands Carl in a black silk robe, and I fist my hands until my fingers feel like they're about to snap. No. I'm not going in there. No fucking way.

The man behind me shoves me forward until I'm in the room, "Get the fuck in there, pretty boy, or things are about to get a lot worse for you."

He and Carl share a knowing look, and my heart speeds up to a gallop. "It's going to get worse anyway," Carl says.

This is different from the usual room I come to when Adriana and I have to film. There are black curtains, a king-sized bed, and a fireplace. It looks too… personal. Lived in. I glance around but promptly wish I wouldn't have. A tripod is situated right in front of the bed, and there's a cell phone attached to it, probably ready to record. What the fuck is he doing? What sick shit does he have planned for me?

Three more men come into the room, along with the one who brought me here, making them a total of four. Carl steps back, letting them walk past him, and I get ready for a fight I know I won't win. I'm outnumbered, weak, abused. I imagine I've been living in these shitty conditions for at least a month. Even still, I'm not letting them do whatever it is they plan on doing without a fight.

They close in on me, coming at me from every side. "Don't you dare fucking touch me," I growl, and Carl laughs at my attempt to get the men to back off.

Even still, I'm grabbed from every side. I try to throw them off, rocking my body from side to side and kicking my legs as hard as possible. The ones holding on to my legs falter, letting me go, and I kick one of them in the face. Their grunts bring me happiness, and I'm ready to kick the other guy holding on to me when I'm shoved face-first into the bed. Someone grabs my right ankle, as I try to kick back with my left foot, but it's useless. Before I can fight back even more, I'm shackled to the bed by one ankle, then the other. Someone sits on my back, stealing the breath from my lungs, as the other men shackle my wrists until I'm at their mercy.

This is the most humiliated I've ever been in my entire fucking life. Lying on my stomach spread eagle for a depraved man who has taken enough from me, but is clearly insatiable, has my anger growing to new heights. Maybe I just need to accept that this is my life and that it will be easier if I just lie down and take it. Not fighting him would mean less pain for me, and then he'd probably lose interest faster if that's what he's into. Something tells me he has depraved tastes, and that's why he buys us in the first place. Since no sane person would consent to the shit he wants to do.

I hear the shuffling of footsteps getting quieter, then the door clicks closed. I rest my cheek on the mattress, hoping that what he has planned doesn't take long. At this point, it's obvious what that is, he's done it before with toys, but I think that's over now.

"Look at you," Carl all but purrs, "Spread wide open for me."

A hand lands on my ass roughly, and the sting registers late. I try not to have a reaction, though, but it only seems to make him want one. So he tries it again, this time harder. I whimper softly, just enough to get him to stop. It seems to satisfy whatever the hell it is that makes him want to inflict pain.

"Why are you doing this to me?" I ask him, wanting answers. Why me? What made him pick me out of everyone else he had the option to purchase?

Suddenly he's between my legs, yanking my hair back until it feels like my neck is about to break. "You don't get to talk to me, boy," he tells me, clearly agitated, and I withdraw into myself. The last thing I need is to piss him off and make him hurt me even more. "But have you seen yourself? With your tight ass and big dick? Your body is made for an audience."

I close my eyes at that. The mere thought of people witnessing the beginning of the end for myself is making me nauseous. I taste bile at the back of my throat. "Please don't do this…" He laughs at me, even as I still beg. "*Please.*"

"I like when you beg for me, pretty boy," He chuckles as he spreads my cheeks and presses a finger to my back entrance. "Although nothing is stopping me today. We have a schedule to meet."

Carl gets off the bed for a moment, messes with his phone, and then returns to the bed. I steel myself for what I'm about to suffer through, and tears sting my eyes when I hear him rip open the condom wrapper. He uncaps the lube and spreads my ass cheeks again, making sure it's all over me. "Don't think for one moment this is for your comfort." He chuckles. "It's for mine."

With that, he nudges my back entrance with his dick and enters me roughly. Sharp pain shoots through my insides as he gets past the tight ring of muscle, and I know even though he has a small dick, I'll probably be bleeding from the assault. This is what he's been preparing me for all along, and I was too damn stupid to see it. I thought he was just torturing me, finding ways to make me hate my life. Never did I think he was going to do this to me, much less film us and put it out on the internet where everyone can see and find it whenever they want to get off on something. How naive of me not to see that coming.

I rest my cheek on the bed and stare off into the distance, willing myself to ignore what's happening to me. He makes it difficult though, and I don't know if he can tell what I'm trying to do, but he goes faster or harder every time I start achieving it. For the sake of my sanity, I need this to be over as soon as fucking possible. It's time to accept that no one is coming for me; there's no way out of this. As long as I don't see his face, I can imagine anything else. Anyone else. There's nothing enjoyable about this.

My eyes water again, the tears falling down my cheeks and onto the bed. Some of them travel across the bridge of my nose and drip off my face, and I focus on them to forget all about Carl. I can't fucking believe this is my life right now. I miss Hallie. I wish I could have her back. All I want is to kiss her once more so I can die in peace. And I *do* want to die at this point, just not the slow death I'm already suffering from.

When I close my eyes, Hallie is all I see. Her soft brown eyes, dark hair that somehow glows red in the sunshine, and the cute little freckles on the bridge of her nose. I remember the time I took her out for a sunset drive, and we sang along the whole way, then she somehow ended up with half her body outside of the car while she let the wind blow in her hair. She was mesmerizing. And she was *mine*.

I've fucked all of that up for myself. There's no surprise in the fact that I'm not good enough for her. It's not even about her. I'm not good for anyone. I understand that now, and I need to come to terms with it. Everything I put her through not only destroyed us individually but also as a whole. I was the one who put our entire relationship on the line and ruined it, and she was always so willing for me to use her, abuse her, and discard her when I was done. Yet even still, she's the only person I've ever loved. Truly loved. She's also the only person I've hurt this deeply. If I were her, I would've left me behind too. And that realization is what's breaking me into jagged pieces on the inside.

He holds on to my neck, pumping into me so fast that it's getting hard to ignore again. I choke back a sob and just let the tears fall. I will fucking kill him. Someday I will get the chance, and I won't pass it up. The pain he's inflicting is almost as bad as the one in my chest, and I wish it would hurt more so I can forget all about how my heart feels physically broken and damaged. I think I heard somewhere about how people can die of a broken heart. Why the fuck hasn't it happened to me then?

With a grunt, he comes into the condom, and even after he pulls out and he cleans me up, I stay still. Maybe if he sees I won't fight, he will leave me the fuck alone. Staring off into the distance, I count to ten for the simple reason that I need to clear my head and not beat his fucking ass. If I get out of these shackles with just him in this room, he will not walk out of here. That's for fucking sure.

I'm not that lucky though, which makes me so fucking sad. The men come back in the room to witness my humiliation and unshackle me. I can't fight back this time, and they know it judging by the smirks on their faces. This time I keep my head down as one of them walks me back to the basement-type room then shoves me into the cage and locks it behind me again.

I lie on my side, facing Adriana, for the simple reason that I don't want her to see my ass. I don't know the extent of the damage, and I'd rather not get that vulnerable with her. A man comes back, throws a pillow and blanket in the cage with me, and then closes it back up.

"A reward for being such a good boy today," The man says in a mocking tone, then walks away.

The pillow and blanket might just be the nicest thing I've had in weeks, and it's fucking pathetic how grateful I am that I can have something so simple. This is how he fucks with my mind, by giving me scraps of something that I shouldn't have to beg for yet making me work for it. Basically, he's treating me like a fucking dog. I'll enjoy the pillow and blanket for tonight, however.

"Are you okay?" Adriana whispers to me, and I nod slowly without opening my eyes. "Come here…"

I scoot closer to her until I'm flush with the bars, and she reaches through to touch my face. My lips tremble when her fingers rub against my cheek. Suddenly I can't help it, I start to cry. Tears trail down my face, and my shoulders begin to shake, but even as I sob, I'm crying so hard that no sound comes out. My abdomen cramps up from the force of my cries, and Adriana wipes my tears gently.

"I know," She shushes me with a low voice, "It's okay to cry, *papi.*"

Adriana holds my face with one hand, and I put mine on top of hers. "It hurts…" I whisper back, and it's not a lie. My ass feels like it's on fire, and I don't want to think about the damage he did this time.

"You need to rest," she tells me, trailing her fingertips over my eyes and between my eyebrows until my body relaxes. It's like she's done this her whole life, instantly relaxing me and making my body feel tired and heavy. "You're done, and you're okay."

I want to scream at her that I'll never be okay, that she can't fucking help me, but I just nod and let her continue to trail her fingertips across my face. Regardless of how much I miss Hallie, how guilty I feel at times for how close I'm becoming with Adriana, she does make me feel better. I need to embrace that, for these moments are few and far between.

Suddenly, there's a commotion on the other side of the room. The cages against the wall begin to rattle, and two girls become hysterical. A blonde girl with blue eyes and a slim body reaches into the cage with the woman who gets injected and shakes her repeatedly, "*Su cara está azul.*"

"*Ayúdala,*" the girl beside her whispers.

"Help!" the blonde screams. "Someone help me!"

Adriana quickly retrieves her hand and moves to the other end of her cage, just in time as one of the men who restrained me earlier walks into the room. His face displays annoyance in its every feature, "What the fuck are you screaming for?"

The blonde girl lowers herself to her knees, her eyes on the ground. "I think she's dead."

The man grunts and walks over to the woman's cage, opening it and shaking her. She doesn't move, and then he proceeds to check her pulse on the side of her neck. He grabs her cheeks with one hand, inspecting her face, and when he lets go she immediately slumps back. "She is," he affirms, closing the door behind him and walking away, back to where he came from.

"Get her out of here!!!" the blonde screams, and the man stops in his tracks and peers over his shoulder. "Please."

"Shut the fuck up, or you'll be next."

I sit up and look at the woman. She's skinny. Her arms are covered in scabs, visible even from a distance. She's been picking them, and some are clearly infected. And yet, I bet that's exactly how she wanted to go. There hasn't been one minute in however long I've been here that she has opened her eyes, gotten up, or even eaten something. They've been hydrating her through a straw, which she was waking up for momentarily, yet I think she was too high to truly function. She was probably going to die regardless, from starvation or dehydration. This was the quickest way to go, presumably the most blissful too. All I can think of, however, is who she left behind.

Did she have kids? What was her life like before she was forgotten?

All I know is that I don't want to rot in a cage for the rest of my days…

CHAPTER 8

Damien

It's been a week since Diego fucked me up, and I had to get stitches. Ironically, now we are together in a van on our way to wherever Carl is hiding. Armando is sitting in the back, where Zayne and Adriana will be later, cuddling with the AK-47s.

After I was stitched and patched up, they took me back to my car to retrieve all my belongings and return to my hotel. I was told to not go back to the bar anymore so as not to draw more attention to myself, and they would contact me in a few days to let me heal a little before we show up somewhere with no idea what security looks like.

We don't know what we're getting into, whether it's a house or an entire fucking compound, but we're determined to get Carl. While I'm technically here to get Zayne out, I'm not here *for* him. Even though it's personal for Diego and Armando, we've all agreed we can equally torture the fucker. Then after I get my answers and they get their pound of flesh, the people he captured can decide if they want to participate.

The GPS has led us into a sketchy ass dirt road surrounded by thick vegetation and no street lamps. Just a long stretch of nothingness. Diego turns the headlights off entirely in case there's security patrolling the roads, and he goes slow as fuck to not draw attention to us. Even after three minutes on the road, there's no building, house, or sign of life. Maybe he knew I put a tracker on him and he just dropped his car off randomly so I couldn't locate him. Or maybe figured out where the tracker was and just threw that shit somewhere to bring me to it.

Goddamnit.

There's a ding, and the GPS says we've arrived at our destination, and yet, I don't see shit. Perhaps we need to hide the van and go on foot? Who knows anymore, but this is making me nervous. I can admit I'm scared, especially if only three of us are going to get fucked up by a whole army of fucking *sicarios*.

"*¿Qué hacemos entonces?*" *What do we do then?* Armando asks, making Diego sigh in irritation. Yeah, I'm already getting pissed off too. If we knew what we were doing, we would've said something by now.

"Maybe it's time to park somewhere and find this place?" I make it sound like a question, even though it's more of a statement and Diego knows it.

He narrows his eyes at me, "Are you fucking with me, *güero*?" Armando looks me dead on when he hears Diego call me that, and now I have both of their suspicious eyes on me. "Did you set us up?"

"How the fuck would I do that?" I look him in the eyes, "And why?"

Diego scoffs, "To get back at us."

"I have too much at stake for that bullshit." I run my hand through my hair. "I don't give a fuck what you did to me. I need to get Hallie."

Armando interrupts, "*Que se joda, estamos aquí por Adriana.*" *Fuck it, we're here for Adriana.*

"*Ni modo,*" *Oh well.* Diego mutters, pulling over close to the trees, partly concealed by the darkness of the night and some bushes.

"When we get out of this van, we're a team, D. You good with that?"

I nod, "Let's do it."

Once parked, we each put on a vest and grab multiple weapons. Aside from the AK-47, I also grab plenty of extra ammo, a knife, and a handgun. Even still, it doesn't feel close to being enough. Whoever says they're not scared to die is a fucking liar. We all have a different reason to be scared, but when death stares you in the face, you cower. My fear isn't death itself; it's what happens after I'm gone. Like Hallie never being free of that sick motherfucker. I can only imagine how traumatized she is now, much more than before, and I worry about what will happen even if we rescue her. What if she can't recover from this? If she can't live with it? Will we survive this? Make it through to the end of the tunnel? Or will we fall? It doesn't matter to me if she hates me and never wants to see me again. I can't live with myself if I don't get her out of the mess I kind of pushed her into.

Armando opens the van's side door, and we all silently step onto the gravel, then he closes it back up. Even though he tried to be quiet, it was still loud as fuck in the silence of the night, making both Diego and I tense up. No matter how much we try to be quiet though, it'll never be enough. Small rocks crunch under our boots, and even that sounds amplified.

I don't know how long it takes to get here, probably at least five minutes, but we finally stumble upon a house. It's not fancy. In fact it's very outdated, but it is large. Carl doesn't seem to have as much money as I thought, or maybe he spends most of it on purchasing people. The thought makes me sick to my stomach at how some people are fucking deranged.

Surprisingly, no men are waiting outside, which seems sketchy as fuck. Either Carl is extremely confident that no one will fuck with him, or there's a whole army waiting for us inside. I don't really want to have to figure out which doors are open. The only thing I can think of doing is letting go of the element of surprise and go in guns blazing. The house can't have that many people in it. Right? Or maybe it does, and we're fucked.

"What do you want to do?" I ask Diego in a low voice as we stalk toward the house. Watching for branches on the ground in the soft lighting is harder than it looks, so we slow down even more.

"Front door," he whispers. "Fuck it."

While that's the attitude I want to have, I find it a little difficult to be this optimistic. Maybe I just have more to lose. Although, if it were for me, I'd leave Zayne here after Carl is dead and not have to worry about his stupid ass ever again in my entire life. Yeah, that actually sounds pretty damn good right about now. The only problem with that is having to tell Hallie that I had the chance to rescue the little bitch boy, yet I didn't. Yeah, that might disappoint her even more, and quite frankly, I can't take any more rejection from her.

We're finally on the front steps of the house, some shitty steep concrete steps that you'd break your fucking neck on if you ran down them. He must be selling his own ass to afford the skin trade. There's no way he has money, unless he doesn't want people to suspect he's rich, or this isn't his residence. Something tells me the latter is probably it.

"*Voy a abrir la puerta,*" I'm going to open the door, Armando says, "*Si no está cerrada, entramos con calma. Si está cerrada, estamos jodidos y tenemos que hacer ruido. Pero vamos a entrar de alguna manera.*" *If it's not locked, we enter calmly. If it's locked, we're fucked, and we have to make some noise. Either way we're getting in.*

He tries the doorknob, and it surprisingly gives way. Something about this doesn't sit right with me. Why the fuck would anyone in this business leave the door unlocked? There's no fucking way they're so relaxed and trusting with this industry. No, something is fishy as fuck.

"Wait," I say, looking at them intently, and hold my hand up as I try to listen for any rustling or footsteps. There's none. "Why would anyone leave the front door unlocked?" Do they somehow know I tracked them here? I didn't think they suspected anything after I disappeared. They led me the wrong way last time anyway, so there was no way to discover this place through that route.

"I will open the door quietly, and we'll go in one by one swiftly."

Diego seems to think about it for a second, "Once we're in, we need to make sure we have a view of everything. All of us need to be back-to-back."

Armando and I nod, though I haven't heard the fucker speak English one fucking time. Does he even understand what Diego is saying? Or does he just know what to do based on what they've done together in the past? Not reassuring at all. Nope, not even a little bit.

Diego opens the door very slowly, and it shockingly doesn't creak very much because he doesn't open it all the way. Or maybe they spray it with WD-40. Not smart of them either way if they have no security on this side of the house. Unless all of it is guarding the treasure.

We make it inside quickly and all get in position just like Diego wanted to. Armando and I are back-to-back with Diego, forming a triangle formation. That way, we have a clear view of every side. The lights are all turned on, which is surprising since they provide complete visibility. It's almost like they don't expect anyone to come for any of their prisoners. Did Carl give all the guards the night off? Or what the fuck is going on? If he did, he's a dumb cunt. Makes the job easier for us though, so I won't complain.

Thankfully the floors are tiled here, which is common in Latin American countries, so they don't creak. We do have to make sure our shoes don't squeak however, so we raise our feet as we walk carefully through the house. It's bigger than the outside indicates, and I have a feeling it will be harder than I thought to find where he's hiding everyone. I should've taken more time to get a blueprint of the house, but I don't have the luxury of making that work into Hallie's schedule.

We stop abruptly at the sound of loud laughter coming from somewhere in the house, and I signal a hand over my ear to tell them to listen. Talking right now may give us away, although they're being fucking obnoxiously loud regardless.

Following the laughter, we maintain our triangle formation, wanting to have eyes in every direction. I glance around and make sure no one is hiding in any corners that we're not paying attention to, and we finally make it to where the men are apparently all gathered. Is this some kind of party or is it a job? I'm so confused, because drinking while on guard duty should be considered reckless as fuck. For these exact reasons: we're about to fuck them up, and they're not going to know what hit them.

Diego signals for us to halt right before we reach an arch that leads into what appears to be a formal dining room. I'm almost sure not everyone will be here, so if we take them by surprise and kill these men, we better be ready for many more to show up as well. I anticipate there's more wherever their prisoners are.

Armando and I look around again, then nod at Diego that the coast is clear on our sides. He then signals for us to get ready to shoot, and at his command, we run into the dining room and riddle them with bullets. About ten men are instantly dead with the number of rounds we just fired upon them, except one refuses to die. It's convenient for us, even though he's trying to reach for a gun in the back of his pants. I walk to him, crushing his hand under my boot, and he screams.

"You scream so pretty," I tell him, smirking when I put more pressure on his hand and his eyes begin to water. "*¿Dónde están?*" *Where are they?*

"*¿Quiénes?*" *Who?*

"*No te hagas el pendejo.*" *Don't play stupid*, I growl, "*Se me está acabando la paciencia.*" *My patience is running out.*

I put more weight on his hand, and I hear a crunch. That's the least of his worries though, and as I think of different ways to heighten his pain, blood starts pouring out of his mouth. He begins to choke on it, which makes me smile. "*En el sótano.*" *In the basement.*

I narrow my eyes at him and look back at the guys over my shoulder, who also match my expression. That was too fucking easy, and not in a good way. "*¿Y dónde carajo está el sótano?*" *Where the fuck is the basement?*

"*Está—*" *It's—*

Dead.

He's dead.

I want to fucking scream, but instead I draw in the deepest breath I have in my entire life. I guess we're going hunting. At least we got them all on this side of the house. That being said, they surely will be ready for us by the time we get to the rest of them. We have to be careful now, more than before.

Leaving the bodies behind, we walk through the house silently. Not a soul in sight, we make sure to go through every nook and cranny before heading to a hallway that surely has the bedrooms. There has to be some in this house somewhere.

The hallway is pitch black, and the only reason we know it's a hallway in the first place is due to the light behind us shining barely any light toward the entrance of it. As we get closer, we can't see shit, so it's either a cell phone flashlight or turning on the light. I'm sure either choice would give us away, so might as well turn on the fucking light.

I point at the ceiling, motioning to the lights, and Diego nods his head. At least we're on the same page. Armando turns them on since he's closer to the light switch, and the hallway is illuminated. It's not very long. In fact, it looks at odds with the rest of the house. It almost makes me feel like I've been deceived. The main side of the house, where the living area is, suggests a huge home, yet this tells me there's only one bedroom and a bathroom. Something is off about it.

As we get closer to the doors though, there's whimpering coming from the side of one of them. I hold up my finger so Armando and Diego stay quiet, then motion at the door. Did I already mention how fucking grateful I am for tiled floors?

Apparently, this motherfucker doesn't know how to lock a door, which is convenient for us, and when I open it, he's fucking a girl against the edge of the bed. Sick fuck.

He looks up from the girl, his beer gut hanging over her ass, and glances back at a camera positioned just at the right angle to capture what he wants them to see. Whoever is on the end of that is going to get tracked down; I promise myself that much. I will no longer participate or tolerate this shit. I can't believe I ever did in the first place.

"What the fuck?" Carl yells, pulling out of the girl who still has her face buried in the sheets.

I advance, walking quickly, and grab him by the throat right in front of the camera. I want them to see what happens to him. "You didn't think you'd get away with this forever, did you?" I smile, and he cringes. "It's time we show your friends," I nod at the camera, "what happens to fuckers like you."

Armando keeps his back to the camera, since it probably wouldn't be good for them to be spotted coming into Carl's house by the cartel they work for, and grabs the girl from the bed, pushing her forward until she's out of the room.

"Wait, wait." Carl puts his hands up in the air, showing his surrender. What a fucking pussy. For someone who does this every day and has guards, he sure as fuck needs to grow a pair. Maybe that's why he needs so many men here. "What do you want?"

"Oh, you'll find out." I grab my knife from my pocket and flip it open, making his eyes widen. "But first things first."

I stab him in the side without remorse. Yeah, I know it hurts like a bitch, it's happened to me. But he deserves it, so I twist the blade until he screams and cries. Then Diego turns off the camera. I pull out the knife and kick Carl in the abdomen, making him fly onto the bed. Blood pours freely out of the wound, and it's a good thing we're not squeamish because that shit is gnarly. Kinda proud of myself for that one, to be honest.

"What do you *want*?" he repeats, and I cross my arms over my chest, knife dangling from my fingers.

Carl tries to put pressure on the wound, but it's pointless. There's no way he can stop the bleeding with a gash that big, and I don't want the bleeding to stop anyway, so I won't let it.

"For you to talk." I shrug, pointing my knife at him. "Or we can keep having fun. It's truly up to you."

"O-okay..." He breathes in deeply, but it's still shallow. He's losing blood and in pain. This isn't going to last very long, so I better get shit out of him and fast. "I'll talk."

"Where's the basement?"

"What basement?"

I take out my handgun and shoot him straight in the shoulder, and he falls back on the bed with a scream. His wails hurt my ears, and I begin to pace. "Let's try this one more time, Carl." I stare into his eyes as I say his name, letting him know I'm aware of who he is. "And this time, make sure you answer my fucking questions, or you won't like what I do to you."

"It's next door."

So that's what that door leads to. Good to know.

"How many people are in there?" I ask him, looking at the blood coating the sheets. I don't have a lot of time. I can tell.

"T-ten…"

His breaths grow more shallow as his face is ashen. His fingers relax against his abdomen.

"Fuck, no. You don't get off this easy, bitch." I walk over to him and slap his face hard, and he snaps out of it enough to look into my eyes. "Who is Michael?" Carl's eyes widen, and he gasps, except I'm not sure if it's for breath, from pain, or the mention of that name. "Who the fuck is he?"

"If you're asking, then you already know…"

"Where can I find him?" I ask, and Carl has the audacity to laugh, yet it just makes him choke on blood again. The gurgling sounds as it travels up his throat don't disturb me, but I want it to stop so he can answer my damn questions. "*Where?*"

"No one knows where he is." He coughs, "We don't even know his last name."

This will not be for nothing. I did not just come here to rescue Zayne for no reason. I came for Hallie. For *her*. The reason I breathe every fucking day. No way is he just giving me this shit as an answer. "Do you want me to save you?" I ask him, and we make eye contact. He's beyond saving, but hope sparks in his eyes for a moment.

"Yes."

"Where can I find him then?" I press, "Don't worry. They can't kill you for talking if you're already dead."

Diego chuckles in the back, and I smirk. The truth is I do enjoy this, no matter how fucked up it is. Yeah, I already know I have fucking problems, but this satisfies the blood lust I feel during my anger outbursts. This one is definitely warranted, however.

"There's an auction…" My face falls, and I listen intently. "At the cultural center…"

"What about it?"

"The day after tomorrow." Carl coughs again, and I fist my hands as I try not to scream at him to not die yet. "M-m-m-ichael… will be… there."

"What is the auction for, and how do we get in?"

"Women."

"How do we—"

Carl's head slumps to the side, and I know my time is up. I don't have to touch his disgusting neck to know he has no pulse. I look back at Armando and Diego who are leaning against a wall in the hallway, waiting for me. I guess now is the time to go downstairs and free Zayne. I'm tempted to take all the girls and leave his ass behind, but I know if I ever find Hallie, she'd never forgive me. I wouldn't forgive myself either for putting her through that, so I guess I'll save the useless fucker.

I sigh and exit the room, noticing now that the naked girl is hugging her chest as Armando talks to her, who then proceeds to whisper something in Diego's ear. I look at them expectantly, waiting to know our next move. I don't want to lead right now. I'm tired and disappointed, and soon I'll have to deal with the person I hate the most. I just want to get out of here. Hallie better fucking see my efforts. This shit is not going to be a walk in the park.

"They're all down there," Diego points at the door to the basement. "In cages." Cages? What the fuck? "She doesn't know where the keys are," he continues, pointing at the girl.

I go back into the room and begin to tear it apart, and after five minutes I end up finding it under the bed. How cliche. I should've checked there first. "Let's go," I tell them, holding up the keys. Hopefully, it's the same one for all of them, or we're going to be trying to get people out for a fucking minute.

Armando opens the door to the basement, and the girl leads the way down the short steps. At first, I can barely see from the blinding lights. Compared to the hallway, it's fucking bright in here. My eyes adjust quickly enough, and I stifle my gasp as I glance around the room. Cages line up two walls opposite each other, and the people are lying down on the ground. Mostly girls. I don't see Zayne.

They have them living worse than animals. There's a smell that makes me gag, and I cover my nose and mouth. What the fuck is that? I look around, trying to place where it's coming from, but can't figure it out.

She starts to lead me to the cages, and I let people out of them. I don't know what the fuck is going to happen now that they're free. Where will they go? What will they do? Will they be captured again? I can't think about it much. I just have to set them free, and that will have to suffice for now. I won't stray from my path right now. Everyone else comes last place to Hallie.

After I've let a bunch of girls out and they make their way upstairs, I notice three people left. A woman lying on her side in the furthermost corner of the room, who seems to be the only clothed person in this room, and a girl lying on her side with her arm through the bars. I walk toward her, and she's holding someone's hand as they sleep.

Zayne's.

What the fuck is she holding his hand for? Solidarity? Companionship? More?

I shouldn't give a fuck; I don't. It would be very convenient if he fell in love with someone else, in reality, he'd make my life so much easier. Still, I doubt the dumbass has it in him to leave Hallie to me. Maybe I'll pay him to leave. Or threaten his life. I don't know; I'll have to think this one through.

The girl lifts her head when I begin to open her cage, and Armando and Diego run towards her. When they reach her, the girl starts to sob and lets them envelop her in their arms. They retreat to the other side of the room, asking what they can do and how to help her. Seeing them care for her this much is touching, but it only makes me burn with jealousy. It should be *me*. I should be getting Hallie right now.

Zayne looks up at me with wide eyes, as mine make contact with his. He seems surprised to see me, probably stunned I'm even opening the damn cage to let him out. Yeah, that makes two of us. I'm confused at my fucking self. No one tells you how far you're willing to go for love. Maybe it should be taught in high school. Make it its own class, because goddamn this shit is too complex for my brain right now. All I know is that when I unlock the cage for Zayne, I can already feel a sense of loss. Like he's going to steal her from me, take her away forever.

"Damien?" Zayne whispers, standing up as I open the gate. "You're here?"

"What do you think?" I ask sarcastically, then take a deep breath. "Yes, I'm here for you. Sadly, you can't die if I can help it."

"How did you find me?"

"It's a long story," I reply, moving out of the way so he can step out of the cage. "We'll talk later. Right now we have to get out of here."

I look back at the crumpled form in the corner, and I can feel the crease forming between my eyebrows. Why isn't she getting up? Something tells me to go to her, to check if she's okay. I have to let her out, she can't be left behind.

As I get closer, that terrible smell returns, and I cover my mouth. Fuck is she—

"She's dead," Zayne announces as I unlock the gate. "Died two days ago."

After opening the door, I look down at her. She looks oddly familiar, I can't place it, though. Her hair covers her face, and I won't lie, I'm afraid to pull it back and look. Mostly because I don't know what she'll look like with how long she's been dead. Is she going to look fucked up? She's clearly decaying since she smells.

Even still, I kneel down and hold my breath. Zayne's footsteps are loud behind me, and I think it's likely curiosity bringing him my way. It's possible he wants to see it just because she's been there this long. Thankfully he stops behind me, not getting any closer.

I gather my courage and breathe in through my mouth, holding my breath again before gently moving her hair out of my face.

All the air escapes from my lungs forcefully, and even with her puffy face, I recognize her. My heart speeds up in my chest and my hands start to sweat.

"Mom?" With shaking hands and blurry eyes, I turn her over to her back. She's stiff and gray, nothing like the last time I saw her. She was so full of life back then… "Mama?" My voice breaks, and when I glance down, I see it. Track marks.

"Mommy," I call out to her, but she's on the couch with her eyes closed and something sharp sticking out of her arm. "Mommy, I'm hungry."

She barely opens her eyes, except the blue I can see looks funny. Like the lights are turned off inside of her. She doesn't look like the happy, funny person I know her to be anymore.

"Baby?" She slurs, "Mommy is so, so tired. Can you get a snack for now?"

"Okay…" I tell her, "Will you cook for me later today?" She hasn't cooked for me in two days, and I'm starving. Whenever I get hungry, she tells me to get a snack, and my belly keeps growling at me.

"Yes," she sighs. "I will. Now please, let me sleep."

Tears gather in my eyes, and she sees them spill down my cheeks. I simply nod, but as I retreat, she grabs my hand.

"I'm sorry…" She looks around for a moment, at the mess my brothers and I have made, and I hope she doesn't yell at us. "Mommy loves you, baby."

My heart flutters at those words, and I smile. My lips meet her cheek for a quick peck, and just like that, I'm whole again…

She put me back together.

What the fuck have I done?

My tears fall fast as I fall back on my ass, and I cover my face in my hands as I begin to sob. I don't hear anyone or anything anymore, in fact, the blood rushes in my ears so quickly I feel like I might pass out.

Realization hits me in full force. I traded my mom's life for Hallie's. I was supposed to get her back all along. That was the deal. Hallie for my mom, and now I've failed them both.

I rock back and forth, trying to get the image of her out of my head, but I can't. I can't. I can't. *I can't.* The palm of my hand meets my face for a hard slap, and I do it again to ensure I'm truly living this. There's no fucking way this is my life, that I've messed everything up to this extent. I refuse to believe it.

Happier memories flood my brain, lighter times when my mother wasn't an addict. Her pink dress, baked chocolate chip cookies, even her kissing my dad goodbye before he went to work. Only none of it is real. Not anymore.

She's gone.

Fucking gone.

And it's all my fault.

Zayne's hand reaches my shoulder, and I flinch, then swat him away. The fucker is persistent and tries again. I don't have the strength to fight him this time, not anymore. I sob as he grips my shoulder again, and the more I shake, the more his hand tightens on me.

He drops to his knees next to me and turns my body toward him; his green eyes have pity in them. Fuck him, I refuse to let him feel bad for me. I wipe my tears and push him away, turning back to my mom. I don't get to be comforted when she's lying dead a few feet from me.

This is all my fucking fault.

CHAPTER 9

Hallie

There are men everywhere.

I'm assuming many of them are part of the Mexican cartel, and they always throw parties like these. The mansion is so big, I see no end to it with its speckled tiles and grand staircase. Rooms that go on forever and open spaces that fit herds of people, but now I see what they're used for. Unfortunately, I have to stay glued to Michael's side. Better the devil you know than the devil you don't or however the fuck it goes.

My naked body shivers but not from the cold. It's the staring eyes that are making me uncomfortable. Michael forced me to be naked and wear high heels, and ever since we've come into this house, not one man has looked away from me. The only thing I can hope for is that he doesn't let a bunch of them fuck me, like he allowed the men back at his house to do. The thought of it makes me flinch, and Michael gives me a knowing smile. He's aware of what he's putting me through, and I bet he wants to make me even more uncomfortable by the second. I won't budge, however. If he wants me to be a willing participant, he's going to wait his entire life.

That shit isn't happening.

Not that he gives a shit. That much was evident by the stunt he pulled the other day. My wrist still hurts from the tattoo, a constant reminder of what my life has come to. I want to skin myself, cut off my hand, anything to take it off. I can't fucking stand the sight of it. Bile rises in my throat when I glance down at it, the barcode still red and angry from me trying to scratch it off, as if I could anyway. Then again, my mind isn't exactly reasoning with logic at the moment. Instead I'm getting rather desperate. I'd do anything to end this.

Anything.

As we walk through different areas of the main living space, I'm unable to tear my eyes away from the disgusting scene before me. Yeah, these people are fucking rich, and in each room, women are in chains being fucked. Some are bent over, some are leashed and pinned against furniture, and some seem to be willingly riding their dicks. Though I highly doubt they have a choice.

Some of the women are moaning, and it makes me want to cover my ears. I can't blame them, in any case. It's a biological urge. These fucking assholes will take advantage of you in any way possible, just to fuck with your head. If they know the last thing you want to do is let them touch you, they will find a way to make you come just to make you hate yourself a little more. I learned this game from Michael and some of the girls back at the house.

Yesterday, I had to suck Michael's dick again, or he would hurt Brittany. He's going to use her against me as much as possible, and now I have to comply. I'll let him do what he wants, but I'll just be a rag doll through it. For some reason, he hasn't tried to fuck me yet. I'm stunned, especially with all the shit he has said, but I think he's prolonging it on purpose. Probably to keep me on my toes, fucking wondering when he will pounce. He's achieving it too. The stress might just kill me before I do it myself.

"You will do as you're told while we're here," Michael tells me, gripping my arm painfully. "There will be no arguing, or you will pay with blood. Men get off on that here, and I won't think twice about it."

"Yes, sir," I reply, my eyes down so I don't piss him off. This is neither the time nor place to start shit with him.

Michael tightens his hand around my arm even more, making me cry out. "Daddy," he growls.

"Daddy," I whisper in agreement.

He guides me to a room with a bar, a pool table, and small couches around the entire space. There are bartenders and cocktail waiters, and I have a brief neurotic moment where I think of asking one of them for help.

Why the fuck would anyone help me?

They're all clearly okay with working for these people, and they don't even bat an eyelash at the brutal rape happening right across from them; the screams so loud that I have to try not to flinch consciously.

Michael watches me closely, as if trying to make mental notes of what seems to affect me the most. I'm sure he will be trying it all at some point. He takes me to a green velvet couch that sits empty in the corner of the room, taking the spot right next to me. There's no space between us at all, he's flush to my side and pulls me closer by my shoulders. His black suit has not one wrinkle in sight, and I begin to wonder what he did to get so rich in the last decade. But it's become obvious to me that it's definitely cartel related as well as… this.

I knew he was already a pedophile long before he started participating in this bullshit, but this is another level of fucking evil and depravity. Maybe I'm naive for not believing he could go this far, although I could have lived my whole life in ignorance.

A young waitress comes our way with a tray, except instead of food or drinks, there's… drugs and paraphernalia. Pills, powder, a spoon, a needle, a straw, and a lighter. What the fuck?

"Compliments of El Capo." She makes sure to look at the ground while talking to him, and disgust floods my body at the thought of what they'd be allowed to do to her if they felt disrespected.

"Thank you," Michael says with a smile, and she sets all of it on the couch next to him then walks away. He moves his hand from his lap to between my legs, cupping me. I flinch when his fingers make contact with my slit, and he laughs. "Don't overreact, baby girl. I haven't even started."

I take a deep breath and try to stay very still. Thankfully though, he doesn't try anything more than that. My hope is that it's a power show, and he's going to leave me the fuck alone. Just to make sure though, I still ask, "What are you doing to me tonight?"

With his free hand, he takes hold of my chin and turns it his way, tipping it up like he's giving me permission. We make eye contact, and his hazel eyes crinkle with a smile. "Whatever the fuck I want." A chill runs down my spine when he leans in to whisper in my ear, "If you want to be doped up, let me know now. Because if I'm invited into the black room, I'm fucking you."

My eyes water and I shake my head at him, making him tighten his fingers on my chin, "*Please*, don't."

"I love it when you beg," he murmurs. "It turns me on more."

I want to spit in his face and show my disgust, but instead, I shut my mouth and close my eyes. "Dope me up," I tell him, regret already running through my body, but it's undeniable that I miss it anyway. It's been a few days, and I need an escape. Maybe one day, his hand will slip and give me too much. I'd rather die and be out of my misery than be next to him for one more second.

Michael lets go of my face with a smile and looks at the drugs, then starts to mix things together. It's clear it brings him joy that I'm submitting to him, that if I'm doped up, I'll be a pliable doll that will be too fucked up to fight back. He's not wrong, either.

I relax further into the couch, knowing that if anything, I'll at least have this one escape. Now I understand a fraction of what Zayne felt, taking refuge in something that could never disappoint you. Maybe I should've been kinder back then and tried to help him instead of leaving. If this is ever going to be over for me, then

I think I'll need help, or I'll be one of the lucky ones who make it out peacefully.

I watch women walking behind their owners, some of them trailing after them like lost puppies and others being forced to. I don't know who I can relate to more at this point. It feels like I'm losing a piece of myself with every passing day. Between the horrors I've seen and the heroin they're pumping me with, I can barely remember the two most important people in my life. I miss them. I fucking miss them so damn much it hurts. There's a hole in my heart that can't be filled, no matter how hard I try to ignore it, it's like I'm missing a limb.

Warm hands probe my arm, turning it over, and I watch him search for a vein. He's going in without a tourniquet, and I know the danger of that. Let's hope he's actually good at finding a vein, if it goes under my skin I'm fucked. That's what sucks about drugs and being a nurse. I know all the fucked up shit that can happen and don't feel reassured by any of this currently. But also, the situation I find myself in cancels out the rest of my thoughts. Side effects, addiction, death... none of it matters to me anymore.

So I willingly give him my arm.

Forgetting about everything is my salvation, the only thing preserving my sanity, and when offered to me, I'll take it each and every time. After all, why would I pass it up? I have nothing left to make me feel good.

He lines the needle up to my vein, and I look at it intently, mesmerized by how it penetrates my skin as he empties the syringe. There's a rush, a warmth that follows the plunge, and it almost feels like my body goes numb. I'm floating into oblivion, melting into the couch. I distinctly feel myself smile, mostly because of the way my brain stops working. It's no longer running a million miles a minute, and there are no worries at the back of my mind. I'm *free*.

My head slumps to the side, and I make eye contact with a man across the room. I know I should look away, but I can't get my brain to obey. Everything's happening in slow motion, and I think he can tell I'm fucked up because he smiles at me and shakes his head. My eyes blur, unfocusing and refocusing until I'm confused and have to close them. I want sleep to take me under, yet I know Michael wouldn't let that happen, even if I couldn't physically help it. He'd find a way to torture me and keep me awake for as long as he wanted to.

After what feels like hours, but surely has only been a minute or two, I open my eyes again. The man from across the room is now standing in front of us, talking to Michael, smiling and nodding like they're best friends. When he walks away, my stepfather pulls me up to stand, supporting me with an arm around my waist. We must finally be leaving, but I couldn't walk even if I tried. These high heels have my balance all fucked up, and my world is tilted on its axis. My blurry eyes are unfocused, and I can't tell where this fucker is dragging me to.

Why are we going in this room?

Where are we going?

Open your eyes.

Scream.

Fight.

I kind of feel someone pushing me down onto my belly, except I can't make sense of anything long enough to speak up. I can't snap out of it. My head is heavy when I try to pick it up, and it just falls back onto the couch cushions face-first. I turn it to the side, trying to breathe, trying to remember why we're in this room. I can't remember.

What can't I remember? *Why* can't I remember?

Exhaustion weighs me down, and I feel my eyes closing again. Staying awake with my low tolerance to this drug is difficult, and I bet everyone in the room is having a good laugh at my expense.

Oh, look at the naked girl who can't stay awake, entirely at our mercy. Let's all get a turn with her, yeah?

Rough hands grope me, grabbing onto my hips, even though it feels like it's happening to someone else. Surely this can't be me if I barely feel it, right? What I do feel, however, is the invasion my body experiences, as it feels like it's being torn in half.

What the fuck is happening?

What is that pain?

It takes all of my energy to pick up my head from whatever surface it's on, feels like a sofa, and it feels like it weighs one thousand pounds. Even still, I manage to look over my shoulder to witness the most horrific sight yet. Michael is between my legs, thrusting in and out of me, smiling like a fucking madman when our eyes meet.

He fucks me harder, draping his body over mine until his mouth meets my ear, "I'm going to fuck you so good tonight. You're going to hate how much you love it."

No.

I will not love anything he does to me, that's for fucking sure.

I try to tell him that. To get off me and fuck off, but once again, I can't hold my head up anymore. It slumps forward, my eyes heavy as well. While I'm conscious that he's fucking me, thrusting in and out, I barely feel it. It's like my body is numb, my ears rushing like I'm underwater. Almost… peaceful. Even through the chaos.

My brain turns off and everything is black again. The peaceful breaths coming out of me are at odds with the pounding I'm sure I'm receiving but can't feel. It's lulling me to sleep. I try to open my eyes again but can't. It's too hard, they're too heavy. What the fuck—

In.

Out.

Sleep.

Wake.

What the fuck did he give me?

My breaths are shallow and slow; it feels as if I'll stop breathing any second. Whatever it is—it's fucking strong, taking over me like a wave. It feels like I'm drowning.

I'm drowning, and I can't go up for air.

Is he still fucking me?

Finally, I feel it. A tingling sensation that starts spreading through my body. A dull… ache. I can't even describe it other than it keeps building up, and it feels like I'm going to implode. A sharp sting slightly takes me out of my numbness, and I can focus momentarily on the room, at the people staring. There's a lot of men surrounding us. During this time though, my mind begins to register what's actually happening. Michael's hand is between my thighs as he fucks me, and what I'm feeling is a disgusting pleasure. He keeps rubbing my clit, and I try to return to that state of confusion again.

I achieve it, going in and out again, barely feeling the build-up between my thighs. It's getting impossible to ignore it, even as I can't open my eyes, even as I fall asleep again.

Michael growls against my ear, which jolts me. "I hope you fucking hate yourself for this tomorrow." More rubbing, faster, more aggressive. Enough that I can't ignore, no matter how hard I try. "But I'll always remind you of it. *I won.*"

Yes.

He won.

The drugs make me feel more dead than alive right now.

What the fuck did he give me?

This isn't H.

With that, he roughly sticks a finger in my ass and continues to rub my clit. I can hear myself, half sobbing, half moaning. I grit my teeth to keep the noise in, not giving him the satisfaction of knowing what he did. Tears soak my face, but I only know this because I'm staring at the couch cushion. When the orgasm takes over my body, I squeeze my eyes shut so hard that my head hurts.

Make it stop. *Stop.* Fucking. *Stop!*

My chest is on fire from my anger, and it's safe to say I want to fucking kill him now more than ever. My body shakes as I dig my nails into my arm, trying to get myself to stop, but I can't. That only pisses me off even more. I want to turn around, claw his face, and gouge his ugly eyes.

The worst part?

He doesn't come.

Instead, he pulls out of me. I don't know what to think about it, and I brace myself. That can't be good. Of course I'm right. His hands spread me wide open for him to look at, and he spits between my cheeks.

Please, God, no.

Please, I know I said I don't believe in you, but if you make this stop, I swear I'll read the bible. I'll go to church. I'll do whatever you want. Please, please, make it stop.

When the head of his dick lines against my entrance again, I whimper, already expecting the pain and getting ready for it. He rubs the spit between me and him, then enters me roughly. And then… he fucks my ass brutally, giving everyone a show.

But I don't feel that either. I don't feel anything at all. I close my eyes and drift off to that place between waking and sleep. The place where nothing makes sense and everything spins, where time doesn't matter because it doesn't make sense.

I'm sure Michael is the picture of joy right now as he fucks me in front of everyone, further stripping me of my dignity. This is why he didn't fuck me before; he was saving the humiliation for me. Storing it in a little bottle so I could drink it like a shot that sets your chest on fire, burning you from the inside out.

And me?

I'm fucking dead inside.

My high is gone.

Actually everything is. As José drags me into Michael's huge house by my arm, I come face to face with my mother. She looks me up and down with disgust, and my face scrunches up in a moment of weakness. The truth is, I'm a fucking fraud. For the last decade, I've been extremely jealous of the relationships I see other women my age have with their mothers. That best-friend bond is something that I've always craved. Needed. No matter how much

I hate my mom, there is a sliver of love in my heart that refuses to die, like a fucking cockroach. It's a weakness, but I firmly believe it's also human nature. Maybe even animals' nature.

"Mom," I say softly, "Come back…"

"It's okay, Hallie," she replies, her eyes full of pity. "You're going to be okay."

"You're going to be okay, baby," Mom tells me, but my knee hurts so bad… "Let's sit down, and I'll rock you for a little bit?"

"Sing twinkle twinkle?"

She laughs, her dimple showing, and begins to sing. "Twinkle, Twinkle, little star…"

Where did she go? The person who put me back together when I fell apart? The one who kissed my boo-boos and rocked me to sleep? I haven't seen her, felt her, in so long. Once upon a time, she used to love me so much. Even when I lived with my grandparents, she still came to see us multiple times a week. She still cared. Does she hate me now? Does she resent her husband for wanting me so much that he fucking bought me like cattle? Or is she completely indifferent to me now?

"Move." José shoves me forward, breaking me out of my trance and the little episode where I wallow in self-pity and sadness over what my life has become.

After a minute and many turns, he opens the door to my room and shoves me inside. I immediately fall to the tile on all fours, my knees taking the brunt and throbbing in agony. My shoulders shake as I let the tears fall, and I begin to sob.

No.

Wail.

The sounds coming out of me are utterly foreign, and I can't control them anymore. Brittany's hands come to my waist, and I feel her kneeling next to me. I try to shake her off, not wanting her to touch me, but she doesn't let go. In a moment of complete madness, impulsivity, and weakness, I repeatedly bang my head against the tile. I feel my skin split on my forehead, and I scream louder. From rage, and pain, and overwhelming sadness. But I still don't stop. There's a numbness in my body, my brain, my heart. Maybe the drug is still in my system after all. I'm still high, not crazy. Right?

"Stop," Brittany cries, attempting to halt my movements. She pins me to the ground, putting her body on top of mine until I give up, so I just lie down with my cheek on the tile. It's slippery from my tears and blood, and I close my eyes to stop the throbbing. "You're stronger than this."

"I'm *not*," I argue. "I can't do this anymore."

Brit kisses my hair, her body relaxing on top of my back. "Then I'll take over. Let me put you back together."

She stands, and my body hurts from the assault I suffered earlier. I crawl toward the bed in the darkness, touching everything as I go since my eyes haven't adjusted. Once I reach the bed and get on it, Brittany gets on the bed behind me. Her arm wraps around my waist as I lie on my side, and she holds me tightly, letting me cry. This time with silent tears, since my throat hurts from all the screaming, and I have no energy left in my body.

"Make it stop, please, Brit." I beg her, "If you love me, smother me with a pillow or something. I need to die."

"No."

"*Please*, kill me."

Brittany slaps my belly hard, and I flinch, my head throbbing in the process. "Shut the fuck up, Hallie."

I'm not lying, though. I've taken as much as I can, and I'm at my limit. I can't do this anymore; I want to make it fucking stop. There's nothing and no one that can make this better. Even if I found comfort, pleasure, or any feelings at all with the men in this house, none of it would be real. It's all a product of captivity. None of it would matter in the grand scheme of things. I'd never find true happiness again.

My body rocks back and forth on the bed, and Brittany holds me tighter, trying to stop my movements. "Someone is coming for us," She reassures, "Shhhhhh."

"No one is coming for us, Brit." I cry, "You need to accept that shit. Zayne is fucking dead, and Damien?" My voice cracks on a laugh, "The cartel probably killed him by now, and if they didn't, he fucking hates me anyway. *I* fucking hate *myself*."

"He loves you." She turns me around to face her, "He could never hate you."

"I *stabbed* him."

"Okay, so maybe he hates you a little bit," She wipes my tears, "But he loves you too. Isn't that how you feel for Zayne? For both of them? Didn't you keep going back for more anyway?"

"Because I'm fucking broken." It's the truth anyway, and I can't deny it. "There's something seriously wrong with me, and I can't fix it. I'll always go back to the things that hurt me. It makes me feel alive."

"And you think Damien doesn't feel the same?" She gives me a kiss on the cheek. "He won't quit you. Stabbed or not."

"What if I killed him?"

Brit laughs, "That fucker is hard to kill. No way you were the one to do it."

I guess she has a point, but I did stab him where he was already hurt. I might as well have stabbed him in the back and twisted the knife, and in a way, I did. The pain in his eyes, the way he begged me not to go even after I did that to him… it lives rent-free in my head. There's no way I could ever forget that. My heart aches for him, and a selfish part of me hopes he's fucking suffering over me. I want him to be unable to eat, drink, sleep, and move on. I want nothing except heartbreak and fucking misery for him. I need him wanting to stop everything just because he lost me.

Going crazy.

Riddled with dreams of me.

Can't let go.

I don't give a shit how toxic that is, if he's not going absolutely insane over losing me, I don't want him.

Hurry up, Damien.

I don't know how much longer I can survive this…

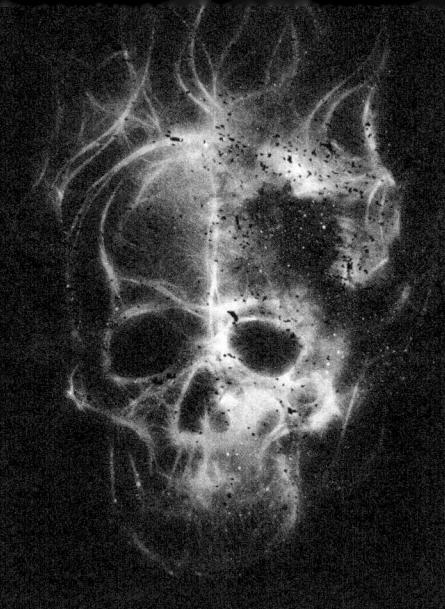

CHAPTER 10

Zayne

I grab Damien's face and turn it toward me. "I'm sorry," I whisper, putting my forehead to his. We make eye contact briefly, then he shuts his eyes and silently cries, his shoulders shaking, his chest heaving. "I'm *so* sorry."

Why do I even give a shit? Maybe it's because he came for me, although I'm sure there were selfish reasons for his rescue. However, if it has anything to do with Hallie, then I don't give a fuck. Let him use me as long as I get her back.

I still can't deny the relief I felt upon seeing him. No matter how much we dislike each other, he is a familiar face. I know he won't leave me to rot. I know he came for me. That means more than I'll ever tell him. I probably won't say shit about it, except maybe thank you.

Letting go of his face, I grip his shoulders and haul him toward me. Damien tries to pull away again, but I don't let him. He said "mom" when he turned her over, and now he's fucking destroyed. How the fuck did that happen? How did she end up here? Didn't he know she'd be here? In a way, it would be worse if he was aware she was here and wanted to get her out. Now all of his dreams would be shattered.

"Get away from me," he growls. This time he's successful with his push, shoving me away until I land on my ass. "I don't want your fucking pity."

Two Mexican men walk toward us, and I flinch, scooting back until one of the cages digs into my spine. Who the fuck are they? I glance around the room, it is empty save for Adriana standing by the basement door. She smiles at me, motioning for me to go to her.

One of the men says, "We need to get the fuck out of here before someone else shows up." He's talking to Damien. I guess he had help to get us out. I'm not surprised; there were a lot of guards in here. There's no fucking way he could've done it all on his own.

I get back up, and walk to Adriana, stopping right in front of her. We're still naked, and even though everyone in this room has seen me this way for weeks, I suddenly have the urge to cover myself. Maybe it has to do with morals or whatever. Who knows anymore?

She looks into my eyes and smiles, her hand reaching for my cheek. "We did it." Adriana says quietly as she touches my face. Tears fill both of our eyes, and she wipes mine when they spill over.

"We did," I affirm, then mirror what she's doing.

Loud footsteps snap us out of the moment, and when I look back, Damien is walking sluggishly with narrowed eyes. It's like he wants to kill me with his eyes, which is nothing new, but it feels like this time is for something else. Yeah, he thinks I'm betraying her, the love of my life. What he doesn't know is that I had to survive this somehow, and I won't apologize for it. Even still, my heart physically hurts like I've been stabbed when I remember Hallie. No, I can't betray her.

When the men pass us, we trail after them until we get outside the house. They begin to stroll while pointing their rifles.

However, Damien stops abruptly and begins throwing up in the bushes next to him. We all stop and look at him, and when he begins to dry heave, I walk toward him. His hand shoots up in the air, telling me to halt, so I do.

He wipes his arm across his face and spits, then picks up his rifle again like nothing happened. We all hurry toward a white van that's partially hidden, and the two men get in the bulkhead. The short one's name is Diego, from what I heard, and he's the only one who seems to speak English. The man has brown skin and a beard, or barely a beard anyway, and dark eyes. He kind of looks like Adriana a little bit, except she has hazel eyes.

Armando, the other man, has his green eyes narrowed on me and looks me up and down. His light skin is a contrast to his very dark hair, and he doesn't look Mexican at all. Yet he doesn't speak any English either, so obviously he's from here.

One goes to the passenger side, and the other to the driver's side. I guess it's me, Adriana, and Damien in the back. *Great*.

Damien opens a sliding door on the side of the van and motions us in, looking around frantically as we climb up to the back. For just a second, I forget all about how his mom is dead, how he just found her, and my hate for him hits me full force again. Just because I empathize and feel bad for him doesn't mean I don't want to beat the motherfucker and put him in a hospital. Hallie is *mine* and will continue to be *only mine*. He stole her once, but I'm not letting that happen again. We need to find her, and when we do, I'll make sure he's out of the picture, forever. Even if that means I'll have to fucking kill him.

Adriana and I find a place to sit, and Damien gets in and shuts the door. It's pitch black back here until he turns on a flashlight and points it at the ceiling. Two backpacks are right next to me as he sits across from us.

"There are clothes in there for you." He says, and I open a bag that has women's clothes and pass it to Adriana. The second bag has clothes for me, and somehow he knows my size. Maybe because we have close to the same build, maybe that's why Hallie is so attracted to him. That thought makes my blood boil, and I get up and put the clothes on roughly. I throw the bag and sit back down, turning away from Damien.

"Watch the fucking attitude," Damien tells me, and even though I'm not looking, I can feel his eyes on me. It pisses me off even more. "I don't have the patience for your bullshit. You're lucky I even let you out. I was going to leave your stupid ass behind."

"So why didn't you?" I spit out, fisting my hands.

"Because she wouldn't forgive me if I left you."

I laugh, "It's a little late for forgiveness, bud." My eyes meet his, "She left you, didn't she?"

He stiffens at that, and I smile. Good girl, Hallie. "Don't make me throw you out of this fucking van, because I will. Hallie be damned."

"Then do it," I taunt. "Bet you fucking won't."

He turns around and begins to fuck with a latch, but I just smile. Adriana, however, doesn't find this funny at all. She jumps up from her spot, fully clothed at this point, and grabs Damien's hand.

"Stop," she pleads. "*Please.*"

Damien looks at her like she has a disease and yanks his hand from her grasp. She doesn't look offended however, and he does listen to her. Maybe there's something magical about women asking for shit. Sure as fuck works on me most of the time. He does lay his head against the side of the van, looking up at the ceiling, then begins to hit the back of his head. After three consecutive and dramatic bangs of his head, he closes his eyes.

I turn to Adriana, wholly annoyed with him at this point and not ready to look at him at all. She grabs my arm and drags me to sit right next to her, which unfortunately, has me facing Damien all over again.

She leans in and whispers in my ear, "What happens now?"

I glance up and Damien is staring at us suspiciously with narrowed eyes and pursed lips, disapproval on his face. Why, though?

Wouldn't he want me to move on so he can live happily ever after with *my* Hallie? Yeah, I don't fucking think so. Not happening.

I turn to her and reply, "I have no idea, but I want to get the fuck out of Mexico."

Her eyes water and a tear spills over. I hate seeing her cry over me; my heart hurts when she sniffles. I turn my body toward her and wipe it away. "You'd leave me behind?" she asks me.

"Not behind, Adriana." I sigh while tucking a strand of her hair behind her ear. "We need to move forward."

"I don't want to move forward." There's truth in her words, and it breaks my heart. The problem is that there's no choice to make for me. It was made for me long before now. I can't let go of Hallie. "I want *you*."

"I like you, Adriana." And that's the fucking sad part. "I really do. I would even go as far as saying I have feelings for you." She smiles at me and cups my face. Only the next words will not be what she wants to hear. I'm trying to do my best to let her down slowly, but the truth is that it stings me too. "Although I think it might be a result of our… *situation*…"

"No." She shakes her head and kisses me softly, her tears getting on my lips. "I know what I feel."

"I feel it too," I assure her. "But my heart belongs to someone else. It has for a long time before you came along."

"So let me try to take it from her."

I smile. That takes guts to be willing to live with the ghost of someone else. I can't though. I want the real thing. I want Hallie. "You deserve someone who picks you over everyone else, Adriana. Being a second choice should never be your place, you're too special. Things would be different if my heart hadn't been taken before I met you. You will find someone who can love you the way you deserve."

This time it's me who grabs her face and pulls her in, and I take her bottom lip between mine and suck on it. Her hands also find my face, and we kiss each other like it's the last time. For it truly is. I don't ever want to see her again after this. Nothing will distract me from *her*.

Damien scoffs across from us, then chuckles. "Of fucking course," he mutters, but the van suddenly stops and any remaining words die on his tongue.

I'm tempted to tell him to fuck off, that he has no idea what we went through together. Instead, I look at Adriana with sad eyes, and her hazel ones fill with tears. "I think this is where we get out." Her face scrunches up, and I try to smooth her features out with my fingers. "This is goodbye, honey." I give her a kiss on the cheek, the nose, and her lips. "I'll never forget you."

With that, I get up along with Damien. She doesn't say anything until he opens the door, and I begin to step out. "I'll never forget *you*..." We smile at each other, and I turn my back on her. "Oh, and Zayne?" I look at her and her face lights up for just a second, then her smile drops and a frown takes over. "If things don't work out with her, I will always be here."

I nod, a knot in my throat. It's entirely possible that it will happen, that Hallie will want nothing to do with me after all of this is said and done. Just because I find her gives me no guarantee that she will want to get back together, especially when fucker number one is still in the picture. I love my Hallie, but she's fucking weak. I know she will give in to him. Especially if he calls her 'love' or whatever the fuck his corny ass says.

"If the time ever comes, I promise I will find you."

Finally, I walk away from her with a knot in my throat. I know I deeply care about her, but it's not enough. I've always believed there's only one person for you in life that you can't move on from. You can be with other people, but it will never be the same as with that person. Hallie is that for me, *my* person. Forever.

Damien begins to walk toward a beat-up car, and I chuckle. I bet he hates that shit. Always with his coupe and motorcycle, he's such a little bitch. Probably crying in a corner about it.

"You sure you don't want her instead?" he asks with amusement. "I would fully support that decision. You know that, right?"

"Go fuck yourself, Damien."

He laughs like he's just so funny. "Nah, I'll be fucking Hallie soon enough."

"You talk a lot of shit for someone she didn't want to be with."

Damien turns around at that and grabs me by the throat, but I don't cower. I tuck my chin and push my forehead against his, not even giving a fuck that I have to get on my tiptoes since he's two inches taller than me.

"You know fucking *nothing*." He abruptly lets go of me, then keeps walking to a car. Once we make it there and he unlocks it, he tells me, "Get in the back, peasant. I don't want anyone to see you."

Bitch.

"Yeah, whatever," I mutter. "Also can't stand the sight of you, but you already know that."

We're parked in an abandoned lot. Whatever grocery store that used to be here is long gone. Windows are shattered and doors are kicked in, and I bet there's either homeless people or serial killers in there. I stare at it for far too long. Damien notices and smirks.

"Scared, *baby*?"

I'm fucking done with him, so I open the door and get in, lying down on the seat and hoping to not hear his voice for the remainder of the trip. I close my eyes, trying to nap, but unfortunately, the ride is short.

We pull up to a dingy ass motel that looks about one hundred years old and like it should be demolished, and when I try to open the door, it won't. There's a fucking child lock on this shit. I huff in annoyance, and Damien looks at me via the rearview mirror and smiles. I'm tired of playing these fucking games with him. I just want some sleep and a shower and some food and Hallie. Not too much to ask for.

He unlocks the motel room door, and I file in after him, locking the door behind me. Three locks—not to be paranoid, but that feels like a little too much. Just what part of town are we in? Personally, I'd rather not get kidnapped yet again. I also don't want to have to rescue *him*. Now I feel like I owe him a debt, and it's not sitting right with me.

I finally take care of business, shower, brush my teeth, and put fresh clothes on. Damien even got me spare underwear. *Aw.* Maybe I'll try to tolerate him now, but probably not, to be honest.

One thing I hadn't noticed before this very moment, which is just the cherry on top of my anger issues, is that there's only one fucking bed in here. Damien and I take a long look at each other, and he raises an eyebrow in challenge. He's fucking rich, and he didn't think of getting a room with two beds?

"What the fuck is this?" I ask, gesturing to the bed with an exasperated wave of my hand. "There's only one bed in here."

"Yeah, well, you try finding a motel in the middle of a city full of cartel sicarios who know you, and then get back to me."

"Don't they have double queen rooms here?"

Damien rolls his eyes. "You really are dumb. How would it look if I had two beds and showed up alone?"

"Whatever, dude. Just stay on your fucking side."

"I wouldn't touch you with a ten-foot pole."

The bed is comfortable, I'll give the shitty motel that much. It's also clean enough, compared to the conditions I've been living in lately. I'm just happy to have a place where I don't have to be naked and abused.

After about an hour, I'm sitting in bed eating the best tacos I've ever had, which he went and grabbed for us, thankfully, and Damien is sitting at a small desk. We haven't looked at each other, and the air is thick enough to suffocate. I don't know how long the peace will last. We seem to be at each other's throats with every other word we utter. I want to say it's getting on my nerves, but I immensely enjoy pushing his buttons. And I want some fucking answers too. Like how the fuck did Hallie end up in Mexico? Maybe it's not the right time.

Faint sniffles come from Damien, and I look up from my food to watch him closely. He has finished eating and is burying his face in his hands. He looks like a lost child, going through life with no direction. Now I'm curious about his upbringing. Did his mom do drugs before getting taken? Is this why he hates them? Why does he judge addicts? And if so, why the fuck did he work in this industry?

"I'm really sorry about your mom," I tell him. "Truly."

"What do you want?" Damien sounds defeated. "To bond over our mommy issues?"

Bingo. He's still an asshole and will always be one. "I only have daddy issues, sorry," I joke, and he actually laughs. He *laughs*. At *my* joke.

Who is he? Did he hit his head?

"I guess I have both." He looks like he would. Damn, just look at us being the perfect pair of damaged prospects. "Maybe we should go to therapy together?"

"That sounds kinda nice." Really, not even a little bit. "Maybe then we can learn to get along."

Damien smirks. "No chance there."

We chuckle together, but I sober up quickly. I finish up my last taco and lean back on the flimsy headboard. Hopefully there's no one next door. If I have to hear this shit bang against the wall from someone getting fucked, I might just spiral into a deep depression.

"I have some questions," I start, but I continue when he doesn't reply. "Where is Hallie?"

He sighs. "If I knew, you wouldn't be here." Okay. Good point.

"So then, how do we find her?"

"How will *I* find her?" Of course. It's so like him to play the fucking hero. "And I don't know yet. There's an auction Carl told me about, and I need to figure out when it takes place."

A shiver runs down my spine at the mention of his name, and I try to keep my face blank. I don't want him to know about what was done to me. It would be one more weakness for him to exploit, to use against me. I won't give him that opportunity. Not willingly.

"How the fuck did this happen?" I run a hand through my hair in exasperation. "How could you let this happen?"

"Me?" He asks, appalled, standing from his chair abruptly. "She stabbed me and left me to fucking die!"

I roll my eyes, "No, she fucking didn't."

Damien lifts his shirt, and there is a stitched cut right below his rib cage. My eyes widen, but then I begin to laugh. I do it for so long that my belly hurts. Oh my fucking God. I didn't think she had it in her, but damn. She really did it.

"She did what?!" I continue to laugh, wiping tears from my face and trying to breathe through it so I can stop. "I fucking love her."

Damien looks me up and down, completely unamused. "I don't get what the fuck is so funny about that."

"My Hallie finally grew a fucking pair."

"She's not yours." He stalks toward me. "She's *mine*, and *I* taught her how to have a fucking backbone."

"She loved me first, dumbass." She did. I don't give a fuck what he says to me; he will never have that. He will never be the guy who took her heart and stitched it back up after breaking it. He shouldn't be proud of being second choice.

"She loves me more."

I stand from the bed, now getting angry. Fuck this. I can't do this shit. Maybe there's a way I can return to the United States and not deal with the asshole anymore.

I smirk. "I fucked her last."

He grins at that, his eyes twinkling, and I narrow mine. "No. You didn't."

At that, I do see red, and the punch that lands on his face is unexpected even to me. I guess my anger issues are coming out at the most unexpected times, but he really knows how to fuck with my head.

Just as fast as I punched him, he hits me back. My entire face twists with the force of it, and I clutch it. Pretty sure something split open. Probably my lip. I lift my hand away to glance at it; sure enough, it's covered in blood.

"I'll ruin your fucking life, you little bitch," Damien says through gritted teeth, like it's exhausting to deal with me. The feeling is mutual. "What are you going to say next? 'She begged for my dick?' Well, guess what? She begged for mine too."

I advance toward him again, and now we're forehead to forehead, pushing against each other, glaring into each other's eyes. He shoves me hard, but I push him away harder.

He walks away first, but I don't feel victorious. I thought Hallie loved me more than this. We shouldn't be fighting over her. She should know who she wants to be with. I guess she did though, since she didn't pick either of us.

That makes me more nervous than if she had.

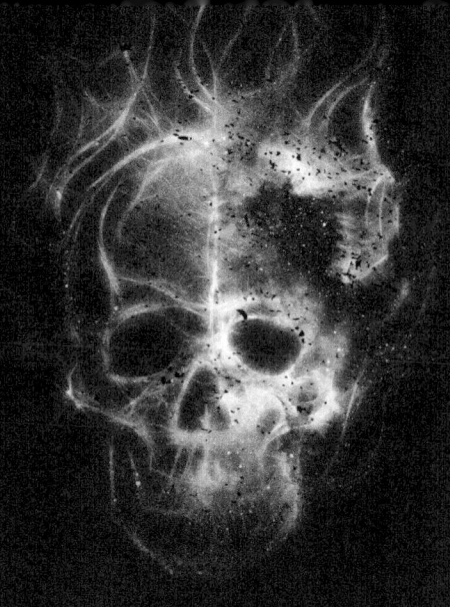

CHAPTER 11

Brittany

I haven't been here very long, but I can confidently say that this shit is for the birds. However long I've been here, I only know I want to go home.

Right fucking now.

Hallie is lying in bed, doped up yet again, with a blissful look on her face. I hate what they're doing to her. She has fought long and hard to escape her addiction, and Xanax is child's play compared to what they keep giving her now. The sad part is that she doesn't even fight it anymore. Instead, it seems like she looks forward to it.

After she came back the other night, all fucked up and talking about dying; she's willingly given her arm over multiple times per day. During those times though, Michael fucked her into the ground. Maybe that's the only way she can escape from the pain, the abuse, the fucking rape. I'm only surprised he allows her to get lost in a bubble instead of forcing her to be present and aware of the depraved shit he's doing to her. Does the asshole have a conscience, after all? Or is it only with her? Does he care about her? Is he in love or some shit?

The thought of me being next is scary, but I've already come to terms with it and made peace in my heart and soul as well. If the time comes where I'm forced to suck dick or take it, I will be obedient and submissive. Unlike Hallie, I won't get special treatment. I'm no one's favorite, thankfully, but that only means that I will have no protection. As far as I can tell, Michael has been using me against Hallie to make her comply as much as he can. Even still, she's fucking stubborn and does whatever she feels like doing. I'll probably die soon. I feel so…at peace with it and I'm no longer scared. There's no getting me out of here now; I'm stuck for life. Nothing matters to me except Hallie.

The friendship she and I have goes way beyond that; she's my fucking sister. When my parents put me in a mental hospital, I never thought I'd amount to anything, but I did. Back then, the only person by my side was Hallie. She's seen me through the ups and the downs, held my hand through heartbreaks and family drama, and even bailed me out of the psych ward when I admitted myself. She said I didn't belong in there, and she was right. She's always right.

Hallie is my rock.

I have been working on the side, all on my own, trying to decipher something. Making a plan to get out of here seemed downright impossible until I met a man named Tomás. He must be tired of his job, or maybe he actually likes me. Honestly, I don't really give a shit. The main focus is getting Hallie and I to make it out of here alive. So, when he said he could help me, I got on my knees and sucked his dick. It's just one more of all the ones I'll be forced to suck, so why not? At least this one was consensual.

I'm not being honest with Hallie, and it bothers me. For now, I just have to keep this to myself until I know for sure when and how we're leaving this fucking place. I can't risk her being forced to talk, whether it's with torture somehow or by withholding something as simple as heroin. I wouldn't say she's fully addicted yet, but she's definitely using it as a coping mechanism, which *will* eventually lead to addiction.

When she called me and told me to leave everything behind and head north, I thought she was full of shit. That maybe she was making up some crazy story for entertainment to get my attention. I still listened to her, but it didn't matter. The cartel must have been watching me for a while, or maybe they tapped her phone and listened in on our conversation. I don't know how they accomplished it, but they caught me in a motel by the Texas state line leading to New Mexico and Colorado. I was heading north just like she said. Unfortunately, they somehow knew that. If we got out of here, we would have to figure out another place to go because they definitely know about her Alaska plan. Maybe we can go the opposite way and head East to Canada by New York.

When those men waited for me and cornered me, I immediately realized who they were and that Hallie hadn't lied. It took a whole day to get me from the state line all the way down here, but they seemed to be doing just fine. I guess it's just another day in the life of a sex trafficker.

Now that I'm here, I've decided to live my life to the very fullest. Which is precisely why I'm fucking Tomás. Not only will I be getting something out of it, but also, his dick fucking slaps. So that's that. I've fucked a lot of dudes in my short twenty-two years of life, but I will say, this guy is one of the best I've ever had. Then again, he looks close to thirty, so he probably has plenty of experience to rival my own. I'd even go as far as saying that somehow I've grown to like him. He usually sneaks in when everyone is asleep, including Hallie, or we fuck when she's gone to do whatever Michael wants for her to do.

"I'm back, *hermosa*," Tomás tells me, climbing in bed with me and putting the covers over us until we're not visible. I guess being naked all the time is a bit convenient when you're into the person who wants to see you that way. "Did you miss me?"

I smile into the darkness even though he can't see me. Yes, I missed him, but I'm not telling him that. He doesn't get to have my pussy along with the rest of me. I willingly spread my legs for him, and he goes down my body, lingering on my tits. It's been years since I got them done, and it was the best decision I have ever made. If I had to choose, I would do it a hundred times over.

His fingers part me, and he takes a long lick from center to clit, lingering where I need him the most. Tomás puts my legs over his shoulders and grips my hips, then eats my pussy like he's starving for it. I breathe in through my nose slowly, even when it feels like I'm going to pass out from how good it feels and try to contain my moans. It's harder than I give him credit for 'cause he's amazing at what he's doing. When he inserts three fingers and hooks them while fucking me with them, I'm a goner. My body feels like it's on fire, and all the blood rushes south. I have to bite the inside of my cheek to keep quiet, and my breathing is so ragged and loud, I wonder how the hell Hallie hasn't woken up from it. Then again, she's also fucked up on H.

When Tomás crawls back up my body, leaving my legs on his shoulders, he rubs my wetness all over his dick and up my slit. "You were made for me, weren't you?" I don't get to answer as he enters me slowly and contorts my body until my knees are touching my chest, kissing me with an urgency that has my stomach bottoming out. Somehow his dick is even better than his tongue, and I'm ready for him to rearrange my insides.

Tomás keeps my legs bent and gets on his knees, making the covers fall from on top of us. It's risky because if someone comes in and catches us in this position, we're absolutely fucked. I don't know exactly what would happen, but I can't imagine anything good. So then why the hell don't I stop him?

Thankfully, the mattress is on the tile and not on a frame. When he starts fucking me hard and fast, the mattress slides a little bit, but it doesn't matter either way. My legs fall right over his arms; they're the only thing anchoring me in place as he thrusts in and out of my body. His thumb rubbing my clit makes my toes curl and my eyes roll to the back of my head.

This is why I don't stop him. The way he fucks me is possibly my favorite thing about my life right now. Actually, scratch that. It most definitely is.

"I think *you* were made for *me*…" I whisper-yell, moaning softly and hoping no one hears.

Tomás leans back in and drapes his body over mine. He bites my neck softly, making goosebumps spread all over my body, "Moan in my ear, *hermosa*. I want to hear when you come."

Either way, it doesn't take very long for me to feel the familiar tingling and shaking taking over my body. I shut my eyes as my orgasm takes over my body, my head lolling to the side.

My legs are sore as they're draped over his shoulders again, and he fucks me so hard I'm momentarily scared he will tear me apart. I dig my fingernails into his chest, and he hisses, speeding up his movements until he can't hold it anymore. Tomás buries his face into my neck as he comes inside me, his dick pulsing as he pants and barely holds it together.

The only problem?

When he pulls out and I open my eyes, I immediately see Hallie's narrowed ones on me. She looks fucking pissed. She closes her eyes again, except I think it might be for the sake of Tomás until he leaves. I'm almost one hundred percent sure that as soon as he walks out the door, she will cuss me the hell out.

Tomás brushes my hair out of my face and gives me a peck on the cheek. "When do you want to leave?" he asks me, hope blooming in my chest.

"As soon as possible."

He nods, "I'll make the arrangements for five days from now."

"Thank you," I whisper. "Hallie has to come with me. That's the only way I'm willing to come with you." He wants us to leave here and live together and make a family or whatever. I've never seen myself doing any of that shit, however with him… maybe I could.

"*Sí, mi hermosa.*" I smile at that, loving how sexy he sounds when he speaks Spanish to me. "Anything for you."

"I know." I grin, and he returns it.

"Don't worry about anything. We will all get out of here, and no one will know it. I've worked here for years and know exactly how to do it."

"Perfect," I smile, caressing his face and running my finger down his jaw, over his lips. "Now, get out of here before they get suspicious."

Tomás walks out of the room, and I get up immediately and run to the toilet so I can clean up. The last thing I need is for someone to check on me or try to force me to do something, and I have cum dripping down my damn legs.

When I return to bed, Hallie sits up. "What the fuck did I just watch, Brittany?" Oh, she's mad. "And don't say 'nothing' because I just watched the entire thing."

"Was I good? Did you like it?"

"Bitch?" Uh oh. "You laid there the entire time. What do you mean?"

I burst out laughing because she's right. I was definitely a pillow princess, and I'm not even mad about it. "You're right."

"How long?"

"I don't know how long I've been here…" I tell her. "But maybe like two days after?"

"You're a fucking slut, you know that?" Wait. I can't tell if she's for real right now or playing. "He fucked me, too."

Oh, so she's jealous.

I chuckle and walk to the side of her bed, "Men tend to do that, you know." I pat her arm condescendingly. "They usually stick with whoever they like most. Not to bring you down or anything, but it's not you, babe."

"What the fuck are you planning?"

"Something fun," I reply, alluding to absolutely fucking nothing. As I said, I'm not telling her anything until the very moment we have to leave. "Besides, I don't understand why you're so hurt. Do you not have enough men pining after you? Leave some for the rest of us, holy shit."

"I love you, Brit, but you're crossing a fucking line."

"And what line is that?" I ask her. "Because I'm being clear. Back the fuck off."

Hallie laughs, "Me? I was here first."

"So what?" I sneer, "You fucked him first. Big fucking deal. You have someone waiting for you outside of this shit hole, I don't. You only want him due to your attachment issues and can't bear to be alone."

I hit the nail on the head just like I knew it would. Hallie shuts up and lies back down on the bed, giving me her back. Suddenly, I feel bad for my outburst. It's not a lie in any case, and maybe that's why she's so sensitive about it.

"You're my person, Hallie." I join her in bed, pushing her aside until I'm spooning her. I rub her hair back as she sniffles and wipes her nose with the back of her arm. "You have always been my person."

I stay awake long after she falls back asleep, thinking of everything that could go wrong if we try to escape. It doesn't matter, though. We have nothing to lose.

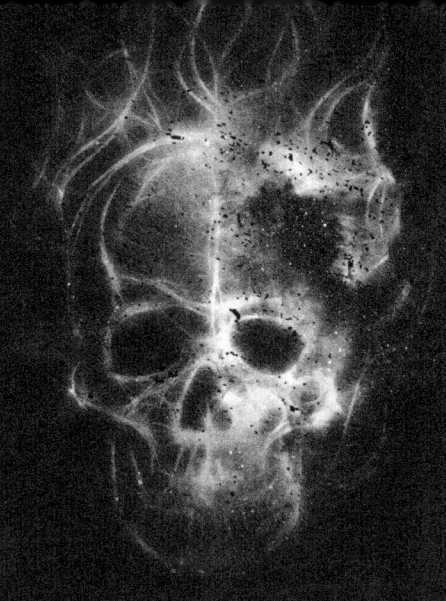

CHAPTER 12

Damien

I have five words.

Get Zayne away from me.

It's not that I hate him, even though I still do. It seems no one could pay us enough money to stop arguing or get along. It's fucking exhausting. Gone are the days when I do a job independently and on my schedule. Now I have to worry about when he eats, how many pairs of shirts I got for him, and whether he washed his balls. Mostly since I refuse to sleep next to someone who smells like a sweaty ballsack.

Has he been here for me about my mom? Yes. Has that stopped him from making offhand comments that he knows will piss me off and make me want to kill him? No chance. Which is exactly why I've been avoiding him like the plague, yet the little bitch is persistent.

Sean finally found out when the auction takes place, which will be tonight, and I've spent two days figuring out how I'm going to get in there, blend in, not be recognized, then somehow follow Michael afterwards. I'm pretty sure this will be my only chance to be in the same place as him for an extended period of time, and I don't want anything to ruin it or get in my way.

So then tell me why the fuck Zayne keeps insisting on coming with.

Obviously, if it were up to just me the answer would be—hell to the fuck no! There are many reasons for that. Some of them being that he doesn't know what the fuck he's doing, and if you look even a little out of place, they will mop the floor with your hair after they bleed you out for fun. Also, what if someone recognizes him? On my life, he doesn't have a fucking brain. He's too impulsive and doesn't think anything through.

How the fuck did she even like this dude?

Either way, he's not fucking going. I'm not budging on that. It's non-negotiable. First of all, he doesn't have a suit, and I'm not going on a scavenger hunt in Juarez, one of the most dangerous places in the country. Zayne will simply have to deal with it.

My phone rings, and it says Sean is the one calling. "Hey, D," he says, but it's not his usual cheery tone. Shit, it's not even the sound he makes when he usually calls me after finding out important information. What the fuck is happening? "There's something you need to see, but you need to remain calm."

Those little magic words instantly put me on edge. "What is it?" I ask him slowly, suddenly dreading his answer.

"I have to send it to you…" he replies. "It's going to be hard to watch, but this is the only footage of him where you can see what he looks like. Since we haven't found his last name, this is the only way I can show you."

A shiver runs down my spine, and I glance back at Zayne sitting in bed, intently staring at me. There's a look of suspicion on his face, and I know I will have to show him or he will lose his shit. I don't have time for that crap right now, so I guess I'll just let him see if he wants to.

"Send it to my email?"

"Done," Sean replies with finality then hangs up on me.

I grab my computer from my suitcase, set it on the bed, and turn it on. This might be a massive mistake. Probably after tonight we will have to move to a different motel, or we will get tracked down, but I need to see what this asshole looks like. The sudden fear in the pit of my stomach is overwhelming, and I'm scared of what's in the email.

"What's that?" Zayne asks as I click on the message, and there's a video. The preview is black, so I can't even tell what this will show me.

"It's a video of Michael," I reply, "We need to see what he looks like."

Zayne crawls over to the spot next to me, and I tense when his leg brushes against my arm. I push him away from me in annoyance, and he rolls his eyes. "Chill, bro. It was an accident."

My head whips to look at him. "I'm not your 'bro.'"

I take a deep breath and open up the video, which leads me to a new tab. No amount of breathing could've prepared me for what I'm seeing, however. Hallie is lying naked and facedown on a velvet couch, wearing only heels, while Michael rapes her. His suit-clad body rams into her with so much force her body rattles with it. Turning her head and putting her cheek right on the couch. It's almost like she makes eye contact with the camera, but if you look closely her eyes are blank. I look over her body, and I notice a thin trail of blood traveling down her arm.

Fuck no.

No.

I'm going to fucking kill him, and I'm going to make it fucking slow.

I memorize Michael for a few seconds. Blond hair, green eyes, muscular build. It's disgusting that he doesn't look like the slimy fucking pig he is, and I can see why some women might even think he's attractive. It's too fucking bad he's a disgusting cockroach that refuses to die.

Zayne gasps next to me, and when I look at him, there are

tears in his eyes. He looks fucking destroyed, almost as destroyed as I feel on the inside. This might be the only time we can agree on something: we need to get her the fuck out of there.

My pain is intensified by the one thing he doesn't feel, and that's the overwhelming guilt riddling my heart. A tear trails down my cheek when she screams and starts to sob. It's unmistakable; he's forcing her to come.

Anger takes over, and it's hard not to throw my fucking laptop against the wall and make it shatter like my heart just did. My chest squeezes my heart, and the knot in my throat barely lets me breathe. *I need to find her.*

"Not her," Zayne whispers. "Never her."

"Yeah? Well, it *is* her," I reply. "And we have to fucking stop him."

I wanted to leave Zayne out of this, but maybe he could be useful, after all. No way am I letting him enter with me, that's too risky for both of us. It doesn't take a genius to figure out who he is and who he's supposed to belong to. We don't know who is aware of his ties to Carl, though as it stands, probably half of the people attending saw him on the live feed.

"I will need you tonight." His face changes to a hopeful expression when I turn my gaze toward him. "We need an escape plan. I'm going in alone."

"Absolutely fucking not."

"Zayne," I growl. "Hear me out for one fucking second, you prick."

He visibly relaxes, like he's used to the familiarity of someone telling him off and treating him like shit. He's more damaged than I thought, which pisses me off since now I can see the stupid trauma bond between him and Hallie. It makes me want to throw up. I can see why she thinks they have many things in common; it's pretty obvious they're both similar in more ways than one. I fucking hate that she may be right. That doesn't make him the man she needs, though. Quite the opposite. Still, I'll have time to convince her of that.

"Are you going to be quiet?" He nods, and I continue, "I need to go in alone just in case someone recognizes you from the live feeds. If they do, you might just be added to the auction for having experience as a sex slave. Let's be real, as much as I hate to say it, you have a pretty face. Anyway, I need you in the car waiting close by and watching your surroundings and paying attention to when I come out. Can you do that?"

"Yes."

"Okay good. Once you see me come out of the building, I need you to haul ass to me. Let me get in the car and then we get the fuck out of that place. We cannot take any chances. I'm there to find out who this fucker is, his last name, and any goddamn information I can get on him. If we're lucky, he won't notice I'm watching him, and then we can follow him to wherever he's going. That is, if he doesn't have ten guards with him."

"We *have* to follow him," Zayne argues. "Hallie can't spend one more fucking night in that house."

"She will have to if we can't safely reach her." Sadly. "We're no good to her dead."

He purses his lips, seeming to consider my words. If he could just follow directions and shut up, we could finally get along. Maybe. I'm willing to try, not for him but for Hallie. Once we get her back, she won't be in a state of mind where she can handle us being at each other's throats. From what I just witnessed on my laptop, I'd be surprised if she's not a shell of a person by the time we get her back.

"I'll do whatever you need me to do. All I want is for Hallie to be okay…"

"That makes two of us."

About thirty minutes later, my suit is ironed, and I've cleaned up and gotten dressed. Now it's Zayne's turn to look normal and not a homeless guy. Much to my chagrin, I have to lend him some of my clothes. To be clear, that's all we will be sharing. Thankfully, he gets ready in record time.

The drive to the cultural center is uneventful. Not much traffic at all on the road, but then again, it's eight p.m. Most people are either at work or at home at this point. Others are buying women and men at a fucking auction. One day I will try to stop this from happening in the first place. Unfortunately, for now, I only have one person I can help. She doesn't stand a chance if all of my attention is not on her.

Zayne goes to the far end of the parking lot so no one recognizes the car when it's time for me to escape. "Don't forget the plan. Once you see me, you get to me as fast as humanly possible."

"I understood the first fifty times you said it."

I smirk and open my car door. "Just making sure." Before I shut it, I say, "I hope the car gets stolen with you in it."

I walk to the enormous building, trying to keep my stride not too quick yet not too slow. My hands shake slightly, and I wipe the sweat off my slacks, looking around to ensure no one is staring at me. I can't afford to appear nervous or suspicious in any way. One pro to this situation is that Sean figured out exactly where Michael is sitting—again, the fucker never puts his last name on anything—but the cons are too many to count. Some of them do include the fact that Michael is sitting in the first row, whereas I had to settle for the third row since the first-row seats were all sold to the rich as fuck capos. Nasty motherfuckers. I did, however, get to sit within his line of sight so I should have a good view of him. Another con to this situation is how hard it will be to get information.

Who the fuck do I get it from? Are there any employees around?

The building is fancy with its circular architecture in the front and some sort of shiny tile on the surface. I wonder who runs this place and if they ever feel guilty about letting women be fucking sold in what's supposed to host plays, ballets, symphonies, and orchestra concerts. Unless they're in on it as well, in which case I should just blow up the fucking building. Those girls don't stand a chance either way.

Murals and beautiful—fucking expensive—artwork lines

most of the walls. Most of them have blood red in them, something that doesn't escape my notice. There's nothing subtle about it. Walking through and handing them my ticket makes me nervous—but I keep my face blank and still my hands. *Don't fuck this up.*

I'm surprisingly waved in, which was easier than expected since he barely glanced at my ticket, and I'm rightly on edge when I hear the music they're playing. There's a pianist, and it's a haunting melody that fills the theater. I shouldn't be surprised by how many people are here, except when I glance up and see that almost every seat is taken in this vast room—there are three fucking levels to seating—I'm outraged. Again, I'm forced to keep my face blank and make my way down the steps and through my row. Men grunt and harrumph as I walk past, making them move their feet. The cultural center should've made it more spacious down here. Now I see why Michael wanted the first row. Only the first few rows are participating in the auction, and the rest are spectators. That's worse. They come here for *fun* or some shit.

The only positive to come out of this so far is that at least the seats are comfortable as fuck. I'm a bit nervous that the lights are so bright, still. I can't afford for Michael to see me here. Now I'm wondering how many rows are participating in the auction, because if I don't, it might make me look suspicious. If I do, however, then it draws attention to me. Damned if I do, damned if I don't. Fuck me.

Every single seat visible to me is occupied, and I keep my eyes trained forward, not even looking at where Michael is supposed to be. Suddenly, the lights dim slightly, which helps me relax. I just hope no one in my row bids for any of the girls.

The MC approaches the stage and grabs a microphone from its stand. Of course, it's a man who does it, and I bet he's been ogling each and every one of them. I'd be surprised if he didn't sample any of them.

"Good evening, gentlemen," His voice booms through the microphone, and he adjusts it so it's away from his mouth. "Today, we will be bringing to you the best of the best, and we hope you enjoy the show." The man proceeds to also repeat what he just said in Spanish, then walks to a corner podium.

As far as the eye can see, there are only men in this fucking place, but something tells me it's not just women here. No, judging by how Zayne was bought, I know there must also be men. I wonder exactly how Zayne got to Carl in the first place, but I won't ask.

The first girl is called by her number, and she comes to the center of the stage, peering down at the ground. She looks around eighteen years old, blonde, and naked. I think all of them will be.

"Number 001." The man proceeds to say something about how submissive the girl is, and multiple people from the front row bid on her. "One million going once, going twice..." Michael didn't bid on her though. Is he saving his money for someone he already knows about? Or does he have a specific taste? Anyone who looks remotely similar to Hallie? We're about to find out.

"Sold!" he all but yells. "Number 001 is sold to Emanuel Garza."

Everyone's eyes turn to the man with approval and a sort of pride. What the fuck is going on? I can't believe I was ever a helping hand in this shit. My regret is deep and will stay with me for the rest of my life. The fear in her eyes tugs at my heart, making my chest feel like it's caving in. I can't take my eyes off the girl—not because of attraction or perversion, but because the trembling of her hands is noticeable even from the third row. Although she now keeps her eyes on her feet, the set of her hunched shoulders and stiff body tells me she knows what's coming. The disgust I feel right now emanates from my body, seeping from my pores like sweat. The fact that I played this game once upon a time—not by purchasing but by enforcing and kidnapping the girls—fucking makes me feel like the biggest piece of shit on the planet. Even worse than them right now. I can't believe that was me—but one thing is for sure: I will never do it again. Over my dead body.

More and more women, men, and teens walk the stage completely naked, just like the first girl, and people continue to bid on them. The catch? Michael hasn't bid on any of them. What the fuck is he doing here, and in the front row, if he doesn't want to buy? If he doesn't, how the fuck am I supposed to track him down?

"Only a few left," The sick fuck on stage wags his eyebrows, and the only reason I can see it is that the light focuses on his face when he speaks. "Get yours now before it's too late!" He sounds like a fucking commercial.

A few people later, everything goes silent. Even Michael sits up straighter in his chair; eyes hyper-focused on the stage. What the fuck is happening? Everyone seems to be on the edge of their seats. Are they saving the best for last or some shit?

I accidentally make eye contact with one of the men sitting next to him, who looks like a guard. Fuck. Not right now. I need to see this through. Against all instincts, I avert my eyes. I hope he doesn't think it's a sign of submission, because he can't sissify me. I refuse to be anyone's bitch, and I won't start now.

Hushed whispers permeate the air, and I keep my eyes trained on the stage, trying to think of what the hell could have people so riled up. The anticipation is palpable, and when I see what is clearly siblings stepping onto the stage holding hands, bile rises to the back of my throat. No fucking way. This is some sick, perverted bullshit. *No way.*

"Fraternal twins," the man announces, and the pair come to center stage and stand at the 'x'.

White, blue-eyed siblings stand on stage. I'm sure they were kidnapped from the United States, and I bet their family is moving heaven, hell, Earth, and fucking limbo to find them. Their eyes are purple, panda eyes as they call it, and they are naked with bruises on them. My own eyes well with tears, and I'm choking on emotion when they hold hands, their fingers reaching for each other in a terrified grip. Fuck. I can't watch this. I can't do this anymore.

"You may make your bids," he tells everyone, and just when I thought it couldn't get any worse, more men make bids on these fucking siblings than they did for any teenager or woman. What the fuck is wrong with people?! I don't want to think of the depraved shit that they're going to make them do to each other.

"One million going once," he says, but someone else immediately outbids to 2 million. Another person outbids that, then another, and another. "Seven million dollars going once… twice," He stops and looks around. "Sold! The twins go to Michael!"

Loud whispers turn to complaints that turn to yelling, and suddenly the crowd is in pure chaos. I watch the twins being quickly ushered off the stage, probably to wait for this fucker to transport them. People begin to get up from their chairs, and within two minutes, many of the rows are entirely cleared out. The men who won bids are talking to each other in a circle with proud looks on their faces.

With each passing second, I hate this more and more.

From my chair, I see a woman cleaning the stage—which isn't even dirty—and I decide this is my shot. I don't look around as I get out of my chair, since I don't want to seem suspicious, and find a way to get backstage. Once there, I spot the girl right away. She looks around twenty years old. Easy prey.

"*Hola, querida,*" Hi, dear, I tell her, and she jumps. It's obvious she knows what these people do. Not only is there skepticism shining brightly in her brown eyes, but also fear. "*No te preocupes, no te voy a lastimar.*" *Don't worry, I'm not going to hurt you.* She visibly relaxes. "*Solo necesito saber dos cosas.*" *I only need to know two things.*

"*¿Qué dos cosas necesitas saber?*" *What two things do you need to know?* She shifts from one foot to the other, avoiding my gaze. As much as I hate it, I need her scared.

"*¿Cuál es el apellido de Michael?*" *What is Michael's last name?*

She shakes her head rapidly, instantly scared shitless. "*Realmente no lo sé…*" *I really do not know…*

"*¿Cuál es su dirección?*" *What is his address?*

"*No tengo ni idea…*" *I have no idea.* Her lower lip trembles, and a tear spills down her cheek.

"*No quiero lastimarte, solo necesito respuestas.*" *I don't want to hurt you. I just need answers.*

"No te puedo ayudar." I can't help you.

The fuck you can't.

"Entonces atente a las consecuencias." Then face the consequences.

I wrap my hands around her neck and begin to squeeze, choking her until she turns purple. It's no skin off my back if I actually kill her. She works for these pieces of shit when she could choose not to. Anything else is more honorable than this. However, when she taps my arm in submission, I smile.

The girl begins to cough, a loud sound that I hope doesn't make anyone come back here and check on her. *"Está bien,"* Okay. *"Te digo dónde vive."* I'll tell you where he lives.

"Gracias, querida." Thanks, dear.

She grimaces but pulls out a paper and pen from her apron and writes something down. I don't even know if it's an actual address, but it's a chance I'll have to take. As I walk back to the theater room, Michael is nowhere to be found. I scan the area with my eyes, seeing that fucking guard yet again.

I hurry to the bathroom and put the paper in my back pocket. This whole thing has me feeling queasy as fuck, and as soon as I open the stall door, I throw up in the toilet. I can't fucking believe this shit. To think these people all waited impatiently to buy *people*, for them to join the stage, is beyond nasty. I don't even have enough words for how much I hate them all.

I *can't* let them go with him. I'll *never* forgive myself.

I kneel on the tile, which is surprisingly clean, and spit in the toilet one more time before flushing it. The door to the restroom opens as I rinse my mouth, and I open my pocket knife with my free hand. I see a man walking toward me with purpose, trying to get me from behind, and I last minute turn on him and stab him in the jugular. Blood begins to come out in spurts, and unfortunately for me, I don't get out of the way in time. There's sprayed blood on my dress shirt, and now I'm fucked because there's no way I won't draw attention.

I look both ways before fully coming out of the bathroom just to make sure no one sees my shirt, and then speedwalk toward the front doors. I don't notice at first, but then it clicks. The man walking through the front doors is Michael. He's about to escape. As the door opens and he steps through, he looks back for whatever reason. We make eye contact, and I don't waver. In fact, I start to speed up so I can get to him, and he narrows his eyes at me and walks even faster. I make it to the door just in time to see him get in a Mercedes van just as the siblings are ushered in. He looks at me out the passenger window with a smile, and signals something with his hand that I don't know the meaning of. Then they speed off.

I run toward the parking lot since I'm not visible from where I stand, and surprisingly, Zayne is quick to get to me. Whatever. I get in the passenger side, slam the door, and Zayne floors it until we're back on the highway.

"Does this mean we're friends now?" he asks with a smile. He looks happy for once, maybe because he's driving super-fast. I can relate to that, in all honesty.

I scoff. "We will never be friends."

"Oh, yeah. Nevermind."

I glance at him. "What?"

"I forgot you're too good to be friends with an addict like me."

"No, I just refuse to be friends with someone who has fucked the woman I love."

Zayne rears back as if he's been slapped, and the car swerves. "*In love?*" he chokes out. I guess that's hard to believe. Fucking tell me about it.

"Yeah," I affirm. "In love, asshole."

He starts to laugh, which only makes me want to hurt him. What the fuck is so funny? "You realize," he starts, "we are *both* in love with her?"

"Yeah."

"And she's in love with both of us?"

My blood boils, but I nod my affirmation.

"I won't make her choose," he tells me, and I instantly freeze.

What does he mean? "She doesn't need that kind of pressure when she comes back to us."

Us.

I hate the way that sounds.

"What the fuck are you proposing?"

Zayne smirks. "That she makes her own choice when she's ready."

"So, what?" I don't like where this is going. "You want to share her?"

"Until she decides who she wants to be with."

That stuns me into silence, and I open my mouth and close it for a second. I almost say yes that she doesn't deserve that, but the truth is she never did pick one of us. I'm not the kind of man who shares. I want my woman for my damn self. So, no, as selfless as that would be for her sake, it's not fucking happening. I wish I could do that for her; I just can't. So, no.

Over my dead fucking body.

"*No.*"

CHAPTER 13

Hallie

I can't believe the fucking nerve of Brittany lately. Not only was she fucking around with someone without telling me, but once she knew he was interested in me first, she still didn't stop. To be completely honest, I'm not sure why it bothers me so much that she's fucking him.

Do I feel betrayed that she didn't tell me? Or do I feel betrayed that she won't stop?

Maybe it's simply that I need that attention for myself, and she's stealing it away. She keeps talking about Damien as if he's some honorable knight in shining armor, which he's extremely far from. Someone needs to get it through her head: he's not coming for me.

He doesn't want me back.

He fucking hates me.

I don't want to think about him or how much I miss him. The hole in my chest is big enough as it is. When Zayne died, and I left

Damien… both halves of my heart crumbled to dust. Now there's nothing left. I'm not sure if it's the circumstances, but sometimes I feel like Brittany is the only person who keeps me going, the only reason I wake up day after day. Then other times, like now, I feel like I want to strangle her.

What bothers me most is that she wasn't entirely wrong about what she said. I mean, I only want Tomás because I'm scared to be alone. I hate it. I've never learned to be alone, to love myself. Maybe this is what I need in order to grow into that person… the fact that I'll have no choice. There will be no one I can lean on or take advantage of. At the end of the day, I don't truly care about him, just what he can offer me *right now*.

However, that's not to say I believe what they have is real. No fucking way in hell she's *in love* with him after a week or two (who knows anymore). Let's say she is and I give her the benefit of the doubt. How can she not see this shit is some kind of Stockholm Syndrome? For fuck's sake. Although knowing her the way I do, she doesn't fall in love easily. Definitely not in a short period of time this way. So, what is she really planning?

Something.

Brittany is planning something for sure. I'm acutely aware of that, and it feels so obvious to me now after he comes in, and they immediately start to make out. To me, this is her way of coping. She doesn't even want to talk to him.

Tomás whispers in her ear about something, yet I can't hear it from here. She nods and smiles, then wraps her arms around his neck. I observe them from my bed, and I guess I can't deny they find each other attractive. They're both hot. However, they've only been together for like five minutes. Even still, Tomás has twinkling stars in his eyes when he looks at Brit, but that's to be expected. His feelings are probably as deep as he says or acts. Her eyes are duller, though. Her smile reaches her eyes, but it's not as potent as his. I'm sure she likes him; there's a lot to like in this shitty situation. Still I'm sure if her life wasn't threatened, or she wasn't on the cusp of abuse, she wouldn't even give him a chance.

I clear my throat and narrow my eyes, and when they turn around to look at me, they let go of each other like they were burned. I wonder if they feel guilty at all, or at least Tomás. Something tells me he's shameless, that there's not one ounce of remorse in his body. He narrows his eyes right back, and it doesn't sit well with me,

"We have to go to the dungeon," Brittany tells me, her eyes pleading. Ever since she told me off, she has felt guilty. I bet she thought telling me I'm her person would be good enough for me. Nothing is good enough for me anymore. Everything is just…shit.

He whispers something in her ear, and she laughs, further pissing me off. "What's funny about that?"

"Nothing is funny about that…"

I scoff, "So why were you laughing?" What was he whispering in her ear? Does it have to do with me? He clearly told her about the dungeon since she knew just now, but they were talking about something else too. I know it.

"Don't worry about it," What the fuck does she mean? Why is she hiding things from me? "We'll talk about it later. Maybe when we get back from the shit show."

Whatever. I don't believe a word coming out of her mouth, but I also know we don't have time to discuss this. When we are summoned, we always need to hurry the fuck up, or we get punished. As it is, they've wasted enough time with their lovey-dovey crap. Yeah, I'm aware I'm being a bitter bitch, except I don't have anything else that brings me happiness. At this point, it feels like even Brit is betraying me somehow. Or maybe I'm paranoid as fuck. I heard drugs do that, and lord knows I've been fucked up nearly every day. Great. Now my hands are trembling with the anticipation of another hit.

Nevertheless, I follow them out of our room, down the hallway, and into a different door that leads to the dungeon. I guess I should consider myself lucky that Brittany and I have a bedroom with a toilet and two beds, no matter how shitty it appears. The other girls don't have any of that and sleep in the dungeon.

Sometimes they sleep on the cold concrete or in sleeping bags. It all depends on Michael's mood. Ever since he got to fuck me, he's been more generous with them, so I guess that's good for them.

As we enter the dungeon however, I begin to doubt his good mood. Michael looks positively murderous with a scowl on his face, and I can't figure out why. There's nothing any of us have said or done to piss him off, so it has to be something else. But of course, he's going to take it out on us. He probably has no friends and no one else he can control. Excluding my mother, of course.

The jeans he's wearing hug his every muscle, and his black t-shirt does the same. It would be highly appealing to other women. But to me...I just want to throw up and kill him on sight.

The rest of the girls are kneeling in a circle, heads bowed, eyes on the ground. Michael stares at us and waves us over, then Tomás forcefully shoves us forward to not raise any suspicions.

"I have some news for you," Michael drawls, his anger suddenly leaving him, and instead a bright smile takes over his face. "I have new ones."

New what?

"Oh, sorry." He chuckles, "Brittany and Hallie probably don't know what that means." I audibly gulp, and he waits for Brit and I to join the circle before continuing. "Two new people will be joining you. I need you to teach them how to behave, to do as they're told, and all will be good. I'm sure you can do that, right?"

We all nod while keeping our eyes down.

"Let's just say they are the most special in the group and will be protected at all costs." I don't know what's happening, but now I'm getting curious. "Even more important than Hallie. How does that make you feel, baby girl?"

"Oh, *no*," I reply sarcastically. "I'm just heartbroken."

"Don't be a cunt about it. By the way, there will be a party in this house in just a few days. If you don't shut the fuck up and do as you're told, I'll share you with the hundreds of guys joining me."

I purse my lips, trying to swallow my retort. I really suck at this. You'd think I would learn my lessons, count my losses, and be obedient. But something about him makes me want to rebel and lash out. Surely, it's our history and my daddy issues. Also, I just plain fucking hate him.

"Bring the twins in," Michael says to one of the guards, not sure who since I'm not looking, and the sound of a door opening and soft whimpers sends a chill down my spine. "Come." He holds out a hand to the twins.

Never in a million years could anything have ever prepared me for the sight before me. Two young siblings, a boy and a girl, who can't be more than twenty years old, stand naked inside the circle. Tears are in their eyes, and they're clutching each other's hands, holding on for dear life. I can't do this. I won't watch this. I'd rather gouge my own eyes out.

"Nina," he says softly to one of the girls kneeling a few people down from me. "Teach them how this all works. They need to learn to kneel, keep their eyes down, and speak only when asked a direct question. And above all, they need to stay still and shut the fuck up when the time comes."

Bile claws its way up my throat, the acidic taste filling my tastebuds. Immediately, I turn around from the circle, giving my back to Michael. The contents in my stomach empty out onto the concrete floor, and my stomach continues to heave repeatedly until I'm crying.

I knew Michael was a monster, but this is another level of disgusting. Siblings? Really? I do not have it in me to let this happen to them, much less fucking watch it. There must be something I can do—anything to distract him from them.

I wipe my mouth with the back of my hand and clear my throat, going back to my spot and kneeling submissively again. The girl begins to cry, screaming that she wants him to kill her, and tears stream down my face. I can't stand it; this shouldn't be happening. They shouldn't fucking be here. He can keep me forever if he wants, but not them. They need to go back home. Where the fuck are they from?

"Shut the fuck up!" I look up when he screams at them, and instinct takes over when I see Michael's hand raise to hit her.

"Stop!" I scream, crawling rapidly toward them and shielding them with my body. Pushing them back as far as I can where he can't reach them. That doesn't mean anything though, and I know it. If he wanted to have his guards bring them to him, they would. But at least I know I did all I could, and I didn't stand around like everyone else in this fucking room and let this happen. "No. Please, no."

Michael tsks, "You always did have such a big heart, baby girl," Michael says condescendingly, then grabs me by the neck with both hands. He squeezes until my chest is on fire, and the deranged look in his eyes makes me panic, which then makes me lose more oxygen. Fuck. "But you need to learn your fucking place."

I wrap my hands around his forearms and dig my fingernails into his skin, but the deeper I go, the harder he squeezes. My head is spinning, and I try to look at him to beg him with my eyes. Instead they feel like they're going to pop out of their sockets. My lower lip trembles, and I mouth the word 'stop'. Surprisingly, he does. With a hard shove, I fall onto my back and begin to cough. The tiled floor hurts my elbows and brings me back to my senses. My eyes suddenly burn, and it's not from tears.

"Please, Michael," I beg him, getting on my knees and grabbing his legs. "Please," I sob, "I'll do *anything*."

"Keep talking."

"I will do whatever you want," I reply, instantly regretting those words, but there's nothing I can do now. "Just spare them. Please."

I look up at him, and he smiles, patting the top of my head like I'm a dog. Disgust and hate travel through my veins, spreading like poison to the rest of my body.

"I'll think about it."

My hands tremble, but I hug his legs tightly, resting the side of my face on his thigh and begin to sob. He sighs like I'm nothing but an annoying fly that keeps buzzing around his food, but he tilts my chin up and wipes a tear with his thumb.

"*Please*, Daddy," I hate myself when I say it, my tongue burning with the need to cut it right off so I can't say any more stupid shit. I can't believe I did this, but I also know I cannot watch them go through what I know he's capable of. I can't. No fucking way.

"What do you want, baby girl?"

I lick my lips, thinking of how I will say this. There's only one chance to get this right. Now that I have his full attention, I can't fuck it up. "I want them to stay in my room with Brittany and me, and you don't touch them. For any reason. Add another bed or something, doesn't matter. I'll sleep with Brittany if I have to."

"And you said *anything* I want?"

I nod, tears pricking the back of my eyes. I'm going to regret this decision for the rest of my life, but I would've, no matter what side I picked. Better to help them, if I have the ability to. "Anything."

That makes him smile, and he offers me a hand. His rough fingers are on my chin, which he turns slowly as he inspects my neck. "I love that everyone can see you belong to me, baby girl."

He grabs my cheeks and pulls my face to his, slamming his lips to mine. All the air in my lungs escapes forcefully from the assault, and when his tongue enters my mouth, I can taste his cigarettes. The sudden urge to throw up again is strong, yet I force myself to be neutral, not have a reaction. Just let it happen. I take a deep breath when he pulls away and nods. "Okay."

"Okay?"

"Yes," he affirms. "But only if it's beneficial for me."

"What do you want?"

"I never know what I want, baby girl. You should know this." Michael grins, even as my vision blurs, making me see double. He looks fucking evil. "I'll decide when I come up with something. Don't worry though, I will keep you busy." He winks, and I swallow down bile.

"One more thing," I request with tear-filled eyes. His face

hardens, and he clenches his jaw. I know he doesn't like to be challenged, but I can't do this anymore. If it were for me, everyone here would have their dignity back, but I have to take baby steps. I can't save everyone. "Please find them clothing. I can't bear to see them naked."

"Any other requests?" he asks with narrowed eyes.

I lower my head and keep my eyes on my toes. "Please feed them," I whisper low enough that he will be the only one to hear.

Again, he tilts my head up to face him, and nods.

"Tomás!" Michael calls out, and when the man comes over, he stands a few feet behind me. "Find them clothes and bring them here."

"Yes, sir."

"Thank you, Daddy," I whisper again, and he cups my cheek this time.

"You better be grateful for this," he drawls. "Don't worry. You'll be thanking me every day, one way or another."

I know what I just got myself into, but I can't bear it. Whatever I can do to help them in any way is what will happen. I can live with myself, and I can take Michael's bullshit.

Tomás comes back into the dungeon with underwear and pajamas for the twins, which he drops on the ground next to me, and Michael begins to walk away.

"You have one day to spend time with them. Teach them how to be quiet, or this arrangement will come to an end. Is that understood?"

"Yes."

Without another word or acknowledgment, he walks away from us, leaving. I grab the clothes from the ground and crawl to the siblings, making sure we all avoid the puke on the floor. Tears are streaming down their faces, and their blue eyes are bloodshot and purple. They even look scared of me, and I'm only trying to help them.

I put my hands up in the air, "I want to help you." My eyes

fill with tears as well, and they visibly relax. "I'm just like you. I don't want to be here."

"I want to leave…" the girl says, her face scrunching up with her sobs.

"I know, baby," I tell her soothingly, "But this is your reality until I can change it." I want to promise them they will leave one day, but I can't bring myself to do that. Empty promises are worse than the truth, and I won't give them either of those right now.

"Let me help you put these on," I tell her, and they wait obediently next to me. "Tomás, can we go to our room?"

Tomás looks around and ultimately looks at Brittany like she has the final word. I look at my friend with tired and sad eyes, and hers water in return. She nods at him, and he motions for us to follow. They hold on to me for dear life, digging their nails into my arm from how terrified they are. I need them to trust me.

Once in the room, I sit them down on the bed I usually sleep in, the one closest to the wall and farthest from the bedroom door. They're terrified and hug their knees up to their chest, looking at me. It's a twin-sized bed, but I'm sure they will sleep just fine on it. It has to be better than whatever living conditions they have experienced since being kidnapped.

I sit on the ground in front of my—their—bed, and Brit is on hers. Once Tomás leaves, they visibly relax. At least their pajamas look brand new and fit, and even though they do have bruises, they're healing. I won't ask what Michael has done to them because I know I will be severely triggered, but I will be here if they want to talk about it.

"What are your names?" I ask them softly, and they both look at me.

"Abby," she answers, her hands twisting on her lap.

"My name is…" He struggles, "is…"

"Kyle," she answers for him. "Kyle Hughes."

"How old are you both?" I ask her.

"I'm twenty-one." My eyes widen, although I expected them to be around that age. I'm confused as to why it outrages me. All of us are around the same age. Maybe it's because their situation is fucking depraved. "We both are."

"Do you want to take a nap?"

Both of them shake their heads vehemently, even though they seem exhausted. "N-no," Kyle replies.

"I will watch over you. You can lay down together and sleep. I will stay right here and watch you. No one will hurt you if I'm with you."

They look between Brit and I. "What about her?" Abby asks.

"Brittany is my friend," I reply, peering back at her. She smiles at me with wobbly lips, and I know this is affecting her too. I suspect any kind empathetic human would be affected by this. "You can trust her."

"Okay," she whispers. "What is your name?"

"I'm Hallie."

"Thank you, Hallie," they both say, and my heart swells. Hope blooms in my chest, and there's a brief thought about what will happen when we get out of here. Only I squash it down quickly. We aren't getting out of here. There's no fucking way.

"You're welcome."

With that, they turn over and take their nap. Brittany lies down too, but I know she's not really sleeping. Neither of us will be able to sleep for a long fucking time. I don't know how to do this or put up a front and pretend I'm okay with this. The only thing keeping me together is the fact that I'm helping them, but I know Michael will tear me apart with his bare hands, regardless.

Someone help us, please.

Anyone.

I can't stay here.

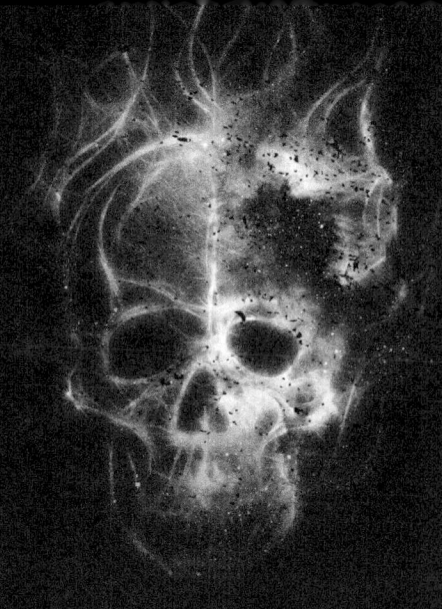

CHAPTER 14

Zayne

I've been trying to talk some sense into Damien. Only he still won't accept sharing her. He doesn't realize this isn't about us but what's best for Hallie. If it weren't for the fact that she's gone through something traumatic and doesn't need that kind of pressure, I wouldn't even be suggesting it. The problem is that I don't believe she will be emotionally ready to make such a choice. Instead, she may make a rash decision she's not entirely sure of.

What if she changes her mind?

If she picked me just to turn around and say she wants Damien instead, I wouldn't survive that. I want her to think about this choice, really think about it, and I plan to give her all the time she needs to reach her decision. He refuses to give her that opportunity, and I think she will be devastated if he backs down and leaves after we get her back. I'll always be her shoulder to cry on, someone to lean on. She doesn't expect this type of abandonment from the little fucker. I wish I could say she feels that way about me too, but I know better. No use in lamenting or crying about it. I just need to show her I'll be the man she has always needed.

"Did you hear what I just said?" Damien growls, annoyed with me, as always.

"Uhh." I shake my head, trying to clear it. Thoughts of Hallie have been invading my mind, and I can't help it at this point. She occupies my every waking *and* sleeping moment. "Sorry, but no."

"For fuck's sake, asshole, if you don't want to be part of this then tell me now." He paces the small motel room. "We don't have time for you to not know what the fuck is happening."

"I'm listening now."

"I got a call from Sean." *Okaaaay?* I nod, trying to get him to keep talking. "He said he knows how we can get Hallie back. It's very risky."

"How?"

"I will tell you, but first, I need to know how serious you are about getting her."

I hold up a hand when he opens his mouth to continue talking, "Are you seriously fucking asking me that question right now?"

"Yes." But the way he says it is not condescending. It's almost like he's trying to protect me. Makes me want to laugh. "We have to go to a party and pretend to be part of this community."

I tense, my mind automatically taking me to the place where I was being fucked in the ass. It's terrifying to think I could be putting myself in that position all over again. What if this all goes wrong and I get kidnapped again? Then what? "Whose party?"

"Michael's." He sighs and runs a hand down his face. "At his house in two nights."

My pause isn't very long, but it's there. I know he can sense the hesitation in my voice, and I hate it. "Does that mean we are getting Hallie out?"

"That's the plan."

Is Hallie the only person he's keeping? If not, how many more are there? Can we get them all out safely? How will we get to her? How will *we* get out? How many people are going to this fucking party? How many guards do we have to get through in order to make this happen?

My brain runs a million miles a second as the questions flood in. Damien must see it in my face because he sits beside me on the bed and drops his head. "I have a blueprint of the house and know all its rooms, including its largest room. Which is probably where he keeps them."

"How many people are attending that party?" I ask, feeling nervous already. What if someone recognizes me? Wasn't that the fear he had in the first place when he went to the auction? "Are there more people we need to help?"

Damien audibly gulps, and my stomach drops. "At the auction... he purchased more people. Uh, twins."

What?

"You're joking." I shake my head no. He raped Hallie when she was twelve. Is he really that sick? He was sick before this, but this puts him at a different level. "Please tell me this is a sick fucking joke."

"It's not."

My stomach drops at his answer. "So, what are we going to do?" This can't end well. There will probably be so many men attending, and somehow we're supposed to go in unnoticed and get to her. The question is how or who will take care of all the men and women attending this party. Everyone needs to die, that's for sure. No one can walk out of that fucking party to continue doing this. I sure hope these are all the sex traffickers in the area. Then we'd be doing the world a service. "How the fuck are we getting her out? There's no way we'd make it past so many people."

"There's only one way." He looks at me and smirks, and I return it for the first time ever. He's speaking my language now. I've always been aggressive, have had anger issues, and this might just be the perfect outlet. I need to release this out into the fucking world. "We kill them all."

"I love the idea of that." However there are too many loopholes. I have to watch my words with him since he's been a little *sensitive* lately. "*But* how are we going to kill all the guests, if there's only two of us?"

"There won't be just two of us." He chuckles, "I'm calling Diego, Armando, and my father's men."

"Your father's men? I thought he couldn't talk to you anymore?"

"He gave me a burner phone in case I needed help. Well, this is it—I need the fucking help, and I need it *now*."

We do need the help, as much of it as we can possibly get. This is about to be an entire operation, and it will take meticulous planning to achieve it. If we don't know exactly what to do… we're fucked. Actually, we're fucked now either way. Hallie shouldn't have ever been put in this situation, and every time I remember he's the one that brought her into it, I get fucking pissed all over again.

"What's the plan after we get her back?" Damien grimaces when I utter the word 'we', and his face hardens.

"We go north."

"To where? Alaska?" I hate the fucking cold, and that place sounds miserable. "Could we go maybe…anywhere else?"

"Not Alaska, Canada. If we want to stay alive, that's the only place we can go." *Great.* "The cartel doesn't have many allies up there, and at least that border is cleaner than the Mexican border. Apparently, they have morals up there."

I highly doubt that's the truth. The drug problem is not just in the United States and Mexico. All of North America is affected. Shit, everywhere in the world is affected. Point is, Canada is not immune to the fucking opioid epidemic, that's for damn sure. I'll hear him out, in any case. Not like I have a choice.

"Okay, so we go to Canada," I affirm, "What the fuck is up there? A house? Or will we just stay in hotels for the rest of our lives?"

"First of all, of course there's a house. I've been making arrangements since I was in the hospital getting patched up for getting the fuck beat out of me and *then* also getting stabbed by Hallie." I snort, trying to hold in my chuckle, and he rolls his eyes.

I'm honestly impressed she did that. I'll never get over it. "None of this ever involved you; you have never been part of the plan."

I stand from the bed and fist my hands. The sudden need to hit him takes over, and I breathe in through my nose. "Well, I'm glad I could fix that for you."

"You're not fucking coming with us."

I laugh, but it sounds like manic Zayne. I need to rein it. The last thing I need is for him to figure out what's wrong with me and admit me to a mental hospital just to get rid of me. Then Hallie will never be the wiser, and she and this fucker probably *would* go to Canada together.

"The fuck I'm not."

Damien stands from the bed, walking toward me now, and stops a foot away. "I saw you on a live with Adriana, you know." His smile brings chills over me, "There was something there between you. I saw it, and everyone else sure as fuck saw it."

"What the fuck does that have to do with anything?" I tuck my chin, ready to swing at this motherfucker, and he does the same.

"You should've stayed with her."

"Of course, there was something there. I thought I was going to die in that place, so I latched onto anything that would make me feel better. Until you go through that shit, don't fucking judge me. I will never feel what I do for Hallie with anyone else." I walk even closer until our chests are touching, and he lowers his forehead to mine, pushing me backwards. "*No one.*"

"Oh?" Damien grins, "Me either. But the only difference is I haven't betrayed her in any way since she was captured. I have not been emotionally or physically available to another woman."

"I didn't have a fucking choice!" My throat burns from how loud my scream is, and I immediately lower my voice. We can both agree that whatever happens between us, we can't draw attention to ourselves in this room. If anyone else knows we're here and they blab to the cartel, then all of our plans will go down the drain. But this fucker is getting on my last damn nerve.

"You had many choices after, and you chose wrong."

"Are you threatening me? Is that what this is?" I ask him, just about ready to ruin his fucking face. "You're going to run to Hallie and tell her everything I was forced into doing and then the product of that?"

"Yeah, I'm threatening you." Damien is such a little fucking cunt sometimes. Just when I'm thinking we can get along, he proves to me yet again that he's not ready or willing to. "You won't be going anywhere with Hallie and me."

My body reacts before I can control it, before I can even think about what's happening. My brain isn't processing, and my fist flies into his face. I hear a wet sound, and blood splatters onto my shirt—his shirt that he let me borrow—which makes me take one step back. Fuck. I need to learn to control myself.

An eerie laugh comes from him, scarier than the shit he talks. I keep forgetting he is skilled in murder. That doesn't seem to deter me, though. I think I'm okay with dying at this point.

Damien grabs me by the shirt and yanks me closer to him, and the snarl on his face makes my body go rigid. His free hand wipes blood from his cheek, "I could fucking gut you right here, right now, and feel nothing. You need to learn your fucking place."

"My place is next to Hallie," I grunt when his bloody hand wraps around my neck, restricting my breath slightly. "There's nothing you can do about that. So kill me, then. She will never forgive you."

"She will never know." He squeezes tighter until my face grows hot and my vision blurs. Then suddenly, he releases me, shoving me hard. I catch myself, saving myself the humiliation of falling on my ass.

I cough and laugh. He doesn't seem to know how smart Hallie is, but she will know. When something feels off with him, she will get suspicious again, and she won't stop until she finds out what he did.

"She will." I'm surprised he hasn't hit me back yet. Maybe he has other plans for me, worse ones. "You say you want to rescue her in two days, but you haven't even tried to get along with me.

Do you think she will be able to cope with herself and the trauma she has suffered if we're always at each other's throats?"

Damien seems to stop and think about that. Fucking finally. Maybe I'm getting through to him and he will make an effort. I've been trying to be friendlier, as much as I don't want to be, but this asshole really is making it hard. He argues and talks shit at every opportunity. I know he enjoys instigating problems between us. He hates me the same way I hate him. Still this shit has to stop. I won't put her through this; I'm also too selfish to let her go.

"Are you delusional?" he calmly asks me, "You and I will *never* be friends."

Never say never. "I'm not asking you to be. All I'm asking is to be civilized for her sake."

"What's your game?" Damien asks, "What do you actually want?"

"No game. I want Hallie." He looks fucking furious at that, and I hold my hands up. "Any way she will let me have her."

I walk away from him, not giving a shit about how he feels. If he doesn't want to even try to be civilized—fine. She's going to notice and reach her own conclusion, make her own choices. I'll just do my damn best to make sure she chooses *me*.

After taking a long, hot shower to take my mind off everything the asshole just revealed, I get dressed and join him again in the room. Maybe we can come to a mutual agreement before we get her back. It's possible we won't though. It makes me sad that he's willing to put her in this situation, but no one can force him, I guess.

Damien pulls up the blueprint on his laptop and turns the screen toward me, waiting not so patiently for me to get a closer look. We go over the plan, how we're dressing, getting the invitation, when we will be going to the big room, how we will get past the guards, and also relying on the men his father will send to kill everyone but Michael. Only we will decide how the fucker dies.

He already has Armando, Diego, and his father's men lined up. He works fast, I'll give him that much. Apparently, he organized the entire squad before I even got out of the shower. I'm impressed, though I'd never admit it to him. Ever.

Since everything has been planned, I don't wait for him to start another fight. Instead I get in bed and face the window. I continue to be terrified of someone coming in this room and taking me away in the middle of the night, and Damien would fucking let them. I know he would. The extent of my fear makes me wonder if it's because I'm in Mexico and this is where my trauma happened or if I will continue to feel this way for the rest of my life.

My mind doesn't want to shut off those thoughts, but at the same time, my body is so exhausted that I'm not given a choice. I'm grateful for that though. I never look forward to sleep anymore. I'm constantly assaulted by nightmares now.

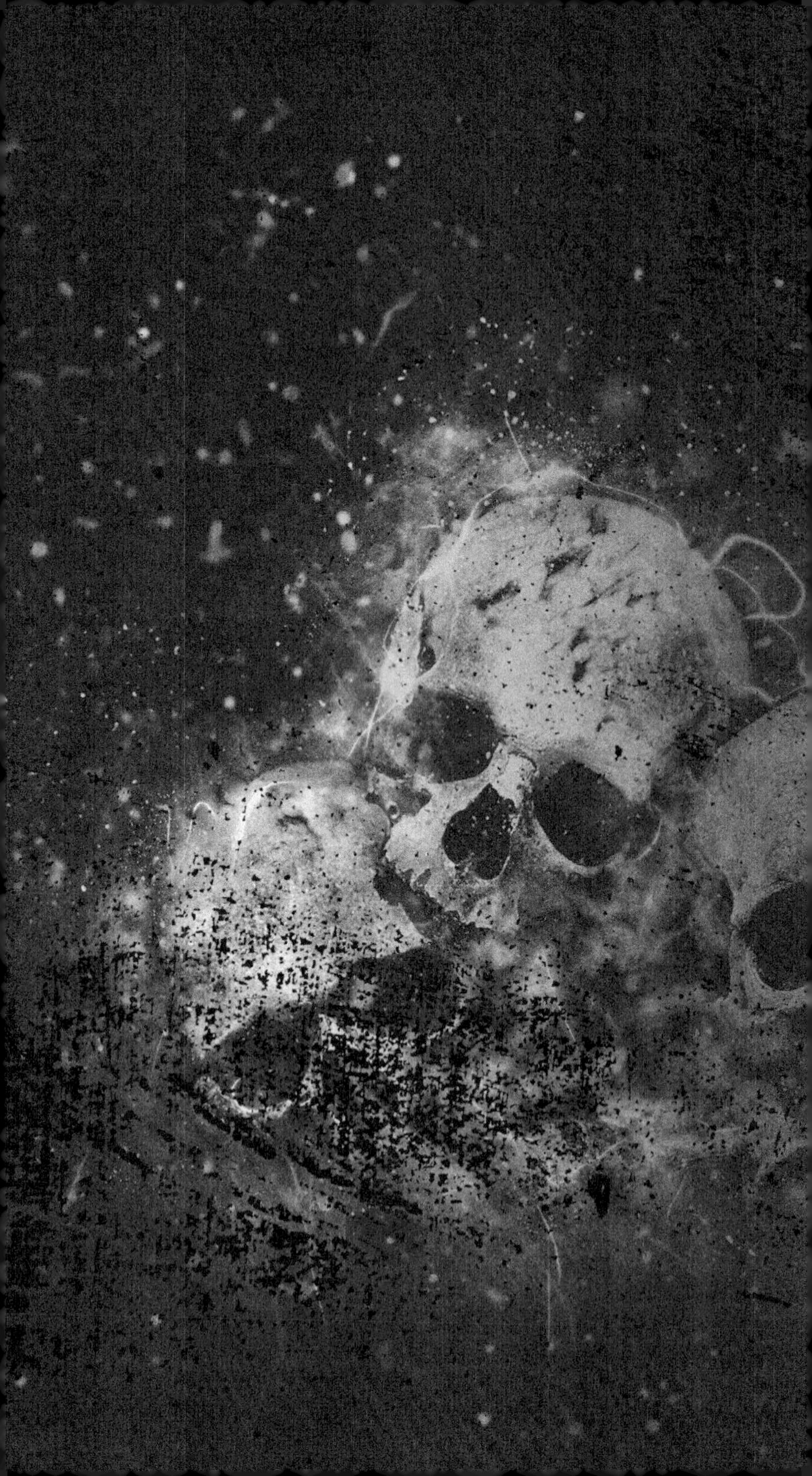

THE
FUGITIVE

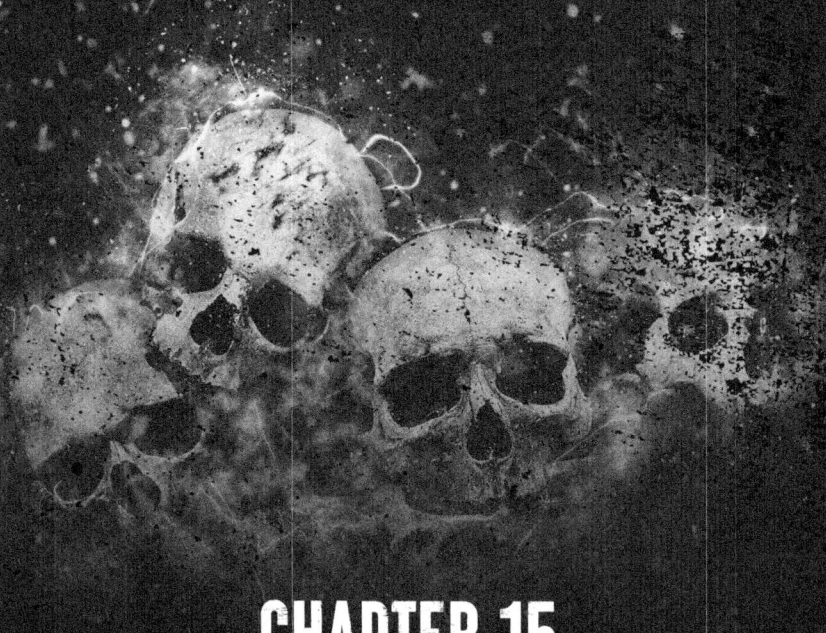

CHAPTER 15

Brittany

Michael has wasted no time when it comes to torturing Hallie. He gave her the twenty-four hours he promised, which I'm truly surprised about, but ever since then he has kept her occupied so much that I've had to stay alone with the siblings in my room.

They're still frightened of me, even after I stayed in bed all day yesterday and have shown them I will not hurt them. I can't fault them for it. They've been horribly abused since they came into this life. I hate it for them, I truly do, but we all go through it. Maybe I'm bitter, but I don't see what makes them so special that Hallie won't allow them to endure the same fate as everyone else. Is it depraved? Yes. Is it worth sacrificing yourself over? Fuck no.

Thankfully, Hallie is here now. It's the only time they sleep, the only time they stop crying. Can Hallie shoulder this type of responsibility? Or will she crumble in the face of struggles?

We've been reminded over and over again that the party will

be two nights from now, and Michael said she's going to have to be part of it. What he doesn't know is that all of us will be gone before then. There's no way I will let Hallie be handed over to whichever men want her at this fucking disgusting reunion. I bet more girls like us will be being used and abused, forced to do things they don't want to.

Tomás barges in, his chest heaving, and closes the door behind him. The twins immediately cower, rushing back against the wall. Hallie tries to console them, offering words of encouragement that sound like inaudible whispers to my ears. What is wrong with Tomás? Why does he look so affected?

"Hallie." He gulps out, "He wants you."

I shake my head, "No." She's done. She can't do this again today. "I'll go in her place."

His eyes widen, and he vehemently shakes his head, walking toward me. He kneels in front of my bed and whispers in my ear. "Please don't do this."

"We're leaving tonight. None of this matters anymore."

"Don't—"

"She's had enough. There's no way she will survive if he keeps touching her. I'll take it this once, then never again." I pull away and look him in the eyes. "I promise."

Tomás nods, and I stand up and follow him out of the room, looking back into Hallie's wide eyes. My hesitant smile makes her eyes well with tears, and one of them spills over. I turn back around and close the door. I can't be feeling sad or regretful already, he hasn't even gotten started. I'm not giving him the damn satisfaction.

I'm taken back to the dungeon, and I kneel on the ground to wait for him. He's going to be fucking furious it's not Hallie, and it's probably going to take a lot of convincing when it comes to leaving her alone. It's possible he won't budge, tell me to go fuck myself, and then go get her himself. I'll probably get hurt for it too, there's no way he will tolerate this.

I hear the door open again, but I keep my eyes on the ground, ensuring I don't break even more rules. Just because I want to spare

Hallie some pain, doesn't mean I want to be punished worse than I already am.

"Now, who do we have here?" Michael's voice is full of curiosity, and I curse myself for allowing him to indeed notice me. "Aren't you a pretty little thing?" His fingers trail my jaw softly, and I close my eyes.

He hasn't paid much attention to me before, but I think that's mostly because he seems to only have eyes for Hallie. The only time he has fucked the other girls has been when Hallie refuses, and he sometimes seems to let it go. At least before the twins came along, he appeared to leave her alone for the most part. Although, she did tell me of how he killed a girl in front of her and fucked many others to make them hate her since she wouldn't let him touch her. What I want to know is why he didn't force her when she first got here.

"Tomás," he barks out, making me jump. "I asked for Hallie, and as pretty as this one is, I want her."

Fuck.

Think. *Think*. "Wait," I blurt, and when his hand comes around my neck abruptly, I quickly regret my decision. "Don't you want to make her jealous?" I can barely get the words out, his grip choking me, making my blood rush in my ears. I don't particularly enjoy being choked, if I'm being honest. If this were any other man, I would've slapped him by now.

"Keep talking."

I lick my lips, suddenly nervous with all his attention on me. I can feel Tomás staring at me, the heat of his gaze burning my bare back. He hates this, the fact that Michael hasn't even bothered with me, and I'm putting myself at his mercy willingly. I can't deny I'm placing myself in a dangerous position, and I don't know what the outcome will be. Is he going to hurt me? Make me enjoy this? Ruin my life?

"If you fuck me, Hallie will get jealous," I reply. "But you have to make sure she can tell I'm enjoying it, or it won't work."

"Hmmm," he says, contemplating. "Are you fucking with me? We both know she fucking hates me."

"She might hate you, but she's clearly your favorite. Hallie won't be happy to be replaced by her best friend." I shrug, making some shit up. She's not going to give a fuck if he does this to someone else. In fact, she will be glad it's not her. That is, until she realizes it's me. Maybe she will understand I'm doing this for *her*. So she doesn't have to feel his dirty fucking paws on her body.

"Bring her to me," he tells Tomás, and I hear him walking away. "As for you, you said she will be jealous if you enjoy this?"

"Yes." I nod my head quickly, hoping he doesn't see my desperation.

"Alright then." He smiles, "Lie down and spread your legs."

I do as I'm told, lying down flat on my back, my eyes finding the cracks in the ceiling. Sex is just a transaction; I've always seen it that way. It's a give and take, and I'm willing to give as long as I get what I want. I've always been someone to enjoy sex, and to be honest, this bothers me less than I care to admit. He's just another notch in my belt. That doesn't mean he's not a sick motherfucker, and I'll probably get chlamydia from this shit, but at least he will probably get me antibiotics if he does give it to me. Maybe. If not, for sure Tomás will give me some.

Michael grabs my thighs and looks at my pussy with a twinkle in his eyes, and I breathe in deeply. Don't think about what he's done. He's just another man. You met him at the bar or some shit, maybe even found him hot. Or he paid for your dinner, so you paid with your pussy. It's fine. You're fine, Brittany.

I finally take a good look at him, his blond hair and hazel eyes. He's not a bad looking man. In fact, he's actually quite handsome. Tall, muscular build, chiseled jaw. It's too bad he's fucking crazy. I can still enjoy playing with him, though.

"I will say..." He smiles, scooting me toward him on the tiled floor. I gasp from the sting but don't dare make another sound. If he gets off on suffering, I won't give him a reason to remind him of it. "You have a pretty pussy."

I force myself to grin, facing the ceiling again and closing my eyes so I don't have to see his face anymore. There's a shuffling sound, and then he's spreading my pussy wide open, blowing on it. His mouth descends on it, and I will say the man knows what he's doing. Thank fucking God. Maybe now I can at least close my eyes and come without worrying about anything.

One of his hands reaches up to squeeze my breast really fucking hard, which makes me cry out in pain, but when he tweaks my nipple and sucks my clit into his mouth, my back arches off the concrete floor. "Is that good, little girl?"

I try not to let that pet name bother me, but I'll say that's impossible. Nevertheless, I reply, "Yes."

He pulls back, and I feel the sting before the loud slap that lands on my pussy. "Daddy," he growls.

"Yes, Daddy." I gulp.

He brings his mouth down on me again, and when he fucks me with his tongue, I moan. He seems to take this as an invitation to continue to do it. When the door opens, I hear a loud gasp, and he picks his head up to see where it came from. I open my eyes to look at him, and he has a wide grin on his face when he coats his fingers with my arousal and runs them up and down all over me. I tilt my head up again as he begins to lick my clit and suck it into his mouth, and Hallie and I make eye contact. I shake my head slightly, and her lower lip trembles.

Michael shoves three fingers inside of me, not gently what so fucking ever, and I won't lie it fucking stings. He moves them in and out of me roughly, but when he curls them and sucks on my clit, I see stars. I let out a loud scream, and my body goes rigid as he fucks me with his fingers and brings me to my release with a flick of his tongue. I want to grab his head to force him to put even more pressure on my clit, but I suddenly remember who the fuck he is and refrain. I don't just refrain though, I freeze.

My head lolls to the side when the familiar sensation of being relaxed takes over my body, and I open my eyes to see the horrified expression painted on every feature Tomás possesses. It's a good thing Michael is too busy with me to notice him, if he saw this, I bet he'd know immediately that there's something between us. The jealousy is palpable even from across the room. Hallie stands next to him, her hands covering her mouth and silent tears streaming down her face.

"Stop," Hallie tells him, "Why are you doing this?"

"Oh," Michael tsks as he kneels in front of me, opens the button of his slacks, and gives me a great view of his dick. It's actually huge, which then makes me feel bad for Hallie. For me, though—it'll do just fine. "She asked me to. Didn't you, darling?" When his gaze falls on me, I make sure to smile and nod, which seems to satisfy him. He looks back at Hallie, "Unlike you."

"You don't have to do this!" Hallie gets on her knees, begging him. "Please don't."

"You're right, I don't have to do this." His hands come to my waist, and he flips me over swiftly onto my stomach. My face almost hits the floor, and I'm grateful I moved it out of the way right on time. It was a close call though, too close for comfort. "I *want* to."

He spreads my legs apart, and the tile makes my knees squeak and drag on them. I have a feeling I'm going to end up with bruises and cuts and scrapes all over my damn body by the time he's done with me. He clearly has no regard for my pain. Doesn't give a shit whatsoever.

With that, he puts his hand on the back of my neck and directs his dick to my entrance. My cheek lands on the tile as he thrusts into me, and I feel the pain of it when the skin splits open. He groans when he speeds up and lets go of my neck, instead pulling me up on all fours. The scrapes on my knees worsen with the movement, and I cry out, tears filling my eyes. "*Owww,*" I whisper. For a moment I think he doesn't hear it, but then he slaps my ass so hard the tears spill over.

"I'll make you hurt if you don't stop that."

"Don't hurt her," Hallie sobs, and my heart squeezes in my chest. "Take me instead. Stop it!"

"I want *her*," he replies. "Not you."

Hallie's face crumples, but I believe it's for me, not him. He seems convinced of what I told him earlier, and the more she cries to him about not fucking me, the more he believes it's 'cause she cares. Because she wants him. Joke's on him; she'd *never* feel that way about him.

His fingers find my clit, and I begin to rock back and forth to make the movements speed up, which seems to entice him to go faster. He chuckles when I moan, and I kind of hate how good he's making me feel. It's just one more man, that's it. No need to make a big deal out of it. It doesn't mean anything. I want Tomás. I'll never actually want this disgusting human being.

"Yes," I moan, and Hallie cries harder, surely thinking I'm faking it. Sadly, I'm not. I just want to come and get this over with. Maybe then he will let us go back to the room and leave us the fuck alone. "Harder."

I'll take the pain for Hallie. I'd do anything for her. I'm doing *this* for her.

"Be careful what you ask for, little girl."

Yuck, here we fucking go again with his nasty pet names. Is this what he's into? But yes, obviously, if we're judging by what he's done to Hallie.

His movements on my clit speed up, and he buries his fingers between my pussy lips to hit the right spot. It takes him a moment to get the rhythm right since I'm slippery as fuck from when he ate me out, but when he finds it, I close my eyes and forget it's him all over again.

It's Tomás instead. He's rubbing my pussy just how I like it, coaxing moans from my lips. I arch my back so he can hit the spot I like, and his thrusts speed up. His groans only spur me on, and when the pleasure builds until it can't anymore, I snap. We groan together as my pussy pulses around his dick. Immediately I'm broken out of my fantasy when he pushes me back down, my ass up in the air and my back arched for him. Grabbing onto my hips, he fucks me hard, and soon I feel him come inside me before he makes a sound that's half groan, half moan.

Hallie sobs at this point, as he pulls out of me. I barely register the footsteps. However, when I turn my head to watch, he's cleaning himself, mine and his come, with his fingers and then shoving them in Hallie's mouth. She gags, and when he pulls them out, he clamps her mouth shut with his hand. On the verge of throwing up, she breathes in through her nose loudly and smiles.

Finally, Michael walks away and out of the dungeon, leaving us in a very uncomfortable silence.

"Why would you do that?" Hallie cries, "I can fucking handle this!"

I shake my head, slowly getting up from the ground. "No, you can't."

"Fuck that," Hallie covers her face with her hands and cries louder when she sees the scrapes all over my face. "I can fight my own battles, Brittany."

"I did it for you." I reply, "It's no skin off my back." I smirk at the irony, but Tomás walks quickly toward me and *slaps* me.

My head whips to the side, the already scraped cheek hurting even more now. "Snap the fuck out of it," he says through gritted teeth. "Are you fucking crazy? Did you lose your damn mind?"

"Do not *ever* fucking touch me again." I'm not weak like Hallie. I do not give a damn what the reason for this assault is, I will not fucking stand for it. "I rather die than be with someone who does that to me."

"You made me watch that." His eyes seem devastated, and I look away from him. "You fucking came for him!"

"So?" I meet his eyes again. "You realize he would've hurt me more if I hadn't. Right?"

Tomás stays silent at that and takes a step back, then grabs my arm and drags me toward the door. Hallie follows quickly behind us all the way to the room, and when we go inside. Tomás shuts the door, as I curl into a ball on the bed and cry.

"Thank you," she whispers, "You mean everything to me."

I hope she knows that, above all, she's my soulmate and I'd do anything for her. The true test of this friendship will come tomorrow when I tell her the plan; if she goes through with it, I'll thank her in return.

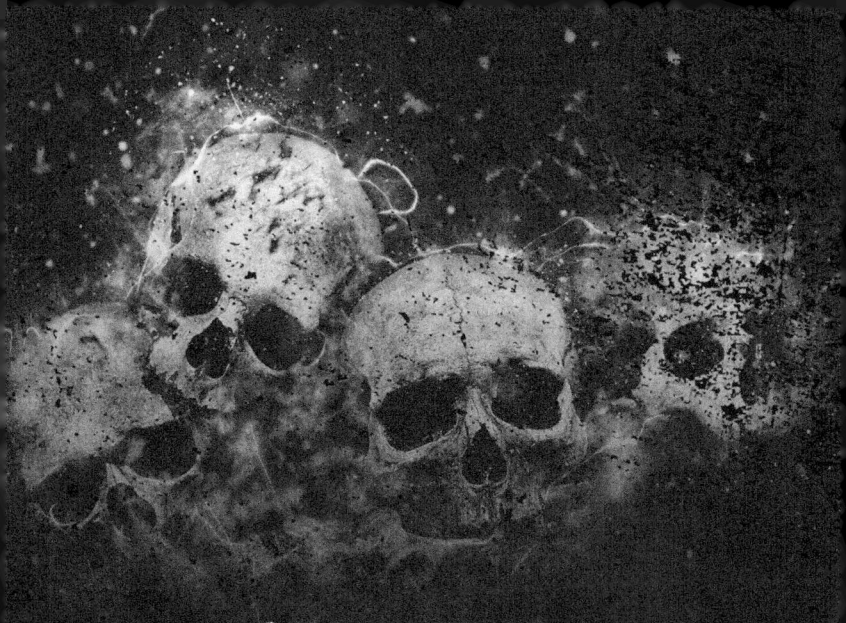

CHAPTER 16

Hallie

Waking up to the scrapes all over Brittany's body is just a bitter reminder of what I witnessed last night. I can't believe she did that for me. The confusion is profound, and I don't know if I should be grateful or fucking pissed for the way she handled that. It should've been me. I know I can take him. It doesn't make a difference in my life anymore.

Brit and I stare at each other for what feels like the hundredth time. She signals for me to get closer to her, and I do, crawling across the small space between the beds to reach her. I lie down next to her, and she puts her mouth close to my ear.

"We're leaving today, and I need you to do exactly what I say."

We're doing *what*?

"What about the twins?" I question, knowing damn well I'm not leaving them behind.

"We can take them."

"Where the fuck are we going?" Seriously though. Doesn't she know there's nowhere we can run? "There's no way we're making it out of here, Brit. You're delusional if you believe we are." Brittany rolls her eyes, which honestly just irritates me. Why is she acting like I don't have a valid point?

"We've had this planned for a week now, Hallie." I look back at them to make sure they don't hear any of this. She follows my gaze, and then when I'm satisfied they're still sleeping, we look at each other again. "Tomás knows exactly where Michael will be today, who is working and their guard posts. He has a vehicle ready for us to escape in."

No matter what she says, what they have planned, or how much they have lined up… it still feels like a shit show. "How did he achieve any of this? How will we make it out if we get discovered?"

"We won't."

"It's not that fucking easy, Brit," I whisper-yell, "It's entirely possible that we'll get caught, so then what?"

"We will *not* get fucking caught," she replies calmly, and I don't understand why she's acting this way. Is she resigned? Is that what this is? She's okay with dying, so she doesn't care if we all do? Well, I'll be damned if this brings the end upon me. I will decide when I fucking die. No one else will put me in that position. "Do you remember how he bought the twins?"

"How?" I ask her. All I know is that he showed up, not how he came to find or purchase them.

"He went to an auction, and that's where he will be most of today."

My stomach turns, and suddenly I get the urge to throw up. I can't think about what that means right now. If he comes home with more people, I won't survive it. How the fuck am I supposed to live with myself while he does that to other women just to get back at me? I've done so much for the ones I've kept safe—for the most part—since they got here. Except when will it be enough? And is he really doing it for that purpose, or is he just sick in the head?

"That's fucking disgusting."

"Yes, it is," Brit affirms, "That's why we have to leave. Whatever it takes."

"What if we get caught?" I hold up a hand when she opens her mouth to argue, "Don't tell me we won't. There's always a possibility. I want to know what the plan is if we do."

"There's no plan. We will escape one way or another."

That doesn't make me feel any better. I have a bad feeling about this, and my gut feelings usually never fail me. There's a pit in my stomach when I think of risking everything for a shot at freedom. Of course, I want it—more than anything—but at what cost? I don't care about my life at this point. Although I do feel responsible for Abby and Kyle.

What if something happens to them?

Either way, I nod. If she leaves without me, I'll never see her again. Maybe I can get out of here and find Damien again. I'll apologize and be on my way. Figuring out how to get back in the United States, back north, is going to be the tricky part of this. I don't even know where I will run to or stay before crossing the border. At this point, I guess I'll have to trust that Tomás has taken care of all that. Does he want Brit to stay in Mexico? Is that what this is? What will happen if she does and they're discovered? No doubt about it—she'd die.

"Okay," I tell her. "Tell me what to do."

She explains the plan, how we will get out of this room, where he will take us to wait until he checks that everything is okay, and how we will get to the getaway vehicle. It sounds well planned, I won't lie, and yet… I still don't know why I don't want to do it. I mean, I still will. This might be my only chance to leave this fucking hell hole.

A few hours later, Tomás appears apprehensive and glances around before closing the door behind him. "It's time to go."

Brit and I nod, and he drops a backpack for us to get dressed. Once I'm done, I wake up the twins and tell them what's going on, explaining that they need to be quieter than they have ever been because if they make any noise and we are discovered, it will end badly for us.

Tomás opens the door, and we make a beeline to follow him. Brittany is first right behind Tomás, and then Abby and Kyle are between us. Whatever happens, I'm protecting them with my life. No harm can come to them, or I'll never be able to live with myself. They're actually doing really well, listening and paying attention to the signs Brittany gives them. They still seem like they're in shock though. Honestly, I don't blame them. Everything is happening so fast.

We stop when Tomás tells us to. When we enter the hallway, he quickly walks toward a door I've never seen before. It takes us into yet another room, and we walk across it at a fast pace. Once we reach yet another door, we stop. He slowly opens it and peeks out, peering from one side to the other before opening it all the way. The sunlight blinds all of us except Tomás, and I realize I can't remember when I last saw daylight. When the fuck did I get here? How long has it been? I lost count of the days. Once they started drugging me, I had no recollection or even a way to recognize the passing of time. I was lost in a haze—literally.

Thankfully, he lets our eyes adjust to the light before ushering us out. The dirt road has little rocks digging into our feet, and Kyle cries out in pain. It truly does hurt, but I shush him and grab his arm. Brittany thankfully does the same for Abby. I don't know how fast we can run with them, but we will have to try. Hopefully, it doesn't come down to that.

Tomás holds his hand up in a halt gesture, and we stop behind him. He takes the gun out of his holster and holds it at his side.

I don't like this at all. Not even a little bit.

He begins to walk and drops his hand, whispering to follow him. There's a blue sedan parked a few feet from us, and we all speed walk toward it. Tomás opens the back door for us, and we file into the back. Brit sits in the front passenger seat and stares out the window with an emotionless face. I can't believe we're in the car and about to get away.

What. The. Fuck. Is this real?

Abby whimpers, and I softly shush her. It has to be scary as fuck to be going through this, so I let my hand drop between them so they can hold it. They each take one of my fingers and close their eyes as if that'll save them from their fear.

Once Tomás gets in the car and starts to drive, my body tenses up. This is going to be the most crucial step of the escape plan. If we get off this property, then we have a real chance of getting out of Mexico. Yes, they could catch us before making it to the border, but if we never leave here, that won't even matter anyway.

"How close to the border are we?" I ask him in a soft whisper.

He covers his mouth like he's coughing, but instead answers my question quickly. "Fifteen minutes."

That feels doable. Truly. Maybe I should trust this, get out of my own head, and focus on the positives. I'm just nervous because this isn't just about me anymore. What would happen to all of us? What would happen to *me*? What if Michael hates me and kills me in a fit of rage? Would he? If he does, Abby and Kyle are fucked.

The crunching of the rocks under the tires as he slightly speeds up has my nerves on edge. Every little noise seems to make me more nervous than the last, until my chest is tight and I can barely breathe. I don't know if it's an asthma attack or anxiety at this fucking point, but I need to get out of here. *Now*.

"We're almost there," he tells us, and I breathe a sigh of relief. "Almost out."

Brittany glances back at me, her lower lip trembling. "I love you," she whispers, tears filling her eyes. She did it. She got us out of here. "You're my person."

I squeeze her hand with my free one. "I love you more, forever. You're *my* person."

Suddenly, Tomás slams on the brakes and says, "Hold on!" He steers left quickly, almost throwing us off the seat and mutters, "Fuck, fuck, *fuck*."

No.

No, please, God. Don't let us be caught. Not now when we're

so close to freedom. I can almost taste it. I can almost feel the sun on my skin again. *Please.*

There's a loud noise coming from the left side of the car, and I quickly realize that it's the sound of bullets hitting the door. Oh, we are so screwed. How the fuck is he going to get away from this without any of us getting shot?

Tomás drives faster and faster with no regard to even our safety, but at this point, that doesn't matter either. I bet we'd all die if he stopped this car right now. He ends up doing what I never thought he would, slamming his brakes and coming to a complete stop.

Goddamnit.

He needs to go.

Keep driving! We have to get the fuck out of here!

We don't dare speak, however. Shit, we can't even breathe at this point. I motion to the kids with my finger to stay quiet, and they scrunch their eyes closed. There's a commotion outside. I hear yelling, but Tomás doesn't say anything. Instead, he's just breathing really hard.

"I'm sorry, Brittany," he says with a somber tone. "Just know I love you, so mu—"

He's cut off mid-sentence as a bullet goes through the windshield and out the back window. Did he get shot? What the fuck?

Brittany whimpers then starts to sob when we see blood on the back of the headrest, a huge hole staring back at us.

Fuck. We are so fucking fucked.

"I'm going to need you both to be brave," I tell the twins, trying to shield them from the people about to open the door, which opens abruptly. I hold my breath, not daring to look at Brittany. She reaches down to hold onto me, and I hear a dragging sound. Her fingernails claw my arm, and I realize the sound is coming from her. They are dragging her out of the car by her feet. A loud thud makes me shut my eyes tightly, and she screams.

"Get her out of the fucking car," Michael barks, and I tense. "*Now.*"

I let go of them so I don't accidentally make the twins get

dragged out with me. "Stay quiet, and don't fight," I tell them quickly. "I'll be right back."

"Someone get her the *fuck* out!"

I get up and raise my hands behind my head so they know I'm not holding any weapons, then step out of the vehicle. Two men grab me as I kick the door closed, not wanting the twins to see whatever happens next.

"You can't save them anymore," Michael says as I'm turned around roughly. "Not any of them."

"Please don't kill them." I beg him, "I will do anything."

"Yes, you will," he replies. "Except not to keep them alive. No, you'll do it to keep yourself alive. I will make no more promises about the others. You fucked this up for yourself."

"No!" I scream, beginning to sob as I fight the men, but I don't have enough strength to do so. "Not them!"

"Someone is dying today, baby girl," he says with a smile, and I hate how happy he looks about it. A renewed sense of hate fills my veins. I don't think I'm ready to face whatever he has in mind. "But it won't be the twins. No, what's coming to them is much worse than death."

I begin to sob, and he walks over to me, wipes my tears, and pats my cheek condescendingly. When he grips my face with one hand, I don't even flinch. I just accept my fate. "Did you think you'd be able to get away from me, baby girl?" I whimper when it feels like he's crushing my jaw, which only entices him to grip it tighter. He wants me to suffer. "Listen closely, Hallie, because I will only repeat this once more for you. There will be no third chances, this isn't fucking baseball." The guys around us chuckle, and he glares at them. They all instantly shut up. "You will *never* get away from me. I own you." He lifts my wrist up to my face, digging his fingers into my forearm. "See that mark? You're not leaving here alive. *Ever*."

My lower lip trembles, but I need to reply, or he's going to take it out on someone else. "Yes, Daddy."

Realizing he said someone would die, my eyes scan the space

across from me, trying to locate Brittany. Tomás is dead, so does he mean she's next?

"Oh, yes," He informs me as if reading my mind. "She will die too."

"Wait," I plead. "Don't do this, please! I will do anything you want. Let her live! Let her live!"

"Hold her tight," Michael instructs the men who have each of my arms, and they tighten their grip on me. "This is how it's going to go, Hallie. Tomás over there will be hung from a bridge to make an example out of him. Everyone will know not to fuck with me." Yeah, that may be tragic, but I couldn't fucking care less about what happens to him. I only care about Brit. "But her?" He points at my best friend and grins. "She's going to suffer."

Brittany begins to sob, and I follow suit. What the fuck have I done? I should've gone north from the beginning, warned her earlier. Left with her. I should've never let her go alone.

"Daddy," I sniffle. "Please. Can I say goodbye?"

He seems to think about it, "You have one minute, then come back or you will regret it in more ways than one." He looks directly at the car and doesn't have to tell me what it means.

The guards let me go and I run to Brit, collapsing on the ground right next to her, covering her body with mine. "You're okay." I try to soothe her, only I realize it's impossible. There's only one thing I'm sure of out of everything. She *is* dying in a moment. I don't know how, what they will do, or how painful it will be. But she will die.

"I love you so much. I want to tell you that you've been the one person who has helped me through everything that has mattered in my life. The good moments, the bad ones, the fucking worst ones. I'm so sorry it came to this. I'm so, so sorry. Please forgive me." I begin to cry, and she hugs me tightly to her body. "I love you so much!"

"I love you too, Hallie. You're the only one who has mattered to me. Without you, I am nothing. Get the fuck out of here," she whispers in my ear. "Find a way and leave." Brittany's voice shakes as she says that, and I hug her tighter. "I will find you in another life."

"I will find you in all of the next ones."

I pull back and kiss her cheeks, tasting her tears. She grabs my head and presses our foreheads together, and we just cry against each other for a brief moment before I'm forcibly yanked off her. The men grab each of my arms again, pulling me back as far as possible, and three men step up to Brittany. When she sees what is in their hands, she begins to cry again. No, not cry. She's *wailing*.

Unable to process what's happening right in front of me, I cry uncontrollably. Two men have long knives, and the other has a machete. I don't understand what's happening.

The men kneel in front of Brit, and she starts to kick, refusing to go down without a fight. That's my girl. Don't give up! Fuck them. They can't do this to her. This must be a sick fucking joke to get me back in line, but he wouldn't do this to me.

Except the two men begin to stab Brittany in her stomach, and she writhes and screams and sobs. They do it over and over until I lose count, and even then, she doesn't die. Oh my God!

"Stop!" I scream, trying to wrangle myself free from the men. I ineffectively pull at my arms, trying to get them off me and begin to kick my legs savagely. I hit them both, making them tighten their grip on me. "Stop, Michael, *please*."

He looks at me and nods, "Let's be done then."

With that, he walks away, and just when I think they're going to let her die in peace, the man next to her head picks up his machete. She shakes her head weakly, raises her hand, and gurgles on her own blood.

The man steps on her chest, and I release another scream. She opens her mouth to do the same, but the machete comes down on her throat as he begins to cut off her head. Her legs twitch, and she still kicks them roughly even as it's halfway dislodged. She shouldn't even be alive.

I bawl and close my eyes, unable to watch anymore. This will be the one thing in my life I will never, ever forget. If anyone asks me what's the most traumatizing thing I've gone through, it will never be about Michael again. It will be this. I don't know how

I'll live with this guilt. There's no way I won't go crazy. Maybe I'll act out and force them to dope me up. I think that's the only way I'll be able to keep myself alive. At this point, I'd do anything to force them to kill me.

When the man grabs Brittany's head by her hair and throws it at my feet, I can't help turning my head and throwing up. I heave and heave, unable to look at it. The man approaches me and grabs my dirty chin, then turns my face so I'm forced to gaze at it. Her eyes are rolled back in her head, her mouth open on a scream, yet I don't dare to look at her neck.

There's no one to console me. There will never be any sort of sympathy ever again. I know that after this I can never be at peace. I take one last look at her, and my vision turns hazy. The corners go dark, and then everything turns black.

The intense pain in my shoulders and arms is what rouses me, and with blurry eyes I look around. I'm back in the dungeon, except I'm the only one here now. Where the fuck is everyone else?

As if on cue, I remember everything all over again. Tomás getting shot in the head, Brittany… I can't even think of that right now, or I'll throw up again. The burning question is: where the fuck are Abby and Kyle? Surely, he didn't kill them too. Although, after what I've witnessed, I wouldn't put it past him. I always thought I knew what kind of monster he is, but now that all of this has transpired, I realize I know nothing. The lengths he will go—they're unthinkable.

My feet shift under me as if I'm trying to distribute my weight somehow, and when I look down, I realize the reason why my shoulders and arms hurt so damn bad. In slow motion, I turn my head and look up. Leather cuffs are secured to my wrists with metal chains attached. My legs give out from under me, and the pain in my shoulders is even more intense when it feels like my arms are going to pop out of place.

I gasp as I try to regain my footing and use my legs to stand again, but I'm suspended enough that my feet don't touch the ground. How did I even get here? I have no recollection of what happened after... Brit. The fact that there's no one here with me worries me more than if there was.

A squeaking sound comes from the far-left side of the room. Then the door opens, but I can't see who it is. With closed eyes, I steel myself for whatever fuckery they have in mind. I'm sure this is just the beginning of my suffering. I'm not delusional enough to believe I got off easy just because he let me live. No. I think it may be worse.

Footsteps follow, and I hold my breath until they stop, yet I don't open my eyes. Loud, shrill screams can be heard when the door opens yet again. A sob threatens to escape when I realize those screams belong to Abby. The unthinkable is probably happening to her right now, and there's nothing I can do to help her.

My face scrunches up and my lower lip trembles, and the people who came down here begin to laugh. It sounds like a woman—probably Penelope—and someone else. I open my eyes to see the evil fucking bitch, and a man I don't recognize.

Penelope tells the man something in Spanish, and he nods, looking between us with a smile on his face. What the fuck is she saying that has him looking so fucking happy?

It's almost like he's reading my mind, and he offers an explanation. "The boss will be here soon when he's done with... the girl." He grins when I weep. "Oh, don't cry yet. Save the tears for him."

They each take a chair and sit on it, waiting for Michael to come into the room, I'm assuming. Penelope takes some items out of her pocket, and I watch her set them on her lap. A syringe, a small Ziplock bag, cotton balls... I can't see the rest. It's enough to get me excited though. Now that I think of it that sounds fucking terrible, but it doesn't matter to me anymore. I just need to forget and tune out the screams that keep bouncing in my head. Between Brittany's, the twins', and my own, I'm feeling overstimulated.

I hadn't noticed before, but the man has a knife and pliers in his hand. I want to say I hope he doesn't use them on me, but I don't think I care much anymore. That will probably change regardless, depending on how much it hurts, I guess.

After a few minutes of agony, Michael enters the dungeon with bloody hands and a smile. My stomach drops, and it feels like I have to throw up all over again. "What did you do?" I whisper, too choked up to raise my voice. Tears trail down my cheeks all over again.

"You know what I did," he all but purrs. "I'm sure you remember."

I yank on the chains with all my might, but all it does is make my arms hurt more and sucks the energy out of my body. He fills the space between us and caresses my face, which I flinch away from, smearing the blood on my cheek and jaw. I know he wants to make me crazy, and I hate to say he's achieving it.

When will it fucking stop? Will it ever? Or is my only escape going to be death? If it is, I will do whatever it takes to make that happen.

The stranger across the room grabs his chair and drags it over the concrete, making the worst screeching sound that leaves my teeth chattering and my head reeling. He sits close enough to touch me if he wants to, and suddenly I'm nervous he will. The man and I make eye contact long enough that I can tell his intention is to hurt me. He actually wants to, whether Michael instructs him to or not. That's not to say he'd go through with it if my stepfather didn't approve, yet you can tell he's thirsting for blood.

"Did you think you could run away?" Michael asks as he circles me like a shark scenting blood. "Get away from me?" When he makes it back to my front, he stops so close I can smell his nasty breath. "You," he says through gritted teeth, wrapping both hands around my neck and squeezing like he wants to kill me. "Will *never* fucking escape me."

Michael's meaty hands continue their assault, and just when I think he's going to let go he squeezes tighter instead. My chest blazes with the desperate need to draw in air, and I can feel my face getting hot. I'll have bruises in ten minutes, that's for damn sure. I try to get him off me by kicking him, but that just makes me hurt even more. Thrashing from up here is useless. I might as well be on a mission to break my arms.

It's almost like he's trying to kill me.

I'd let him at this point.

"Now tell me, baby girl," he says as he lets go, and a coughing fit takes over my body. I want to clutch my throat, but my hands are not available. "How long were you planning this?"

I shake my head quickly and take deep breaths so I can try to answer, "I—" More coughing, more tears. "I didn't plan this. I found out about it t-t-today."

When Michael's arm rears back I steel myself, but my body stands no chance when his fist lands on my face. My lip splits open and so does my cheek. Surely, I'm going to need stitches from that, and I know he won't let me have them. Or maybe he will. It's not like he wants me disfigured. I think.

"You might want to start telling the truth, Hallie, or this won't end well for you."

"Please," I sob, "I swear I didn't plan this. I didn't even know!"

Michael laughs and punches me in the face again. I change my mind. I do care about the pain. I'm not lying; Brit did keep me in the dark until a few minutes before the escape. The fact that I thought about staying… I should've listened to my gut. None of this would've happened if I had. I would've been spared Brit's death, which will live on in my mind forever.

I can't open my left eye anymore, and my entire face is throbbing and feels like it's on fire. The urge to hold on to it is driving me crazy. I can't even feel the blood running down it at this point, which worries me.

With my right eye, I can see Michael looking at the strange man across from us, and he nods at him. That can't be good. He has a knife with him and pliers. While I don't know much about torture, it's obvious that I'm about to be in a world of pain. I've watched crime television before, and it doesn't take much imagination to figure out what he's about to do with those pliers. Although that scares me, the unknown is more terrifying. What the fuck is he going to do with that knife?

"Go ahead," Michael tells the man, "Let's get the truth out of her."

I don't wait until the man makes a move. Instead, I start kicking my feet. There's no fucking way I'll willingly let them hurt me. The man grabs me by the ankle while I kick out with my other leg, and I'm momentarily proud when my foot lands on his face. That pisses him off though, and he yanks me until I'm suspended by just my arms. I scream when my shoulder feels like it's dislocating, and I can't move from how much it hurts. That gives him the opportunity he needs, so before I can move away or try to fight him again, he squeezes my foot and slowly pries my toenail until it tears away from my skin completely. This time I scream and sob from the pain, and I don't think I've heard myself be in so much agony ever in my life.

It feels like I'm in a haze, almost in limbo, unable to focus on anything but the pain. They all begin to laugh, and I take deep breaths to stop crying. It's inevitable. Pain is all I feel. It's taking over every single nerve ending, and I can't seem to be able to tune it out.

"Are you sure you don't want to talk?" Michael asks in a mocking tone. "There's more where that came from." I think he's rather enjoying this, and I hate that I'm giving him the satisfaction of hearing how much he's affecting me. I won't beg, though. That's the one thing I won't give him.

"I really didn't plan it. Brittany and Tomás did." I cry out when the man positions the pliers to the next toenail and rips it off. My sobs follow the movement, but I don't open my eyes. "I swear. They were fucking right in front of me, and she told me about it five minutes before we left the room. I had nothing to do with any planning."

I can feel the tears in my eyes, yet I don't feel them trailing down my face. I bet there's something wrong with it. So much is wrong with me at this point. What's one more thing to add to the list?

"I want to believe you, baby girl," I open my eyes at that, "But you're a fucking liar. So, you will be treated like one." He looks at the man and Penelope, "Leave the room."

Both of them nod, but he holds out his hand, and the man gives him the knife and pliers. My lower lip trembles as fear holds me within its clutches, and I silently cry as he circles me. My toes are throbbing, and I can't bear weight on them. Oh yeah, I'm pretty sure my shoulder *is* dislocated. What the fuck else does he want from me? How much more does he plan on hurting me? I have told him all I know.

The door slams when they exit. As he positions himself behind me, I feel the tip of the knife on the skin of my back. I bite my lip, which only makes it hurt more, and force myself to release it. The sharp end of the knife digs into my skin softly, then a little deeper when he puts more pressure on it. I wince and gasp, already scared of what comes next. When he drags the knife down my back in a shallow stroke, I scream yet again. It could be worse, but it damn well doesn't mean it's good. Everything fucking hurts.

"Are you sure that's what happened?"

"Yes!" I yell, "I didn't fucking know!"

Michael drops the knife on the ground and grabs my hips, which only makes my shoulder hurt more from how I'm hanging from the restraints. "Don't fucking yell at me, Hallie," he grits out in a low voice. "I'll hurt you more."

As he unbuttons his pants and lowers the zipper, I realize I no longer have clothes to protect me. I wish I would've been brave enough to get in the front seat and drive us away, but what's done is done. Now I have to live with my reality.

Michael enters me from behind and begins to thrust into me furiously, but I'm so numb to the pain. There's not one thing he can do to me at this point to make this worse for me.

Everyone I've ever loved is dead, or I'm dead to them.

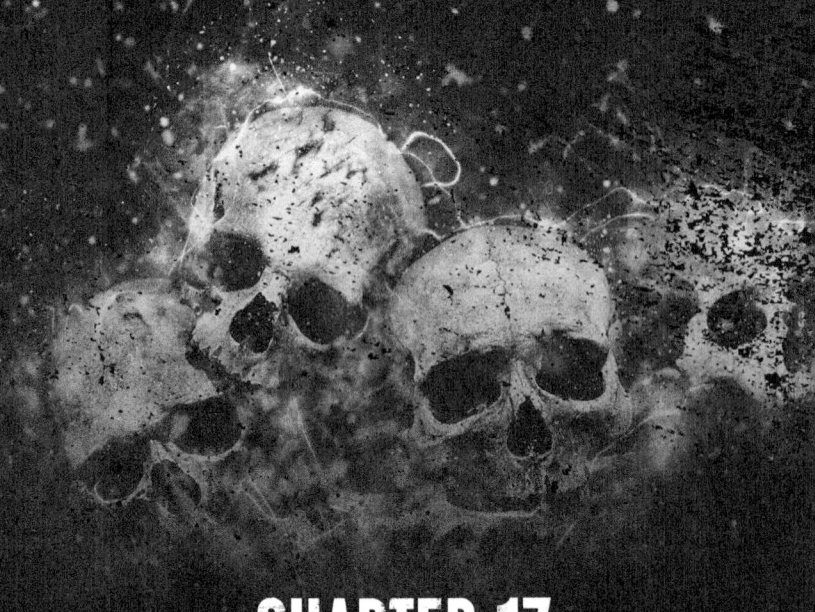

CHAPTER 17

Damien

One thing that sucks about cheap motels is the shitty excuse they call curtains. Although it's only seven in the morning, the bright sun still makes its way into the room and shines on my face. Tonight is when we are going after Hallie. That's why we need our rest, but of course I'm right next to the damn window.

I flip the other way just to roll over Zayne's arm. Are you fucking kidding me? There's an unspoken agreement when two men share a bed, and that's for everyone to stay on their damn side. So, tell me then, why this fucker is all over the bed while I'm falling right off the edge?

Goddamnit.

I'm trying my best to get along with him, but shit like this irritates me to no end. What he said about not forcing Hallie to choose yet… I hate to say it, even though he's right. Just thinking of sharing her is giving me a fucking aneurysm, but the alternative will kill me just as well. Either way, I can't win this one. All I know is that I can't just let him have her, especially not after the lengths I've gone to so I can get her back. I didn't travel to another country, stay in sketchy ass places, almost get killed, rescue her ex, follow her stepfather… for nothing. Now it's my turn to save her too, and there's no way in hell I'm *not* getting her back. Whatever it takes. If I have to share her attention for a few days, then whatever. I'll do it.

Is it delusional of me to believe Zayne will only be with us for a few days after we rescue her? Would she even pick me? What if she chooses *him*? Most importantly, what if she won't make the decision? Does that mean I have to bring the asshole to Canada with us?

Fuck, this is way too much to think about right now. Yet, I have to think of it at some point, and it seems like I won't have much time after tonight. Once we get her out, we really have to make a run for it. We have to figure out how to exit that fucking house in record time and then disappear. The tricky part will be getting to the border without drawing attention to ourselves, but once we're at the checkpoint, my father will have a man wave me through without checking my identification or passport. A lot of people owe Victor favors, so at least I have that going for me.

There have been many perks to working for the cartel over the years, and that was one of them. Now I'm a fucking nobody, and I can't wait to disappear from the universe that is the Sinaloa Cartel and now Juarez too. I just wonder if I'll ever see my father again. I'm not stupid, our last encounter felt like a permanent goodbye. Still, is it too much to ask that we get one more meeting? Something that doesn't feel like a breakup that's trying to end on "good terms," but no matter how much you try you know where it's leading.

It feels like my father opened up about how much he cares for me since now he doesn't have to deal with me anymore. He doesn't have to make an effort to keep our relationship afloat or to keep in contact. I get it. It's too much shit to deal with, work through, forgive, and ask for forgiveness. But damn, at least let me think you hate me so I don't have to wonder about the what-ifs for the rest of my fucking life. All in all, everything that has transpired with him has been terrible timing.

I only have two hopes at this point: that we get Hallie out safely and make it to Canada without getting followed to the safe house. The first one, I will do whatever it takes to make that happen. As for the second one, well, that's a little more complicated. I can't control who follows us or has connections to go after us across the border, especially since I don't have that kind of intel. Sean helps me a lot, don't get me wrong, although it's not the same as doing it myself. It always feels like there's a gap in my knowledge. I can't complain, he has aided me with so much as it is. I'm fucking lucky to even have found him.

Zayne's hand touches my arm, and my skin crawls. Fuck. No. I shove it away and growl, "Get your filthy hands off me."

Zayne opens his eyes, confused as fuck, and yanks his hand away from me. "Sorry, dude." He turns over the other way and gives me his back. "I'm sleeping. I have no control over that."

"You need to learn some boundaries," I reply. "Or do you need us to divide this big ass king-sized bed equally down the middle?"

"How the fuck would you even…?"

His lack of imagination makes me want to laugh, "Wait, you're serious?" I chuckle. "Pillows, Zayne. Fucking pillows."

"Of course, you'd do that."

"Yes, I would." I roll my eyes. "Also, has anyone ever told you that you sleep a lot? For fuck's sake, princess, it's time to wake up. We have shit to do."

"Well…" He smiles, lifting his head to look at me. It feels like he's mocking me, and I already know I won't like what comes out of his mouth. "Hallie—"

I slap him upside the head. "Shut the fuck up."

"Alright, alright." Zayne chuckles and gets out of bed.

"I thought we were making progress, asshole!"

He looks at me over his shoulder, "Us? Progress?" I want to punch the smirk off his face but ball my hands into fists instead.

Patience, Damien. Also, calm the fuck down. He hasn't even done shit to me, and I'm already riled up. I really need to learn to live with him. "I never knew that was possible. Did you think about what I told you? About sharing?"

I instantly feel the intensity of rage take over my body and sweat beads trail down my spine. Fuck. I don't want to talk about this or do it at all, but now I feel like I must go through with it. For Hallie. "We can get along—I think. Right?" Fuck no. "I think you're right. We will have to share for a little while." His stunned face is priceless. He wasn't expecting me to give in and probably wanted her to choose him for readily considering her needs. "But we aren't touching dicks."

"Fuck, no. There are limits to my generosity. In fact, I don't think we can fuck her at the same time. Just separately," he replies, and I can't say I disagree. I don't want her attention on him when my dick is inside her.

"Yeah, absolutely no fucking threesomes here."

"Cool with me." He enters the bathroom, and right before he shuts the door, he yells, "Unless Hallie wants it!"

Nah. Nope. Zero chance.

Hallie can get over that real fucking quick. There's no way I'll give in to that. I'm too possessive, and this sharing situation makes me itchy and uncomfortable. The thought of his dick being inside her right after mine makes me sick and see red at the same time. Even if we weren't sharing her in one bed, it feels awfully close to crossing swords. Goddamnit. Not to mention, what the fuck do they expect me to do? Wait outside the hotel room in my car while they fuck? Absolutely not. There are more important matters at hand, so I need to shelf this for later when it becomes a problem.

Once Zayne is done with his shower, I take mine as well. We have a long day ahead of us, and we have to ensure everything is in order and absolutely perfect. We can't afford any mistakes, not when Hallie's life is on the line. Ours too, and if we die, no one will free her.

Sean managed to get me a physical invitation to this party,

which I don't know how the fuck he did. Apparently, this shit is very exclusive and even has a formal invitation that looks like it should be for a wedding. Elegant and gold foiling adorn the edges, and the text reads:

You are cordially invited to our Christmas Eve party where you can celebrate with us and open your presents before midnight!

Yeah, I fucking bet they will be opening presents. My only concern is that Hallie will be one of them. What if she's part of the party and being sampled? I don't think I can witness that. I'd lose my fucking mind and mess up the plan. I would kill everyone in sight before I have backup.

The next few hours go by quicker than I thought they would, and Zayne looks more nervous by the second. I'm starting to think he's not ready and might fuck this up. Maybe I should leave him here where he's safe. I never thought about how badly this may affect him since he said he'd be fine, but the PTSD is showing through right now.

Finding a tux while laying low in this country was harder than I anticipated, but we had to do whatever was necessary. I'm thankful I've had help on the side, or I'd be totally fucked. *We*, I guess, would have been totally fucked.

By the time we get in the car, Zayne is a fidgeting mess and visibly sweating. I crank up the AC even higher, especially since it's hot as fuck in the winter here too. "Are you good there? Do I need to turn around and drop you off?"

"No. I'll be okay. I just need a moment to get prepared."

I nod, but he's looking out the window, so he can't see me. "You can talk to me about it, you know. If you need to get it off your chest." I'd rather he didn't, but he needs to go in here with a clear head. Can't have him thinking about the shit he's been through or worried about it happening again while trying to kill everyone in there.

"Why would you offer that?" Zayne scoffs, "You don't actually give a fuck."

I mean, I do and I don't. He's not entirely wrong. "Because you need to get the fuck over it."

"Oh yeah?" He laughs sarcastically. *Here we go.* "Would you get over being fucked in the ass against your will over and over? By a goddamn *man*? Would you be okay with being kidnapped and forced to be on live streams while he's doing it?"

I stiffen, tightening my hands against the steering wheel. I did not know the extent of it. I just thought he was fucking that girl, and that's it. I only saw him on the live stream with her, and they looked perfectly happy about it. Why didn't Sean mention the other part? *Fuck.*

He must have seen my stunned look, or I may not have concealed my thoughts well enough because he adds, "I don't need your fucking pity."

"You don't have it." I lie through my teeth. I do feel bad for him. Perhaps I'll be nicer. Probably not, though. "He's dead, Zayne. You need to get through this, over it. If you fall back into drugs, I will personally make sure Hallie never sees you again. You catch my drift, fucker?"

"I will not fall into drugs again."

It would be convincing for someone who didn't know him, but not for me. I've seen what he's capable of for a slam, and it's not something anyone should be proud of. He'd give up everything he loves, all his belongings, his money. His ass, let's be real here. Everything goes out the window when meth is under his nose or, in his case, his veins.

"It sounds like you're trying to convince yourself."

"Maybe I am," he replies. "I *will* do better by Hallie."

"You have to. We don't know how she will be when she gets out of this place. All our focus and attention needs to be on her. We can't fuck this up, and we can't make this about us. I fucked up enough, and so did you. It stops now."

He sighs long and loud, "I agree."

"Glad we're on the same page then." It's progress. If we're ever going to make this work, we have to actually put in the work.

He surprises me by saying, "We need to stay that way."

The rest of the drive is silent, and my mind starts to wander. Is this what bonding with him feels like? Surely we aren't becoming friends. There is no fucking way that's happening. And yet… I think we're coming to terms with getting along as much as possible. That's not to say we will agree with things or not fight, but I no longer hate him to the point where I want to shoot him on sight. Maybe now we're down to stabbing or possibly medium torture.

A woman's voice comes from my phone's GPS, which I hate that I have to use but have no choice in the matter. Zayne and I both startle when it tells us we have arrived at our destination.

Even though it's dark, I can tell a few things about this party. Number one, there's a fuck-load of people here. I can't even count how many cars are parked in the middle of the street as if it belongs to them. Maybe Michael owns the entire neighborhood for all we know, but damn. It's a good thing we know where we're parking and anticipated, at the very least, that we needed to be out of sight yet close enough for a quick and seamless escape. Number two, the man is rich. I'm not talking 'I have money and can flaunt it' type of rich. No, more like the 'I can afford a four-million-dollar house and buy people' kind of rich. Based on the floor plan, I expected a huge house; I did not expect it to look this pretty. It is an enormous Spanish-style home with columns and steps leading to the front entrance. A black wrought iron gate secures it, but it's wide open at the moment, which is convenient for us. Number three, there are many more people than anticipated, and I hope my father came through and got me at least ten people to help out. Otherwise, we're well and truly fucked.

I loop the car around and park near the back entrance of the house, which seems to be on a dirt road. For some reason they decided not to have this area gated, which is just about the dumbest shit I've ever seen. But hey, whatever. They're making my life easier as it is.

"Now what's the plan, Zayne?"

I stop and park the vehicle, trying to conceal it slightly by the trees. The color doesn't help, making it stick out like a sore thumb. That being said though, it's not my fault I couldn't find anything else around the same price on such short notice. A flashy car is not going to help me stay under the radar.

"We go in," he says slowly, breathing deeply through his nose. "We mingle and pretend to like the same shit as them. Don't act nervous or suspicious. We look around and locate the people, then we go back to our spot and get our weapons."

"Then?"

"We fucking kill everyone," Zayne says with a maniacal smile.

"Good boy."

He smirks, and I roll my eyes then open the door. We have to be really fucking smart about this, and if everything is going according to plan. Diego and Armando already took care of the side door we can use to enter and hide the weapons. Yes, more than one. We'll need a lot of firepower to take everyone down.

We grab rifles, ammo, and two handguns each and walk toward the side door. I test the knob by twisting it, and it is thankfully unlocked. I don't open it yet. Instead, I look back at Zayne who has a somber expression on his face.

"Lighten up," I try to put him at ease and smile at him, "We're about to see Hallie. This is it."

His eyes light up, and fuck me. It reminds me of my fucking self. He's a lovesick puppy, just like me. Goddamnit. "You're lucky I've gone hunting before, or you'd be shit out of luck."

"I guess we'll see how much you remember. For our sake, let's hope it's a lot."

I bring my finger to my lips to gesture for him to be quiet and then open the door slowly. Surprisingly, it doesn't creak. It doesn't make one sound. It's a little eerie and puts me on edge, but maybe this is the advantage of being rich as fuck. I'm trying not to read into it too much.

Stepping into the house first, I don't know if I'm glad the light is on or if that freaks me out even more. Zayne comes in after me, shutting the door behind him to make sure no one sees us from outside. The room is empty save for some boxes, which I don't even want to fucking know what's in them. Most likely it's drugs. Hopefully. Either way, we take advantage of them and set the weapons down behind a tall stack, entirely out of sight if someone were to come in here. Unless they actually are looking for something and walk between the boxes. Then we're fucked.

We leave everything as it was when we came in and exit the room through the side door once more. While it's convenient that we're in the house and we already know the floor plan, being caught in the house without going through the guards at the front door is the last thing I need. Drawing attention to ourselves must be avoided at all costs.

Looking around, I check that no one has followed or is near us before we go around the house to the front. There's a group of about twenty people—maybe even more, what the fuck—and we're able to blend in and stand in line behind them. Once at the front, I hand my invitation over, and we are both checked for weapons, cameras, and bugs. Thankfully, they don't force me to hand my cell phone over. That's what I expected to happen anyway, although I was praying it didn't because I need the damn GPS when we get out of here.

When we reach the threshold, the house opens into what looks like a damn ballroom. What the actual fuck? Did they purposely purchase this home for this sick shit? I wouldn't put it past them. There's a smaller living room to the right of the foyer with a sofa and a loveseat, a coffee table, and a large window behind the setup. The floors look like marble tiles, shiny as fuck, and it gives a glimpse at the kind of money they have. I don't know why I keep thinking about his money, though. It doesn't fucking matter in the long run. He's dead tonight, no matter what he does. My only regret is that we might not have enough time to raid his house.

That's not entirely true however, and I smile as I text Diego to do it for me. If this motherfucker has hurt Hallie, then he can pay for it with his life *and* his money. She deserves that much. No matter what she decides, whether it's to stay with Zayne or me or neither—at least she will have her own money and will never have to depend on us for it. Or me, anyway. Zayne is a broke-ass bitch.

As we walk into the ballroom, I stop in my tracks, and Zayne runs into me. When he comes around to stand by my side, he gasps. The twins I saw and talked to him about from the auction are completely naked in the middle of the ballroom. There are bruises, cuts, and dried blood on their bodies, and I literally feel the bile rising to the back of my throat. I'd never profess that I'm a good person; I know I'm not. Even still, I could never be capable of this level of depravity.

Zayne grabs my arm and digs his fingers into it painfully. Only I can't even swat him away. First, I don't want to look suspicious, even if it bothers me. Second, I don't even feel like it bothers me right now. This reminds him of what he just went through, and he needs some damn emotional support if we're going to make it through tonight in one piece.

I lean into him and get close enough to whisper in his ear since I don't want to be heard. "Stop looking."

He turns his head, and we stare at each other. "I have to." Tears are in his eyes, and his nostrils flare as he breathes deeply to keep them in. "If I don't, it'll look suspicious."

"It's worse if you look at them and cry."

He does have a point. Maybe he should pretend to look but instead stare at something beyond them. Like a wall or a light fixture. Whatever he needs to get through this shit. My phone vibrates with a text from Diego telling me he's scouting the house, and I reply with a thumbs up. His code to get ready to take this fucking place down will be a fire emoji, so I make sure I'm keeping an eye out.

"Is it time yet?"

"No," I mutter, "You will know when it's time. All of my father's men will turn and start shooting the shit out of the place. Then when I get the signal, we'll get our things. We won't be left out of this shit."

"As long as that motherfucker is left for last," he replies.

"Already on that."

This time, I look away from the twins, as they are ogled enough by everyone in attendance, except their gazes are approving and longing. I can't be here much longer without shooting someone. The man and woman are visibly in distress, crying and shaking. No one has touched them yet, at least not the guests. Michael clearly has done way more than touch them. They are going to be so traumatized after this.

Who do they even belong to? Are they from the United States? How do I get them back to their homeland without the cartel finding out? Will they live their life on the run? I don't know what to do for them. I usually take people, not rescue them. I don't ever return them to their families, that's for damn sure.

We walk through the ballroom, keeping our eyes averted and watching the party fucking go on in just about every corner of the room. At first glance, you'd never think these women are unwilling. If you dig deeper and look closer, you'll realize just how well-trained they are. The men who purchase them usually have someone who takes care of that for them, or the girls are already trained before going to the auction.

A waiter comes to us with two flutes of champagne, but I shake my head at him and smile. He looks stunned for a moment, then carries on. I've made it a point to Zayne that our thinking cannot be impaired in any way while we're here, but really, I'm more worried about him being too tempted. Any drug is a gateway back to hell for him, and I won't let that fucking happen. Not until Hallie decides what she wants. I've thought about sabotaging him like I did a while back. It would be so fucking easy to get him out of the way, but I think I'd feel guilty now. Fuck me. I think I'm going soft on the asshole. What the fuck.

I spot Michael in the corner of the room, mingling and laughing with a group of men smoking cigars. I bump Zayne discreetly, and he follows my line of sight, stiffening when his gaze clashes with the monster who's been haunting Hallie in the corners of her mind for a decade. He's more real than any monster under the bed a child could be scared of, and yet, he was literally her monster under the bed. Now that he's caught her again, terrorized her, I don't know if there's any coming back from this. Will she ever recover? This might be her last straw.

"Wait here," I tell Zayne, and he looks at me with wide eyes.

"No fucking way." He shakes his head, "You're not leaving me here alone, and you're definitely not going to go talk to him either."

"I want him to see who I am." I smirk, "It'll be even better when we kill him."

I don't wait for Zayne to reply. Instead I make my way across the room and stop a few feet from the men to observe what seems to be a live stream. What the fuck is up with these people and their goddamn live streams? How much do they make off them? Is the market that big? I mean, I know people watch porn all the time, but this seems a little extreme.

Someone taps me on the shoulder, and when I turn around, I come face to face with the fucking devil himself. Hazel eyes and a bright smile stare back at me, but I'm not a fool. The prettiest teeth take the sharpest bites, and he's a fucking shark. I can tell he's scenting the water, looking for blood, but I won't bleed for him.

"Cigar?" Michael asks me, extending a cigar my way. I take it to be polite. He lights it for me, then I take a hit of it. "I think I've seen you before. You are?"

"New," I reply, "This is my first time in Juarez."

"That makes sense." He nods, "Well if you need anything, I'm here. Feel free to sample my girls."

My spine stiffens at that, but I nod. "I will." Michael smiles like he approves, and I mutter, "Thanks for the cigar."

With that, I walk away, back across the room and to Zayne's side. I can't keep my eyes off the people here. I want to make sure each and every one of them dies first. I will have their blood on my hands, if that's what it takes to bring my Hallie a semblance of peace.

My phone vibrates repeatedly, and when I check it, the fire

emoji fills my screen. I pocket it once more and look around, and when I see that no one is watching us, I tell Zayne, "It's time."

A stiff nod is all the response I get from him, and we begin to walk toward the room where we have our weapons stashed. I make sure to look all around us for signs of being followed, and so far, we're in the clear. When we enter, Diego and Armando are standing in the middle of the room, waiting for us. I shut the door behind us and begin to gather our supplies, holstering one handgun at my hip and the other in the back of my pants. One rifle each will have to do.

Zayne is actually holding his own with this, which I'm entirely surprised about, and it must show because he chuckles and says, "I'm from Texas. Not like you little Colorado boys that grow up snowboarding and drinking beer with your pinkies up."

"Alright now," I almost snort at the accuracy. "The beer is damn fucking good, though."

"Are you ready, or will you two be talking shit to each other all night?" Diego asks, and Zayne and I share a brief, amused look.

We sober up quickly when Diego begins to go over the plan one more time though, and once done, we open the door and step out of the room. Diego and Armando lead the way, since they're going directly to the security guards, and we're turning the other way to fuck everyone up. Hopefully the guards have done their jobs and none of the guests have weapons. Then again, my hopes are not too high. I bet if you're the right person or friends with Michael, they would let a lot slide. Michael, on the other hand, will definitely be armed. Unless he's a pussy who relies on everyone else to protect him. Actually, that scenario sounds the most accurate now that I think of it.

Diego looks at me one more time and nods before stepping out of the hallway with his weapon ready, Armando following closely behind. They open fire on the security guards, and we quickly follow behind and open fire on the guests right in front of us. There's a herd of people dropping to the ground, and I open fire again as I run over the bodies. I shoot toward the left side and

Zayne shoots right. I can't lie, we do make a damn good team. I'm happy to say he has not disappointed me in this department.

I can see Michael running away, looking for a hiding place, and the dumbass chooses a couch that I definitely saw him run to. He crouches behind it and pretends to be invisible. Lucky for me, I get to make him pay for everything he's ever done to her.

Multiple gunshots echo in the ballroom, but it's not mine or Zayne's that I'm hearing. I look back and see Armando and Diego engaged in a standoff with the guards, some of them shooting at the guys. Fuck. It's too bad I can't help them, but for now we have to finish what we started. Everyone in this ballroom has to die. I don't care about their reasons for being here. As far as I'm concerned, if they're present, then they condone what he's doing.

I look around the large room but don't see them. I point my weapon at a small group of people, the last ones left, and get ready to shoot.

"Wait!" Zayne yells as the kids run to the other end of the room, screaming and crying. "Don't shoot the naked girls!"

"I won't," I reply, although they're lying flat on the ground, trying to get cover either way. "Now, let's finish these parasites."

Zayne and I open fire on the last few people and then look around the room to make sure no one's left. Everyone dropped like fucking flies, and within minutes, we literally cleared out the entire ballroom. I turn around to look for Armando and Diego, but they're already walking back toward us.

"I'll get the twins," Zayne says, hurrying towards them.

Once in front of them, he crouches and holds out his hand. I see his lips moving, but I'm too far away to hear what he's saying. I make my way closer and stop behind him. There's a commotion across the room, and Zayne turns around as we all watch Michael trying to escape.

Zayne lifts his rifle and shoots, smiling when the shot meets its intended target. Michael immediately drops to the ground and screams, and I notice the blood pooling around his legs on the ground comes from his kneecap. I start to laugh and pat him on the back, which makes him smile.

Diego and Armando grab the nearest chair and sit him on it as he keeps screaming in agony. They tie him with some rope, which I'm assuming they either found somewhere or hid really, really well. I see Armando going to the twins with a small backpack I prepared for them earlier that has clothes and shoes. Then I begin to back up and walk back the way we came from.

Zayne follows me, staying close behind. We stop abruptly when we reach the door to the room where we think Hallie is being held captive since it's the only one left. I take a deep breath and look at him. His hands shaking is heightening my anxiety, but I try to calm down.

"Are you ready?" I ask him, my voice hoarse as I turn the door handle.

"No."

"Me either."

I push the door open and go down the stairs, almost tripping on each step as I try to get to Hallie as quickly as possible. Her arms are suspended above her head and looking like they're at an unnatural angle. She's also covered in blood and bruises, her perfect skin now marred thanks to that degenerate. Her feet barely touch the ground, and her head is slumped to the side. I can't imagine how the fuck she's sleeping this way. She has to be in so much pain, yet her face is peaceful.

Hallie lifts her head and makes eye contact with me, her face confused and completely swollen. Even one of her eyes is swollen shut. She glances between me and Zayne, back and forth over and over. Her lips tremble, and she gasps. When she realizes that we're real, as we advance on her, she begins to sob uncontrollably.

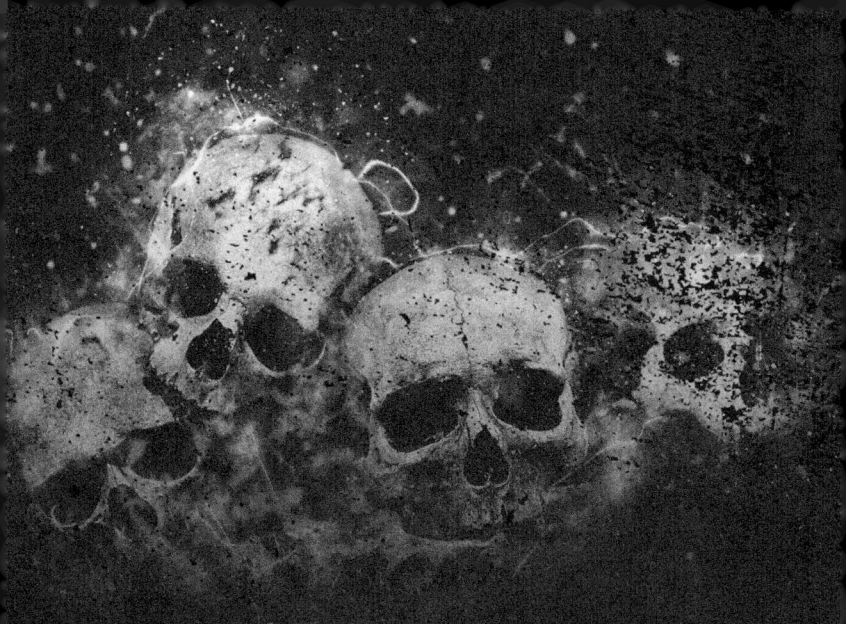

CHAPTER 18

Hallie

What the fuck did they give me?

That's some strong fucking heroin they've been giving me, I guess, and now I'm clearly hallucinating. Just what I need right now. *Was* it just heroin? Surely not? I've never hallucinated before. I guess it beats being in pain all day.

Honestly, life has a way of playing cruel fucking jokes on me.

The two most important people in my life, the loves of my life, are not visibly standing in front of me. Yet, I see them.

I close my eyes, hoping that they will be gone when I open them again. It's too painful to see them in my waking *and* sleeping moments.

Footsteps get closer and closer to me, and now I wonder if guards are coming my way, and for whatever reason I thought I saw *them* instead. I brace myself for what will surely be another beating, standing on my tiptoes. Unfortunately, no matter how I position myself, I can feel my shoulder out of the socket. It's fucked up. Screaming at me in pain, more painful than the rest of my body. My face and eye are still throbbing, the cuts on my back still burning. I'm pathetic.

Rather than the expected beating, someone touches my face tenderly. Even still, I flinch. My face is throbbing to the rhythm of my own heart, and one of my eyes is still swollen shut. I don't even want to talk about the damage to the rest of my body. It feels insignificant.

I feel insignificant.

"Look at her face," Zayne's voice again, and it sounds hoarse, almost like he's in pain.

"I'm going to fucking kill him." The icy voice sounds like it belongs to Damien, but surely it can't be real. What the fuck is wrong with me? They hate each other. They wouldn't be caught together, dead or alive.

I want to bang my head, claw my face, let myself hang from these chains, and feel more pain. Anything to get their voices out of my head.

"It's not real. It's not real, it's *not* fucking real. Get it together, Hallie," I mutter, trusting the guards don't think I'm bat-shit crazy. Then again, I might just be at this point.

"Hallie, baby." Zayne's voice again. "We're really here." He touches my face again gingerly, and I cry out, tears beginning to stream down my face. "Please, open your eyes."

"You're not real," I tell the voice. "Leave me alone, *please*. I can't do this." My bottom lip trembles, and so does my body. I can't let myself believe this lie; it'll be too painful later. I know for a damn fact that my chance of getting out of here is long gone. Brittany and Tomás thought they had planned our escape well, but we never stood a chance.

"I'm real, baby."

"You're dead," I cry. The cuts on my cheeks and lip sting, but he's still there when I open my eyes.

"Fuck, no," Zayne says, laughing. "You can't get rid of me that easily."

"Show me you're real," I tell him. But how can he show me? "I don't believe you."

Zayne comes close to my ear. "What do you want me to do, baby? How can I prove it?"

"I don't know…" I sob.

"Let me help, Hallie," Damien interjects. "We will show you we're real."

How is this even possible? How did they find me? Why are they together? How is Zayne alive? Why is Damien here? Doesn't he hate me? I would hate me. I *do* hate me.

"Calm down, baby," Zayne tells me. "Breathe how I breathe." He puts his hand on my chest and shows me how to inhale and exhale slowly. It takes me back to another day, another time, when he did this exact thing on my bed after a nightmare.

I try to mimic him, and I do at first. After a few seconds, though, Damien releases my good arm. Thankfully, Zayne catches me when my knees buckle.

My other arm is still suspended and bent at an unnatural angle, and I scream when he starts messing with the restraint around my wrist. "It's broken!" I cry, "Stop!"

Damien stops briefly. "Zayne, hold her arm up. Don't let it fall, whatever you do."

Zayne nods, "Eyes on me, baby. You're okay. I got you."

"Oh God, you really are real!" Damien releases my wrist, and Zayne holds onto the arm tightly, making me scream again. Once Damien comes to my side, he takes the arm, and Zayne lets go.

"You did so good, love," Damien says, and when I gaze at him, he seems sad. "Now comes the hard part. But you're a nurse, so you know what I need to do." I do know, and that terrifies the shit out of me. I know it's an emergency, and he has to pop my shoulder back in, but I don't want him to. Goddamn it, *I don't want him to.*

Zayne places me down slowly while Damien holds onto my arm. They don't mean to pull on it, but they do, and it makes me wail in agony all over again. Once I'm sitting on the disgusting tiled floor where I've seen the vilest acts occur, I take a deep breath and nod.

Damien lowers my arm to my side slowly, but even still, I cry and sob again, my body shaking from how much it hurts. Once at my side, he and Zayne lie me down on my back.

"Okay, love. You know I have nothing to give you for the pain," he says, but maybe the H will make it better. Isn't it just like morphine or some shit? "But I have to do this now."

"Okay…"

He grabs my forearm, and with his other hand, he puts pressure right below my elbow. Raising it so my hand points to the sky while keeping the rest of the arm flat on the ground.

"Ow," I cry out.

"It's okay," Zayne says as he sits beside me and holds my hand. "I got you." Damien's eyes shoot daggers at Zayne, and of course, Zayne just rolls his.

"Okay, I'm going to start moving now, love." I cry harder but nod, "It'll be over soon. Just a minute, and then you'll be done. I need you to keep your arm to your chest until I can get you a sling, okay."

"Diego!" Zayne yells, and a man comes to the door a few moments later. "Get a clean bed sheet, please. We need to make a sling for her." The man nods and leaves once more as Damien gets to work.

Damien rotates my arm outward in a slow motion while still keeping my upper arm on the ground. Pulling me by elbow and forearm, he moves it back and back and back. It feels like someone is slicing me from the inside out. This might just be worse than what I've endured in the past few days, or I don't even know how long at this point. Whenever the fuck we tried to escape.

He keeps going, and when it doesn't work, he brings it back to my side and starts over again. I breathe with Zayne even though I'm a sobbing mess, so it's a pathetic attempt at it. Once Damien has my forearm all the way rotated again, I cry out.

"Almost there, babe." He tells me, and my belly flutters even through the pain. He's calling me babe again. He came to *rescue* me. He loves me. He *still* loves me, after everything I've done to him. "Almost...there."

I scream when I hear it pop back into place, partly because it fucking hurt, and also because it stunned the fuck out of me to hear that loud cracking sound. Damien drapes my arm across my chest tenderly, and the man shows up again, this time with a sheet. He walks out of the room once more without a word.

Damien rips the sheet in half, turns it into a makeshift sling, and then puts it on me, placing my arm in it slowly. "Thank you," I tell him. He smiles at me with tears in his eyes and scoots closer to me on his knees, leaning over my body. "I'm so sorry."

"Don't worry about that right now. I don't fucking care about any of it." With that, he leans into my face and gives me a soft kiss, and even though it fucking hurts, I don't give a shit. I needed this and him. I don't want to be without him ever again.

He came for me.

They came for me.

Both of them help me sit up, then stand as well. Once I can put weight on my feet, Zayne drapes my good arm over his shoulder to help me walk. Except he's rooted in place. I look up at him, confused, and he kisses me. Except he doesn't give a shit about my pain. He never has. His kiss is rough, claiming, "I love you." He tells me as he pulls away. I look at Damien without replying.

I'm stunned into silence. I don't even know what the fuck just happened. Damien's nostrils are flaring, and he looks fucking angry. He doesn't say anything; he swallows hard and turns away, walking in front of us. I don't reply to Zayne, and I know that probably pisses him off. But I won't tell either one that I love them when they're right in front of each other. It just feels wrong.

Out of nowhere, it hits me. The twins. It took me this long to fucking remember them! "Where are the twins? Zayne? Where are they?" I start freaking out again. My chest begins to hurt from how fast I'm breathing, and my hands start to shake. "Are they dead?!"

"No, Hals," he soothes, stopping again and brushing hair out of my face. "They're okay. We have them."

"Let's go, Hallie. We have something for you."

Damien leads the way again while Zayne carefully helps me walk. I'm still out of it, and my legs feel like they weigh a thousand pounds. Now that the adrenaline rush has passed, my body is exhausted again, still drowsy from the drugs I've been given repeatedly for the past few days.

We go through the same hallway I've used to get back to my room throughout the whole time I've been here, and Zayne basically half-carries me out. He sits me down on a dining chair and pulls clothes out of a backpack. Between both of them, they get me dressed from the waist down. When it's time to put on a shirt however, Damien seems a little hesitant. I obviously need it, though. I can't go shirtless if we're trying to get out of here.

"Just do it," I assure him, "I'm high as fuck, so that'll probably help my pain."

Damien tenses, his lips pressing into a thin line. "Zayne, I need you to hold her arm when I remove the sling."

"Got it."

I look between him and Zayne repeatedly, watching every interaction closely. They're both cooperating, seamlessly working together. *Holy shit!*

When and *how* did this happen?

I disappear for a little while and now suddenly they're a team? Also, I saw Zayne get taken. I *saw* it. So how is he here?

"I have so many questions…" I voice my thoughts.

Damien undoes my sling, and Zayne grabs my arm, gently holding it still while Damien gathers the shirt. "Well, those are going to have to wait a while, Hallie," he replies. "We have to get out of here as soon as possible."

He successfully puts my shirt on, except for the arm that hurts, and slowly begins to pull it through the hole. I cry out, fisting my hand as he finishes putting it on. My shoulder fucking hurts, but it's nowhere near as bad as it was before he put it back in place.

Once my arm is back in the sling, Zayne half carries, half walks me to a giant room I've never been to. At least if I have, I've either been too high to remember or had a bag over my head. I do recognize the marble floors; I'll say that much. Although they're barely visible right now. There are too many dead people—and blood—taking up most of it.

The further we walk into the room, the weirder I feel. Something is off. I don't know what it is, but I don't like the feeling. "What are we doing here?" I whisper to Zayne, but he keeps his eyes forward as I look at him. He's still dragging me along in silence, and I plant my feet so he can't move me. At least it's an attempt to make him stop anyway. "Where the fuck are we going?"

"To make things right."

I move my legs this time, even though I'm completely unsure about what he means. Soon enough, I see the man who brought the sheet to us earlier, but he's not alone, for there's also another man with him. They're standing in front of someone, laughing, and as we get closer, I realize who it is.

Michael.

They have him. He's here. That makes me grin, the fact that he's not in charge anymore—he's the fucking captive. I want him to suffer. Even a decade of suffering won't make up for what he's done to me, what he's put me through.

I walk faster now, wanting to see the pain he's about to be in. I know Damien won't disappoint me in that area, and if I ask him to, he will make him suffer.

"Coming through," Damien yells, and the men move out of the way to reveal Michael strapped to a chair and blood pooled under him on the ground. His pant leg is soaked, and I look at Damien in confusion. He raises an eyebrow at me and smirks. "How's that knee feeling?"

"Please," Michael licks his lips and looks at me wide-eyed. "Don't hurt me. I'll do anything you want!"

It's my turn to answer, "You did enough already."

Zayne and Damien both have a smile on their faces as if they approve of what I just said. I look around the room at all the dead bodies piled up and shake my head. He did this to them. Zayne and Damien probably both participated, but it was Michael's fault for being such a piece of shit.

Disgust radiates from me, "What did you do to the twins?" I ask him, almost stunned at my possessiveness over them. They might as well be mine though, I've looked after them. Michael's face morphs into that of what I can only describe as a monster, and I suddenly regret asking. "Where are the fuck are they?!" I scream.

"You don't really want me to tell you what I did to them."

"Yes—" I stand directly in front of him, "I do."

"I raped them both. Are you fucking happy?"

"Am I happy that you hurt them?" I ask in disbelief. "No, but now I get to hurt you. Now I get to make sure you never hurt anyone else."

"Good luck." He smirks, his face smug.

"I won't need it," I smile. "But you will." I don't give a shit that I can barely walk or move, he's tied to the chair pretty good with his arms bound to it, his chest and legs too. He's motionless, and he can't fight me. It's perfect, truly. "I don't care if you suffer or not, to be honest. I just want to be done with you. You're not worth my time. You're a waste of fucking air and space."

Michael has the audacity to laugh. "You don't have it in you, baby girl."

Zayne steps forward and gets behind me, whispering in my ear. "Yes, you do." His arm comes around my chest possessively, although he's still careful with my hurt arm. I lean into him instinctively, a smile on my face.

When I look back at him, I see nothing but love in his eyes. "Yes, I do." He smiles back. "Someone get me a knife."

"Here, love," Damien says, handing me a knife. He looks at Michael and grins, "You're about to see what she's fucking capable of, and you should be scared now. There's nothing a person who hates you wouldn't do."

Zayne lets go of me as I take steps forward, but he still stands behind me, getting closer and closer until he's right behind me.

"Thank you," I tell Damien. "Hold him for me, please."

Damien goes around to the back of the chair and grabs him by the hair, yanking it back until his throat is exposed. But I don't want his throat. I want his fucking brain. I want to feel and see as the light fades from his eyes. This will bring me closure, I think. I hope anyway.

I take more steps forward until I'm at his side, since I can't support myself without my arm working. I won't be able to use my dominant arm for this, which means he will only hurt more. But the good thing is I don't care how sloppy this is as long as it gets done.

"Anything you want to say to me?" I ask him, but he just grins.

"If you're expecting an apology, I won't give it to you, bitch."

I smile back. "I didn't want it anyway."

Damien yanks his head back harder, and I lean over Michael as best as I can. My hand doesn't shake, in fact, I feel a rush of something going through my body as I slice from his eye all the way down his chin. Blood trickles from the wound immediately, and he holds back a scream. I can tell he held back, so I do it again on the same wound, going deeper this time. A lot deeper. He does scream now, a piercing sound that fucking delights me. I wanted him to scream for me at least once before I killed him. Every time I remember how he fucked me, I'll think of this moment to make me feel better.

"This is where you die, motherfucker."

"No," he pleads. "I *am* sorry."

"Take it up with whatever deity you believe in."

I rear my hand back and drive the knife through his eye until I feel a crunch. It's all the way to the hilt, and I feel nothing. No happiness, no rush. I'm just numb at this point. Honestly, I thought I would feel better, but it's like it never happened. He doesn't even scream from it. He's dead just like that.

Leaving the knife in, I take a step back to see cerebrospinal fluid leaking from his ears. Now *that* makes me smile. Maybe I'm a sick bitch, but nothing brings me more joy than making him hurt, just like he hurt me. Maybe stabbing him through the eye didn't make me happy because it was too anticlimactic compared to all the suffering he inflicted upon me.

I step back and begin to turn away when Damien says, "That's my girl." I twist back toward him and smile.

Zayne gets closer until his front is flush with my back and says, "*Our* girl."

I look back and forth between them, very, *very* confused. Damien looks pissed, his lips thinned. Zayne? He looks fucking giddy, like he enjoys pressing Damien's buttons. Nothing new there.

With a frown on my face, I open my mouth to say something but swiftly close it. I don't have time to figure this shit out right now. I need to find the twins.

"Where's the twins?"

"The men who came here with me have them," Damien replies.

I don't trust anyone enough to leave them alone now, and needless to say, they will never trust another man again. Not after what they just went through. I want to ask them what happened, how he hurt them, but I also don't want them to have to relive the whole thing.

"So where are they?"

"Outside in the car."

My anxiety spikes until it's hard to breathe, the tight feeling in my chest returning with a vengeance. "Where is the fucking car, Damien?"

Zayne sighs, "Side of the house, baby." I know exactly where that is because they used it to get me to that fucking party. I walk back to the hallway as quickly as I can, which is probably slow as fuck since my entire body is throbbing. I guess the heroin is wearing off, which I'm a little afraid of.

I'm almost at the door, about to open it, when I'm suddenly

yanked by my hair into a room with an open door. I scream as loud as I can, and I hear the thumping of boots as Zayne and Damien run to me. Someone has my back to their front, and it's a smaller frame. So it can't be a man.

Damien and Zayne both stop in their tracks abruptly when, suddenly, a gun is pressed to my temple. Damien also raises his gun, pointing it at the person behind me. I breathe in slowly, trying to keep calm, yet I can't deny that my heart is racing. I can hear the thumping in my ears, the beating erratic. I might just pass the fuck out.

"Drop your gun." My mother's voice is the one that belongs to the woman behind me, but that can't be right. She wouldn't do this to me. I don't believe she would after how she acted the last time we talked. "Or I will kill her right here."

"You won't," I whisper, my stomach dropping. Would she, though? "I'm your daughter."

"You're no daughter of mine."

Tears prick my eyes, and I look at Zayne, with his stony expression. Although, he's not looking at me, he's looking at her. Damien begins to lower his gun, but I yell, "Don't do it!"

My mother digs the barrel of the gun deeper into my face, and I whimper. Damien tenses at the sound, his hands repositioning on his own gun and his grip so tight his knuckles are white. He raises the gun back up.

"Damien," Zayne growls. "You're going to get her fucking killed. There's not many options here."

I beg Damien to kill her with my eyes, and he shakes his head. I don't give a shit if I'm in the way. I want her dead. She says I'm not her daughter. Well, she's no mother of mine either, so she can rot with Michael too. He shakes his head again.

"Please," I whisper, "Kill her."

My mother laughs behind me and shifts her body. Damien hasn't lowered his gun this whole time, and when she keeps laughing, he shoots. The ringing in my ears makes me clutch my head and groan as I drop to my knees. Damien and Zayne both run to me and pick me up from the ground. When I look back at her, she has a hole in her forehead and blood pooling all around her.

Damien opens the side door and holds it for us while Zayne helps me walk out. I turn around to look at my house of horrors with disgust, but at least I'll never have to come here again. Looking back at it makes me shiver, remembering everything that happened there. I want it destroyed.

"Anyone else in there that we need to get out?" Damien asks the men waiting in front of a white van.

The girls that were in there with me are in the back of it, and I feel relief coursing through my body. I look around for the twins, and they're in a different car—a Kia.

"Hallie?" Damien asks, "Anyone else in there?"

Suddenly, I remember Brittany. My chest tightens again, a knot forming in my throat, and tears spill from my eyes.

"Baby, what's wrong?" Zayne asks me, but I can't reply as the sobs wrack my body. He pulls me in and hugs me tightly, and even though it hurts, I find comfort in the pain.

"Brit-t-tany was here with me. She's dead."

"*What?*"

"When did this happen?" Damien interrupts. I try to breathe and calm down, but it's no use, I can't. Damien can tell because he comes to my side and pulls me away from Zayne, cupping my face gently and looking at me. "I need to know what happened, love."

"A few days ago?" I sniffle, "I don't know, Damien. I've been out of it the entire time. We tried to escape, and they—" I start to sob again, a broken sound that I don't even recognize. "Killed her."

"How the fuck did this even happen? How did she end up here?" Zayne asks as Damien begins to hold me close to him, my head on his chest, his scent in my nose. It makes me a little dizzy when the coconut and sea salt invade my senses, but it feels like home.

"I called her before I went to my hotel, or maybe after I was there… It doesn't matter. The point is I told her to run, to get out of Texas. I guess she didn't get very far."

"I'm sorry, baby," Zayne says and comes to me, kissing my forehead.

Damien stays silent for a beat, then tells Zayne, "Please, go wait in the car. I have one more thing to do."

"Alright."

"You too, Hallie," he tells me with a somber expression. "I don't want to put you in danger."

"I'm staying," I tell him through gritted teeth, although I don't know what he has planned, regardless.

Just when I think he's going to tell me no again, he nods. He takes out a box of matches from his pocket and lights one, then throws it on the ground at the edge of the house. The flames erupt quickly, rising taller and taller before our eyes. We take a few steps back to not get burned, and the flames engulf the house. I turn toward Damien with tears in my eyes again. He did this for *me*. He came for me. That has to mean something, right?

I grab his face roughly and pull him down toward me, standing on my tiptoes to reach him. When my lips meet his, he's stiff and unmoving, but when I brush my tongue against his lower lip, he readily opens for me. Damien pulls me close to his body, his hand on my lower back, and thrusts his tongue into my mouth. I don't care that it burns, that my lip hurts where it's busted, or that I'm most likely bleeding right now. Our tongues are warring with each other, and I win, tangling it with his.

He pulls away first, leaving me slightly disappointed, and opens the car door for me. However, when I get in the car and the twins hug me, I forget about everything else.

I got out.

We got out.

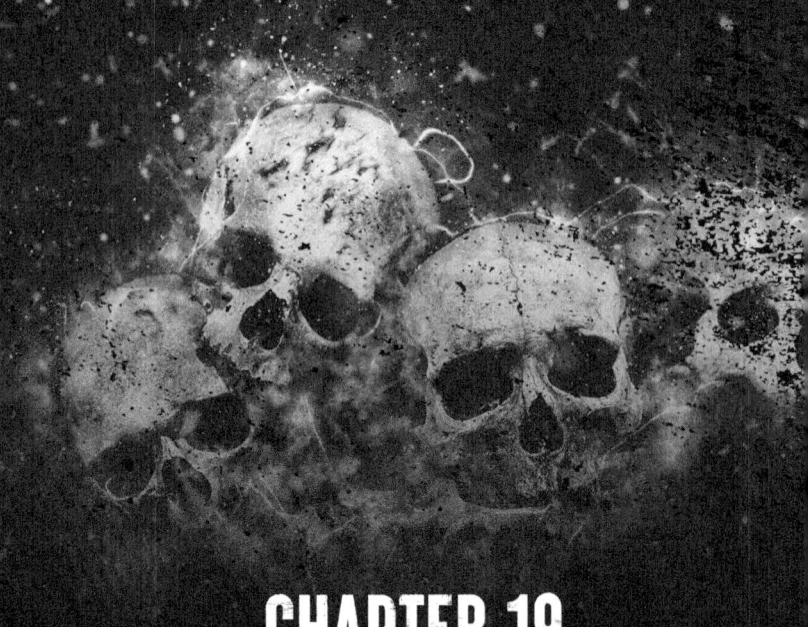

CHAPTER 19

Zayne

I can't believe I finally have her back. Being without Hallie is like trying to breathe without lungs, staying alive without a heart beating in my chest. Every moment of being without her has been agony for me. Even when I had a distraction, it was never enough to keep my mind off her.

Now that we're in the car and on our way to the border, it feels bittersweet. We're finally leaving, and I couldn't be gladder. Mexico will always be a fucking nightmare for me, no matter how much time goes by. There's no way I could ever forget the horrors I lived in this country, and I would rather die than come back.

Hallie is quiet in the back, rubbing the woman's back on one side, and on the other side, the guy sleeps on her lap. They seem to feel safe with her, and I wonder how much she has cared for them if they seem to trust her this much. Judging by how she looks right now, I'd go on a limb to say she gave herself over for them. Or maybe she didn't have a choice. All I know is that the cuts on her face and lip, her swollen eye, her bruised body, and her dislocated shoulder tell a story of how she spent most of her time. I can't think about everything else that happened at the moment. I know it might be selfish of me, but I also need time to process. She's never been the kind of person to give up; that's always been me. Was this another act of bravery? Did she refuse something, and that's why they tortured her? Knowing Hals, it's entirely possible.

Damien is driving at a steady pace to not raise any suspicions. I personally don't think there's anyone else following us, especially since they wouldn't know about all the people that just died in that house yet. All the bodyguards were taken out, and so were the guests.

What pisses me off is that Damien's father's men never showed up. We would've never made it out if it weren't for Diego and Armando helping us. There's no way I could've taken out all the guards while Damien shot everyone else, without one of us getting killed. It would've been a colossal failure. But these guys came through, and that's all that matters to me. As for the guy sitting next to me... well, that's a different story.

His expression is somber as he drives, and I almost want to pat his shoulder. I know he would hate it though, so I refrain. It's funny how much we hated each other not too long ago, yet now it feels like we can actually get along. We haven't been fighting, and even though I felt a surge of jealousy and rage when I saw him kissing Hallie outside the car, I knew to stay back and shut the fuck up about it. Pressuring her right now isn't going to make anything better, mainly when she was the one who kissed him. I saw it—her—grabbing his face. He stayed still for a moment. It wasn't him. I can't hate him for it. All I can do is hope she sees that I'm doing this for her and that she gives me a chance to stay in her life.

"Are we going to be okay?" I whisper to Damien, leaning in so hopefully Hallie doesn't hear me. "Those men never showed up to the house."

He looks at me briefly, "I'll make this happen."

I nod because I don't want to have a conversation about this and make her nervous if she hears. At this point, I trust Damien enough to know he will not only keep her safe, but he'll also get us back to the United States.

The border checkpoint is not at all like I envisioned. It's almost like trying to go into a military installation. Multiple lanes that seem never ending greet us as we cross the bridge, and I bet this shit would be packed during the day. As I look around, barbed wire lines the sides of the border where the bridge ends, closer to the checkpoint gates.

Damien seems to know exactly which lane he's going to, and I steel myself for the chaos. What if we don't make it through? What happens to us then? Will I be recognized if we're sent somewhere to wait for deportation? My hands start to visibly shake, and my legs do too. He reaches across the console and grabs my arm, squeezing it once in reassurance. "Chill." He tells me.

I look back at Hallie once he lets go, and she watches me with narrowed eyes, her gaze going back and forth between us. She doesn't have time to ask any questions though, because right as she opens her mouth, it's our turn at the checkpoint.

"Time to be quiet," Damien tells us, and we agree. "I need to see where we stand with them."

He lowers the window halfway, and there's a white man with dark hair and blue eyes with his hand extended toward the window. "Passport and vehicle registration."

"Red," Damien replies, and the man looks around nervously. "What did you say?"

"*Red.*"

The man steps back. "Lower all your windows."

Now I'm really fucking fidgeting, and I don't want to admit it, but I'm scared as fuck. This man doesn't look like he's going to help us. In fact, he seems like he's going to turn us in. A Mexican man approaches the vehicle from behind him and tells him something. The white man—Jacobs is his last name according to his name tag—turns to talk to him. They spend about a minute conversing, and I look back at Hallie, who looks just as scared as I feel.

"It's okay, love," Damien says in a low voice, and a tinge of jealousy fills my insides. Calm the fuck down, you told him to share. *You.* "We're going to get through. That's my guy right there."

Jacobs leaves, going inside some kind of building, and the other man comes to the driver's side window. "You can put your windows up," he tells us calmly. "You're D, aren't you?"

"Yes."

"I was told it would only be three people."

"Impromptu change of plans." Damien says slowly, "These people were kidnapped along with my wife."

What now? *Wife*? Who the fuck does he think he is?

"Is that true?" he asks Hallie.

"Yes, sir," she replies, and I want to smash Damien's face into the steering wheel. If anyone is marrying her, it's *me*. We've talked about it a million times.

The man looks around. "Show me the registration so this doesn't look suspicious."

I get the registration out of the glove compartment and hand it over to Damien, who then gives it to the man. He looks it over for thirty seconds, I'm assuming pretending to read it over, and gives it back.

"You're good to go."

"Have a good night," Damien says, although I can tell it's forced. Hopefully, we will never have to do this again. Although it's safe to say the United States is equally dangerous for us right now.

We're waved through and cross the border, but the *Welcome to the United States* sign doesn't make me feel better. It just feels like a bad omen. Everyone is silent in the car, except for the twins stirring. When I look back in the mirror, they appear very confused. Hallie soothes them, and I can't help but think about how great of a mother she would be. We've always said we didn't want kids, and I've never wanted them. Not really. I'm an addict with bipolar disorder, and Hallie is well…she's Hallie. So, it didn't feel like it could work out. But now, everything feels different.

"Where are we going?" the man in the back asks.

Hallie shushes him softly, "We're going to go find someone to help you both."

Oh fuck. If we didn't want to give ourselves away before now, only we indeed will if we stop by a police station. Then again, if we don't and the twins are discovered with us, we'd be accused of kidnapping. Yeah, no. No fucking way.

"We'll find a station," Damien assures her.

"Not in El Paso, please. I want to be as far from the border as possible."

"Okay, babe."

I can't help myself, my head whips toward Damien, and the little bitch smiles. *Fuck. Him.* He knows exactly what he's doing. Then again, I can't necessarily complain because I've been calling her baby and shit. So I guess I'll rein it in.

After about an hour of driving north, Damien pulls into a police station parking lot. Hallie is sniffling in the back, and the twins are crying and holding onto her. My heart squeezes in my chest for how she must be feeling; all fucked up physically and now emotionally as well. She clearly has formed a bond with them.

"Please don't leave us," the guy pleads.

"You're going back to your family, the one missing you both and looking for you."

"We don't want you to go!" the girl tells Hals, her eyes welling with tears.

"It's not safe, Abby," she tells them. "They will try to find us again. You need to go with your family somewhere no one will follow."

They begin to cry, well more like sobbing, and Damien turns off the car. Hallie embraces both of them tightly, and they cling to her.

"Come on," Hallie says, "let's get you back to your family."

Damien gets out of the car and opens the back door for them to step out, then I get out as well and follow them into the building. It makes me nervous to step into a police station as if somehow they will figure out everything that transpired in Mexico just a few hours ago. I bet they'd be suspicious of why Hallie looks like that too.

The police station is empty save for a woman at the front desk, and she asks what we need. Hallie tells her that the twins had been kidnapped. How they need to find their parents, which then leads to the woman calling someone on the phone. Not even a minute later, a sheriff comes to the lobby and asks her and the twins to go back with him to his office.

We're somewhere in bum-fuck New Mexico, and the chances of anyone knowing how to contact those twins' parents feel close to none. I won't argue with Hallie; we can't be caught with them if anything happens. It hurts Hals, though, I can tell.

She cooperates and walks to the back with him, but when Damien and I try to come with her, the man raises a hand to stop us and shakes his head no. Now I really am nervous. Hallie looks like shit, and so do they. If she gives them the real story, that they were kidnapped together, her wounds will make it believable. I guess that's the only bright side of this. Her credibility won't be put into question.

Damien and I wait an hour in the waiting room, sitting beside each other, our legs shaking from nerves. We don't talk to each other, shit, we don't even look at each other. I think we're both so afraid of how this will go that we just have nothing to say. After the hour is over, Hallie comes out alone, sobbing. Damien and I both get up at the same time and come to either side of her.

"What happened in there, love?" Damien asks her, and she cries harder.

"There was a missing person's report for both of them. Their parents have been contacted."

"Then why are you crying, baby? This is good, right?" Hallie looks at me like she wants to hurt me, and I shut my mouth.

Damien interjects, knowing I'm about to get fucked up. "Let's go, Hallie," he tells her with finality, "We need to get away from this place."

Hallie looks back at where the twins are still with the sheriff, and tears stream down her face. "Goodbye," she whispers.

The walk to the car is silent except for Hallie's sniffles. The air is thick enough to choke us, and I have so many questions I don't see her wanting to answer. I open the door and she gets in the back seat, not sparing me one glance. There's something different about her. Not overall, but just little things here and there I've noticed over the last few hours that make me feel like something is wrong. Other than the paleness settling over her face and the sweat glistening on her forehead, it's not quite obvious. If she felt like something was wrong, she would tell us. Right? I think she would, but I've come to the conclusion that I'm wrong quite often nowadays. I just hate that she's pushing me away.

"I'll drive," I offer Damien. "Just tell me where we're going."

Surprisingly, he nods. I thought he'd tell me no, but he must be exhausted. Neither of us got much sleep last night between being anxious about today and talking about dumb shit. At least we can talk like normal people now, though.

I catch the keys when he throws them, and he chuckles. I bet he thought they'd hit me in the face. He would've never let that go. "We have a twenty-nine-hour drive to Canada," he says, and I pause mid-step. "Drive for a few hours until you get to the New Mexico state line, and once you do, we need to get a hotel. I don't want to risk us being back in Texas to stay the night."

"Sounds good." Anything to stay out of that fucking state.

Just when I'm thinking we're getting along, he doesn't join me after we get in the car. Of course not. Instead, he goes to the back to sit with Hallie. *Motherfucker*. It's no wonder he wanted me to drive. Although I'm fuming, I don't want to stress Hallie out, so I don't say anything. That's not to say I won't cuss him out when we have some one-on-one time.

I pull out of the parking lot and get on the highway. Thankfully, we have enough gas in this piece of shit to get us to the New Mexico state line all the way up by Colorado. The downside—I know we need a new car to get us to Canada if we want to make it there. No fucking way this car will get us halfway to the place we need to get to. But also, what if someone recognizes it from Mexico?

I try to clear my mind as I drive through the deserted towns—it's fucking weird. An eerie feeling settles in my stomach, like we're being watched. We just got here so that can't be right, yet I can't help but be paranoid. I need fucking meds before I spiral again. It's not my fault I'm crazy. All I know is that if I don't get help now, it'll be tough to get me back in line, and Damien will abandon me. He will also convince Hallie to do so. This isn't about the cartel anymore. If I die, I die. However I can't live without her. If she willingly leaves me again, I won't survive it, and if he convinces her to, I will kill him with my bare hands. Or at least attempt to.

The roads have no damn lights to illuminate my way, and this car is so old—I fucking hate this damn piece of junk, but at least it's driving so far—so I have to manually go from low beams to high beams and vice versa. I guess I've been spoiled by my car for too long. Unfortunately, the next car will still have to be modest, which is sad as fuck, but hopefully, it's new and with more specs than this. Maybe I shouldn't be complaining in the first place, considering I'm jobless and have no belongings as of now. Also don't have any money, so there's that.

I look at Hallie from the rearview mirror and see her and Damien whispering to each other, their faces close together. I try to force myself to glance away, but my eyes are glued to them when he kisses her. Fuck. I want to swerve us off this damn road just so he can't have her. Maybe this whole situation is a mistake. I don't know if I can do this; share her. Jealousy has always been my most major flaw, and I've never been able to overcome it. For Hallie, I'd do anything though. Clearly.

Damien and I make eye contact, and he smirks, but drops it when I narrow my eyes at him. I think there's an unspoken communication between us presently. I told him to cut the shit, and he said yeah, okay. As he should. A full-blown competition is not what she needs from us right now, and personally, I'm not insecure about my dick, so there will be no measuring contest here.

Hallie, on the other hand, doesn't look at me. I think she's ashamed of what's happening. Going from one to the other, being affectionate. I'm not sure whether it's due to what I just went through or because I'm trying to put Hallie first, but I will say that a few months ago I would've had an aneurysm if she pulled this shit in front of me.

I focus back on the road so I don't kill us all since there are no lights out here. Within minutes, I hear Hallie's soft breathing. She's sleeping, my angel—the love of my life. I can't believe I get to see her again. After everything we've both been through, it feels surreal to even be out of that hell hole.

The rest of the drive is quiet. Damien isn't sleeping, but he's also not talking to me. Honestly, I prefer it this way. There's nothing either one of us can say to make this less weird or awkward. I suggested the whole sharing, but now that I'm actually doing it, it feels very different from what I envisioned. I knew I'd feel jealous, but my possessive side is screaming at me and the rational side is trying to keep my monster caged in. Maybe that's progress. At least I'm keeping myself in check and having some self-control.

My body begins to feel heavy and relaxed, and I'm thankful when Damien tells me to find a hotel since I've been nodding off more times than I can count. I'm fucking beat, and I can't wait to go to sleep. I pull into a parking lot that doesn't have that many cars in it but still enough that you can trust the establishment. It definitely doesn't look as questionable as the places we were staying in Mexico. Anything we find here will more than likely be better. Even the ugliest motel.

I park right in front of the entrance, closest to the doors but not the handicapped spot. Once the car is stopped, Hallie begins to stir. Damien extricates himself from her hold and scoots up on the seat closer to me.

"She doesn't look so hot right now," he whispers, and I look back at her. She looks like shit. I wince at the sight. What the fuck is wrong with her? "I'm going inside to check in since I have my fake ID."

"I'll try to figure out what's wrong with her." Damien rolls his eyes in the most condescending gesture he's ever directed at me, like I'm fucking stupid and can't figure shit out on my own. "Don't fucking look at me like that again, motherfucker. I think I know a thing or two more than you about what's wrong with her."

"Oh?"

"She's detoxing."

"Fuck." He breathes and wipes a hand down his face. "I'll be back."

Turning around, I observe Hallie for a minute. She honestly doesn't look good right now. How the fuck is she even sleeping? Her face is the palest I've ever seen,-she looks like a damn ghost. Although she's deep asleep, she's shivering and shaking.

"Hallie." I reach out to touch her, and when I make contact with her skin, it startles me. She is burning the hell up. "Baby, wake up."

"Hmm?" Hallie stirs, stretching her arms above her head and making a sound between a groan and a moan.

"What did they give you, baby?" I ask her softly, hoping her headache isn't too bad. "What did they make you take?"

"H," she whispers, lifting her sleeve and showing me the track marks on her arm. "Something else I don't know. Maybe Fentanyl."

There are easily ten of them, probably even more. "No," I reply, shaking my head. *Not her.* Anyone but her. I can't bear to see her going through this just like I have. I don't want her to be an addict like me. She doesn't deserve this; she didn't do it to herself.

"I'm sorry." Her voice is hoarse, and I can't understand why the fuck she's apologizing right now. "I understand everything now."

I know what she's referring to. My addiction. My relapses. My behaviors. "It's in the past now, baby. There's nothing to forgive. I don't blame you for how you acted. That was all *my* fault. None of this is yours."

"I should've taken you up on the offer to leave together."

"We wouldn't have made it." I smile softly at her as she shivers again, and my heart physically squeezes in my chest from how much it hurts to see her going through a pain I know so well. "Damien is the only one who can keep us alive."

She chuckles, "You're not wrong."

"I just want you to know something, Hals," I tell her, emotion clogging my throat. "No matter what has happened between us, I still love you. I don't care about any of it. I'll leave it in the past. If you give me another chance, I swear I'll do right by you this time."

"Really?" Hals asks in disbelief. "You still want me after everything that happened? I'm used up. Disgusting."

Tears spill from her eyes and trail down her cheeks, getting in the cuts. It looks fucking painful, but her expression doesn't give away her feelings. I wipe her tears with my thumb and grab her arm, pulling her in toward me as gently as possible. She willingly gets closer, and I bring her wrist to my lips, her soft skin brushing against them. When I kiss her wrist, it takes me back to when we first met, when I first fell in love with her. I can still remember every detail from back then. I wish I could go back to the car ride when she was singing along in my car and looking like it was the happiest day of her life when she leaned out of my car window and let her hair blow in the wind.

When I look at her wrist, however, I see the brand on it. A tattoo with a name on it.

Michael.

Motherfucker.

How fucking dare he?

I take a deep breath, though, trying not to show emotion because I don't want her to think it's directed at her.

"I will never think that of you," I reply, my voice firm, leaving no room for argument. "You are the love of my life, Hallie. I will love you until my last breath. No matter what has happened."

"No one can love me this way, Zay," she sniffles, and I climb back there and sit beside her, soothing her. "Even I fucking hate myself."

I will not let her go down this downward spiral. There's no way I can watch it happen before my own eyes and not intervene. I'm still nervous about what happened to me and how to bring it up, but there's no time like the present. Maybe she needs to feel like she can relate to someone, and that can be me. While I'm sure we didn't go through the exact same thing, I think both of us being kidnapped brought forth similar feelings.

"I'm used goods now, too, Hals," I inform her, turning her face toward me so I can look into her eyes, "Do you love me less?"

"What are you talking about?"

"They took me too, you know." Her lower lip trembles at that revelation, making me want to cry along with her. "When the car crashed, they took me to Mexico."

"No." She shakes her head. "What the fuck?"

"It's okay, baby," I reassure her, rubbing her back again. "I'm okay. But just know I will never love you less."

And it's not a lie. Nothing in this world will make me stop loving her.

Not one fucking thing.

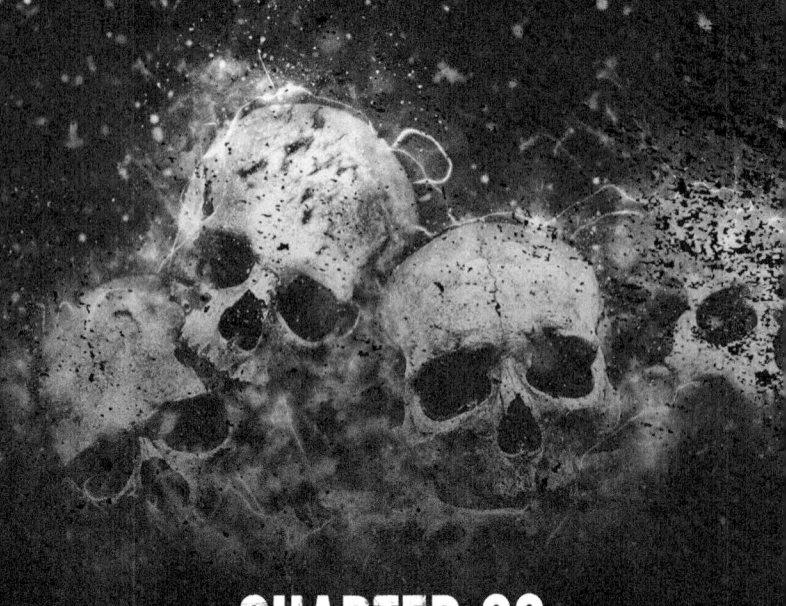

CHAPTER 20

Hallie

I never realized before this moment how unfair I've been with Zayne. This is fucking miserable. As I shake on the bathroom floor with my face on the cool tile, that's probably dirty as fuck, I try to think of all the times I told him I wouldn't be with him if he were on drugs. The fact that I didn't help either while he was going through withdrawals… I just walked away. I was such a bitch, and now he's here, rubbing my back when I throw up, sitting on the floor next to me as I shake and shiver, my teeth chattering, and the cold sweats enveloping my body. Who would've ever thought the roles would be reversed? I don't deserve him.

"You… don't have to do this," I tell him, my body shaking as I fight the nausea. "Please, go wait outside and get some sleep."

"No fucking way, Hals." Zayne replies, "You're not going through this alone."

Zay holds my hand, and I try to pull it away. Instead, he holds on tighter. I don't want him to see me this way. What if it triggers him? I don't even know what he's been through since the last time we saw each other, but from what he hinted at earlier in the car, it sounds like it was miserable. Did they give him drugs? I wonder if he had to go through this again.

The way my hands tremble is scary. It feels like the tremors are taking over my body, no matter how much I try to keep them still. He doesn't seem phased by it though, doesn't even pay attention to them. He rubs my hair with his free hand, making me feel slightly better. The problem is that no matter what I do, I can't drink anything. I feel weaker by the second.

There's a knock at the door, and Damien comes in, looking at me sadly. I know this is hard for him, seeing me in this light like he saw his mother. Forcing this onto him with his trauma feels wrong, so I've been trying to stay away from him. I want to spare him from this as much as I can.

"Is she able to keep drinks down yet?" Damien asks Zayne, looking away from me. There're tears in his eyes, but I can barely focus on them when my body fucking hurts. It feels like I got hit by a truck and barely survived it.

"No, and she's not going to. I can say that from experience."

"I have something to help her."

"Whatever works." Zayne nods, and Damien goes back to the room.

It feels like I missed something crucial between them. I've been left reeling at how calm they've been with each other. Not exactly friendly, but also not unfriendly. They used to hate each other, and part of me still feels like they still do, at least a little bit. However, they're oddly civilized for two men fighting over me for so damn long. How did they even meet up? Did they find each other by chance? I need explanations, desperately.

Damien returns with an IV and a saline bag, which I should've known he would have. He's always so damn prepared that it blows my mind. I wouldn't be surprised if he's prepared for a damn apocalypse. Although, it feels like that could be the case for us on any given day. I'm still terrified of them finding us and hauling me back to Mexico. Damien wouldn't let that happen, not willingly. I know that now. I just wish I had understood it back then. He went through hell probably to get me back. There's no way it was that easy to find me.

I feel self-conscious of the puke smell in the bathroom, and also the odor coming from me. Maybe it's just a girl thing, but I don't get how they're not gagging or thinking I'm gross. They may be just acting this way to make me feel more comfortable. Damien, however, even with all his trauma when it comes to heroin, manages to make me feel like he's not bothered by this. Deep down, I know he is. I saw his face when he first came in; he was hesitant and clearly distressed.

He still manages to insert my IV without me feeling a damn thing, then hangs the bag from a towel hook so it can flow well. Although he's giving it to me by gravity, he really doesn't have to calculate any drops per minute because he wants to slam me with the fluids. I'm probably dehydrated as fuck though, so I can't complain. Maybe after this, I'll feel better, but I don't have high hopes. I've heard that detox can take days, and I don't believe we have many days to stay here unnoticed. We have to move and fast. I just don't think I can tolerate being in a car right now. The mere act of turning my head makes me want to throw up.

"I hope you know I love you," Damien tells me as I close my eyes. "I just can't watch this happen. I hope you understand."

Tears prick the back of my eyes, but I don't nod because I don't want to throw up again. Instead, I whisper, "I understand." Although it sucks. I kind of saw this coming though, and I can't be angry for something he has no control over. Forcing him to be here for me when all it does is remind him of what he went through with his mother is out of the question.

Damien exits the bathroom, and Zayne lifts me slightly so he can stretch his legs. He positions my head on his lap and continues to rub my head when the bathroom door clicks closed. Tears stream down my face, and I'm grateful I'm not facing Zayne right now.

"Hals," he says softly, "he really does love you."

"Why are you telling me this?"

Zayne sighs like he's exhausted. I get it, so am I. "We found his mother, you know."

"What the fuck are you talking about?" The nausea is taking over again, gripping me tight. However this is important, so I breathe through it.

"She's dead." His tone is somber, almost like he cares. "She overdosed a few feet from me when I was with…" He stops abruptly.

"With?"

"It doesn't matter right now, baby." I turn my head to stare at him and feel the bile rising in my throat. "Just know he's going through something, and this is causing him pain. Don't blame him for it."

Even though I know it's not my fault she overdosed, I can't help crying. I should've been here for him. I should've never, ever, fucking left him the way I did. I *stabbed* him. Almost killed him. How can he even stand to be in the same room as me?

That thought throws me over the edge. My body starts to tremble, and I begin to get up from his lap. I'm struggling to crawl to the toilet because I'm weak, and I guess he notices because he shoves me toward it. Somehow, he manages to not rip out the IV as I puke and heave until there's nothing left in me, which wasn't much, to begin with. Then Zayne brings me a cup full of sink water to rinse my mouth. I swish the water and spit it out in the toilet before flushing, and then we return to the same position as before.

The embarrassment never comes back again, at least not in full force. That's the good thing about being with someone who has seen you at your lowest, you don't give a shit anymore. There's nothing else they could see about you that will push them away. Except maybe everything that happened in Mexico. I'll never talk about that. Not with Zayne and definitely not with Damien. It's not that I would prefer to speak with one over the other, but I think it's a sensitive topic for Damien, considering he was supposed to hand me over, changed his mind, tried to protect me, and I still managed to stab him and get kidnapped. So yeah, not the best idea to remind him of all of that if I can avoid it.

Silence settles over us, but it's not awkward. It's more peaceful. At least as much as it can be when I have body shakes and hot flashes. Zayne continues to rub my head as I close my eyes, playing with my hair in a way that makes me super sleepy. I'm afraid to sleep, however. My mind has always betrayed me in both my waking and sleeping moments. All that comes to mind right now are the twins, and it makes me emotional all over again.

Saying goodbye to them was the hardest thing I've done in a long time, even harder than saying goodbye to both of my men. It was heartbreaking to explain why I had to leave them and never see them again. Is this what it feels like to be a parent? My heart may as well have been ripped out of my chest when I left the police station. Even worse, they kept begging me to come with them instead of going home to their parents. That really got me thinking, and at this point I hope the attachment is from the trauma we suffered together and not because their parents are abusive. Now I regret leaving them behind. I should've stayed until they got picked up just to see what kind of people their parents are.

If their parents are anything like mine, then they're fucked. It makes me so damn sad I even had to do that, but if they're good parents, would I be any better than Michael for keeping them apart? For kidnapping them? No, I wouldn't be.

When my mom stopped me in that brief conversation before she walked away from me, the only encounter we ever had in the shit hole of a mansion, I thought it was because she cared. I had a glimmer of hope that maybe she would let me escape—how naive of me—but she let me down as she always has. So, I truly hope they will be okay for their sake and my emotional stability.

All I know for now is that I need to figure out my life. Navigating whatever is happening between me, Zayne, and Damien is proving to be more difficult than I thought. There's a palpable strain between us, and I don't know how we will survive together if we don't fix it. I'm not confrontational… but it feels like I need to be in this scenario.

The past several days in the hotel were absolutely awful as my body screamed in agony for just one more taste of heroin. I still feel guilty about delaying our trip by days now because of this, yet the guys keep telling me it's out of my control and not my fault. At least now I don't have to worry about a sling. My arm isn't healed all the way, but I can sort of use it now.

Damien also mentioned that while he and I have paperwork since he planned for us to leave the United States, Zayne has nothing yet. Some guy named Sean is apparently working on getting Zay a fake ID so we can cross the Canadian border. However, it could be a few days, maybe even a whole week, before we get anything back from him. This means, either way, we can't leave the country so we might as well take our damn time. Personally, I don't want to be in the car all day, but that's just me. I understand if we have to do it, but it doesn't feel like we're in that much of a rush right now.

It's almost night time now, the sun setting in a beautiful explosion of pastels and bright orange across the sky. It reminds me of Texas and Zayne, those days when we only had to worry about getting him sober. I'm not saying that's not a big deal or that it's insignificant in any way—it's not. However, running from a Mexican cartel and killing one of their bosses feels like a much bigger problem if you put them both on a scale. That's just me though. The cherry on top of the cake is that now we are all stuck together for who knows how long. What if Zayne wants to leave? Or Damien? I have no money. I know damn well Zay has no money. What the fuck do I even do if *I* want to leave? No. What the hell am I even thinking? I can't leave them again. They got me out of my prison in a foreign country, for fuck's sake.

"Can we stop?" I ask them from the back seat.

Damien looks at me from his place in the driver's seat via the rearview mirror. "Do you have to pee?"

"No." I sigh. "I'm just tired of being in this car. I want a damn bed."

"Don't be a brat," Zayne turns in the seat and tells me with a smirk on his face. "Say please."

Must I? I mean, my request is not that unreasonable. My body fucking hurts, and this car is small as fuck. My legs are cramped back here, and I am a tiny person. "Why?" I raise an eyebrow at him, and his eyes darken.

Maybe something is broken in my brain. The only explanation as to why I'm feeling a spark between him and me is that there's something very fucking wrong with me. There's always been an attraction, obsession, and love between us, and that probably will never change. I'm just questioning why I want him to pick me up and fuck me against a wall. Sex is a coping mechanism for me; it always has been. When shit hits the fan, I have sex. It's what I like to do. I fucking enjoy it. So why don't I feel an aversion after everything I just went through? Shouldn't the trauma incapacitate me?

The truth is it doesn't. Yes, the entire experience was traumatic. Between the drugs, the rape, and my best friend dying… It was too much. Only Zayne and Damien don't trigger me. They're my safe harbor. I just feel weird having to choose between them, and I know it will be a problem if I do—so I won't.

"Alright—" Damien interrupts, "How about we stop for the day then, babe?"

Zayne's eyes stay on me when I look at Damien, almost jostled at the fact that he called me babe. I know he's probably done it multiple times by now, but I'm just confused as to why he isn't rejecting me. Why is he being so damn nice? Doesn't he hate me? I would hate me. I already do.

"Yes, *please*."

Damien and I smile at each other, and when I look away, I see Zayne's eyes on me. They're narrowed into slits for a moment. Then he relaxes his face almost immediately. I try not to overthink it. There's just a lot going on at the same time, and I can't focus on everything at once or solve it.

"You got it," Damien replies, looking at the road now and no longer at me.

I'm genuinely surprised when he parks the car at a hotel that looks decent but is probably on the worst side of town for all we know. At least the cars don't look that bad. In fact, ours might be the worst one in the whole parking lot. Thankfully, there are only about five cars here besides this one.

"I'll be back," Damien says. "I'll get a room, and then we can all go inside, yeah?"

"Okay," I tell him, and as soon as he exits the car, Zayne locks all the doors.

I desperately want to know what happened to him. Where did he go after they took him? Who was he with? How did he get out? I can't quite put the puzzle pieces together because I don't have much information. Zayne, however, mentioned that Damien's mom was with him when she overdosed. So clearly, he was being kept somewhere against his will, and if Damien saw his mother die, then he must have been in that same place. Why, though? What was so important about that place that Damien showed up?

"Is this how it's going to be then?" I look up at him when he asks the question, and my belly somersaults when his piercing green eyes stare at me with such intensity it feels like I'm being burned from the inside out. "You won't kiss me, touch me, look at me?"

"I—"

"Don't give me your shit excuses, Hals." Zay shakes his head. "I fucking know better. This has nothing to do with what happened to you in the past month, but the fact that you don't know how to act—"

"You're right," I interrupt him. "I *don't* know how to act. You and Damien are confusing as fuck, and I won't choose between you."

Zayne smiles. "So don't."

"Huh?"

"Don't choose if you don't want to." He looks so serious it's a little scary. "Just don't push me away because you don't know who you want more. There's only one thing I know about all of this, Hals. I've never wanted you more than now. I can feel my heart breaking in my chest whenever you look away from me. Every time you ignore me."

"I'm sorry…"

"You're hurting me, baby." He taps his chest. "In here."

"You're right, Zay. If you can deal with me not being able to make up my mind, then I can stop being weird. I don't see this getting better if you and Damien always fight over me. I'm trying to avoid it as much as possible."

"See, baby," He chuckles. "This is where you're wrong. He and I have an agreement. We're not getting in the way of each other or making you choose. Whatever you want to do with us, is up to you."

"There's no fucking way you're friends now."

"Never say never." Zayne smirks. "Although, I don't think he believes we're friends."

"Do *you*?" I almost gasp at the thought.

"Maybe a little bit. He's really helped me a lot."

Friends? Them? Hell will freeze over before that happens, that's for fucking sure. I could never see them being friends, yet I could never see them getting along even remotely before now. They're weirdly civilized with each other, and I would even dare to say *friendly*. Apparently, when I think something could never happen, life likes to prove me wrong. That's been happening a lot lately, and I get it. Lesson learned. Now if it could just stop fucking me with no lube, that'd be great.

"Did you hit your head or something?" I ask him, still incredulous. "What the hell is going on?"

"You're more important than whatever he and I were doing before," Zayne replies, grabbing my arm abruptly and pulling me toward the middle console so we're face-to-face. "And I know you,

Hallie. You can't control that tight little pussy, so I won't force you to."

I stay very still as he brings my wrist to his mouth, giving it a soft kiss that makes me shiver. He smiles as he pulls away but doesn't let go of my arm. I feel the heat of his gaze like my skin is on fire. It's making its way south, and I don't know how I'm going to control myself if he keeps doing this to me.

"Kiss me, Hals," he begs. "Fuck me." This time he turns all the way around until he's on his knees in the passenger side seat. "I'll take whatever you will give me."

I'm weak.

I close the distance between us and pull on his hair lightly, then our lips meet. There's nothing gentle about it. It's urgent, needy, just like it's always been between us. I missed this. The rush he always makes me feel is like snorting cocaine, hitting me instantly. When I open my mouth to let him in, he sweeps his tongue into my mouth, and I twirl mine around his. Zayne's hands come to my face and pull me in, and when I thrust my tongue into his mouth, he moans. I almost disintegrate on the spot, and there's now a pulsing between my legs that needs relief. I haven't felt like this in way too long. I need it. I need *him*.

The driver's side door opens abruptly, and we pull away from each other. I launch myself back until I'm seated again, and Damien purses his lips. The guilt hits me full force when he turns off the car and opens my door. I can't even look him in the eyes. This is the problem; I can't do shit like this and face them after. It clearly bothers him, and I won't force it on him. I cannot do it.

How the hell do I fix this now?

Zayne and I get out of the car silently, and I swear the air is so thick it's hard to breathe. Damien opens the trunk, gets his luggage out, and then shuts it harder than usual. I flinch, and my heart sinks when he locks the car and walks ahead of us to go into the building.

A hand wraps around my arm and squeezes lightly, "It's okay, I promise. He just needs a minute."

"I don't know how to do this."

"I do," he reassures me. "Go do the same with him."

"Fuck, no," I huff. "What is wrong with you right now?"

"Hallie," Zayne sighs, "I lost you and thought I'd never see you again. Now that I have you back, I'm not letting go. I don't have time for jealousy right now. I just want time with *you*. Fuck him for all I care, if that's what you need to do. Just come back to me."

"You can't be serious." I shake my head and try to walk faster. I want this conversation to be over. Now. "I don't get you. Your jealousy has been over the top, and now you want me to fuck someone else?"

Zayne yanks me toward him abruptly until our chests meet. I peer back, and Damien is nowhere to be seen. We need to go back in before he leaves us, and we have nowhere to sleep. He's petty enough to do it, I just know it. Especially after what he saw in the car.

His fingers brush my hair away from my face, and I melt into him, despite everything wrong. Fuck my life. He has so much power over me that it's scary. "I almost died, Hals. And all I could think of was you." He almost died? How? What the fuck happened? "I just want you. However you'll let me have you doesn't matter."

"He doesn't feel the same, Zay." I cry, and tears start streaming down my face.

"Shhh." He kisses my tears away, and I close my eyes tightly. "Deep down, he does."

"So, what do I do?"

"Go to him tonight," Zay replies, and my stomach bottoms out.

He lets go of me gently, and I walk away and into the lobby. I can hear him walking closely behind me as I wipe my tears, and thankfully I see Damien waiting for us by the elevator.

Damien frowns when I make eye contact while I wipe my tears, but he doesn't ask me what's wrong when I reach him.

Instead, he pushes the button to go up in the elevator. It dings, and we all go in.

"I need to warn you," Damien says, and I tense. "All they had left were king bedrooms. So, I'll take the couch, and you two can share."

"It's okay," Zayne interrupts. "I can take the couch."

Damien looks at me briefly, then drops his head. "I'm good."

My heart breaks in my chest as we leave the elevator, and fresh tears stream down my cheeks again. It's like a fucking waterfall that can't be controlled, and the weakness makes me feel humiliated. Worse than that, he doesn't seem to care.

Damien taps the key card to the scanner on the door, and it buzzes open. I hold my breath when he groans, dropping his suitcase forcefully on the ground and kicking it out of the way. Why is he so mad? As we enter the room though, I see the problem.

There's no pull-out couch. In fact, there's no couch at all. Only one king bed takes up the entire room. It's tiny in here, with barely any space on either side of the bed. The only other thing in the room is a television mounted on the wall and a mini fridge.

"I guess we're all sleeping together, then." Zayne smirks, and it makes me want to punch him. Does he just want to aggravate him? Or is he really just clueless about what he's doing? No. Zay is not ignorant. He knows what he's doing.

"Hallie will be between us," Damien replies, visibly annoyed. "I won't be cuddling you in my sleep."

"I don't think you'll be cuddling anyone if the way you've been acting for the past ten minutes is any indication."

"You're right." Damien opens his suitcase and gets out a pair of boxers. "Now leave me the fuck alone. I'm taking a shower."

He slams the bathroom door, and I go sit on the edge of the bed, exasperation consuming me from the inside out. I don't know how to fix this anymore. Maybe this is a mistake, running away with them. I should go away on my own and avoid even more pain.

Footsteps draw me out of my thoughts, and Zayne walks over to the curtains to close them. The lights are dim in here, and for just a brief moment, I imagine fucking him on the bed. I shake my head, trying to dispel the image. Zay knows exactly what's going on as he leans against the wall with his arms crossed and grins.

"I can read you like a book, baby," he tells me. I kind of love it, not having to explain to someone everything I'm feeling. He's always felt like my other half because he understands everything I've been through. "But you're on the wrong side of the room."

"What do you mean?"

"Go in the bathroom and talk to him."

If I go to the bathroom, there won't be any talking. Then again, I could be wrong, considering he can't even look at me. Will he even talk if I go in there? Or treat me like shit again? I swear I can't take any more rejection than I've already received from him since I was detoxing. If I cry over him one more time today, I might just run out of tears.

"*Go*, Hals."

That snaps me out of it, and I get off the bed and walk toward the bathroom. Maybe he'd be more willing if he sees I'm coming to him. Damien did kiss me when we were leaving that house. Maybe that was just in the heat of the moment, when the emotions were heightened. Except it meant something to me. It felt like he cared, like he still loved me.

I take a deep breath and release it when the doorknob turns. He didn't lock it. He wants me to come in. That's what this means, right? He wouldn't have given me this opportunity if he wanted me to stay away. I take it, and I go to the bathroom. I'm surprised the door makes no sound, and I only open it slightly, enough to fit my body so that there's no gust of wind. I'm not brave enough to make myself known before he's out of the shower. We can talk after.

The lock is silent as I turn it, then lean against the door as my hands shake from nerves. Even though the water is running, it feels like I'm breathing so hard I will give myself away. But then I hear a groan, and I forget all about waiting. I stand on the other side of the shower curtain, closer to where I can watch him, and hear skin slapping. I stay very still to make sure I'm hearing this right, but when I hear his moan, I lose my composure and yank the shower curtain open.

Damien drops his hand, his thick, long cock standing at attention. I lick my lips, my mouth dry from how good he still looks. His body is carved from fucking stone. Capped shoulders, perfectly shaped chest, deep abs, defined Adonis belt. Goddamn. I want to take him in my mouth and make him see heaven.

"What the fuck are you doing?" I ask him, whisper-yelling. I'm hot all over and want to go in with him. Thankfully I'm bare now, having gotten razors from the store yesterday.

He gestures to his cock with one hand, but his facial expression is stony. "I don't think I have to explain this to you."

"You don't get to do this without me, Damien," I tell him as I start to drop my clothes. My shirt and bra go first, and he watches my face, refusing to look at my tits. When I drop my pants and underwear in one go though, he does look. I feel a sense of accomplishment when his eyes linger on my pussy, and he balls his fists. He's trying to restrain himself. I can tell.

"I can do whatever I want, Hallie."

"What? I'm not your love anymore?" I taunt, getting in the tub and pushing him out of the way until I'm under the spray of water. I close the curtain because I don't want to get cold, and when I take a step back his cock brushes against my ass briefly. I'm so fucking hot for him that it feels like someone put me in an oven, and I'm about ready to beg him until he fucks me. I won't lie, his rejection cuts deep. "You don't want me anymore?"

Damien looks away, and I have my answer. "You left me, Hallie."

"You kidnapped me, Damien," I reply. "How about we call it even?"

"It's about more than that."

I turn around and get close to him until his back is against the tiled wall, his cock fully erect and between us. I get so close it is pressed to my belly, and the urge to grab it almost takes over my body. "Tell me how to fix it, babe."

Damien grabs my tit forcefully, and it really fucking hurts, but I still let him. "You're a little fucking backstabber." My heart sinks as he pinches my nipple, and I gasp from that pain.

I remember how I stabbed his side with the knife, how slick it felt in my hand, and exactly how he dropped to his side. Truth is, I don't deserve his forgiveness, but I'm still selfish enough to want it because I want *him*. Something tells me he's not talking about that, though. It's about Zayne.

"How can I make you forgive me?"

His eyes flash, even as his expression doesn't change. "Pick *me*."

Fuck. That's the one thing I can't do, and of course he'd ask that of me. "No. I pick *me*." It's not what they want to hear. Shit, it's not even what I want to hear, but I won't be forced to decide. I have a feeling that once I do, everything will fall apart.

"Then I don't forgive you."

My heart hurts at those words, so I turn around and begin to wash myself, focusing on what matters the most. Yeah, he wants me to pick him. He won't forgive me until I do. That only means one thing to me, he still loves me. I'll break him tonight. I don't know how, but I want his cock, and nothing is stopping me from it. Not even him.

Once I rinse my body, I turn around and put my hands on his shoulders, running them down his chest and to his pelvis. Unexpectedly, he slaps my hand away. I'm persistent in any case. So instead, I grab his cock and begin to pump it hard and slow. His nostrils flare, as I go rougher. A little moan slips out and his hips buck against my hand, but he removes it again.

"You want this, Damien," I say with a hoarse voice. "Let me."

"No."

"Fine." I glance behind me. "Give me the showerhead."

Damien narrows his eyes at me but grabs it and hands it over. I keep my hands on him as I plaster my back against the wall and put my foot at the edge of the tub, spreading my legs. I know he knows what I'm about to do, but he doesn't move either way. I point the shower head toward my pussy, adjusting the pressure to make it stronger, and putting it right over my clit. Immediate pleasure floods me, and I close my eyes tightly as I feel the urge to rock back and forth. I rock my hips the way my body is screaming at me to do and open my eyes to see Damien staring. We make eye contact, and I drop my head against the wall as I feel the orgasm about to rush through me, my mouth opening on a gasp. Except he yanks the shower head away from me before I can finish and puts it back up where I can't reach it.

My pussy throbs with the need to come, and I groan. "What the fuck? I need to finish."

Damien stalks toward me angrily, closing the distance between us. His hand reaches behind me and grabs a hold of my hair, yanking my head back forcefully, aggressively. "You're fucking *mine*, Hallie."

He stares into my eyes, the blue being swallowed by the black of his pupils. "I don't belong to anyone but myself."

"That's where you're wrong, love." My insides melt all over again. He's calling me love again. His hand reaches between us, and two of his fingers find my clit, which he begins to rub forcefully. "You belong to *me*."

His fingers dig into my hips, and before I can process what he's doing, he drops to his knees. Damien's warm breath hovers over my pussy, and I press my thighs together. It's a physical need at this point for him to make me come.

"I told you to make men get on their knees for you, Hallie," He licks up my slit then kisses it. I grab onto his hair and pull him hard, trying to get him closer. He growls, "I'll be the first one to do it."

"Wait." I lick my lips, suddenly having doubts. "Get up."

Is this wrong of me? It feels like I'm playing games with his heart and mine at this point. What if I can't choose between them? I love them both. What's wrong with me? This is worse than it was before.

"Let me show you how yours I am."

At that, I look down at him. His bright blue eyes tell me a

million things he won't vocalize. I need you, I want you, I love you. There's no way to say it back, though, so I just spread my legs for him. He puts one of them over his shoulder, giving himself access to my pussy.

When he wraps his lips around my clit, I throw my head back and gasp. Damien sucks it slowly, softly, and I want it harder. I need more. "More," I beg. "Make me fuck your face."

Damien lowers himself even more and thrusts his tongue into my pussy, driving it in and out until my eyes roll to the back of my head. I reach down and rub my clit, wanting to come already, needing to.

He slaps my hand away and licks a path up to my clit. The way he devours it is like he's kissing me, practically making out with my pussy. His tongue is everywhere, and so are his lips. The hint of his teeth on my mound is slightly painful, yet it adds to the pleasure when he sucks my clit back into his mouth, then grazes it with his teeth as it comes out.

"Oh, *Damien*," I whisper. "Fuck, yes. Just like that." I try not to moan, but it's fucking impossible as he focuses on my clit, swirling his tongue around just how I like it. "Yes!"

I grab his head and push it harder into me, making him clutch onto my hips harder. His fingers dig so deeply and painfully I'm sure I'll have bruises in the morning, but I don't give a fuck. I want the pain.

He goes faster, harder, when he sucks on my clit as he makes me see stars. The white spots that dance around my vision brighten up when he grabs my ass roughly, and my moans get louder, closer together, as I feel the orgasm about to hit me.

"Damien," I repeat like a chant, "I'm right there."

His lips wrap around my clit again, and he pushes three fingers inside my pussy forcefully. My legs begin to shake, my knees buckling, while he holds me up with one hand on my belly and my leg over his shoulder.

"Make me come, baby. Fuck!"

With that, he bites my clit, and my orgasm detonates through me. I buck my hips fast on his face as he holds onto my clit with his teeth, then sucks it back into his mouth, prolonging the orgasm. I can hear myself panting as I fuck his face. When I finally feel myself coming down, relaxing, he puts me back in a standing position. Except I can't stand up. All I can do is slide down the wall until I sit in the tub, face-to-face with him.

I grab his face and kiss him. Long, deep, with lips, tongue, and teeth. I can taste myself on him, and it makes me want him even more. "Please, Damien." I don't know what I'm begging for exactly. He already gave me what I needed.

"If you're not mine, why did you come for me like that?" I *am* his. But I can't say that. I'm also Zayne's. "Why are you begging me so pretty to put my cock inside you?"

"Fuck me, *please*."

"Maybe later." He smirks. "If you're a good girl."

Damien's eyes drop to my tattoo, and the blue of his irises flare like someone set them on fire. He doesn't say anything about the branding, just turns around to leave and exits the bathroom.

I get up slowly as my legs still feel unsteady, then turn off the shower head. At least he left me a towel, but I don't have any clothes. In fact, I think I used all my clean clothes and underwear at this point.

I dry myself and wrap the rough towel around me, opening the door so I can maybe find something to wear. Damien and Zayne both do a double-take when they see me. Damien probably didn't expect me to come out in only a towel, and Zayne didn't because he knows what I did. Jealousy coats his features for a short moment before he forces himself to relax.

"I need something to wear," I announce, then begin to dig through Damien's suitcase. He doesn't stop me, not even when I bring one of his shirts to my nose and inhale deeply. "This one will do."

I drop my towel to the ground in front of them, it's not like they haven't seen all of me before, and put the shirt on. Then I walk to the bed and lie down in the middle, facing the window. Zayne pulls the covers back behind me, turns off his bedside lamp, and then joins me. He's not touching me yet, but I can tell he wants to. Honestly, I want to touch him too. He's only wearing boxers, basically close to nothing.

Damien stares at me for a full minute before he walks toward the only empty spot on the bed, right next to me, and turns off his light as well. It's awkward for a few minutes, and no one dares to move. I don't think I'm even breathing for fear of spooking Damien away. He might just sleep in the fucking car.

Zayne makes the first move, getting close to me, his hard cock pressing against my bare ass. I push back against him slightly, and he does it back to me. "I want that pussy, baby."

"I can't," I reply, and Damien still doesn't move. I hope he can't hear this conversation, but Zayne is quiet, whispering in my ear.

His fingers come to my pussy, and he rubs my come all over it, "Fuck, Hals," he breathes into my ear, and it makes me even hornier. "Be a bad girl for me." I turn my face slightly as I try to figure out what he means. "He wants you too."

Zayne pushes me toward Damien, and I go. It's not a difficult choice. This doesn't mean we have to fuck. I just want to cuddle and kiss him for a little while before bed. It sucks not feeling wanted, and he's been pushing me far, far away.

I run my fingers over Damien's face, tracing him from his forehead, down the slope of his nose, all the way down his lips and to his chin. He grabs my wrist, stopping me, but I get closer and take his bottom lip into my mouth. His hand comes to the back of my head and pushes me closer to him as his tongue meets mine. I moan low and deep and get on my belly to kiss him deeper.

Zayne clearly feels jealous because he touches my pussy, rubbing my clit with one finger as he thrusts two more into me. I moan louder as Zayne fucks me hard with his fingers, and I can hear my wetness.

Damien clearly doesn't like that, and he pulls me closer to him, kissing my neck and biting it hard when I moan again, "Shut the fuck up," he whispers. "You only make those sounds for me."

He hikes me up higher, trying to get me away from Zayne, but it only gives him easier access as I get on my knees slightly.

I think Zayne heard that because the next thing I know his breath is right between my ass cheeks, and he darts his tongue out to lick me there. His tongue then thrusts into my pussy, and he bites my ass cheek. He repeats the process a few times until I begin to push back into his face, trying to get his tongue deeper inside me.

Damien yanks my head back as I moan again, "Fuck me, Damien," I beg again. "*Please.*"

"Not right now, babe. I don't want him in the room when I do."

"So, let's go to the bathroom."

"*No.*"

Zayne pulls me forcefully toward him and spreads my legs wide, pushing the tip of his cock against my entrance. "If you don't fuck her, *I* will." He thrusts hard into my pussy, making me cry out.

"Damien," I say, "Please."

Zayne fucks me harder, pushing my face into the mattress until he smothers it. "Don't beg him while my dick is inside you, baby." His hand goes under me, and his fingers rub my clit, making my eyes roll to the back of my head. "I fuck you better anyway."

"Goddamnit," Damien growls. "Fuck this. You can't just fuck her in front of me on the bed we're all sharing."

My stomach bottoms out at his words, and Zayne just fucks me harder as if he's taunting him. Damien doesn't get off the bed, though. Instead, he sits up and looks right at me. I can't even imagine what I look like to him right now, getting fucked by another man. The guilt begins to creep in again, except Zayne rubs his fingers faster over my clit, and I forget what's happening. My mouth opens on a gasp when Zayne moans and that seems to make Damien snap.

Damien grabs me by my arm and pulls me hard until I'm on his lap, effectively getting me away from Zayne. I tighten my legs on either side of his waist, refusing to move. Now that I'm here, I want him to see that I need him. He lets go of my arm slowly and sighs, briefly looking up at the ceiling. I can't tell if he needs a minute to compose himself or if he's already done with me.

I pull the shirt off over my head and throw it on the ground, but I don't know exactly where since it's dark in here. All I see is whatever is right in front of my face, which happens to be this beautiful man. Maybe I should feel bad that I'm begging him in front of Zayne. It's probably hurting his feelings, but at the same time, he told me to. He's somehow okay with this.

"Damien," I whisper, rubbing my pussy over his abs. "Look at me."

He doesn't, and I support my weight on his pecs, digging my fingernails into him. I continue to rub myself on him, rocking back and forth until I moan. His hands come to my hips, his fingers digging deep into my skin, and he begins to help with the motion.

"Yes, love," he whispers, "Fuck."

"I want you," I tell him, sliding myself lower toward his cock. I make it to it and lift myself slightly so it can be under me, then glide back and forth on it. "Stop playing games with me and fuck me already. We both know you're dying to."

"You're very demanding lately." He reaches between us, and I get on my knees, lifting up and off him slightly while he grabs his cock and directs it to my pussy. I slam down on it, moaning when it's all the way in. "Don't worry, I'll fuck the attitude out of you."

Damien slams his cock into me from underneath, fucking me from the bottom. I stay still as he drives in and out of me with so much force that I'm barely hanging on, and I fall forward until we're chest to chest. Even still, I don't do any of the work. I let him get this pent-up rage out of his system. I grab his face and close the distance between us, taking his bottom lip into my mouth and sucking on it. He moans when I do, then slaps my ass hard when I bite it. I gasp, and he does it again.

My hips buck of their own accord as I swivel slowly in figure eights, then faster when he stops fucking me from the bottom. I'm lost in my own little world, feeling the pleasure take over my body, and don't realize that someone else's hands are now on me too.

Zayne holds me down so I can't get off Damien, and I continue to move back and forth, biting Damien's chest from how good the friction feels on my clit. While Damien holds my face between both hands and brings my lips to his, Zayne traces my back hole with a wet finger and thrusts it into me. I moan when he drives it in deeper, and Damien tenses when he gets right behind me. I'm assuming their legs are touching because of where Zayne is positioned.

I don't think this is going to work. Any moment he's going to shove me off him and leave the hotel room. He's going to hate me for letting Zayne touch me while he's inside of me. Fuck, I can't even blame him for it. I'd probably be so angry if someone else was touching him too.

Zayne, however, doesn't seem to care about anything but putting two fingers in my ass. I hear the cap of something open, and then I jolt when something icy is rubbed between my cheeks.

"Wait," I say, trying to stop him. "We can't—"

Damien's hand wraps around my neck tightly, and I stop moving. "We are so perfect together, love." I try to breathe but can't, so I tap his arm. He doesn't let up. "I won't just let him fuck you. So, I'm fucking you too."

I shake my head quickly, trying to get him to loosen his grip, and he finally does, just enough to let me talk. "I don't think we should."

"Maybe not," Damien replies gruffly. It makes me wish I could see the expression on his face right now, but the angle isn't letting me. "But we will anyway."

He begins to top from the bottom again, and I stay very still when Zayne grabs my hips, trying to still me again. Damien gets the hint and stops, and I begin to get up to see what the hell is happening. Zayne pushes me back down though, and Damien wraps my hair around his fist, rendering me immobile.

"Let me see that pretty ass, baby," Zayne breathes as he pushes the head of his cock against my back opening. "Put it up for me."

The air whooshes out of my lungs when he enters me slowly,

stretching me as he begins to fuck me with shallow strokes. "Damien," I cry out, "Are you sure?"

Zayne stops his thrusts, leaving everything up to the blond God under me. I'm genuinely surprised, as Zay isn't exactly patient enough to wait for consent. Not really. He doesn't usually ask for it.

"Quiet, Hallie, or I'll fucking gag you." Damien pulls my hair that's wrapped around his fist, and tears spring to my eyes, one falling on his chest. "Be a good girl and let us fuck you."

I whimper, and Zayne chuckles. Then he grabs my hips and begins to drag me back toward him while I push forward to feel the friction on my clit. I grip Damien's shoulders and suck on one of his nipples, and he moans, letting go of my hair to grab my face. I bite down gently and let him tug me away.

"*Fuck*," Zayne says from behind me, his fingers digging deep into me as his pace increases. He fucks me harder until my entire body is jolting on top of Damien.

"Faster, babe," Damien begs, "This feels good, but give me *more*."

I plant my knees on the mattress and begin to rock back and forth faster, and the way Zayne is fucking me makes me go even harder with how he's rocking my hips already.

"Oh, God," I cry out loudly, and I'm sure the entire hotel probably heard. "That feels amazing." And it does. I've never felt so full in my entire life, and the combination of both of their cocks hitting deep inside of me, as well as the friction on my clit is already bringing me close to an orgasm. I never thought fucking them like this—at the same time—would feel this damn good.

"Look at me, Hallie," Damien says, grabbing my face until I'm staring straight into his eyes. I can't see their color since it's so damn dark in here, but the expression I see almost stops my heart. He looks like he's in heaven and hell simultaneously, and I want him to only feel good right now. "I want you to look at *me* when you come."

Zayne puts some of his weight on my back, hitting deeper, and I groan as I rub harder on Damien's pelvis. "Oh, baby," I tell him, then grab his face when I feel the familiar tremors taking over my body. I suck on his bottom lip, moaning loudly and crying out. Damien bites my lip hard as I moan, and he begins to push me against Zayne, and they work together to make me come. The faster he pushes me against Zayne, the harder the friction on my clit becomes, and the deeper Zayne hits inside me. My eyes roll to the back of my head, my toes curl. Everything is heightened. Their hands on my body, their dicks inside of me, it all feels like too much and not enough.

Damien pulls me up slightly until we're face to face, and Zayne follows, chasing us. I'm panting, moaning, groaning. The sounds coming out of me aren't familiar to my own ears; it feels animalistic. This feeling of urgency, pure fucking desperation blooms inside of me, and with one last thrust and Damien's eyes looking into my own, the orgasm detonates me from the inside out.

I scream so loud Damien kisses me to muffle it, hard, wet, sloppy. Teeth and tongues and lips. Hands everywhere. Zayne's balls slapping against me. It's an intense overstimulation, and I fucking want *more*.

My body shakes on top of him, and when I feel the aftereffects of the orgasm, he lets go of me. Zayne pulls me up against his chest, wrapping an arm around my waist as he pounds into me, and Damien does the same. They hold onto me, gripping me wherever they can reach, as their groans and moans fill my ears. I'm a toy for them to play with, a hole to fill, and I'm more than happy to oblige.

"Oh my fucking God," Damien groans, his panting echoing through the room as his hips slap against me. "Hallie, yes!"

Zayne slows down as if savoring the moment, and I drop my head on his shoulder. His moans in my ear make me clench, and both of them moan louder. "I fucking love you, baby," Zayne whispers for my ears only, and he moans again when I push my ass against him, "Oh, baby, I'm about to come."

The moans crescendo again and, this time, Damien holds on to my thighs for dear life, and Zayne's hand comes to my neck, squeezing me tightly until I see spots dancing across my vision. Both of them come at the same time. I can feel them emptying inside of me, their cocks somehow following the same rhythm.

Tears begin to fall down my face as Zayne pulls out, slumping over on the bed right next to us, and I just stay in place. Damien pulls me down gently as I begin to cry in earnest, and he rubs my back.

"You're going to hate me, aren't you?" I whisper to him. This is a conversation I don't want Zayne to be a part of.

"Never," Damien replies.

Deep in my heart though, I know. This could never last. They won't share me, not really. There will always be a competition between them, a rivalry that won't die, and if I don't put a stop to it, that means I'm feeding the chaos too.

Only I can't choose, it's not possible right now. I betrayed them both, left them both, and I *love* them both. How do I choose one and not the other? Whatever I do. I know one thing: I will never get over the one I walk away from, and that won't be fair to whichever one I choose.

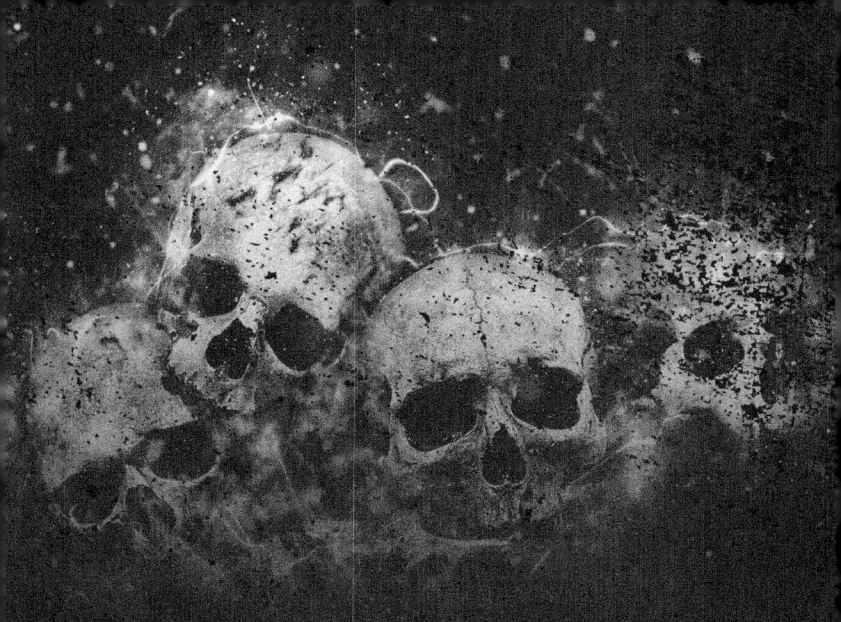

CHAPTER 21

Damien

It's been two nights at the hotel, and the plan is to leave this morning. We've wrapped up some loose ends, have planned our route, and reserved an Airbnb this time, so we don't have to deal with having only one bed.

Never in my life did I imagine I'd *ever* come close to sharing Hallie, but I did. I'm not sure what got into me, maybe the fear of her letting Zayne fuck her in front of me. Hell, he already was. It's almost like he was trying to make me jealous and instigating me into going through with it. That asshole has no shame; he wants her as much as I do.

The only difference is that I'm better for her.

He's weak as fuck and will hand her over for an ounce of meth in a heartbeat. I'd never trade her for anything in this world—not even my mother. Hence, why she's fucking dead. I know I'm a selfish motherfucker, although it hurt me deeply to see my mother, dead, in a cage. However, it actually hurt me more to know Hallie was beyond my reach, suffering because of me.

That's why I felt so damn triggered when Hallie was going through withdrawals and looked like she was dying. Something about it reminded me so much of my mother, and I couldn't handle it. I fought so hard for so long to keep that time of my life hidden deep, never to be opened. Yet here I am, questioning all of my life choices because of one fucking drug. It's not Hallie's fault, I fucking know that. Still, it didn't take away that she was dependent on the same drug as my mother. The same substance that I despise the most.

Which takes me back to the guilt I feel every time I gaze at Hallie. I should've stayed away from her after I caught feelings, should've refused to do the job even before then, but I was selfish and wanted more time. More, more, *more*. The greed I feel for my little backstabber is astounding. I'll take whatever she gives, even a morsel of her love.

I'm well aware of how hypocritical it sounds for me to have told her I don't forgive her. It's not fair, yet I can't help feeling hurt. I have a scar on my ribs to prove how much she wounded me. Yes, I lied to her, deceived her even, but goddamn. After everything I've done for her, how I protected her, got her a new identity, and an opportunity to leave the country and start over, she'd see that she's the love of my fucking life.

But no, she wanted to make me her villain all along. Someone to blame for everything that went wrong. I take accountability for my actions; I fucked her over in a way. Nevertheless, she fucked me over too. So, excuse me if I'm a little sensitive about the way she left me, high and dry, with a throbbing side *and* blue balls. That was kind of shitty to use sex against me.

Now, she looks sad since the *incident*, and won't talk to either of us. The way she's acting reminds me of when we were staying in Breckenridge, and she was sleeping her life away with no energy or will to live. I hate to see her like this, knowing she can be so full of excitement and love, ready for anything life throws at her.

Seeing her in pain is like being in pain myself, and all I want is to make it better. Only she doesn't want that. In fact, she's isolating herself to the point that she won't let either of us near her. It's as if a switch has been flipped. Scary as fuck.

Whenever I ask her what's wrong, she says she's okay. That nothing is going on… Except I know better. All the smiles she freely gives don't reach her eyes, and there's no longer a spark in them. How did we get here? Is it my fault? Zayne's and I's fault? Did we fuck something up? I thought she'd be happy I shared her willingly. After the shit I talked, I decided to let it go and show her how much I love her, but maybe I was wrong. It's possible she doesn't want us to share her at all, and she just wants time to make up her mind.

Either way, I won't fault her. I'm willing to wait until she knows what she wants, even if it's not me. All I need from her is to stop giving me mixed signals. If she doesn't want this from me, from *us*, then she needs to say that.

Hallie comes out of the bathroom with wet hair and a towel wrapped around her torso. We're finally alone, yet I'm almost sure she wants nothing to do with me right now. I asked Zayne to go get us some donuts and breakfast, which are two different stops in town so I could have her all to myself for a little while. But of course, she spent most of that time in the shower, not wanting to face me.

"Hey, babe," I say as I walk toward her. Her whole body goes rigid. I stop in my tracks so she doesn't feel uncomfortable. "Hallie, I just need to know if we're okay. Are you upset with me? Was the other night too much?"

She finally looks at me. "No." Her quiet voice is hard to hear, but I read her lips. "I just—" A long sigh, "Didn't expect it."

"I didn't either." I nod, trying to reassure her. "Do you regret it?"

"No." That makes my heart sink slightly, only I don't know why. Do I want her to regret me? Him and I? Just him? "I'm just waiting for the heartbreak."

"Heartbreak?"

"I know you won't be able to look at me the same anymore." Tears gather in her eyes, and I take a couple of steps until I'm right in front of her, catching a lone tear with my thumb. "You hate me, don't you?"

"You're the love of my life, Hallie," I reassure her, and it's true. "I could never hate you. Not really."

"Are you going to leave me since I can't choose?"

I drop my hand to my side, staying still while looking at her. Although I don't say anything, she's already putting words in my mouth. Her face scrunches up as her cries fill the room, and her knees buckle. I catch her before she hits the ground, holding her to my body tightly.

Will I leave her if she can't choose? I don't know if I'll be able to. I suspect I won't ever be able to walk away from her, especially now that I know she will never be safe again. As of right now, I'm stuck between love and agony. Sharing her was much easier in my head than in real life, and every time Zayne touched her or made her moan, my insides felt like they were going to combust.

"Damien?" Hallie snaps me out of my racing thoughts. "Are you leaving?"

"Hallie." I kiss her forehead and grab her hand, pulling her to the edge of the bed. I sit down and spread my legs, letting her stand between them. "I could never leave you. Do you not remember all the trouble I've gone to just to get you back? To make you mine again?"

"I thought you just felt guilty…"

"Guilt is not an emotion I feel for people I don't care about." I cup her face, and she closes her eyes slowly, as if savoring my touch. "I don't want to live in a world where you're not by my side."

Hallie's eyes snap open, and her bottom lip trembles. "I love you," she tells me, and my throat tightens with emotion.

I don't think she will ever understand the depth of my love for her. I'd do literally anything to keep her safe. In my opinion, I've already shown her that. Whether it's kidnapping her and keeping her in a basement or going to another country and killing everyone in sight—I'll fucking do it.

I grab her by the waist and pull her toward me until she's straddling my lap, her towel long gone. She cups my face, and I grab the back of her neck as we meet each other halfway. The moment our lips meet, I feel a zap of electricity vibrating through my body. I kiss her like I'll never get to again. Knowing her, it's entirely possible that one day I'll wake up and she won't be here anymore. It's like I need to sleep with my eyes open, and even then, it's not enough.

She groans into my mouth when I gently pull her hair back, and we both open our eyes as we kiss. I bite her bottom lip gently as we look into each other's eyes, and she smiles. "I adore you, Hallie," I reply, pulling away. She needs to know it. If she picks me, I'll never fail her again, and if she doesn't... Well, I don't want to think about that. "There's no one else and nothing else I care about."

"I'm so sorry, Damien," Hallie mumbles, her words tripping over each other. "I have to say it before I don't get the chance to."

"What do you mean?" My eyebrows crease in confusion, trying to figure out what she's talking about. Something doesn't feel right.

Her lips purse, and she says, "There's no way we're outrunning the cartel. I'm not delusional enough to believe that."

"We will, babe." I will do everything in my power to make it happen, even if I get killed in the process. She will get out of this fucking country. "I swear I will make it happen for you."

Hallie sighs. "Either way, I truly am sorry. I should've listened to you when you said you wanted to keep me safe. I should've run far away from this place with you." I wish we would've. Then she wouldn't have been taken, and we would be together, alone, forever. "I shouldn't have stabbed you."

I chuckle at that because when she left me, it hurt way more than when she stabbed me. "Hallie, look at me." I tilt her chin up with one finger and kiss her lips softly. "I will let you stab me a million times over if it means you will stay."

My eyes water as she begins to sob, and we lean into each other, foreheads resting against each other. I hate that she's going through this and was taken and hurt. I'm too much of a coward to ask her everything they did to her, mostly because I know it's my fucking fault. I'm not oblivious. It doesn't take much effort or imagination to comprehend what they were doing to her. I can't think about it, though. If I do, all I feel is rage. It's too bad I can't go back to Mexico, bring them back from the dead, and kill them all over again.

Seeing the tattoo on her wrist made my body catch fire and burn from the inside out, renewing those thoughts all over again. I wanted to torture Michael again and kill him my fucking self. I can't bring the tattoo up; she already looks ashamed of it and still needs to heal. I won't be the one to make it worse.

Hallie wipes her tears and gets off my lap, and just like that, I lose her again. She goes to the suitcase and grabs some clean clothes for herself and puts them on. Immediately after that, she goes back to the bed to lie down.

"Are you okay, love?" I ask her when she closes her eyes.

She smiles. "I'm fine. I just need time to process everything that happened in Mexico and after."

That's fair. She did go through a lot. It's only normal that she'd need to process it. "I understand, but you're not okay."

"Maybe not."

I walk away when she snuggles into the blankets, and just as her breaths deepen and her chest rises and falls slowly, Zayne walks in. I meet him by the door so I can talk to him and gesture to the bed where Hallie now sleeps. He walks around me to watch her for a moment and then turns around to face me with an eyebrow raised.

"There's something seriously wrong with her, Zayne. She's acting like she's depressed again." I sigh. "This is exactly what she did when we were in Colorado. She was moping and sleeping. That's all she ever did for the first few days. We definitely need to keep an eye on her even more than usual."

"I agree," he says, even though his body is tense, and he looks like he's about to pounce on me. "She undeniably looks depressed. From now on, someone needs to be with her at all times. Except maybe when she's using the bathroom. Let's be serious, she'd never let us be with her in there."

"No more Airbnb's." Fuck my life. I guess I better start planning this trip better if I don't want only one bed in the room. "There's too much space. We need to watch her at all times, so that means we have to alternate sleeping with her. Every other night we switch so we can get rest. On the night we're sleeping in bed with her, we need to pay attention to when she leaves."

"So, you're saying we need to stay up all night every other night?" Zayne asks with a stunned expression. "Do you understand what that means for our driving?"

"Do you even care about her?" I retort.

"Of course I fucking care!" Zayne yells back. Yeah, having a conversation right in front of Hallie was a terrible idea.

She sits up in bed and looks around, rubbing her eyes like it'll help her find us. "What the hell is going on with you two?" she mumbles.

"Nothing, Hallie," I lie. There's no way we can let her know our plan, and even though Zayne is a pain in the ass, I know he won't tell. He wants to protect her just as much as I do. "It's time for us to go. Let's eat breakfast and get on the road."

"Where are we going?"

"We're getting the fuck out of the United States, that's where we're going." We make eye contact, and she smiles. "As fast as possible."

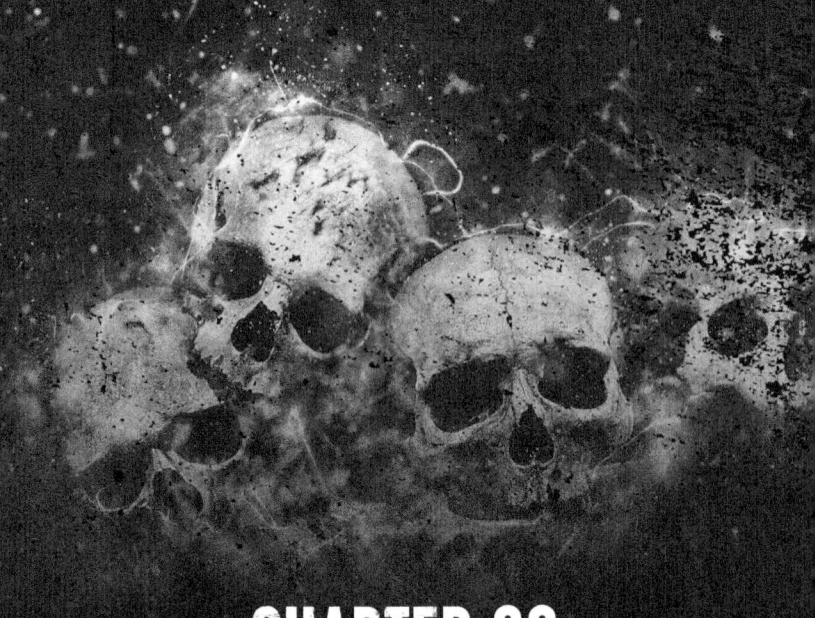

CHAPTER 22

Zayne

I've been driving for about eight hours now, and I know Damien said he has already reserved a hotel room, so we're set. He also said we need to go out tonight to lift Hallie's spirits, and I'm more than willing to do that after what I've witnessed today. She's been lying down in the backseat of the car, not once opening her eyes except for when we stop for breaks and she has to use the bathroom. Other than that, she's made no conversation and hasn't even looked at us. This isn't the Hallie I know and love, and my heart hurts knowing that she's probably struggling with what she's been through.

Watching her go through withdrawals a few days ago was an eye-opening experience for me. I never thought the roles would be reversed. Fuck, I never even thought I'd get sober. Knowing what she felt like when I went through this, the feeling of helplessness… I'm a piece of shit for putting her through that. What she went through wasn't her fault. The drugs she was given weren't willingly taken, so it's not exactly the same situation. I, on the other hand, chose to start using it, and I knew how it could end. I did it, regardless. Whatever consequences I suffered, well, I did it to my damn self.

Nighttime in St. Louis, Missouri, isn't as bad as I thought it would be. There's not much traffic downtown right now, even though it's a Saturday. I'm sure it's because it's only six in the evening, and no one goes out before ten p.m.

The hotel I pull into has garage parking and is much nicer than the ones we've been staying at. How much was this a night? Damn. I guess I must be used to living in the shit now, since I would've never batted an eyelash at this before. It's not even fancy. I make my way into the parking garage and slide into a spot right next to the elevators in case we need to make a quick escape. You just never know with these people chasing us. I haven't noticed anything unusual, but that doesn't mean shit. They could be tailing us for all we know.

I turn off the engine, and we get out of the car. The echo of the car doors closing is loud as fuck in the garage parking. Damien grabs two suitcases out of the trunk and a bunch of shopping bags—probably ten—from when he stopped by the mall earlier. The funny part, that's actually not funny at all, is that Hallie didn't even wake up when we were stopped for about an hour and a half. I wanted to ask him what he bought her, but jealousy took over that I wasn't the one to do it. That I have no way of doing that for her.

I've never had to think about the future before, not really. My mom used to always be there for me to fall back on. Which reminds me, I hope she's okay. Hopefully she doesn't think I'm dead, but more than likely, she will. Anyway, after never taking college seriously, and then being an addict, I never even thought I'd be alive long enough to consider my options on what I needed to do to get by.

Once we settle down, will I be able to work? Will we even be able to leave the house? It's not something I have thought about before, but I don't want to live life being stuck in a house.

I press the button for the elevator, and Hallie comes to stand next to me. When Damien walks around the car and toward us, her jaw drops. Ugh, great.

"What is all that?" she asks him, with love in her eyes. Of course. This is exactly what he wanted. Or... or he saw she needed clothes. *Fucking chill out.* "And when did you get it?"

"You apparently sleep like a rock lately." Damien chuckles, "You slept through the whole thing."

The elevator dings, and we get in. I inhale slowly to not lose my shit at witnessing this bullshit. It makes me want to throw up. Yeah, I can share her body, but her heart? That's the hard part. The way she looks at him doesn't go unnoticed by either of us. I'm sure he knows what he does to her, and he's trying even harder than usual to make her smile.

"What the hell..." Hallie says softly. "Who is that for?"

"Who do you think?" I roll my eyes at the question, and Hallie catches me. I turn away from them and watch the numbers go down to the lobby. "You."

There's no time for Hallie to say anything as we enter the lobby, and the lady behind the desk looks momentarily stunned at seeing all the shopping bags. Yeah, lady, same here. Sometimes I forget how much money he had before this shit happened, but now I really want to know how much he has. Surely he had to sell his shit. His car, his apartment, his motorcycle. I'm sure there's much more than that, which likely means he could live off that money without working for the rest of his life. That benefits Hallie. I have nothing to offer her anymore, with no college education, no money to depend on, and no job. It fucking sucks to compare myself to him, but I can't help but see how he'd be the better choice.

He checks into the hotel, grabbing the key card, then we follow him to wherever the hell the room is. It's on the first floor, right next to the door leading to the indoor pool. Memories of the last time I was in a pool with Hallie flash through my mind in quick succession, and I smirk. Hallie and I make eye contact, and she raises an eyebrow at me. She's healing quickly, her cuts mostly mended, and the bruises are now fading to a light-yellow color. Nothing some makeup can't fix.

Damien opens the hotel room door, and we single-file into the room. This is the largest room we have stayed in so far, with two queen beds, a couch, and a television. There's an open closet to our left with a mirrored door and a very small kitchenette. He sets both suitcases in the closet, one empty, and takes the bags to the bed and begins sorting through them. He separates them for some reason, and I count how many there are. Turns out there are *seventeen* bags, not ten. Six of them are on one bed, and the rest are on the other. Out of the six bags on the bed, he puts one in the closet, then sits on the chair facing the desk.

"The right side is yours, Hallie," he tells her, and her eyes almost pop out of her head. "The left one is yours, Zayne."

Huh?

Now it's my turn to be stunned, confused as fuck, and grateful all at the same time. Why would he do that for me? I guess, yeah, I have been using his clothes way too much. Maybe he's annoyed at this point. It bothers me that he knows Hallie enough to purchase clothes for her. If there are bras in there and he knows her exact size, I might just lose my damn mind.

"For me?" I ask incredulously. "Are you sure?"

"Yes, I'm fucking sure. Now open it before I keep them instead." He smiles at me, and I relax a little. "They're fucking nice."

"Hallie can open hers first," I tell him, and he nods. "I don't want to steal your spotlight, baby."

It looks like he got her a lot of what she needed, and I'm actually grateful for it, even if I can't deny a part of me hates it. She begins to go to one side of the bed that doesn't have bags all over it and dumps the contents of a few of the bags. The scary part is that these bags are filled up to the brim. I think she's going to need another suitcase. The one he just got for her won't be enough, no matter how big it is.

I sit on the other bed and watch her sort through what's already unbagged, her jaw basically on the floor. It's as if he purchased everything someone without any belongings would need—from scratch. It makes sense, since that's precisely the predicament she's in currently. He probably spent thousands of dollars.

A pink hygiene bag, lotions, chapstick, makeup, skincare, and I guess stuff for her hair are all on the bed in disarray. Damien gets the suitcase out of the closet and helps her sort everything out by putting things in the hygiene bag that opens into three parts. It's the kind that has a hook and can be hung from the door.

She continues to dump things on the bed for what feels like forever. Underwear, comfortable clothes like sweats and t-shirts—I guess he knows her after all, to my dismay—pajamas, other clothes for going out. When she sees the fuzzy slippers, she squeals, literally *squeals*. The fucker really did get her all the shit she likes. He even got her Vans and Converse; one pair looks like they could go in the snow, which I guess is kind of cool.

"One last thing," Damien tells her, turning around and getting something out of the bag he took away from the bed I'm sitting on.

He hands her a long Harry Potter t-shirt, and he has a matching one. Ew, what? Is he actually serious? Wait, she doesn't feel the same as me because her face lights up, and she does a little bounce before throwing her arms around him. He lifts her from the ground and spins her, kissing her forehead on the way down.

Damien actually turns around once more and hands her a medium-sized white box with a picture of a mirror on it. Is it for doing her makeup? She opens it, and it has a cord to plug into the wall. When she turns the box, it says it's a happy light.

Hallie looks at the box and back at him; this time, she doesn't smile. "What are you trying to say, Damien?"

"Maybe with a little self-care, you will feel better in a few days."

"A fucking light isn't bringing Brittany back, Damien." Tears explode from her eyes. "And it's not going to erase everything that happened to me."

"You're right—"

"I know I'm right," she argues, her tone icy.

"Hals," I intervene. "He meant well. Give him a damn break…"

"Oh?" She laughs. "You too? I love to see it. I thought you fucking hated each other but turns out you're besties now. At least you have each other."

"You need to chill the fuck out," I reply.

"And how do you suggest I do that?"

"Let's go for a drink," Damien suggests. "And then let's dance. All of us together."

Hallie laughs again, long and loud. "Have you both lost your fucking minds?" She puts her hands on her belly like it hurts from all the laughing. "You know I hate clubs."

"So? Give it a chance, Hals." I start going through the clothes and pick something for her to wear. "It's not like you have anything else to do. We need to do something other than being in a fucking hotel room for days at a time."

"If you hate it, we will come back," Damien reassures her. She rolls her eyes, grabbing her hygiene bag and the clothes I picked, and heads to the bathroom to change. "I promise."

Hallie closes the door behind her, and the lock clicks. It makes me nervous whenever we don't have access to her, but I'm trying to tell myself to calm the hell down or she'll get spooked.

Damien begins to change his clothes as well so I walk over to the bed and ask him, "Is this all for me?"

"Yes," he replies gruffly.

I clear my throat and gingerly begin to open the bags. There are also hygiene products in here for me, clothes, underwear, and shoes. I can't even keep up with it. He even considered the cold weather because I have snow pants, a snowsuit, and boots. It's funny in a way that we share the same size pants, shirts, and even shoes. The irony doesn't escape me. What a cruel fucking joke. It's as if we couldn't be more alike, but simultaneously, we also couldn't be more different than we are from each other.

I grab a pair of jeans and a nice shirt from one of the bags and the Vans he got me. A small part of me wants to believe he only did this so he could have his things back, but I know deep down he cared enough to make sure I'm okay.

After both of us are dressed, I walk to him and offer him my hand. He shakes it and looks at me a little stunned. "Thanks, man," I say, trying to play it down a little. "Seriously. That was really nice of you."

He smiles softly and nods his head, then unexpectedly clasps my shoulder and pulls me in for a very brief hug. I return it and take a step back when we break apart. "You're welcome," is all he says before we hear the bathroom door open and Hallie comes out.

She's wearing ripped black jeans with pink Vans and an off-the-shoulder pink long-sleeve top. Her hair is down in waves, and she has subtle makeup on, which only enhances her features. I firmly believe that makeup doesn't make her prettier, it just highlights all the beautiful things about her even more.

Damien's sharp intake of breath makes her smile, and when our eyes meet, my stomach drops at all the feelings coursing through me. I fucking love her so much. I'd do anything for her. In fact, I already did. Following her after she left me behind at the hotel is something I will never regret, even if I did get kidnapped because of it. I could never regret fighting for her. When I was rescued, I could've just gone home. That was a choice. Instead, I chose her again. I *want* to choose her because I love her. I've also been choosing *me* a lot lately as well. Although it's only been about two months, I have stayed sober even when things feel really challenging for me. I want to do it, not just for Hallie but also for myself. I deserve to have a better life, one where I don't have to worry about overdosing every time I plunge the needle in. That's why I'm determined to not fall again. I will do whatever it takes to stay sober, no excuses.

"Are we leaving or what?"

I smirk, and Damien chuckles. She's sassy today, although it's much better than how she's been acting the last few days, so I'll take it. I genuinely thought she'd be happy that we shared her, that she didn't have to choose between us. Even though I did hear her in the bathroom, moaning. I don't think they fucked, but I'm sure she would've if she wanted to. Or maybe he's the one who didn't want to. Who fucking knows anymore. There's a weird vibe going on between them, and I can't quite figure out why they're acting that way with each other.

"Yeah, but we're not driving," he replies. "It's within walking distance. That's why I chose this hotel."

"I guess it's a good thing I'm not wearing heels." We all laugh together, and it's music to my ears to hear the joyful sound coming from her.

Hallie and I are led to the bar by Damien, except when he says we're there, there's no bar in sight. We're only one block from the hotel, and I want to tell him it's not too late to turn around and go back. Is he serious right now? Where the hell are we?

"Where's the bar?" I ask him, and he smirks.

"You're looking at it."

"This is a hotel." I look up at the very fancy Hilton Hotel then back at him. "Is it in here?"

"No." He points up at the sky. "It's *up* there."

What the fuck. I'm not usually scared of heights, but that looks way up there. Suddenly, I really do want to go back. They can do it without me.

"Nuh-uh." I shake my head repeatedly. Zero chance. "There's no way—"

"Zay," Hallie pouts, "Please come up with us."

Fuck. Of course she's going to ask me nicely, with her little doe eyes. I sigh. "Whatever."

We go up to the bar, which is actually not that bad compared to what I had in mind. The view is quite impressive, with all the buildings lit up like Christmas trees, and you can see the entire city from up here. We sit in a secluded area with a sofa and a firepit right in front of it and huddle together. Damien sits to her right, and I sit to her left.

"So, was I right?" Damien asks me with a smirk.

"It's nicer than I thought it would be, yes. I guess you're right."

Hallie looks between us, alternating from side to side, as if she can't quite understand what's happening. She's been doing that a lot since we got her back. It's as if she can't fathom how we can even stand to be in the same room. She clearly misunderstands what we're willing to do for her, what people are willing to do for love.

"You guys are acting fucking weird," she tells us. "First, there's been barely any fighting since we left Mexico, and then you both fuck me?" Her voice raises a bit with the last sentence, and I shush her. She looks around to make sure no one's heard. "Tell me what's happening *now*."

"Should I tell her?" I ask Damien. "Or will you?"

"I'll tell her," he replies, turning to face her. "Both of us love you and want to be in your life. Neither one of us wants to let you go. We either walk away or learn to live with each other. That is, unless you're making a choice."

"Yeah, baby." I grin. "Me or him."

"Uh, I—" she stutters. "I guess I see why now. Thank you?"

"You're welcome," Damien and I say in unison.

We spend the next hour in comfortable silence while we admire the beautiful view of the city. I can't remember the last time I did this, and in a way, not everything about being on the run has been negative. At least I'm with Hallie. That's all that matters to me now. I meant it when I told her I'd do anything for her.

Drink after drink, I start becoming a little more relaxed, as does Hallie. Damien, of course, doesn't take one sip of alcohol. I'd like to say he's being annoying, but I know one of us needs to be sober in case someone from the cartel comes after us. We never know who it's going to be. Coming out is definitely a risk right now, but I think it's necessary to keep Hallie sane. Staying in hotel rooms is like still being trapped in a cage, at least for me. The only difference is that she spent more time there than me and just got out. She needs some freedom, a little bit of fun. A life.

Damien takes the drink from my hand, "That's enough."

Need shoots through my body, a familiar tingling sensation in my veins pulsing to the beat of my heart with *need*.

No.

I can't give in.

I grunt my complaint but nod in agreement. I'm not putting Hallie at risk when I know I need to stop. She looks at me with curious eyes, and it's evident she's wondering why I didn't fight him or even protest. Earlier, she did make a little sense when she said Damien and I have each other now. We might not be 'besties,' but I know for a damn fact we can count on one another. I trust him enough to lean on him and know he will protect me, just like I'd do for him now. How the fuck did we get here? Well, beats me, but I'm not going to complain. The more time we spend together, the more I notice there's peace between us. Obviously, there will always be jealousy when it comes to Hallie, but if she wasn't in the picture, I believe we would be very good friends. We may not have much in common, he's kind of a nerd and I'm kind of a junkie, but we can get along fine. That's not a frequent occurrence for me.

"How about we go to the next place?" I ask him, and he nods, taking Hallie's hand. She's walking slightly slower than usual and with a slight sway. We should've limited her alcohol intake, especially since she hasn't drank in a while. It wasn't the smartest idea to let her keep drinking half the bar's liquor stock.

Getting out of the bar is a little difficult with everyone crowding the space and bumping into us. Nevertheless, we finally manage to get through and out of the hotel.

"Where are we going?" Hallie asks, her words slightly slurred. "Are we going d-dancing?" She snorts, and Damien and I look at each other.

He smirks, "Yes, love."

I roll my eyes at that because what a stupid pet name. Seriously? He couldn't come up with something more original? I don't care that I call her baby. It's cute. I keep my mouth shut though. This isn't my problem, so I won't make it that way.

The club is not far from our hotel, being only about a block from the Hilton as well. If we needed to, we could run quickly back to safety. Although, I'm not delusional enough to believe our hotel is safe either. At least there will be other people to witness whatever happens, but that's not to say they won't kill them all as well.

There's a long line, but it actually moves very quickly. Within a matter of minutes, we're at the front of the line and being let in. Surprisingly, they don't even card us, which is a relief because I don't have any identification. We're still waiting on Sean to make it happen, according to Damien.

As we enter, the bass shakes the building, its vibrations reverberating through my body. It's dark as fuck in here, but neon lights illuminate us in intervals, going away and then coming back to us every few seconds. It's enough to see Hallie's face as she looks around in awe. I know it could just be the fact that she's drunk as fuck, since she usually hates these places, but to me, it looks like she's enjoying the vibe. I'm enjoying watching her already, and I can't wait to be grinding on her.

Though I can't hear it, I read her lips as she says, "Wow," in awe of her surroundings. She looks up at the round structure above us with multiple strobe lights facing in different directions, switching colors every few seconds. It goes from blue to green to purple. Hallie looks perfect under all of them, but I must say purple is her color.

Damien grabs her hand and pulls her toward the middle of the dance floor, and I follow them like a lost fucking puppy. I don't even care though, because when it comes to her, I'll be whatever I need to be. They begin to dance, her arms going around his neck, and they're moving against each other to the beat of the music. I begin to feel left out, watching from a foot away and dancing on my own for the sake of not feeling stupid, until Damien motions for me to come with them. I close the distance between Hallie and me, pressing my front to her back, and grinding against her. My dick instantly gets painfully hard. I don't understand how people like to do this shit every weekend. Goddamn, it just makes me want to fuck.

His hand comes to the back of her head, and he yanks her hair back hard. It reminds me of me, in a way, of Hallie and I. And it makes me wonder if that's why she wants him so much. The more I spend time with him, the more I see we have some things in common. I hate it a little.

Damien's mouth crashes against hers, and her body jerks back toward me as they kiss. I don't watch them; I just keep dancing against her. Unexpectedly, she turns my way as soon as they break apart and kisses me too. Tongues, teeth, lips. The urgency I feel is bone-deep, and I wish we weren't here at all. I want to go back to the hotel room and try this again. It's sad how much I'm hurting for her affection, for anything she will give me at this point, but when she's been pushing me away for days, I think it's probably normal for me to feel this way. Or maybe not, and I'm just being a little bitch. Wouldn't be the first time, anyway.

The way we move against each other to the beat of the music is hypnotizing. It doesn't even bother me that Damien and I are both pressed against her, our dicks touching her at the same time. I think it should bother me, but it no longer does. Our sweaty bodies are tangled, her arms in the air, head thrown back. She's a vision, and she doesn't even know it.

After about ten songs and a thousand kisses, Damien yells at me that we need to leave. The club keeps getting more packed the later it gets, which makes me think of all the college students getting here at almost midnight. Many, many shoves later and pushing eighteen-year-olds away, we make it out of the club.

Hurrying past the sudden rush of people, Damien hoists Hallie up and over his shoulder before speed-walking toward our hotel. She's too drunk to walk on her own at this point, and he keeps looking around to make sure no one is watching or following us. This entire situation has all of us being paranoid as fuck, but I believe it's warranted.

We go through the lobby and to our hotel room, and when we make it inside, Damien drops her in the middle of one of the beds. She gets up on her knees and starts to strip, taking her shirt and bra off first. Damien and I can't take our eyes off her. I don't know when this turned into…this, but I won't be the one to tell her no.

Once she's completely naked, I'm done for.

Damien and I look at each other as if trying to come to an agreement, and our silent exchange tells me everything I need to know. He's on board for whatever she wants to do, and so am I.

I nod my head, motioning toward her, and his eyes darken. He walks to the bed and grabs her by the ankles, then yanks her to the edge and gets on his knees. When he buries his face between her legs and her back arches off the bed, I unzip my jeans and take them off along with my underwear.

Damien pulls away from Hallie, pausing briefly to look at me, and smirks. I never thought sharing her could be this damn hot, only it really fucking is. He goes back to eating her out and pushes her knees all the way to her chest, knowing it's exactly the right spot to make her come faster. It feels more intense in that position for her, and I'm ready to hear her scream.

My hard dick throbs from the need to come already, and I begin to pump it slowly. I don't actually want to finish yet; there are only two places I want to come in tonight. Her mouth or her pussy. Preferably both.

The sounds of her wetness as he continues to eat her pussy fill the room, and I just stand here and watch as Hallie's legs tighten around his head. Her hands grip the sheets, her back is arched, and her head is thrown back. She looks like a fucking goddess. He spreads her legs far apart, keeping them bent toward her chest, then sucks on her. I know she's about to come when her mouth opens, and she begins to pant. I can see her body starting to shake even from a few feet away. Hallie grabs Damien's head and pulls him closer to her, and within a few seconds, she screams as she comes.

Fuck. Me.

Holy fuck.

Pre-cum leaks from my slit, trailing down the head of it, and I press on it so I don't come on the spot. Hallie's lying on the bed spread-eagle, waiting for us. We don't move, though. Instead, we wait for her to say something. She doesn't, and when she smiles, Damien looks at me over his shoulder.

"I think she's ready for you."

I grin at that, walk to the bed, and spread her legs further. I position myself against her entrance and thrust into her, her warm heat enveloping me. The way she clenches around me and looks into my eyes as I fuck her riles me up, and I wrap my hand around her neck as I begin to pound into her in earnest.

Hallie's moans fill the room, but I pull out of her, flipping her onto all fours. "Come here," I tell Damien, and he gets behind Hallie.

I hear his zipper and the rustling of his jeans as he drops them to the floor, and I get on the bed, kneeling right in front of Hallie's face. She jerks forward as Damien drives himself into her, and I wait until he's situated before grabbing her head and holding her in place.

"Be a good girl and open up for me, baby."

Hallie looks up at me with innocent eyes when I know she's anything but, and I grin when she does as she's told. She wraps her lips around me, and my toes curl when her tongue glides up my shaft, shivers skating down my spine when she sucks me as deep as I'll go.

I hold on to the back of her head and watch her head bob up and down as she takes me all the way down her throat. Damien and I make eye contact as she takes both of us. It's like a competition between us at this point, and he fucks her harder.

She looks up at me, and I thrust into her roughly, making her gag. I don't give a damn though and force my dick down her throat over and over, fucking her mouth. She moans against me, the sound vibrating through my body, and I realize it's because Damien is rubbing her needy little clit.

I fuck her mouth harder until she grunts, then moans around my dick. Damien pushes her head down until she's choking and drooling all over me. Tears stream down her face, and I enjoy seeing them, feeling the tingling sensation starting at the base of my spine. She grabs onto my thighs, digging her fingernails into my skin, doing what she knows we do best: inflict pain. My girl is clearly about to come because she opens her mouth and yells, and I take the opportunity to go as deep as I can.

My balls rise, and my dick throbs as it pulses in her mouth. I throw my head back with a groan, and all I hear from her is choking and gagging as I keep pushing her head down on my dick. Once I'm thoroughly done, I pull out of her mouth and sit on the bed.

Faint moans come from Damien, and then suddenly they get louder and louder until they stop. Hallie slumps forward, falling face-first in the bed, and Damien gets up and goes to the bathroom. The faucet runs briefly, and he returns to the bed with a wet rag. Hallie flips over as he begins to clean her, but she shakes her head.

"I'm actually going to take a bath."

"Are you sure?" I ask her, "You're kind of drunk…"

"I don't think it's safe, love." Damien has a point. We don't really care if she showers or not right now.

However, Hallie still gets out of bed and walks to the bathroom, uncaring of what we have to say. She locks the door behind her and starts the water right away. It's a loud sound since she's filling up the tub.

"What the fuck just happened?" I ask, thoroughly confused. "Do you think she's pissed off?"

"I don't see why she would be," Damien replies, running a hand down his face. "She came like two minutes ago."

"Yeah, that's why I'm confused."

We both sit on the bed and wait around. Except nothing happens, she never comes out of the bathroom. It's been about twenty minutes of waiting, and both of us are getting antsy. Damien begins to pace, and I can't keep my legs still. There's a weird feeling in my gut that tells me something is wrong.

"Damien…"

"I know." He walks to the bathroom door and begins to pound on it. "Hallie!"

No reply. No sound. Nothing.

"Hallie!" I yell, walking to the door too now. "Open the fucking door!"

Damien begins to pound on the door, but no sound comes from the other side. I definitely feel like this door needs to come down. Now.

"I don't have a good feeling about this," Damien announces, and I pull on my hair, my scalp stinging in the process.

"It's time to kick down the fucking door."

He nods and counts to three, then we both kick the door off its hinges. At first, nothing seems amiss. Except for the fact that when we step into the bathroom and turn the corner, the water is ruby red and Hallie isn't visible.

"What the fuck!" I yell, running toward her, reaching in elbows deep in blood for her in the water.

Damien is frozen to the spot behind me, seemingly stunned. He doesn't know this side of her, not truly. He may have witnessed her at her lows briefly, when she was weak and vulnerable, but he doesn't know her as I do. He doesn't understand her the way I do. I know what she's capable of because I'm capable of the same too.

I give her all my demons, and she dances with them in return.

I pull Hallie up by her arms and throw her over my shoulder. Then Damien finally snaps out of it, helping me lower her onto the floor. Blood flows freely from two vertical cuts, one along each forearm, and he gasps. I don't. I expected this at some point. What I didn't expect was for her to get away with it.

Not Hallie.

Not *my* fucking Hallie.

"No," I tell her, slapping her face. "Don't do this to me!"

The clanging in the background snaps me out of it, and Damien brings multiple towels and wraps one around each arm. "Hold those here." He tells me, showing me how to put pressure on the wounds properly so she doesn't bleed out. Although, to be honest, I think we're a little late for that.

Tears fill my eyes and cascade down my face like waterfalls, "I don't think—"

"Yeah, don't think," he replies, kneeling and placing his hands over Hallie's chest. "In fact, how about you shut the fuck up?"

I do actually shut the fuck up, mainly because I have nothing positive to say. Hallie is cold, bleeding profusely, and her face is blue, along with her lips. The way he's pumping her chest is scaring me, but I also know if anyone can save her, it's him. I've never praised him before, but I know he's a good nurse—at least according to Hals.

He taps a phone number into his screen and dials it, then sets it on speaker phone and puts it on the ground next to him. Hallie's chest rises and falls with the force of Damien's compressions, and before I know it, someone else knocks on the door. I open it, not caring about who it is as long as they help her.

A man in scrubs comes in and begins to work on Hallie, and I exit the bathroom. I sit on the bed instead, contemplating how I went wrong. How didn't I see this coming? All the signs were there, but maybe I just didn't want to see it because I wanted to pretend everything was okay. The thing is, there's no way anyone could be okay after everything she went through. Even after everything I've been through, I should be more fucked up. I'm wondering why I haven't cracked yet and lost my shit, but I know it's coming sometime.

When I finally break, my pieces will be pulverized.

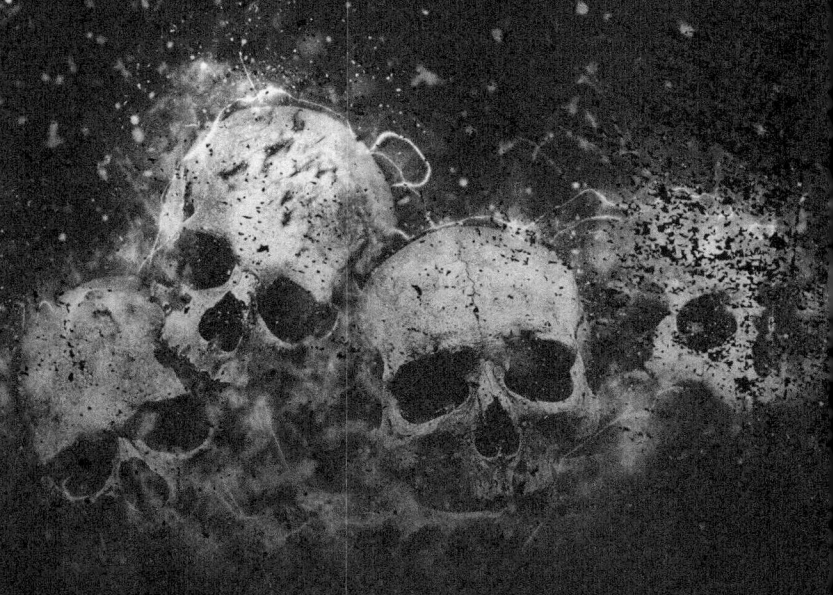

CHAPTER 23

```
Hallie
```

E verything hurts.
It's hard to open my eyes. In fact, it feels like I'm too weak to. Maybe this means I'm in hell, that there was no limbo, reincarnation, or heaven. I know I made a lot of mistakes, but damn, this is another level of pain.

Except, I hear voices in the background. That can't be right, not after what I did in that bathroom. I still remember how deep I cut, how far, how much blood poured out of my wound.

Why did I do it?

I honestly don't fucking know. The intrusive thoughts won. The little voice that was telling me how unworthy I was of living after the way Brit died. I couldn't seem to get that out of my head or the way they *took* hers. So, I decided it wasn't worth it to keep going, *I* wasn't worth it. Yeah, I know I'm a horrible person for leaving Zayne and Damien behind yet again, but I couldn't even stay for myself.

"Stay with me." Damien's voice stirs something in me. "You don't get to fucking die on me."

I feel pressure in my chest, something compressing my lungs, and somehow, I manage to open my eyes even with how heavy they are. There's a bright light above me, identical to the one I stared at right before my world faded to black. My eyes are blurry though, so that's all I can see. And white. So much white.

"She's back!" Damien yells, his anguish palpable. Suddenly I feel like the worst person on the planet for causing him pain yet again. But even still, I can't regret it. I don't want to be here. "Hallie, can you hear me?"

"Let me—" I cough violently, and it feels slightly like I'm drowning from the inside out. "Die."

Zayne grabs my face and squeezes my cheeks together with one hand, "Listen to me, baby, and listen real good." I look into his eyes and try to ignore the pain. It doesn't bother me, it only grounds me. I don't want to be grounded right now. "We will *never* let you die."

I smile at that because I know he means it. At least I think I smile. My lips are stiff, barely able to make the movement. I cough and water spurts out of my mouth, which I begin to choke on. Damien quickly turns me onto my side and pats my back hard like you would a choking baby. Zayne, on the other hand, grabs my forearms tightly, and I yelp and cough simultaneously from the pain.

Fuck. This. Shit.

I wanted to die. They should've fucking let me. Why are they always making shit so damn difficult? I locked the damn door. I did everything I could. I even let them have one last time with me—even if it couldn't be individually, it's better than nothing.

A man enters the bathroom behind them, telling Zayne to get out and Damien to step away. He looks me over and begins chest compressions even though I'm awake. What the fuck? That shit hurts so fucking bad.

Suddenly, it feels like I have to throw up and I gag. However instead of puke, water comes out. I spurt water all over my face, and the man lies me down on my side so I don't keep choking on it again. That would be pointless after all the effort he has made.

My eyes begin to feel heavy again, and I fight to keep them open, shaking my head from side to side in an attempt to make it happen. I fail though, and Damien's worried face is the last thing I see before my world turns black again.

When I wake up again, I hear faint whispers from Zayne and Damien. The pain in my arms is overwhelming, but I manage to take some deep breaths anyway and focus on what they're saying.

"You're such a fucking nerd," Zayne jokes with a laugh. "Who the hell likes Lord of the Rings anymore?"

"What are you even talking about?" Damien replies, clearly offended. "Plenty of people, you asshole."

"Nah." Zay is clearly convinced there's no one out there with the same interests as Damien. It's actually kind of funny how stupid he sounds right now, which is probably why Damien sounds so annoyed. "No way."

"Listen…" Uh oh. I know now this is going to offend someone. "Smoking weed isn't a hobby, so maybe tone it down on the judgment."

"It makes people feel better than watching that movie, though."

"Just in case I hadn't told you lately," Damien smirks, "You're still a dick."

Somehow, they still haven't noticed I'm awake. Not once have they looked at me even though my eyes are now wide open. I observe them quietly, their body language, and the way they speak so freely to each other. For a few days I thought they were putting on an act for my benefit—to not stress me out. It turns out that they can tolerate each other now and enjoy each other's company. This is fucking weird. Maybe something *is* wrong with me. I mean, it's not that far-fetched, considering I was literally dead. I think. Probably. Anyway, I think I'm seeing things because there's no way this is happening.

"I know," Zayne replies. "The only thing I care about is her."

My stomach drops at his words, and Damien clenches his jaw and looks down.

"I love her, Zayne." Tears gather in my eyes at his words, and my hands begin to tremble. He hasn't really acted that way with me. He's been pissed off at me, rightfully so, and therefore not wanting much to do with me unless it's on a bed. "I didn't think I could share her, but I know her too well. She's not going to pick. Neither one of us will get her if we make her choose."

"I know. That's why I said to not force her to."

"Yeah." He nods slowly. "Except, I don't know if I can do this, man."

"Do what?"

"Share."

"You can, and you will."

"I think I should walk away," Damien says, rubbing a hand down his face the way he does whenever he's frustrated. My heart aches at those words, and I want to scream at him not to even think about it. He can't fucking leave me behind, I won't survive. A world without him, a *life* without him, is no life at all. "Let her go."

"What the fuck are you talking about?" Zayne retorts, "Do you have any idea what that would do to her? And the abandonment she deals with every day?"

"I don't know what to do—"

"Leaving is more my thing than yours, let's be serious." Zayne gets up from his spot and begins to pace. How they haven't seen me awake is beyond me. "You're the kind that stays."

"Yeah, how very on-brand of you," Damien says sarcastically. "However, this isn't about what fits my personality. I need to think about myself too, you know. Not everything is about her. What about me and *my* fucking heart?"

"Oh, get the fuck over it already!" Zayne yells, and I make a sound at his outburst.

Both of their heads whip in my direction, and my eyes widen significantly under their attention. I kind of wanted to keep listening in, even if it was wrong. It's hard to figure out their true feelings most of the time, especially now that they seem to be walking on eggshells around me. No one wants to speak their mind for fear that it'll be the thing to push me over the edge, and now look at me. I guess I proved them right. Except they couldn't push me over the edge. There were more gruesome things on my mind than worrying about two men. No matter how much I love them both.

I hate how weak I've been, walking through life constantly thinking of dying. It's always nagged at me like a little fucking mosquito that just won't go away, sucking me dry. The things I've seen, lived through, and thought about since being in that hell house will forever be ingrained in my mind, and I don't know if I'm strong enough to get through it or move on from it. The memories of Brittany dead with her head severed haunt me daily, and the only thing that could stop it was death—for myself. But of course, they had to ruin that for me.

"Why did you ruin it for me?" I ask them both. "Do you have any idea what memories I have to live with?"

I try to sit up on the bed, but it's futile. My body weighs a million pounds, and I'm in so much pain with every movement I can't even see straight. They both walk toward me at my outburst, seeming more serious than I've seen either of them, ever.

"I don't give a fuck what memories you have to live with," Damien snaps. "Because I can't live without *you*."

"So, get over them, Hals," Zayne says, just a tad bit insensitive as fuck. "Get the fuck over them and live."

"You have no idea what I lived through, what I had to see!" I say through clenched teeth.

"Then tell us!" Zayne yells, his voice carrying through the room.

"I can't."

"Then don't fucking cry about it," Damien says in a cold voice. "If you don't want help, if you won't share your pain with us, then that's on you. But I swear on my life, Hallie, if you try this shit again, I will tie you up in a basement and feed you bread and water for the rest of your life. I will keep you alive no matter what you fucking want."

"Shut up." I roll my eyes at his display. "You can't do—"

"I'll help him, Hals. So stop playing these fucking games. Time to grow up and face your damn problems."

"You're really going to talk about facing your fucking problems?" I laugh loudly, "You're the king of suicidal thoughts and drowning your problems in meth."

As soon as it's out of my mouth, I regret it. I clamp my lips shut as I watch his face fall in slow motion. His eyes fill with tears, and he turns around and begins to walk away.

"Wait," I tell him, "I'm sorry."

"You don't know shit, Hallie." Zayne scoffs, and Damien glares at me, taking his side. "I went through a lot in Mexico before Damien came for me, but I have stayed strong. I've even stayed sober this entire time. So, if I can fucking do it, so can you."

With that, he exits the hotel room with a slam of the door, making the walls rattle. Somehow my head seems heavier from the emotions coursing through me, and it feels like it's sinking into the pillow. I look around to see an IV in my upper arm, which I hadn't noticed until now. Since my arms are bandaged and hurt so fucking much, all the other pain is probably muted at this point. There's a bag of saline hanging from a metal hook attached to the wall, and I remember the man who put me on my side when I was choking up water. Who was he, and where the hell did he go? Is Damien still using the cartel? Would they even help him? Is the man going to tell on us now?

"Calm down," Damien says, coming to my side and stroking my face gently. The way I feel when his fingers meet my skin, this searing hot zap of emotion lodging itself in my chest cavity, leaves me fucking breathless. "I can see the thoughts running through your mind. We are okay."

How does he always know how I'm feeling? What I'm thinking? It's as if we're connected, tethered to each other by a flimsy string that may just break at any moment. "We aren't."

"Let me deal with that. I will take care of whatever needs to be taken care of," he replies, and I sigh. I'm tired of running, tired of everything it means for us. I just want to settle down and make a choice—if I even can.

"Why are you doing this for me?"

"Because I'm nothing without you." *Lies.* Fucking bullshit.

"I heard you," I reply. "You're leaving me behind just like everyone else." How dare he tell me I'm the most important person in his life, that he can't live without me, that he's nothing without me. Yet he's willing to leave me so easily. As if we're nothing, and I never meant anything. No, he's full of shit. I don't even matter at all.

"What?"

"Don't *what* me," I snap. "I fucking heard you tell Zayne you were leaving me." A traitorous tear falls out of my left eye, and he catches it with his thumb. "You said you were going to walk away!"

"I should, Hallie."

"The fuck you should." I sniffle, trying to reach for him but unable to move. I can wiggle my fingers, but my arms are useless. What have I done?! "Please, don't leave me."

"Babe—"

"*Please.*"

Damien leans over my body and kisses my forehead and cheek, then runs his lips over my tears, kissing them too. My body shakes from the force of my cries, and I can't contain them anymore. He can't leave me. I'll be lost without him. He's the compass that guides me through life.

"Okay," he replies quietly. "Just know that every day you don't choose me, it hurts. Is that what you want? To hurt my heart?"

I shake my head quickly, giving myself a headache. "Never. But I want you. I *love* you." If looks had the power to heal, all my wounds would close and go away right now. "You said you felt the same. Do you not mean it anymore? Am I not enough to make you stay? I know I left you, and I'm *sorry*. I can't lose you again."

"So, what do you expect from me?" The hardness of his voice snaps me out of it, and I gaze into his eyes to see them full of pain.

Pain I inflicted upon him, and no matter how much I regret doing it, I can't undo the harm I've caused. It will be something I'm going to regret for the rest of my life. However short it may be. "To wait around forever until you make up your mind? You want me to be your puppy until you choose which one is the prettiest in the litter?"

"Why would you say that? I love you both. It's not something I can control. Whoever I choose… I will still mourn a loss. I can't endure it right now, Damien. I'm too weak for it and am not afraid to admit it. The thought of losing you makes me sick, but I feel the same about losing him. In a perfect world, I wouldn't have to pick. But you want me to, so I guess I must. Just not right now."

He's silent for a beat then takes a step back. "I won't wait around forever."

Damien walks away, leaving me alone in the hotel room as I stare at the ceiling with snot running down my face and mixing with my tears. Someone will have to help me because there's no way I can clean myself right now. I don't know how long it's going to take me to recover. I do know I can't take too long because we have a timeline, and we need to get the hell out of this country. I won't be the one to stall us, not when I want to get far away from here more than either of them. The thought of being kidnapped again makes me sick to my stomach, and the anxiety I feel just thinking about it is not healthy. I don't know that they will come for me since Michael is dead, but I know for a damn fact I'm not sticking around to find out.

At this point, I can only hope for the best and not be a pessimist, but that's never helped me.

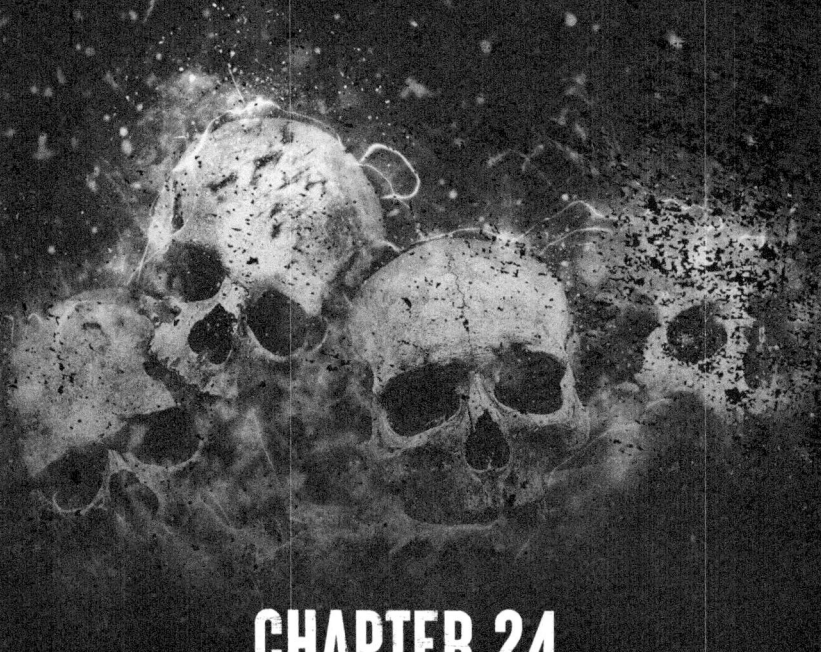

CHAPTER 24

Damien

The helpless feeling coursing through my body when we found Hallie in the tub, completely submerged under the water, with her wrists cut vertically... I never want to feel that again. Not one more time in my entire fucking life. What bothers me the most is that she knew what she was doing; she truly wanted to die. This was not an impulsive decision. She put a lot of thought into this. So much so that she made sure to cut the one way that would ensure her death.

Finding her submerged, with bright red water engulfing her body, just might be the most traumatizing event of my entire life, even more than finding my mother dead. I know she's going through something, that she suffered a lot when she was captured, but I still can't believe she would throw her life away over it. She's capable of healing, I fucking know it. If she wanted to, she could attend therapy when we get settled, take medications, fucking meditate, or something. I've never been depressed, but I could help her get through it, even if I don't fully understand what she's going through or feeling. We could go on walks in the snow, drink hot cocoa by the fire, and do all the things she loves. If she'd just give me the fucking chance, I would do anything for her. I would give her the world.

At least I'm trying, though. I've been driving for hours as Zayne sits in the backseat with her. Her head is on his lap as she lies on her back so her arms don't hurt. Unfortunately, she's doped up since she's still unable to move her arms from the pain, even after three days. I don't know what the fuck she was thinking, but she must be delusional as fuck if she believed I'd let her die that way. She shouldn't have cut her wrists like that. Now she's alive *and* in pain.

We're currently entering the state of Ohio at least, which makes us yet another state closer to Canada. Only Pennsylvania and New York to go, which brings me back to now. Unfortunately for me, we have to stay at yet another hotel because no Airbnb's were available tonight. I only plan on us staying here two nights maximum, one if we're lucky, but I figured I should probably let Hallie heal at least a little before we attempt to cross the Canadian border. The last thing we need is for them to think either one of us did that to her, or worse, that we kidnapped her or some shit. She has been missing for a little while, after all. We don't know if she's on posters, social media, or the news.

Luckily, we don't have to wait any longer to cross over because Sean came through and got me the passport, birth certificate, social security card, and even a driver's license for Zayne. It was all mailed to the hotel where we were staying, and we got it this morning before leaving. I made it a point to stay once I knew it was on the way, otherwise we would've left much earlier.

We only have about fifteen minutes left of the drive to get to the next hotel, and I'm already having anxiety about it. I don't know why this one makes me feel apprehensive, but I just have a bad feeling about it. I know it can't be real though, because we've covered our tracks and haven't done anything to give us away.

Unless you count the only time we went out in Missouri, then I guess we could be fucked.

Hallie begins to stir, and Zayne runs his fingers through her hair, trying to work out the tangles she's accumulated over the course of one night. Seeing them together doesn't quite piss me off as much as it used to, and maybe that's a problem. I still want her to choose me, of course. There won't ever be a day that I won't wish for me to be her one and only.

The gas light turns on, signaling that we're almost empty. Fuck. I should've fueled up the last time I saw a gas station, at least thirty minutes ago. Thankfully at least there's one coming up. I see it on the GPS. We're switching after this, Zayne and I, and he's going to be the one driving.

I pull into the gas station and park at the furthest pump. I'm not waking Hallie to use the bathroom. She's probably so fucking high she won't be able to walk straight. No, it'll have to wait for the hotel. The gas station is oddly empty, with us being the only ones here, and the hairs at the back of my neck stand on end. I ignore the feeling and begin to pump gas, watching the numbers on the little screen go up until it clicks, and I take the nozzle out, putting it back where it belongs.

A blacked-out SUV parks two pumps away from us, directly in my line of vision. I knock on Zayne's window discreetly, and he lowers it slightly. "Are you good?" he asks me as I continue to watch the vehicle.

One Mexican man begins to walk our way. "No. Grab a gun, someone is coming, and I don't want to find out who he is the hard way."

There's a commotion behind me as Zayne gets his weapon, and I move out of the way of the door so he can open it. He opens the door slowly, puts his window back up, and closes it behind him. At this point, the man walks faster toward us, not even concealing that he's here for us, and goes to grab a weapon from his side.

Zayne shoots his arm. "Don't fucking think about it."

The man grunts loudly and stumbles, but other than that, he

rights himself quickly and continues on his way towards us. The door on the other side opens, and I tense, looking around frantically. A different man is on the other side of the car, and I run to it. "Kill him!" I scream at Zayne, and thankfully he doesn't hesitate.

A shot rings out, and a thump lets me know the body of the man advancing on us has hit the floor. I make it to the other side of the car just in time for the man to start getting in, and I grab him by the collar of his shirt and yank him back, choking him with it. I move him out of the way and close the car door, forcing him back onto it.

"Touch her, and I'll fucking gut you," Zayne tells him, putting the barrel of the gun to the man's head.

I chuckle, kinda proud of him, to be honest. "And then I will feed you your tongue and slit your fucking throat."

The smell of urine is overpowering, and when I look down, I see it running down his pant leg. I get him away from the car and shoot him then drop him on the ground. We don't have time for these fucking games, we need to get out of here. There's probably more coming if I remember how this works.

Zayne runs to the driver's side, and I rush to replace him where he had been positioned, needing to get another magazine with more rounds ready just in case this goes south. I don't bother putting my seatbelt on, but Zayne does, and that's good because we might need to peel the fuck out of here. It's inconvenient, but there's no way in hell we're staying in this state now. Unfortunately, that means we're driving the rest of the way to New York, which means I need to reserve lodging for us.

I look at the SUV while Zayne pulls out of the spot, needing to drive right in front of it or behind it. "Go in front so I can see how many of them are left."

He does as I say, going in front of the SUV slowly so I can get a good look. There's one man in the car on the passenger side, but no one else is visible. Suddenly, bullets riddle my side of the vehicle, the door denting from the force of them. I can't see where it's coming from, but I shoot the man in the passenger side just before he gets out of the vehicle to go after us as well, I'm assuming. The shot strikes true, right in the head through the windshield. Guess they don't have bulletproof glass. Dumbasses.

There's another man hiding somewhere around or behind the SUV, and I can't fucking see him. "Get us the fuck out of here!" I scream at Zayne, who floors the gas.

Hallie attempts to get up from the seat, moaning in pain. "Stay down, baby. This isn't the time to get up." Zayne has a way of making her listen that I don't think anyone else can achieve, not even me.

She lies back down slowly just as Zayne gets us on the highway, which is inconvenient because it's dark as fuck, and I have no idea how I'd get rid of the man if I can't see him.

The SUV tails us closely, and I hold my breath as Zayne drives faster to try to not get hit. Even still, the fucker behind us manages to hit us, making the car jolt forward violently. Hallie almost falls off the backseat, and I can't see shit with the headlights behind me. I get down just in case he tries to shoot me, and I hold my gun tightly.

I remember when Zayne got hit back in San Antonio, and he spiraled all over the road until the car flipped over, and my stomach drops. There's no fucking way I'll let them take Hallie again. This isn't about her anymore or even about Michael. He's dead. But the cartel's ego is wounded, and they can't let her escape.

We're hit from behind once more, but to the man's dismay, Zayne keeps control of the vehicle this once. Thank fucking God. Except the asshole behind us changes tactics and goes over to my side of the car, hitting us and almost running us off the road and into a huge ditch. I wouldn't even consider it a ditch at this point, it looks like falling off a damn mountain.

Righting the car, Zayne hits the gas even harder and attempts to accelerate with this piece of shit box of a car, but it's lagging a little. For fuck's sake, we need a new vehicle, something less… shitty. I only got this one to remain inconspicuous in Mexico, but now that we're back in the United States, it'll be much easier to get a vehicle where we're not suspicious at all.

The car finally catches up, accelerating roughly until the SUV is a few feet behind us. It accelerates too though, and I lower my window and point my gun when the passenger side seat is right across from my line of sight. "Go faster!" I yell at Zayne, my voice slightly muffled from the wind. He does as I tell him though, and when I'm slightly in front of the SUV, I let my bullets loose. I shoot seven times in a row until the SUV swerves and does a 360, crashing into one of the metal walls that keep you from falling off the edge of the road.

"You're a bad motherfucker, you know that?"

I laugh at that, putting my window up. I actually do know that, and he hasn't seen the half of it. I'm happy not to be part of that lifestyle anymore though, and I'll do whatever is in my power to not put those skills to use. "I try sometimes."

"I'll drive for eight hours, and then I need to stop." Zayne sighs, running a hand through his hair briefly. "Seriously, I'm fucking tired."

"Just drive us to a rest stop," I reply, putting Hallie on my lap so she can be comfortable and then lying my head against the back seat headrest. "If you can't stay awake, just let me know. We don't need to die tonight."

"I'll get us there."

I fall asleep, unknowingly, because the next time I wake up it's by bright lights streaming through my window. I look at my watch quickly and realize it's been four hours since Zayne started driving, and he's pumping gas once more. I sit up abruptly on high alert all over again since I'm still freaked out about what happened the last time we stopped. No funny feelings course through my body however, and no weird vehicles prowl in the night. It's time for Hallie to use the bathroom though, considering we have four more hours to the rest stop, and we can't stop before that.

Thankfully, I haven't medicated her at all in the last few hours, and she hasn't even woken up since the incident earlier.

No mentions of pain have been made, which doesn't prove much, considering how gnarly the cuts looked when we found her. She's going to be in pain for a fucking minute.

Hallie stirs when I gently shake her, trying to cause her as little pain as possible, but she still groans. "We have to take you to the bathroom, babe."

"No," she moans, refusing to get up. I still poke her, trying to get her to at least sit up slowly before I force her out of this damn vehicle and to a toilet. "I want to sleep."

"No, love," I reply, lifting her slowly. She doesn't fight it at least, which is helpful because I don't want to hurt her. "We're not stopping again for a long time, and you saw what happened last time we did. We have to take advantage of when shit is calm around here."

"Fine."

I go around the vehicle to help her out while Zayne continues to pump gas, and I notice she's finally starting to walk normally. She's no longer hunched over or crying and has a normal pace. I take her to the bathroom and go in with her since it's a family one, helping her sit on the toilet.

"Leave, please." There's no fucking way I'm leaving her in here all alone to faceplant when she feels dizzy. She has no idea how much blood she lost, and the one bag the doctor brought with him was not enough. Neither was the saline I put in her IV. "This is embarrassing."

"No, it's not," I reassure her. It's not, though, honestly. First off, I'm a nurse. And second, I've seen everything I could possibly see when it comes to her body. "I'll turn around if it makes you feel better, but I'm not leaving."

"Then turn around and cover your ears."

We make eye contact, and her face begs me to comply. I smirk as she narrows her eyes, but I turn around and cover my ears. She's actually very quick though, and before I know it, she's tapping me on the shoulder after she washes her hands. Surprisingly, her bandages are still intact, no longer bleeding, and she seems to be using her arms better. This is what I'm fucking talking about;

she's so resilient that this shit is unnecessary. Why would she do something like this when she can get through whatever she sets her mind to? I know she can do it, Zayne knows she can do it, but she's the one person who doesn't realize her potential.

"I'm done."

"Let's go back to the car." I look around as we exit the bathroom, making sure no one is watching us. "Do you want anything? A snack?"

Hallie nods and grabs a pack of Oreos, the family pack, and hands it over along with a peach slush. What the hell? She's going to have to pee all over again. As if reading my mind, she says, "I'm a nurse. I'll pee when I decide to."

I raise my hands in submission. "Yes, ma'am."

With narrowed eyes and head held high, she reaches for the door leading to the gas pumps, and I hold it open for her, ensuring she doesn't hurt herself. Her arms might be getting better, but they could always take a turn for the worse at any given moment. She doesn't realize how far she went this time with her cutting fixation, but once she's better and we're settled in the house I bought, I'm making her listen to me. I have the right to have an opinion about it, and I won't sugarcoat the truth.

Zayne gets out of the car and opens the back door for us, looking tired as fuck. I honestly feel terrible, but I've been driving a lot too. I need a damn break. In a few days, it will be me trying to get us through the Canadian border, and I need to be rested. Before we go to the next Airbnb, I need to get us a new vehicle. This one is not going to do. It can't wait until we cross the border, especially since we won't be citizens yet and are there on a 'vacation'. We have six months to become citizens, but I need to think of short-term for now. Once we're safe and settled, I'll figure out how to make the rest happen. Until then, I have to make sure we can get through the damned border intact.

Hallie and I get in the car, and I shut the door behind us, making sure to help her scoot over as much as possible without putting weight on her hands while doing it. I open the pack of Oreos for her, and she smiles, grabbing one and putting it against my lips. I take a bite, savoring it while she puts the rest in her mouth. I'm just happy she's perked up a little. Between the depression she felt before she did this, and now this whole situation, it's been a rough fucking week. I'm ready for it to be over.

"Four more hours to go," Zayne says as he closes his door and locks all of them. He cracks his knuckles, neck, and back, and Hallie looks at me and smirks. She thinks it's funny, so I give her a smile. "Fuck me."

"It's fine, Zayne." Fucking cry-baby. "You will survive. I promise."

"I know. I just hate driving."

I roll my eyes and let Hallie lie on my shoulder, eating her damn Oreos like she hasn't been fed in months. She's practically inhaling the damned things. I wipe some crumbs from the corner of her mouth, and she leans into me instead, kissing my lips softly. I relish in it, in her, the damn cookies, and close my eyes. Hoping she'll do it again. She doesn't disappoint me, kissing me again so softly it makes me dizzy with the need to take her face and kiss her in earnest. I won't though. I truly don't want to hurt her—not right now, anyway.

She doesn't fall asleep for the rest of the drive, surprisingly, and once four hours come around, we stop at the nearest rest stop to sleep. We have to be careful as fuck. In fact, this genuinely freaks me the hell out. But, unfortunately, it's necessary. Sleep is crucial for survival.

Zayne parks behind the building, and we go in briefly to use the bathroom. Once back in the car, I go to the trunk, grab blankets and pillows, and give some to Hallie before setting up the backseat. I also hand a pair to Zayne, who reclines his seat a little so he can sleep. We lock the doors, hoping the tree in front of us shields us from whoever comes looking. I'm not delusional enough to believe that will keep anyone away. If they're looking for us, really looking, they'll find us regardless of what we do. Now *that* is fucking scary.

We finally made it to our Airbnb in upstate New York, which only took three more days. We're staying near Niagara Falls, waiting until two days from now to make the move. I reserved two days here and will be damned if I waste that money. Hallie needs to see the world, and I want to show it to her. We're going to find something to do while we wait here. I'll make sure of that.

I actually figured out that the doctor who came to help with Hallie was the one who ratted us out, which is how the cartel had our exact location. I don't know how I missed it; I never realized they were tailing us until they were right in front of my face. Either way, it's too late for regrets, but damn. I have to do better, that's for damn sure.

Planning this out has been very time-consuming and draining, but I know getting out of this country is what's best for all of us. I still wish I could kick Zayne out. I don't even care if I leave him stranded—okay, maybe a little—but apparently, it would break Hallie's heart. So here I am, putting up with the little shit. The lack of trying to get rid of him is how I end up standing next to him at a car dealership while he gives me a thousand and one reasons why we should not get an SUV, even though it's the best choice for us.

Between prices and drawing more attention to us, he didn't make any great points. I've paid close attention to people in this country. Unless it's flashy, you'll be left alone. We have to learn how to blend in and make sure we don't draw too much attention to ourselves while still having exactly what we need. Especially if we have more days of sleeping in the car ahead of us.

Hallie points to one vehicle out of all the ones we've looked at, and I know this is the one, just because I can see the way her eyes light up when she looks at it. She points at an army-green Toyota 4Runner with a luggage rack on the roof and black wheels. It's fucking gorgeous, and I've never been an SUV guy. This one is a four-wheel drive, so it's perfect for Canadian winters, as in the current season and shit weather. My only hope for the trip to Canada right now is to not get stuck in a snowstorm.

"This one," Hallie breathes. "I like this one."

"Can we see the inside?" I ask the man as I walk around the 4Runner. I want it all the way open so Hallie can get a good look. Me too, since I'm buying it after all. I want to make sure it's what we need before I pull that trigger, considering this little bitch is over fifty thousand dollars. I have money, but I also need to make it last. The house was also quite a bit of money, so after this I need to chill. There's no hope of trading the shitty car either, so I'm stuck getting no cash back.

"Absolutely," the salesman replies, unlocking the car.

I go around and open all the doors and trunk, really liking the inside already. I love the leather seats, the moon roof, and the spacious trunk. The stereo has a touchscreen and can connect to Bluetooth, which is always convenient. It also has built-in navigation, which is better for us than using a phone that can be tracked. That's yet another thing on the list to get rid of.

"It's actually really fucking nice," Zayne says. "It even has heated seats!"

He sounds like a kid on Christmas morning, even though I'm sure his last car also had heated seats. Maybe it's because the car we have been driving is a piece of shit with absolutely no specs, and it's clear we need something better anyway.

Hallie is still looking inside the car so I come up behind her, plastering my front to her back. She leans against me and looks up at me with a smile that melts me. "Is this the one, love?"

She nods with enthusiasm, "Yes!"

"Okay, we'll take this one," I tell the man, handing him the keys to the car.

"Do you want to test drive it?"

No way in hell am I getting in a vehicle with anyone. "No, we'll take it."

"Very well," the man says. "Let's get started on paperwork."

Three hours and thousands of dollars later, we drive out of the lot with a brand-new Toyota 4Runner. I'm actually really excited about how smooth it feels when I drive it and how much nicer it is than the last car. The Airbnb I picked is pretty close to here, just a few minutes from Niagara Falls.

Once there, I park the car out front, since there's only one parking spot option. I can only hope we were discreet enough that we won't be found here. The cartel is pissed off enough at us for running away. For killing everyone, including top bosses, and escaping them left and right when they find someone new to tail us. It's ridiculous that this has become our lives.

We enter the apartment with all our luggage, not wanting to leave anything behind in case someone sees it and recognizes it. Pictures don't do this place justice. As you enter the apartment, you see the small black couch against the end wall and two matching navy-blue accent chairs. There are two end tables with lamps, a circular coffee table in the middle, right across from the sofa, and a rug right under it. Two poufs also sit right across from the coffee table. A soft light from the windows illuminates the space, making part of the back wall glow yellow and orange, bouncing off a small piano in a corner. How they fit that in here, I have no idea.

We go from room to room, admiring the small dining room with the table that matches the living room's coffee tables and the very, very small kitchen. The entire place is tiled. It's honestly not much, but it'll do. We have to stay low-key if we want to make it out of this country. It doesn't help that they tailed us to Ohio. It's more than likely those men let other members of the cartel know where they saw us, and they've now figured out that we're on our way to Canada. That would be very bad for us. If they tail us and find our hiding spot, we might as well be dead. We would never stop being on the run, in fact, they will never stop coming after us. Disappearing from the face of the earth is our only option.

"I want the small bedroom," Hallie announces. "You both can fight over the other one or sleep together for all I care." She shrugs with a smirk.

No fucking way will I be sleeping with that asshole again, unless absolutely necessary.

"Or… I could just sleep with you." Zayne tells her, making my hackles rise.

"No." I'm not letting that happen. Not every night. If I have to hear them fucking every single night, I might just fucking lose my mind. I'll kill him, or torture him until he wants to die, then kill him.

"I think we can alternate days," Hallie tells us. "Damien sleeps with me tonight and Zayne tomorrow."

"What the—" Zayne starts.

"Or you could just sleep on the couch, Zay."

I smirk, then let out a low chuckle. Zayne shoots daggers at me with his eyes. "Hell to the fuck no."

"Then it's settled. You can alternate." She shrugs and strolls away, wanting to see the rest of the house. "Figure it out, but I don't want to hear you complain."

We tour the rest of the house, which is pretty uneventful. Only a small bathroom was left to see, anyway, and a *very* tiny balcony/deck that's big enough to fit two chairs and a little table.

A few hours later, we ordered takeout and just finished eating. It's refreshing to be in an apartment rather than a hotel, and I'm glad I took the time to look for this. All I want now is to give Hallie as much of a normal life as possible, so tomorrow we're going exploring, then we can go to Canada the next day. This is taking longer than expected. Shit, it's taking way longer than planned, but to say there have been setbacks would be the understatement of the year. It doesn't matter anymore. If Hallie could just stop playing these games, that would be great though.

She's comfortably sitting on the couch discussing with Zayne what he should play on the piano, and she looks so cute with the wrinkle between her brows as she argues with him. Her upturned little nose and pouty lips that beg to be kissed taunt me, and I have to sit on the other end of the couch to keep myself from touching her.

Zayne dims the light—yeah, I'm surprised that's even possible here—and begins to play something he said he learned a while back. Hallie wanted something else, but her face completely changes when he starts playing it. Instead, she looks like she's in awe of him, utterly mesmerized. I can't even blame her; it really does sound beautiful. It's too bad my only talent is killing people, and maybe saving people too. How fucking ironic is that?

He starts out slow and light at first, and then his fingers begin to go faster and faster until they look like they're flying over the keys. Evidently, the song is called *Interstellar*, and I'm quite impressed at how well he plays it. I look at Hallie, whose eyes are glued to him, and she seems on the verge of tears. I take her hand in mine, and she looks at me briefly, a tear trailing down her cheek. I kiss it away, trying to tell her without words that I'd do anything for her. If she hasn't noticed by now, I need to try harder to show her that she's all that matters.

Hallie looks back at how his hands fly over the keys, her mouth agape, and tears continue falling down her cheeks and onto her sweatshirt. I swear there will be a puddle when he's done, which is apparently now.

"That was so—" Hallie sniffs, "Beautiful."

Zayne gets up from the bench, a look of concern on his face, and kneels right in front of her between her legs. "Why are you crying, baby? What's wrong?"

"I just remembered…us."

A tinge of jealousy spreads from my stomach to all my limbs like wildfire, and my jaw clenches without my permission. He sees it and shakes his head slightly.

"There's still us, Hals." He grabs her hand and plants a kiss on the inside of her wrist, right below her bandages. Every time I see them is like a punch to the gut, knowing she tried to end her life, to steal herself from us. "I promise."

"You do?"

"I do." He leans in and kisses her tenderly, and they look into each other's eyes. She smiles at him as my heart breaks a little more, another piece falling out.

When he pulls away, she smiles at him, and I swear to God, I can see the hearts in her eyes when they gaze at each other. It's kind of disgusting. Except it would be perfect if it was with me—I want it to be me so *badly*.

"I'm going to bed," I announce, then get up from the couch and head to the bedroom, shutting the door quietly.

I don't make a scene or act angry. I just simply can't sit around and watch them. I don't know why I thought this was such a great idea. It doesn't feel that way to me now. Sharing her is like cutting off one of my limbs and handing it over to Zayne, and it simply won't do anymore. It might work for a while longer until she makes up her mind. I just don't know how much longer I can truly take this pain. I have to tell her how I feel even though I already told her in the hotel room that I want to walk away. I don't really want to, but maybe then she'll figure out what she fucking wants.

The clock strikes midnight right as I lie down, and I look at it over and over for what feels like hours but has only been fifteen minutes. My eyes begin to close of their own accord, and I decide to let sleep take me under for the simple reason that we've been traveling non-stop and will continue to.

Only five minutes later, I hear the door creep open, and I'm automatically on high alert. I see Hallie's figure and relax again.

"Sorry, I was in the shower."

Thoughts of what we did last time in the shower flood my mind, and I tense at the thought of her sharing a similar moment with Zayne. Surely, she didn't fuck him before coming to bed to me. She wouldn't do that. Hallie's better than that.

"What's wrong, Damien?" she asks me softly from in front of the bed.

"Nothing," I lie through my teeth, and just as I say it, I see Hallie's silhouette as she takes off her clothes and drops them on the ground. It's so damn dark in here, and I wish it wasn't. I want to see her so badly my hands itch to touch her all over. And that's why I turn over in bed and pretend to stare at the wall. My eyes are closed as I remember all the moments when I loved her in the dark, just her and me. I miss it. I *need* it.

Hallie gets on the bed, and it slightly dips from the weight she's putting on the mattress. For a moment I think she's going to lie away from me and go to sleep, but instead she comes to me, gluing her front to my back, the softness of her enveloping the hardness of me. I sigh at the contact, melting into the mattress as she begins to rub my hair, and I feel tears threatening to come to my eyes even though I don't cry.

"Tell me," she demands. "I need to know."

"What do you want me to say, Hallie? That I wish you loved me more? That I want you all to myself? That every time you look at him with love in your eyes, I wish it was me?" Tears do gather in my eyes now at the confession, and I sniffle. "Are you happy?" My voice cracks at the end, and she gasps.

"No, please don't cry." She gets closer, which I didn't think was possible, and hugs my waist tightly. "I'm not happy. I love you too. I do. I've just gone through something that is fucking hard for me, and I don't want to make a rash decision. The wrong choice…"

My stomach drops at her words and clenches when I ask her, "Are you saying I'm the wrong choice?"

"I'm saying I don't know who the right one is."

I turn over now, because I could never be the wrong choice. Zayne, on the other hand, could be a bad choice any day. He's lied to her, deceived her, and he's a fucking addict. He's weak, she'll never come first to him. It's just a matter of time before he fucks it all up again.

I grab her hand and place it over my chest, doing the same back to her. "Can you feel my heart? How it pounds every time you're near me?" I ask her with a hoarse voice, and as if on cue, her heart beats faster too. I know I affect her. She yearns for me just like I do her. "It only beats for you, Hallie. That's forever."

She sucks in a sharp breath, her nails digging into my chest, her fingers tightening against my bone. "You're going to promise me forever?" She asks quietly, "Do you realize how long that is?"

"I'd be blessed to spend it all with you, love," I reply, feeling my own words in the depths of my soul. "That's all I've ever wanted."

"Then show me," she tells me, and my cock hardens.

I flip her onto her back and get between her legs, on my knees for her yet again. Hovering over her, I make sure I'm careful with her arms while I pepper kisses all over her face. I just want to show her how deep my love goes for her, deeper than the ocean. When I press my lips to hers, she opens up for me, and I take the opportunity to thrust my tongue into her mouth. We stay like that, kissing each other until I can feel her soaking my sweatpants, then I rub myself on her.

Hallie begins to claw at my pants, pushing them past my ass, and manages to get halfway down. I chuckle against her lips. "If you want my cock so much, be a bad girl and ask for it, Hallie."

"Give me your cock, Damien."

I pull down my pants the rest of the way and line myself up to her entrance, but instead of giving her what she wants, I gather her wetness on me and rub the head of my cock over her clit in slow, torturous, circles. The problem is that it feels like torture for me too. "I said ask."

"Please." She licks her lips, her tongue swiping over mine in the process as well. "Give me your cock. *Please.*" My spine tingles as she begs, and the need to fuck her takes over my body.

I spread her legs wider and thrust into her roughly, fucking her into the bed so hard that the headboard hits the wall from the force of it, of me. She digs her fingernails into my arms, my shoulders, my ass. I'm sure I'm bleeding all over, but I don't give a damn. This animalistic need to claim her has possessed me and no amount of talking myself out of it is going to exorcize it. I bite her on her neck, hard, then suck on it until I know it'll leave a bruise from the pressure of my lips and teeth on it.

"Go slow, Damien," Hallie pants into my ear. "I want to feel all of you."

I slow down because how can I even argue with that?

My spine tingles again from the pleasure coursing through my body, reminding me that I need her to come before I do. She grabs my face with both hands and looks into my eyes. I can't actually see it, but if I could, I bet all the love she feels for me would be pouring out of that one look.

"You've ruined me, love," I tell her, and she kisses me slowly. I continue to fuck her to the pace of our kiss, rubbing myself all over her clit, and she moans loudly when I stay on the spot she likes. "Ruin me more."

Hallie grabs my ass, pushing me harder into her and fucking me back, making herself come. She thrashes on the bed, her legs spreading even wider to accommodate me, and I know she's done for when her body starts to shake under me. Her groans and moans make my stomach flip.

I pull out of her and flip her over onto all fours, spitting on her ass and rubbing it on it. She tries to get away from me, crawling away, but I grab onto her hips and hold her still. I slide myself back into her tight heat, wetting my cock once more, and then begin to push my way into her tight ass.

"No way," Hallie squeals, still trying to get away, even though my grip is not letting her go anywhere. "You're too big."

"I've seen you take it before, Hallie."

"Not like you."

I laugh. "Well, you're going to." I push her back down until her face is buried in the sheets. "Now open up for me, pretty girl. I'm going to show you how good I can fuck this tight, little ass."

I go in gently, not wanting to hurt her since she said she needs time to get used to it, and once I'm about an inch away from being all the way in she says, "It hurts, Damien. It hurts bad."

My hips piston forward until I'm all the way to the hilt, and she screams loudly. For a moment I think I break her, but she's fine and wrapped around my cock so beautifully it's hard to peel my eyes away from where we connect. Somehow my eyes have adjusted enough to tell where we begin and end together.

"You can take it, babe." I pull back and then thrust forward again, hard. "So, fucking take it."

My thrusts are slow and steady, although with force behind them, and Hallie is already moaning uncontrollably within one minute. It feels too fucking good for me, and I feel my balls tightening from the need to come. I know for a damn fact I'll try my best to hold out until she has another orgasm though because she has one more in her.

"Play with yourself, love," I grunt, moaning when she moves and her ass tightens even further around me. Goddamn it all, I'm going to fucking come. "Rub that pretty pussy and make yourself come."

Hallie plays with herself, rubbing her clit aggressively, "Yes, Damien!"

Fuck. Me.

She comes again, her ass tightening around me, and I see black. My toes curl, and I throw my head back when my balls tighten again. I'm just at the edge of release. All I need is a little—

Push.

Hallie fondles my balls while I thrust harder and faster, and that's exactly what drives me over, making me moan so loud it fucking shocks me. Goddamn, that may have been the most amazing sex I've ever had with her or, hands down, *ever*.

I'm not usually an ass guy, anal has never been something I've wanted to do in general, but seeing her with him, the way she came when he fucked her in the ass, I couldn't not claim her there too. There's not one part of her that he's taken that I won't have, and that's a fucking promise.

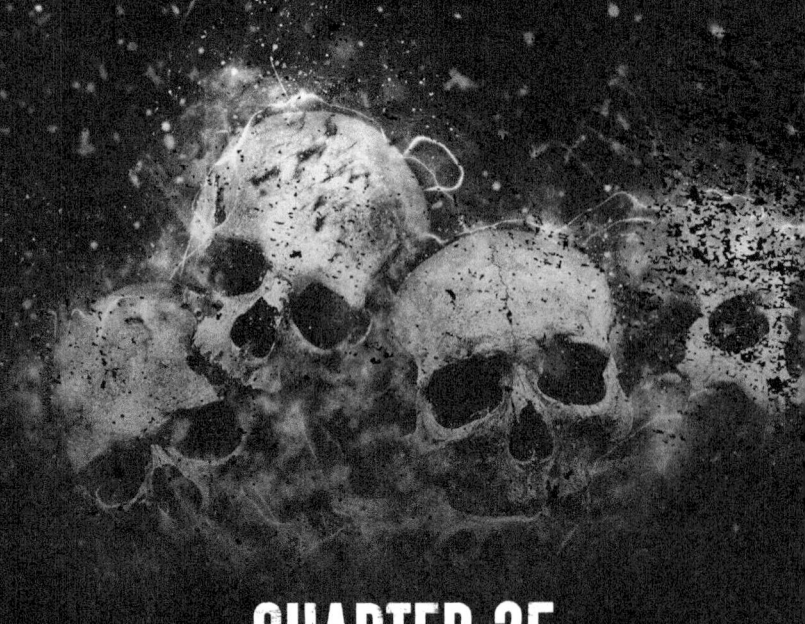

CHAPTER 25

Hallie

The way Damien fucked me last night, I swear it was a spiritual experience. I've never been fucked that way before, with so much lust and love. The way he talked to me—well, only he can do that. No one's ever been able to make me feel butterflies in my stomach from just words.

I didn't want the night to end, but as all things do, the sun rose in the morning, popping our little bubble. Neither of us got any sleep, worshiping each other's bodies to the brink of exhaustion. But I don't care; it was worth it. I'd do it again, over and over, if given the chance.

Now in the shower, while washing my body, I can't help but think of all the dirty fucking things he did to me last night and how much I liked them. I want *more*, but I don't think I'll be getting it any time soon, not with the way Damien wants to be the only one in my life. With every day that passes, I can tell he's getting impatient with me. He needs me to make a choice, and I can't promise that I can do it right now. I don't even know what the choice will be, who I will pick. Hopefully he understands for just a bit longer and lets me think about it.

I finish the shower and get dressed, putting on an extra warm pair of sweatpants and a sweatshirt because it's fucking cold in New York. There was so much snow on the way here it was scary, but I'm glad now we have a reliable and *very* nice vehicle. Honestly, I never thought Damien would get the one I wanted just to make me happy. Although, with the way he was looking at it, I don't think he would've given in if he thought it was the wrong choice.

The SUV is perfect, in any case. Between the spacious trunk for our luggage and other activities that I shall keep to the deepest darkest corners of my mind, I was sold. But the tires, the color, the leather seats… they're all a dream. I've never seen a nicer car, then again, I've never had enough money to. I could tell the moment Damien fell in love with it, and it was when he saw the luggage rack on top as well as the moon roof. I can only imagine all the snowboarding and skiing equipment we can strap to the top without worrying about the inside of the car getting snow all over it. My dream is also to go see the Northern Lights, and I know for a damn fact that you can do it in Canada. When it's possible, that's the one thing I want to do, and the moon roof will be the perfect way to watch it. While I know I will be getting out of the car, I want to fall asleep in the comfort of my back seat while watching the lights dance across the dark sky.

My guys are both sitting at the round, tiny as fuck, breakfast table wearing nothing but pajama pants. Pretty sure I can see both their dicks from here, so they didn't even bother wearing underwear. I bet Zayne knows what happened last night, and he's fucking mad about it. He won't even meet my gaze right now. The walls are paper thin here, so he for sure heard the bed hitting the wall over and over for hours on end. I'd be surprised if he even slept. I guess I should stop being such a selfish bitch and put an end to this already. Apparently, it's hurting them both, and seeing them hurt is hurting me too.

There are pancakes, bacon, and scrambled eggs waiting for me when I walk into the kitchen as well as a mug of coffee just the way I like it. I don't know when either of them went to a store this morning, but it couldn't have taken long. I was only in the shower for thirty minutes.

I sit beside them, afraid to make a sound while pinching my scrambled eggs with my fork. Honestly, I'm afraid to breathe, the air feels thick as I chew my food, and they're in some kind of staring contest that I don't want to be a part of.

"What the heck is going on right now?" I ask, looking between them and then taking a sip of my coffee to not choke on my food. "I thought you both said you could handle it."

"I didn't think it would be that fucking loud, Hallie." Zayne rolls his eyes then pounds one fist on the table. "I couldn't even fucking sleep."

Damien gets up from his chair abruptly, making it fall back to the floor. "Watch the fucking attitude. If you so much as touch a hair on her fucking head, I'll kill you right here."

"Let's fucking go then, motherfucker." Zayne gets up too, and they're suddenly in each other's faces. "She's mine, and I'll touch her whenever I please."

Damien's nostrils flare at this, and he looks at me beggingly. Eyes that plead with me to contradict Zayne, to say the same thing I said to him in the shower not long ago.

"I'm not yours, Zayne," I tell him, and I see Damien's body deflate with relief. "I belong to my fucking self now."

Zayne narrows his eyes at me while Damien smiles, and I think he's proud of me for saying that, even though it was technically for his benefit. I can't deny I had no choice though, not after what I said to him. It's only fair I treat them equally.

Finally, they both backdown, taking a step away from each other. "What are we doing today?"

Damien's head snaps toward me at the question, and he smiles. "We're going to Niagara Falls."

Excitement courses through me, filling my body. "No way!" What the fuck, I've always wanted to go there! "*Really?*"

"Really, babe."

I squeal, jumping up and down in excitement and go to him, throwing my arms around his neck and my legs around his waist. He hugs me to him, grabbing onto my ass firmly while burying his face in the side of my neck.

"God, Hallie, I love you so fucking much," Damien tells me, and my stomach swoops, dipping low and then high again. It's crazy what his words do to me, and I can't get enough.

I smile, pressing his face harder into my neck, and he bites me where he did last night. I hold in a moan as he lets me down, and then run to my room to look for some clothes. I don't know exactly what to wear, but I know it needs to be waterproof and warm. It's cold as fuck here, and I know we will be getting wet one way or another. I won't be the one to get hypothermia. Not today, Satan.

All I have on hand are snow pants and snowsuits, which aren't exactly ideal but will have to do. Better than not having anything at all when you need it. Snow boots will also have to do the job, considering they're waterproof. I have no fucking clue what I'm getting myself into, but I trust Damien wouldn't take me if it's not safe.

Once all of us are ready, we go down to the 4Runner, a dream truly, and get going to the Niagara Falls State Park. It seems Damien has reserved us all a seat to go on a boat tour, and I'm not going to lie, I'm kind of scared shitless.

The drive to the state park is peaceful. Seeing the snow and the trees is a calming experience for me, and knowing that soon enough I'll be surrounded by it, is even more reassuring. Damien really did buy me all the essentials. I can't complain at all. Between the base layers, the wool socks, the snow boots, and the insulated and waterproof North Face jacket, I'm set for whatever comes my way.

We pull up to the parking lot, which is fucking full, by the way, and slide into a spot. Damien peers back at me with a grin, and Zayne rolls his eyes, huffing and puffing. He's not exactly an outdoors person. Moreover, I don't think he'd do what Damien and I do in our spare time together. Breckenridge was the best experience for me because I learned how to do so much, including doing the things I love, without caring what other people think. It just so happens that Damien and I have a lot in common.

"It's okay, Zay," I tell him with a smirk, and he narrows his eyes at me. "You can rest assured you won't be forced into doing anything else. If you hate something, Damien and I will have fun doing whatever we want."

The look he gives me says, *'over my dead fucking body'*. It's a good thing I really don't care nowadays. There are a lot of things I still want to learn to do, especially now that I was given a second, or a hundredth, chance at life. I won't take it for granted. I will make sure to achieve all my goals, check off all the items on my bucket list, live away from everyone, and be happy. It's all easier said than done, especially when I have to live with other people who disagree with what I want to do.

"Whatever, *Hals*. I'm coming with, don't worry."

Damien chuckles as he takes the key out of the ignition and steps out of the car, coming to my side and opening my door. I step out, being careful on the snow since I don't want to be laid out in the middle of the sidewalk. Knowing my luck, it would be me.

Zayne and Damien flank me on each side as we walk down a sidewalk and into an area where there's a crowd. We wait for a few minutes before we get in line, and once at the front, he shows our online reservation, letting the man scan our barcodes. We all gather around to get on the boat, and they give us some kind of plastic bag material poncho, which, in my opinion, is flimsy as fuck.

We get on the boat, Damien holding my hand to make sure I don't slip and Zayne looking like he's constipated. I nod my chin toward Zayne, and Damien laughs, shaking his head. Yeah, maybe it's a bit much to make fun of him, but damn, dude, have some fun for once. Damien wasn't exactly wrong the other day when I heard them talking, and he told Zayne his only hobby was smoking weed. He kind of hit the nail on the head with that one, no matter how embarrassed Zayne may be about it. I still don't know of anything else he likes to do except play the piano, drive fast cars, and fuck. That's about all his hobbies right there. I guess, at least he's consistent.

It's cold and windy. Actually it's pretty fucking miserable, if I'm being honest, and suddenly I'm questioning my life choices. Maybe it was a bad idea to come here. Holy fuck, it's cold. As if he knows, Damien comes closer to my side and hugs me to him, shielding me from the wind, taking the brunt of it himself.

Before we know it, the boat takes off, going around and stopping near the waterfalls, where they proceed to spit out facts at us and bore us to death. Not that I don't like knowing the history of something, but damn, I can barely focus with this cold. I wonder if anyone else can, but then again, I'm sure Damien will be the one who feels just fine. Growing up in Colorado helped him develop a thick skin, and I swear he will go out in short sleeves in thirty-something degrees.

The tour didn't actually last that long, although it was positively breathtaking. I still find myself glad to be out of the cold though, and once in the car, Damien blasts the heat for us and makes me forget all about it.

"Let's go back to the apartment and warm up, yeah?" Damien asks me, I guess *us*, and I nod.

"That was really nice, babe." He does a double take at my words, not expecting the term of endearment. I don't usually do it, and that's probably why he's so surprised. "Thank you for taking me. I will never forget how beautiful that place is." And it's true, it's so fucking gorgeous.

"Anything for you, love."

"What about me?" Zayne whines, "What if I didn't like it?"

Damien smirks at that. I can tell he's trying hard to keep his mouth shut and not be a smartass, but it's definitely difficult. Zayne isn't the kind of guy who likes doing this stuff, and Damien knows that. He told Zayne he could stay behind if he wanted to, but Zay refused, saying he wanted to spend time with me. Well, low and behold, he did not spend time with me. Instead, he huddled in a corner, looking salty as fuck and also cold.

"What's your point?" I mean, yeah, Damien is right. "You never like anything."

"Yeah, I do." Zayne and I make eye contact through his mirror, and I give him a warning look to shut up. "I like anything that doesn't involve being out in the cold. I'm from Texas, for fuck's sake."

"Hey, so am I, and I love being outside. Cold or not."

"Okay, I get it, I get it," Damien says as we get on the highway to go to the Airbnb. "Zayne can stay next time. No need to make him miserable."

"Exactly."

Zayne doesn't like me taking Damien's side. I can tell by the clench of his jaw and his unwillingness to meet my eyes or even look in my direction. It's nothing against him, but being around someone who hates an activity you're trying to enjoy is kind of a downer. I can definitely compromise with him; I don't want all of our plans to be outdoors anyway. The ones who need to get it together are the guys, but that will probably prove nearly impossible, considering how much they argue. In a way though, I guess anything is possible at this point. They might still not *love* each other, but they can be in a room together. Shit, they slept in a bed together. I'd say that's progress.

Either way, I don't care. I have more pressing issues to worry about. Like how the fuck to stay under the radar of a Mexican cartel that wants to kill you for killing their capo.

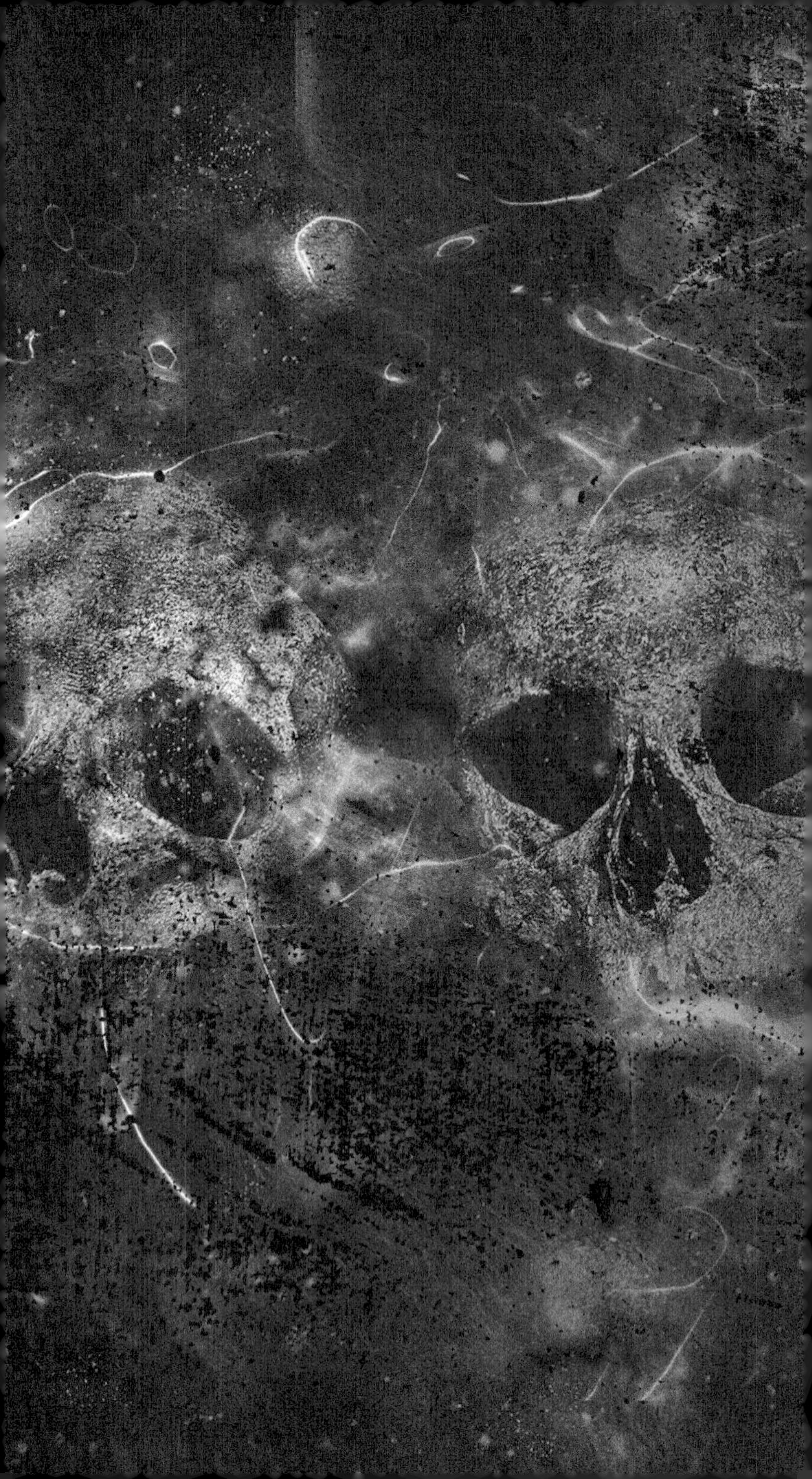

THE SURVIVOR

CHAPTER 26

Zayne

Hallie and Damien have been teaming up against me, which they think genuinely bothers me, but it doesn't. Okay, maybe a little bit, except I'm not taking their bait. Hallie, on the other hand, has it coming. If she thinks she's getting away with teasing me all day and talking shit, she's delusional. I'm just biding my time, waiting for the right moment to snatch her away and punish her for playing these little games. I can play too, so much so that she'll be begging me to let her come later.

Unfortunately, our time in the Airbnb has been cut short because Damien says we can't stay here too long, just in case the cartel knows where we are… yet again. I can't lie, I'm getting a little tired of this shit. All I want to do is move on with my life and forget everything I had to go through in Mexico. I've been pushing it to the deepest, darkest corners of my mind so I don't fall prey to depression or worse.

I know I'm not the strongest person to walk this earth. At

some point, I will fall victim to my mania or depression, and I'll need help. In fact, I think I should get on medication as soon as we settle down so we can avoid it all. I don't want to have to put Hallie through another one of my episodes, and I certainly don't want to give Damien a reason to kick me to the curb. He already wants to, I can tell. Sharing is not coming naturally to me; still, I'm doing it. I hated hearing her with him. Telling him sweet fucking nothings, and him making her come… repeatedly. But him? He's not even trying. Not really. I mean, a three-some is one thing; he's still part of it. However being okay with something as simple as a kiss seems challenging for him. We need to get on the same page, or this shit isn't going to work at all.

The past few months have shown me what's most important to me: Hallie. No drugs, no vice, nothing in this world could ever replace her. Not anymore. I don't want anything to distract me from her, to cloud my judgment. I've been distracted enough that the itch hasn't been there, although I bet that could change in the blink of an eye under the right circumstances. It could be boredom or something as simple as knowing it's accessible. Hopefully, since we live so remotely, I will never see another fucking drug for the rest of my life. I don't want to brag, but I've come a long way. Three months ago, if any of this had happened to me, I would've thrown myself face-first into a baggie of crank. I'd say this is growth.

The crunch of the tires on unplowed snow drags me out of my thoughts, and I stare straight ahead as we cross the Rainbow Bridge to the Canadian border. The longest line of my life greets us as soon as we cross the bridge halfway. Holy shit, it's like everyone wants to cross the border. What the fuck is so interesting about Canada? I bet Niagara Falls looks exactly the same in this country. I won't talk shit about it though, because I'm truly hoping it treats me well. I need this country to be everything Hallie and I have ever dreamed of, except there's an extra person with us now. There's no reason to think about how I feel about him, she's not changing her mind, and I'd rather have her in my life than be too proud to share her.

"This line ..." Hallie sighs from the backseat, stretching her legs with the incredibly ridiculous amount of space, just how she wanted it. Then again, if Hallie told him to get a Mini Cooper, I bet he'd still have done it and made up an excuse about how great of a car it is.

"It's a good thing you have this car to keep you comfortable." Damien senses the sarcasm in my tone and narrows his eyes at me, then punches my arm. *Hard*. "Ow, fucker. What the hell?"

"Watch your damn tone with her."

Oh, great. Now Hallie can't even defend herself for trivial things. He's going to do it for her. Her savior. "Right."

"No, not again." Hallie shakes her head, and I smirk. "No more arguing over me. Please and thanks."

Damien huffs but says nothing more, and I'm thankful for his silence. The way he's been acting the past few days is getting on my last fucking nerve, but I honestly think it's normal. He's probably burnt out from this whole shit show and can't wait to get to the next place. The permanent place. He would probably hate it if I told him I got it. I *understand* why he's so pissed. I'm getting there too.

Before we know it, we're at the border entrance, with the border patrol officer asking for our documents. Damien hands over all of our identifications and passports, and Hallie and I stay very still. The air is charged, and we don't move for fear of drawing attention to ourselves. Fuck, I can't even breathe properly, so I hold my breath instead. What happens if they figure out it's all fake? Will they know? Will we be arrested? Banned from the country? Put in jail? What the fuck did I get myself into?

Somehow, by a fucking miracle, we get waved through, and we are in Canada. We're *in* fucking Canada. My body relaxes into the seat, and I gulp in some breaths, my head dizzy from how I held it. Fuck, that was probably the scariest moment of my entire life. With any luck, this means we're free and that no one can follow us here. I'm not crazy enough—I'm crazy but not *that* crazy—to think we will be safe in this country forever. A few months will do, or even a year if we're God's favorites.

"You good?" Damien asks, and I nod, my hands still shaking from the anxiety this situation just slammed me with.

"Yeah," I nod again. "Yeah, of course."

He smirks but doesn't say anything, and Hallie looks at me again through the mirror. "Now what?" She looks around at the city before us. "Where do we go from here?"

"Now I drive far and far away."

"Okay..." I ask, "How far are we talking?"

"North," he replies. "I'd rather keep it to myself for now." Hallie's mouth drops open as she begins to argue, but he holds up a hand to stop her. Surprisingly, she does. "I'll tell you both when we get closer. Only if we get captured, I don't want either of you to know where this house is. Just in case you get tortured," he looks at me, "or whatever."

"North will do, babe."

Whatever, Hallie. You'd do anything he says as long as he fucks you again.

God, why am I so bitter?

I've been sharing her just fine. Maybe it's because he's not willing to do the same. Or am I understanding why he doesn't want to? Who fucking knows anymore, but if I keep thinking about it, I'll probably figure it out. Right now, though, I don't want to. For now, I just need to get my shit together and stop thinking this way.

"All I will say is our next stop is in eight hours, so by all means, get some sleep."

"It's five in the afternoon." I roll my eyes. "There's no way I'm falling asleep any time soon."

"Then I guess you won't be sleeping because when I get tired, it's your turn."

I want to argue that Hallie can drive too, but then I remember her wrists being fucked up all the way up her forearms. Jesus, this girl will continue to give us all heart attacks, won't she?

While I don't fall asleep, I see that Hallie does within minutes of him saying that. She takes off her seatbelt and lies down on the seat. If a cop were to drive past us, they would be none the wiser, considering she's so tiny you can't even see her with the blankets over her. It just looks like someone threw them on the seats and now they're messy.

I look out the window and keep an eye on the side mirror, making sure no one is tailing us. Damien and I make a good team when it comes to protecting Hallie, and I think sooner or later—hopefully sooner—he will get on board with whatever she needs. Even if it's both of us. Unless he truly wants to walk away, which I highly doubt. Then again, he's very unpredictable. One of these days he might just snap and leave us.

Four hours into the drive, we stop for gas again. Damien says it's not time to switch yet. Nonetheless, it will be in a few hours, so I should get some sleep. This time I do listen to him, reclining my seat and letting my eyes close, drifting and drifting until I'm completely gone.

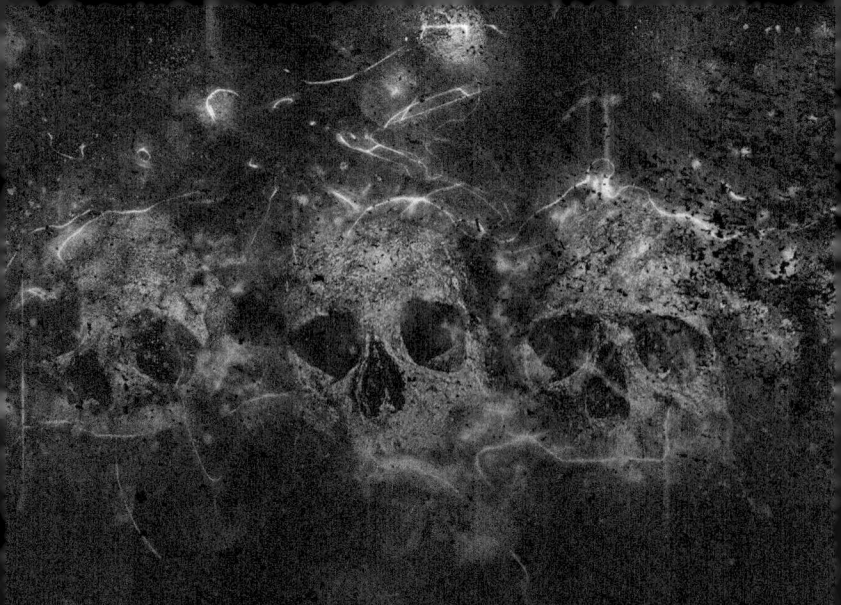

CHAPTER 27

Hallie

Four hours later, we're at a place called "Kettle Lakes," and apparently, we are camping here. Not *really,* since we have a car where we will sleep, but it might as well be camping, considering we're in the middle of a park with tents and RVs around us.

Damien, however, goes to the most secluded spot possible and parks. I've been wanting to do this though, so I don't mind. The temperature outside, however, tells me that if we don't have some kind of sleeping bag, we are completely fucked. It's in the negatives, and surely Damien doesn't want to leave the vehicle on for the entire night.

"Alright," Damien says as he shifts to park, "We're here."

"Home?" I joke, knowing damn well it's not in a park.

"For the night."

I continue to try to look around, but there are no lights on this side of the park. There's just a dirt road that leads who knows where, and I sure as fuck won't be finding out. I lie back down on the seat and close my eyes, hoping we can just go to bed and not have any awkward moments tonight. I've had enough of those to last me a year in just the past two weeks.

"Think there's a bathroom that way," Damien says, and I get up to look even though I don't have to use it. Thank God I don't because he's pointing at that dark dirt road I refuse to walk toward. "With showers. Wanna come?"

"No." Noooope. I shake my head and lie back down. "I'm good."

"You?" he asks Zayne.

"I'm good, man," he replies.

"'Okay," Damien says, coming around and opening the trunk of the 4Runner. The gust of wind that hits me in the face is unlike anything I've ever felt, and suddenly moving to Canada feels like a fucking stupid idea. What the hell?! "Sorry, babe. I need to put the seats down so we can sleep. Can you go climb in the front?"

I nod, climbing over the middle console and over to the driver's side. Zayne looks at me with a brief smile before redirecting his attention back to Damien, and I watch him too.

Damien takes all our luggage and moves it to a pocket compartment in the trunk that's another secret trunk? Or something. It looks similar to a false floor, and all the luggage really does fit in there. He pulls three big blankets out and throws them on the trunk after closing the compartment.

He comes around to my side and opens the back door, putting the seats all the way down until they're totally flat, then grabs a bag from the floor and hoists it over his shoulder.

"I'll be back later. It's probably a mile walk to the bathroom, and I need to shower. I feel nasty."

"Alright. We will be sleeping."

Damien narrows his eyes at Zayne when he makes the comment but doesn't say anything to him. Instead, he looks at me. "Leave the car on for heat until I get back."

"Okay."

With that, Damien closes the door, effectively heating up the space once more, and walks away, disappearing into the night the further he walks into the trail. There's no fucking way I'm going out there.

I crawl into the back of the car once more to lie down, grabbing one of the blankets and spreading it out, just to notice it's actually a sleeping bag. He got me a *blue* sleeping bag. My eyes tear up, knowing he remembers my favorite color, the sweet gesture making a lump form in my throat. He truly is so perfect. He's the kind of man any woman would be lucky to marry. The kind that would make an amazing dad. I don't know if that's what I want, so who am I to hold him back?

Zayne follows closely behind, sitting beside me and arranging his own sleeping bag. Just when I'm about to get in it, he grabs my upper arm. "Hallie, wait."

I stop moving, turning my head toward him and seeing the most somber, sad eyes I've ever seen from him. "Yes?" I breathe, not ready to know what he's unhappy about.

The thought that it's me making him feel that way, that I'm the problem, makes my stomach flip. *I'm sorry*. I don't know what I'm fucking doing. Is he going to ask the same questions as Damien? Does he expect me to pick now? The thought of shutting him down as I did to Damien makes me physically ill. I don't want to. Does that mean *he's* the one?

"Do you still love me?"

What? I thought for sure he'd know the answer to this one. "Of course, I love you." I search his eyes, wondering what could have made him question it. Yeah, it's me. Fucking someone else. That's the one. "Why would you doubt that?"

"I don't know…" Zayne wipes a hand down his face. "Maybe because I heard you telling him."

"Zay—"

"Tell me you love me." God, I love him so much. Why can't he see that? How? "Even if you don't feel it anymore. Please…" Zayne tips my chin up with his fingers, but then looks away as if anxious about my answer.

"I've always felt it, baby."

He snaps his gaze back up to mine. "You have?"

"What we have, you and I, that's forever." And it is. I can't live without him. I just also can't live without Damien.

They each represent a puzzle piece to my heart, and if they're not here to complete it, then I'm hollow, empty, *incomplete*.

I grab his wrist and lower it to his side, then get on my knees and cup his face. "I swear on my life, Zay. You're everything and more."

Zayne kisses me, long and passionate, his tongue stroking mine as we lose ourselves in each other. He flips me over, making me land on my back with him between my legs, then rubs himself against me. The pajama pants I've been wearing since before we crossed the border are thin, and so are his sweatpants. Probably not the smartest attire for negative temperatures, but I wanted to be comfortable while traveling. Either way, I feel everything, every single fucking inch of him, and I want *more*.

"God, Hals." Thrust. "I heard everything last night."

I stop breathing, my heart stops beating, and I look into his eyes. There's anguish in them, pain. He's hurt that I fucked someone else. I'd be hurt too. "I'm so, *so*, sorry."

"All I could think of was how much better it would be if it were me instead." He nuzzles my neck, "I can do so much better than him, Hals."

Tingles spread through my body, down to my core, all the way to my toes. I begin to pull down my pajama pants, getting them right under my ass, and he helps me get them off the rest of the way along with my underwear.

I don't need any foreplay; I'm fucking ready for him. He can tell when I open my legs as he spreads me with his fingers that my arousal is pooling and trailing down my ass.

"Fuck, Hallie. What are you doing to me?"

"Driving you crazy," I moan when he pushes two fingers inside me, gently rubbing a sweet spot. "Just like you do to me."

Zayne pulls down his pants and grabs onto my thighs, pulling me down and closer to him. He pulls me apart, making my knees touch either side of the floorboards, and thrusts into me roughly. He pushes my face to the other side, leaving his hand on my cheek, and bites my earlobe. An electric zap runs through me, and I savor the pleasure mixed with pain as goosebumps break out all over my body.

"Yes, you do," Zayne whispers against the shell of my ear. "Fuck me back. Drive me crazier."

I grab his ass, kneading it with my hands, enjoying the way he feels against me. All of him and all of me. Planting my feet on the floorboards, I raise my hips and meet him thrust for thrust. At first, I just imitate what he does, but after a few thrusts, I begin to circle my hips while doing figure eights just the way he loves.

Zayne groans against my ear, and I want to hear it again. I want to make him come harder than he ever has before. "Oh, hell." He lets go of my face and gazes at me, stilling his movements. "I want you on top, baby."

He flips us over again while we are still connected, effectively getting me on top of him and lying on his back. I start out slow, riding his cock back and forth, then in circles again. He moans, making butterflies erupt in my stomach, and I swear they fly so wildly without escape that I can't breathe.

His hands find my thighs, and he digs his fingers into them, his nails raking them, inflicting pain the way we always do to each other. It's the only way we know how to love, showing each other all the ugly parts of us and hoping the other will accept them. It's funny how he can be my salvation while simultaneously being my ruin. I give him the parts of me that I know I could never give anyone else. I give him my demons, knowing damn well he's the only one who'd take them. The only one who'd play with them.

I fuck him harder, leaving him breathless and panting, his mouth wide open on an 'o' while he throws his head back with his eyes closed. "You like that, don't you, baby?" I ask him as I go faster, my breathing ragged. He doesn't reply. In fact, he doesn't move at all. "Slap my ass if you do."

Zayne immediately slaps my ass hard, then kneads it with his fingers, pushing me into him even harder. "Yes," he hisses, "Right there."

"Harder, baby. I know you can do it harder."

My ass stings from the next slap, but all it does is make me feel a heat in my core that I hadn't felt in a long fucking time. I crave his violence, the way only he can make me feel because we're fucking dysfunctional. Toxic. Bad for each other. Yet, we work so well together.

My legs begin to shake when I rub myself on his pelvis, my clit on fire as I get closer to my orgasm. I throw my head back too, savoring the feeling of falling, jumping, flying, soaring. I claw at his chest when I come, my hands squeezing him, my legs trapping him.

I come down from the high he always inflicts upon me, mesmerized just to see him watching me. No one's ever looked at me that way except for him, like I'm the last hit of his favorite drug, and he wants to make me last as long as possible.

"Your turn," I say in a breathy moan as I pick up my pace again.

My hands circle his neck, and his eyes widen when I squeeze hard. He's not expecting that, for me to do what he does to me back to him, and that makes it even better, sweeter.

I watch his face as I put more pressure on his neck, and he turns red. His Adam's apple bobs, his neck veins straining as I fuck him hard. Within a minute, he's coming inside me, trying to breathe but also not making a move to make me release him. He shudders as he empties himself inside me, and his eyes roll to the back of his head.

My hands loosen from his neck as soon as he stops jerking inside of me, and I let go of him. He's in shock, in awe of me and what I've just done. I think he liked it more than he will probably admit, and I bet he'll make me do it again another time. Knowing him, my savagery turned him on even more, and now he won't be able to get enough of it. We're fucking sick, but our only cure is each other.

I collapse on top of him, my ear to his chest, letting the fast pounding of his heart soothe me. It's running at a gallop, but so is mine. He makes me feel alive, so much so that it feels like I'm floating on a cloud while also being set on fire with his every touch.

"Happy birthday, baby," I tell him, and his eyes land on my own.

"You remembered?"

"Of course, I remembered," I reply, slightly offended. "I remember everything about you."

"Thank you, baby." He grimaces, "Please don't tell him."

Why? Because he doesn't want him to think he's getting special treatment?

"Okay." I sigh. "If that's what you want."

"As much as I want this," he sighs, "I don't want Damien to walk in on us."

Surprised, I lift myself up as much as my hands let me anyway. Now that the adrenaline rush has passed, they feel kind of weak again. "Really?"

"He doesn't deserve it."

"You're right." I get off him, quickly wiping myself with my underwear and putting my pants back on. "Thank you for that."

"It's not for you, baby." Zayne puts his pants back on as well, "He's been very good to me too. I don't want to fuck up whatever this is between me and him, even if he kind of hates me right now."

"I get that." I open the secret compartment in the trunk and stuff my panties in the pocket of my luggage as fast as I can, then close it back up. "Fuck, I have to use the bathroom."

I don't want to walk all the way to wherever Damien is. I'm genuinely tempted to go in the woods, but I don't think I can. Number one, it's negative thirty or some shit out here. Number two, I'm dripping cum. I don't know what animals are into that, but I'm not willing to find out. Number three, ew. I don't want to be that girl. I refuse to get that comfortable around them. I guess the only choice I have left is to fucking walk. Goddamn it.

"I'll take you."

"Okay."

We put on a jacket and take the key out of the ignition, locking the doors and making our way into the trail. Zayne shines the phone flashlight while we walk, making sure no animals jump on us as we walk. Not that it would make any difference since we don't have a weapon on us.

After what feels like twenty miles and an eternity, we finally make it to the bathroom. There's no fucking way I'm doing this again tonight, so if I have to pee again, I'm holding it in until morning. I don't care if I get no sleep from it.

I go into the bathroom, which is surprisingly clean, and take care of business. Once done, I freshen up a little with the sink and someone's toothpaste they left behind. Yeah, gross, but beggars can't be choosers, and I'm not about to have nasty breath at night.

When I come out, both my guys are waiting for me outside of the bathroom, talking to each other. My stomach sinks at the thought of Zayne telling Damien what we just did, but then again, I remind myself that Damien probably knows exactly what happened. Maybe he took even longer on purpose, not wanting to walk in on something he didn't want to see.

"There she is," Damien says with a smile on his face. It reaches all the way to his eyes and soothes the broken parts inside of me. His smile is the best. "Let's head back before you freeze."

"Yes, please." I groan. "It's fucking colder than my mom out here."

They both laugh at that. Hysterically might I add, and I guess it is funny. Dark humor is a coping mechanism, according to my therapist—or former therapist—and I use it frequently to forget about my misfortunes. Something tells me it will now become a regular occurrence since everything went down in Mexico. This is the first joke I make about it, and honestly, I feel good now that it's out into the world.

The walk back to the car is as cold as it was to get to the bathroom, if not colder. Probably colder considering it's getting later into the night. It's dark as fuck on this path, and no amount of brightness from the flashlight is enough to illuminate our steps. I'm trying not to freak out; I've never been scared of the dark. I *thrive* in it. So why then am I so fucking scared right now? Maybe it has nothing to do with the dark and more to do with what will happen once we get in the car again. Will Damien suspect what happened? Will he take one look at me and know? Fuck, I hate this. I really do.

As if on cue, as if he fucking knows and can sense something is amiss, Damien comes to my side and tenderly holds my hand. I look up at him, finding his dark blue eyes even in the darkness, and I try to give him my most genuine smile. I fail. My lower lip trembles so violently his face morphs into a frown. I look away quickly though, hoping his mind doesn't spiral and go down a rabbit hole of possibilities.

Why do I have to be so weak?

Why do I have to care so damn much?

We get to the car and my eyes water. I try to blink back tears as I open the back seat, and the smell of sex hits me right in the face like a sharp slap from my mother. I get in and refuse to look back. Instead I grab my sleeping bag and go to the farthest corner of the car. I hear them climbing in behind me, and we're all lying down together within the next minute.

There's rustling, and then someone wraps their arms around me. I sniffle, then more tears fall. A hand comes around to my face and wipes my tears, and that's when I feel him, smell him. His coconut and sea salt smell fills my nostrils, and my shoulders begin to shake.

"Shhhh." He whispers in my ear. "It's okay, Hallie. I'm here."

"I fucked up."

"No. You didn't," he reassures me. "I still love you."

But for how long? Until he can't take it anymore? Until he decides it's not worth it? I can already feel the heartbreak approaching, and my heart isn't ready for it to be him. He's not the one who breaks me, that's Zayne.

So why does it feel like this time will be the exception?

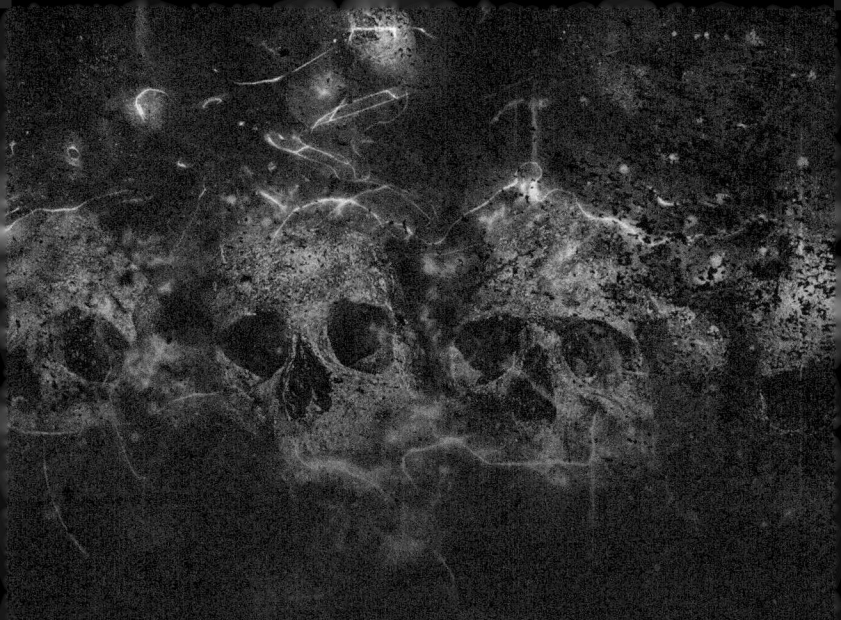

CHAPTER 28

Damien

Kettle Lakes Provincial Park is fucking beautiful in the daylight, just like I knew it would be. Hallie isn't scared to go to the bathroom this time since the trail isn't as intimidating now that the sun is shining. Last night? It was creepy as fuck.

Now even the picnic tables and park are visible. She squeals when she sees the swings but realizes it's way too cold and windy to play today. I love the inner child in her. She thinks she's broken, but I see all her pieces coming back together. She's making herself whole again without anyone's help, and I think that's beautiful.

The lake is right next to the restrooms, which I didn't even realize yesterday, and when we walk toward it, I notice the abandoned kayaks strewn about in front of the shore. I wish we could go in the water for a little while, but there are two problems. One, there's no oars anyway. Two, the lake is frozen solid. So, I guess that's that.

We spend about an hour out here just watching the sunrise.

The pinks and oranges in the sky are gorgeous as the colors bounce off the frozen lake. The ice looks incredible when the golden hour reflects across the entirety of it, and I sigh in contentment when Hallie sits next to me and holds my hand.

Although I cuddled her all night, I barely slept. Going in the car to the smell of her fucking him… was a punch to the gut. I knew before entering, however. The moment she met my eyes before we reached the car and her lips trembled, I knew. I fucking *knew*. She felt like she betrayed me; that's why she acted that way. And even though I reassured her, I can't say I didn't feel the same way.

My heart physically hurt. It's like what they call Broken Heart Syndrome. I never thought it was real, but now… now I believe anything is possible. It can't be normal to feel this much anguish over someone. I'm starting to doubt everything. Fuck, I'm doubting my very own existence. My place in her life, her love for me. Even the way she lets me fuck her, feels fake in comparison to what I'm seeing between the three of us. This dynamic isn't working for me, yet I have no idea how else to voice it. The last time I talked about walking away, she didn't exactly shut me down. Although she made me feel guilty about it. At that point I just dropped it. I don't know that I'll be able to move past this entire situation, and I'll be honest, I might not be able to handle it for much longer.

Now as I look at her, gazing at the lake with a smile, I feel a deep love for her. I wish I could change it, push a button and turn it all off. It would be so much easier than sitting in this suffering with no end in sight. It doesn't matter though. I have to tough it out. After everything I put her through, I can't just walk away. I went to hell and back to retrieve her from the monster that lives in her nightmares, and I'll be fucking damned if I'm not the one who continues to save her. And she *does* need to be saved, mainly from herself. I owe it to myself to try after everything I've sacrificed to be with her, to get her back after she discovered how I lied to her and deceived her for months. I'm surprised she's forgiven me, but I can't forgive her back. I have to try now.

The stabbing me was not the part that hurt me, it's that she left me. I can't believe she did that after how much I tried to protect her. *That's* what I can't seem to forgive her for. Now to add salt in the wound, I also have to witness this bullshit between Zayne and her.

Speak of the devil. He's looking at me with curious eyes. Like suddenly I'm a fucking unicorn or sprouted a tusk or some shit. What the hell? I raise an eyebrow at him, and he glances away, not meeting my eyes. Maybe he's wondering how the fuck I cuddled Hallie to sleep last night after knowing what they did. He shouldn't worry, I don't know how the fuck I did it either. I guess my love for her won over the pain in my heart. It kind of felt like I was getting stabbed all over again, the pain sharp and long as it gutted me over the course of the night.

I couldn't sleep just thinking of all the ways he probably fucked her, how many times she came, and how the fuck do I get out of this? The biggest problem is I don't want to get out of this situation bad enough. Yes, it bothers me, but losing her would hurt worse. Fucked if I stay, fucked if I don't. Either way, I'll be gutted.

I grab Hallie's hand and bring it to my lips, gazing at her with a sad smile, and her eyes turn sad along with me. She knows how I feel, she can tell. Maybe she'll stop. Maybe she'll love me just a little more. Ugh, I don't know when I turned this pathetic, but I fucking hate it. I've never been so low over a woman.

"Time to go, love," I tell her, and she groans. "I know. Just a bit longer. We will be there tomorrow at the latest, I promise."

"I just want to be done already…"

"We're almost there, Hals," Zayne interjects.

Fire runs down my spine, and I begin to sweat even in this morning's negative temperatures. For fuck's sake, I need to chill. Zayne and I were fine just a few days ago. What the fuck got into me now? I don't understand why suddenly everything he does gets on my nerves. Maybe it's because I've realized this sharing thing won't last much longer.

"Let's go," I say, walking away and heading back up the trail toward the 4Runner.

I hear their footsteps behind me so I know they're following me at least. The crunch of the small rocks on the dirt road is the only thing keeping me grounded, and I try not to think about how he fucked her—yet again. I need to get the fuck over it if I stand a chance of staying for even one day longer.

Once in the car, I get back on the highway and begin our trip to our forever home, for now, anyway. The ride is silent as fuck, an eerie silence, and I have a feeling they both feel like they fucked up. I don't think they did. Hallie hasn't promised herself to me or some shit, and it's not like I didn't fuck her just a few days ago, anyway. That being said, it still hurts. *A lot.*

After a few hours, I pull up to a gas station where Hallie goes in to use the restroom while I pump gas. Zayne stays in the car like it's awkward between us now, because it is. At least he can read the room. It's a newly acquired talent for his dumb ass.

Once Hallie returns, Zayne goes inside, and I get in the car with her. The silence is also awkward between us, and she clears her throat.

"I'm sorry," she croaks, then clears her throat once more. "I didn't mean to hurt—"

"Me? Hurt me?" I scoff. "You know damn well what you're doing, babe. Don't worry, though, I can handle it."

"I'm sorry for more than just that."

"What, then?"

She takes a deep breath and lets it out, sighing before she says, "Everything. Stabbing you. Running away. Getting kidnapped. Making you come after me."

I chuckle. "You didn't make me come after you. I did it because I care about you."

"I know, Damien." I turn around to look at her with her face in her hands. I reach back and pull them away from her to see her eyes are bloodshot and her face is red and splotchy. Has she been crying? Over *me*? "And that was the most noble act of all, that you came for me even after everything I did, how I left you. I really am sorry for hurting you."

"And I'm sorry for kidnapping you," I reply. "I'm not sorry for my involvement in everything, because I never would've met you. Now you take over my every thought. You're the air in my lungs, Hallie."

"You're an amazing person, Damien. You're kind and sweet, and you love fiercely." We stare at each other as she searches my eyes for my feelings. She looks at me like my heart is a window, and she's trying to peer into my soul. "And that's only a few of the reasons I love you."

My heart stutters in my chest, the wind knocking out of me. I wasn't expecting that. Anything but her saying that, really. My hands shake as I reply, "I love you too, babe."

Zayne opens the door, and I twist around, straightening in my seat as he climbs in and sits in the passenger side, no longer in the back with her. I think he wants a truce, a little show of putting some distance between them.

We're only four hours down, which is about how long it takes to get through half a tank. I'm paranoid about letting it get below that, so I always fuel up by then. One more stop after this, then we'll be in our new hometown. Eight more hours to go, and I'm sure as fuck not looking forward to them. Let's just hope they go by quickly.

It's nine at night, and we're finally pulling up to the house. The headlights shine on it, which I'm doing since I want Hallie to see the house when we leave this car. I know she's tired, but I'm looking forward to seeing the look on her face when I show her what I bought just for her. Yes, I bought it, but this house has always been for her. I've been wanting to give her a place she can call home without having to worry about anything. Somewhere she knows peace and doesn't have to question what a home is.

Tadoussac is a small town in Quebec that stole my heart the moment I saw the pictures of it. I was looking for something remote but still close enough to a town for activities and essentials. Living near the United States is not an option, especially anywhere with border patrol nearby. I had to find something further north, and I'm glad I did. The place is unreal, with the water right in the middle of town. It looks like something out of a postcard. I can't wait to explore it. For now, though, I'm excited about the house. At first, I bought a little cabin near a lake, but then decided it was too small for all three of us since it only had two bedrooms. I am saving it for a rainy day, for myself, just in case something happens.

"Close your eyes, love," I tell her, and she shuts them. Zayne sits there, his mouth agape, looking between me and the house. I can't lie, it's fucking gorgeous. "And I'll come around and let you out. You can open your eyes when I tell you to."

I get out of the car and open her door. Then I help her get out, grabbing her upper arm and making sure not to hurt her wrists or forearms. It's a steep step for her to descend, so I hoist her up and let her down in front of me. Holding her hand, I direct her to the side of the car, right next to the headlights, so she can see the house with the lights shining on it. I'm honestly surprised she has kept her eyes closed this entire time.

"Okay, now open them."

Watching her face take in the house has been one of the best things I've seen in a very long time. Her mouth is wide open, her jaw slack, and her eyes alive. They shine with a light I haven't seen since I got her back. I know it has nothing to do with the material things. It's not about the house. It's about the gesture, and I'm a man of gestures. I will always do my best to make her feel loved, whether that be through a house she deserves or something as simple as taking her on a mountain hike.

"Holy fuck, Damien," she says in a breathy voice. "What the hell? When did you get this?"

"The moment I rescued you, I closed on it," I admit. "It was only a phone call away. I've been looking at it for months and bid on it before knowing where you were."

"It's gorgeous."

"It's *yours*."

She gulps and looks at me then back to the house. "Why would you do that for me?"

"Because, Hallie." I turn my body toward her and lean in to whisper in her ear, "You're my sunshine. The reason I wake up every morning. Without you, my light is gone."

She steps back and looks at me, her lower lip trembling again, and I hold her chin between my thumb and forefinger. "Do you truly love me that much?"

"You're the love of my life." Without a doubt, hesitation, or thought. Hallie is it for me, the only one that exists in this world. No one else could *ever* compare.

"Wow." She looks back at the house. "I can't even believe this is happening. I thought for sure we'd be staying somewhere super small and low-key. But this? Damien, this is truly unexpected."

"You deserve the unexpected, Hallie." I look at her in awe. Her perky little upturned nose, full lips, wavy hair. She's perfection in one tiny package. "I thought about buying a small house, but then realized… What if this is our forever home? What if we love it so much we never want to leave? It's helpful if it's bigger. You'd never need more than this. You could have an office and sketch or do what you like."

"How expensive was it?"

"Less expensive than you think. These people have been trying to sell it forever. I kind of lowballed a little, and they accepted, which I didn't anticipate. In hindsight, it was probably an asshole move, but it was the only way I could afford it. I've already spent money on this house and a car. I don't want to run out of money. It's supposed to last us forever. I plan on going back to work in a hospital nearby."

"If you're going, I'm going," she replies, just like I knew she would.

"No way, babe." What if she gets kidnapped again?

"So, why can you go but not me?"

"I know it's not fair." I sigh, "But you can easily get hurt, kidnapped, or worse. I never want to see you go through that again. Maybe in a few years, after things have died down. I don't plan on working right now."

"You're right…"

She takes another look at the house. The modern exterior and the beige-colored bricks, the black siding at the top by the windows, and the one-car garage's black door. I didn't want to draw too much attention to ourselves, so I had to keep the house to the average size. It's nothing like my cabin in Breck, which is still on the market and driving me crazy. Once that's sold, my future—our future—is basically secured. That house is worth a million dollars, just like many houses in that expensive fucking state. Breckenridge, though, is way more costly than people realize. A small house would still be half a million dollars.

"Wanna go inside?" I ask her, and she squeals, jumping up and down with excitement.

"Yes!"

I open the front door with keys left under the mat, since I didn't have a way to come get them before now, and Zayne finally gets out of the car. I have a gnawing suspicion he was trying to give us some space for the surprise, so she could truly appreciate it without him hovering or making her feel bad about her reaction. I appreciate that more than he knows, but I won't acknowledge it.

Thankfully, I had all the utilities turned on before heading to Canada. So when I open the door, I smile at myself before turning on the light. This place is fully furnished. I bought it that way while keeping Hallie's tastes in mind. I couldn't do all that Farmhouse bullshit though, not with a modern house and architecture. However, I still know what she likes, so that was helpful.

Hallie comes in behind me, her body heat searing my back, and I turn on the light. The rich, deep brown hardwood floors greet us, and I look at the space. The foyer is simple, with a gold mirror and a black entryway table. It's not a big space, and we move on quickly to the living space, going around the wall that separates the foyer from it. There's a tiny beige sectional couch with the chaise attached, but we don't need anything big. It's actually large enough to fit three people just fine. A glass end table flanks one end of the couch, the one that doesn't have the chaise attached, and the legs are the same color as the hardwood floor. It looks understated and elegant. There's also a matching coffee table in front of the couch and a short, modern, white television stand against the wall below a massive, mounted flat-screen TV. The plush carpet under the coffee table is perfect because we don't have to worry about super cold feet during the negative temperatures—such as now.

Hallie stares at everything with wonder, her eyes lingering on the dark gray accent wall where the television is mounted, and she looks back at me in awe. "Holy shit, Damien." I guess that's the only phrase she knows right now.

I chuckle, "Just wait until you see the kitchen, love."

I take her around the couch and to the dining room, which has the kitchen in the background, as it's an open floor plan. She doesn't look at the kitchen, focusing on each part of the house. Each room, before moving on to the next one. Right now, she's focused on the glass table and suede, beige dining chairs. They match the bricks outside perfectly. There's also a beautiful modern set of lights right above it, hanging low.

Hallie looks toward the kitchen, gasping as she takes in the white subway tiles that go all the way to the ceiling. The cabinets are understated, and there are only two of them, making sure all the attention is on the backsplash. The hood also makes a statement for sure, with its gray charcoal color. The fridge has a built-in pantry with floor-to-ceiling cabinets on either side of it. The large sink also has a beautiful silver faucet; all the appliances are brand new. Lastly, the kitchen island really steals the show with its wooden planks as the countertops and siding.

"Look at this kitchen!" She goes around opening cabinets and the fridge and freezer. "The marble counters! What?!"

"I'm glad you like it, Hallie." I walk around the island to face her. "I got it with you in mind, so I hope you love it."

"It really is beautiful," Zayne says, speaking up for the first time in thirteen hours. I don't even know how his voice works right now. If I didn't talk for that long, my voice would at least crack with the first word.

"Okay, one more thing," I tell them both, heading for the backyard door right next to the dining room. "It's outside."

"No way, Damien." Hallie groans, "I can't go outside right now, it's fucking freezing."

"You don't have to go outside," I open the backdoor, and they both come to my side. "Just look."

"What the actual fuck is that?" Zayne asks, and I laugh outright. This dude has no fucking clue what's happening around him. I'd be surprised if he could find his own dick sometimes.

"It's a—"

"Is there seriously a rink in the backyard?"

"Yes," I tell Hallie. "You can skate. It's basically a rite of passage to have that in Canada."

"This is fucking weird," Zayne tells us both.

"You're no fun, Zay." Hallie rolls her pretty brown eyes at him, making me smirk. "Live a little, damn."

"Yeah, okay. Well, if that's it for today, I'm tired as fuck."

"First bedroom on the right!" I call out as he heads up the stairs.

He doesn't reply, but I'm sure he will listen for the simple fact that he doesn't want to steal Hallie's room and doesn't know which one that is. It's obviously the master bedroom with the bathroom attached to it. Actually, all the bedrooms have a bathroom attached, and there's one extra one downstairs as well. I kind of thought of everything. Although I didn't want to admit it, I had a feeling Zayne was going nowhere. Especially with Hallie just now escaping, she'd be even more attached. It is what it is, but at least there are two extra rooms for whatever we want. I want a gym in one of them, but I'll have to ask Hallie what she'd like before I make that decision.

"Thank you," Hallie tells me, snapping me out of my thoughts. She comes to my side and hugs me, arms tight around my waist. "This is amazing, and I don't deserve it."

"Shhh." I lift her chin until she's looking at me, her dark brown eyes almost black even under the lights. "You deserve it more than anyone I know."

I kiss her, sucking on her bottom lip, then the top. And lastly, thrusting my tongue into her mouth. The way she kisses is more erotic than fucking, and right now is one of those times. This kiss is my lifeline. It's the only thing keeping me grounded.

Sane.

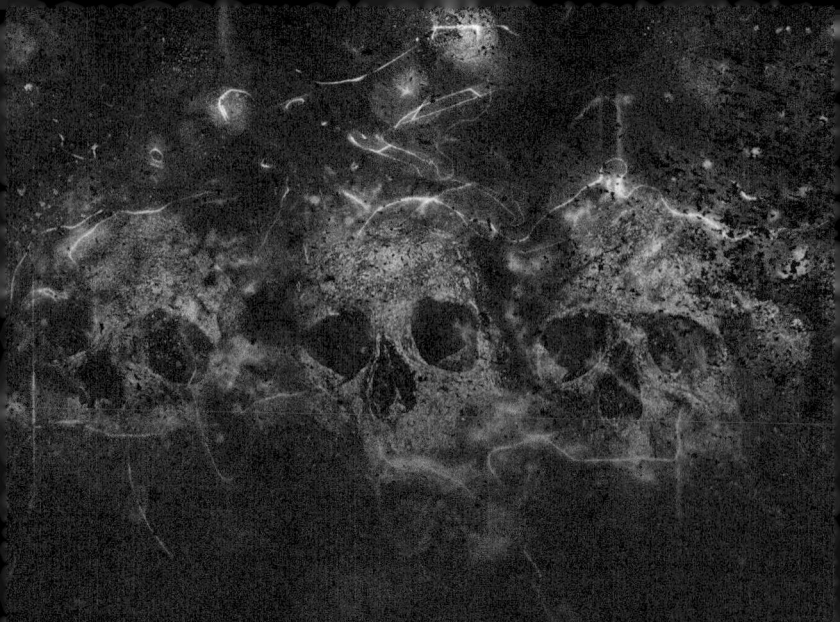

CHAPTER 29

Zayne

Jealousy burns through me as if I stuck my arm in acid, and it's fucking making me angrier that I even feel this way in the first place. I knew what I was getting myself into when I agreed to share Hallie. What I didn't know is he'd do something this big for her. Purchasing a house for her is a big fucking deal, and while I want to be happy for her because she deserves it, I find myself feeling angry that it wasn't me who got it for her. That it couldn't be me because I have nothing left to my name except for what Damien has bought for me, which means I've been living off him too, to top it all off. It makes me feel inadequate to stand in on their relationship, always the shadow in the corner. I'm playing house without contributing, without a fucking clue if I'll ever be able to again. I need to get a job, and it needs to be as soon as possible. In a few days, I'll bring it up to him. That is, if I can control myself until then.

I go down the stairs to find Hallie in sleep shorts and a tank top, sitting at the kitchen island with Damien, drinking coffee and rubbing elbows without a care in the world. One of her legs is draped over his lap, and it makes me want to tip the bar stool over just to make her stop. Not because I don't want to share her—I mean, if she picked me I obviously wouldn't—but because I'm tired of all the praise she's directing toward Damien. Because he bought her this house. I bet this was his intention all along, to snare her in his trap and make her see his love for her. And he does love her, at least. I guess I should be happy about that, but instead it makes me sad. He's willing to do anything for her, and I am too. He just has the means to, while I only have my heart, soul, and love to offer her.

"Good morning," I tell them, making myself known. I don't want to witness any bullshit this morning, so telling them I'm here ensures that nothing weird happens in my presence. Though if I were him, I wouldn't give a shit.

"Mornin'," Hallie replies while Damien nods as I walk by.

"Is there anything to eat for breakfast?" Fuck. I'm starving.

"No." Damien shakes his head. "I just ordered us something. Hallie picked for you."

My body relaxes at that, knowing that Hals is aware of what I like and don't like, so she won't fail me.

"We will go grocery shopping later," Hallie says with a smile, beckoning me with a finger. I smile. "We need to see where we live, even if it's for a little bit."

"You're right, baby." I get closer to her, rubbing her lip to get coffee off it. "You should go get dressed. Aren't you cold in that?"

"Okay, yeah. A little."

She gets up and walks back up the stairs, leaving Damien and I alone. I don't actually care what she wears, but I need to talk to him alone without her hearing us or interrupting. What better way than to ask her to go to her room and take thirty to thirty-five business years?

The silence is a little weird between Damien and me, almost forced. It's as if he wants to talk but also doesn't so he's making himself be quiet. We look at each other for a minute, and he arches an eyebrow, making me grin.

"Are we gonna talk, or are we just staring at each other?" I ask him, trying to start the conversation in a way so he doesn't get defensive.

"Stare." Damien gives me a one-word reply. He's such a pain in the fucking ass.

"Yeah, I don't think so." I take the seat where Hallie was just in and stare straight ahead. "We *need* to talk. Not optional."

"Since when do you give me orders?"

"Since I realized what you're fucking doing." I scoff, leveling him with a look. "You're giving Hallie everything she needs. A house, a car, money. What the fuck are you playing at?"

Damien narrows his eyes at me. "I just want to make her happy."

"Bull fucking shit." I know he knows I'm onto him. "I know better than that, and I thought you were fine with sharing her."

He wipes a hand down his face. "You're right. I'm fine with it."

The fuck he is. He's been distant, acting weird, even when doing nice things for her. My spidey senses are tingling, and I can tell something is off. I just can't quite put my finger on what it is. "You're such a fucking liar."

"I mean it. We can fuck her together again, if that's what you want."

"It's not what I want. This isn't about me." Clearly, he doesn't get it. "It's about Hallie and what she wants. What she *needs*."

"You're right. It is." He sighs, "I'll do better."

He's full of shit, and I know it. He knows I know it too, that's why he won't meet my eyes. "Prove it then."

"That takes time."

"No, it doesn't." This fucker is just full of excuses today, isn't he? "Let's all cook together and act like our normal selves."

"So… you want me to act like I fucking hate you and want to stab you the way she stabbed me?"

I smirk, thinking of her doing that, and he punches me in the arm. Goddamn it. "I want you to act like you love her. I'll sit on the sidelines if I must."

"Don't do it on my account."

"Whatever, I was trying to be nice." I push off from the table just as Hallie descends the stairs again and returns to her coffee. I pass her on my way up, "I'm taking a shower, baby. You know, in case you'd like to join me."

Hallie shakes her head quickly. "No, thank you."

I nod once and walk up the stairs, not going to the bathroom when I reach the top. Yeah, real smooth of me to spy on them, but I don't give a shit at this point. I need to know how he's treating her.

"Good morning," Hallie says.

"Good morning, love." Damien replies, and I have to force myself to not roll my eyes. "How did you sleep?"

"Could've slept better with you in my bed."

A chill runs down my spine, remembering the last time he did sleep in her bed. The sound of the headboard hitting the wall still haunts me. Mostly because she won't do it with me. She hasn't shared a bed with me since him, and there has been nothing else since two nights ago, not even a kiss. Yet here she is, constantly chasing Damien's dick. Is it because we as humans always want what we can't have? Is that how she perceives him now? As unattainable?

"Maybe we can remedy that tonight?"

Motherfucker.

He probably knows I'm listening. Yeah, I'm sharing her, whatever. But it's one thing to share and another to give over all of the attention you want to another person. That's no longer sharing; it feels like a choice. She said she won't make one, but I know her. I know *her* even when she doesn't know herself. If she were going to choose, she'd choose him. She's plunging her knife, twisting it into my heart, then yanking it out for me to bleed out.

"Yes," she says in a low, seductive voice. "I'll be waiting for you."

There's a shuffling and some steps, and I just imagine him

stepping up to her and holding her in some way. "What do you have in mind?"

"Sucking your…"

I know how that sentence ends, but I just can't stick around to hear the rest of it. I make my way back to my room and shut the door quietly so they don't realize I didn't get in here until now. I lock it just in case because, if I'm being honest, I'm not exactly in the mood for Hallie right now. I need to be alone.

My room is very… not me. That's okay though. It'll get there. It's hard to make something that fits you when you have no money at all, but I'll figure it out. I'm going to find a job and fucking soon. I don't care what they have to say about it. I'll move out if I have to. I refuse to be here letting Damien financially support me.

The white walls stare at me, screaming that they need paint. I can almost hear them begging me to give them a dark color. I haven't decided yet, but it's between gray and black. There will be curtains, of course. I need blackout curtains to survive. Luckily, it's been gloomy this morning so the sunlight did not peek through the blinds. I hate being woken up that way unless it's Hallie waking up right next to me.

I open the bathroom door to a glass shower similar to the one from my room in the basement. It's fucking incredible, but sadly takes me back to when Hallie sucked me off in my own shower. Fuck, it was terrific. I know what she's capable of, how hard she can make a man come, and I think that's the problem. I want it to be me again. I want to melt under all her attention until I'm nothing but a puddle at her feet. I want to worship her like the goddess she is.

Something he's clearly not willing to do.

Damien might say that he's all in, that he's not having doubts, that he'll be better and act nicer. At the end of the day, though, I know him, know that he's full of fucking shit. He's having doubts. I can feel it. I just hope he doesn't leave her high and dry. That would be fucked up and unforgivable.

The faucet is cold as I turn it, letting the cold spray hit me right in the face instead of waiting for the water to warm up. It feels like a metaphor for my life lately. I wash quickly, mainly since the water is hot now, the bathroom feels cold as fuck. It's probably those negative temperatures. Oh, and the fact that I didn't turn on the heat vent right above me.

I get out of the shower, drying myself quickly as well so I don't freeze my fucking balls off. I already feel them shrinking the longer I take to get dressed. Somehow, when I come out of my room to look for underwear, Hallie is sitting on my bed with a smile on her face. A knowing face that tells me she knows what I was trying to do.

"What the fuck?" I ask her, confused about how she got in. "How did you get in here?"

"I can't tell you all my tricks." Hallie shrugs, and I narrow my eyes. Now I have to know what she did. I'll have to pay closer attention. Possibly pretend to go in the shower and have her wait in the room instead.

"What are you doing here?"

Hallie frowns, taken aback by my attitude. Same, baby. Same.

"Damien left. I just wanted to talk for a minute."

"Why? Because Damien left?" I scoff, "You don't want him to know you talked to me?"

"It's not like that, Zay. He's just..."

"A pussy? Sensitive as fuck? Refusing to share? Yeah, I know all of that."

Hallie sighs, long and loud. "I just wanted to tell you that I love you."

My body relaxes slightly, but then I tense again when I remember how she's been treating me since we last fucked. "Doesn't feel that way."

I begin to rummage through my dresser drawer, looking for the underwear I have already unpacked and organized. Hallie comes up behind me, crowding my space, grabbing onto my abs from behind and raking her nails across them. I wince from the sting, but I like that shit and she knows it.

"It should," Hallie says, her hand going lower until she cups my balls with one hand. My dick springs to life, twitching up immediately at her touch. "Because I do."

I turn around abruptly, and I grab her roughly by the throat, drag her back, and throw her on my bed while still holding on to her. I straddle her and release her throat slightly but not all the way. "Show me how much you love me then."

Hallie grins, knowing exactly how she can. "Put your cock down my throat."

"No."

She narrows her eyes at me. "*No?*"

"You're about to let *him* do that too. No."

Her eyes are wide with surprise, but she should've expected me to listen in. Next time she should be more careful if that's not what she wants.

I get off her as quickly as I straddled her and put my underwear on, the rest of my clothes following. The sound of her footsteps follows me down the stairs, and when I make it to the bottom, Damien is standing in the living room pacing like a creep.

"Zay!" Hallie yells after me. "Wait for me! What is wrong with you?!"

I don't reply. Instead, I roll my eyes and go to the backyard with wet hair and no jacket. That's how bad I want to get away from her right now. She can suck his dick all she wants, yet I refuse to be treated differently than him. If Damien is who she wants to be with, by all means, then. I'd let her be with him, but if she wants us both, she needs to get her shit together. I don't like feeling like one of us is more loved than the other.

There will always be a favorite.

I grip my hair and pull, trying to get the intrusive thoughts out of my head that even the freezing cold weather won't get rid of. You'd think my brain would be frozen by now, unable to think or let me feel after being out here for five minutes with a wet head of hair and no coat, but no, this shit just keeps running uncontrollably like a broken record.

I just want to make it stop.

This is precisely why weak people like me seek refuge in the drugs that take it all away. I want it so bad, but I refuse to go down that fucking rabbit hole again.

I shouldn't even be bitter. We just fucked, her and I, and Damien knew exactly what happened as soon as we went back to the car. It was evident by the guilty expression on Hallie's face, but it also smelled like sex in there so we weren't going to be able to pretend it didn't happen.

The back door opens, and I look back, "You can come back in, you know." Damien says in a soft voice, coming out with me and closing the door. "And if you didn't fuck her due to bro code, shame on you. I would've fucked her without thinking of you."

I laugh at that. "We both know you and I don't share a damn bro code."

"You're right." He smiles. "We're leaving for the day. Try not to freeze your ass off out here."

"Fine, I'll go back inside." I sigh and my breath is entirely white in front of me. Fuck, it really is cold. I'm not made for this weather, and yet just because Hallie and I fought, I fled right to something I hate. Love that for me. "Since you asked me to so nicely," I tell him sarcastically.

"Don't make me lock the damn door on your ass."

"Alright, I'm coming."

They leave quickly after, and Hallie won't meet my eyes anymore. We'll have to talk later once I've calmed down, but she needs to stop giving someone who doesn't care about her enough to do what's best for her right now so much importance. She'll see reason soon enough.

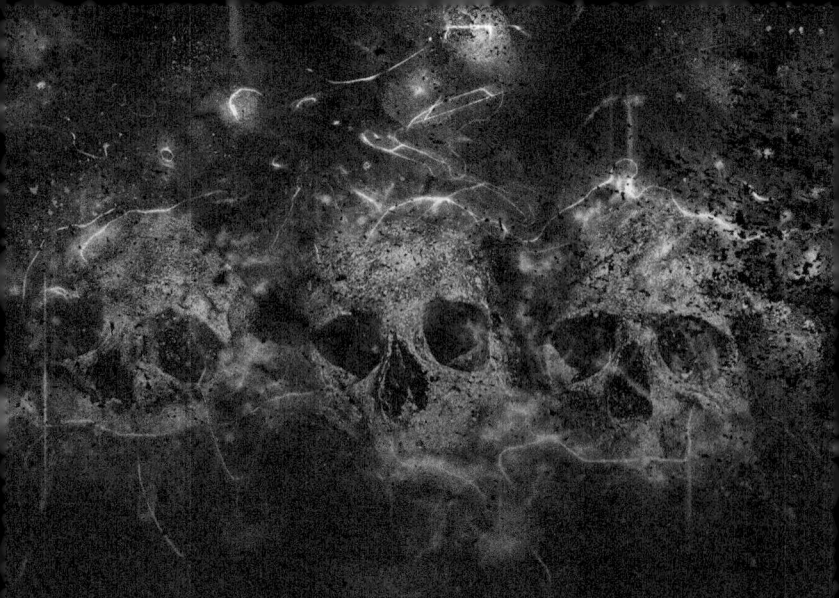

CHAPTER 30

Hallie

I thought coming here would give me a fresh start with Damien and Zayne, but it turns out they're both now pissed at me instead. Damien because he doesn't want to share… and Zayne, well, who fucking knows? He's Zayne. The reason might be similar to Damien's, or jealousy, or irritability from who knows what. Now I have to think of a way to make them both happy in one night, and I can only think of one.

There's a loft upstairs that serves as a second living room, and I told Damien I wanted to turn it into a movie room just like the one at Breck. So, he took me shopping for furniture, a television, and a nice plush rug. I also said I wanted to cook tonight, so we went to a big grocery shop. All in all, we took literally all day, about ten hours for this shit. It's going to be worth it, though.

Damien insisted on checking these companies out before letting them deliver. So he did, and finally all of our furniture is being installed while I prep dinner. I'm making honey, garlic glazed pork chops with Caesar salad and rice pilaf. It's not much, but it'll have to do while I figure out what meals they both like. Until then, they can either feed themselves or eat what I make.

I pull the pork chops out of the fridge and set all the ingredients to make them on the kitchen island, when Damien calls me up. I practically run up the stairs when I realize he's trying to show me our new movie room, and I stop dead in my tracks to see that it's painted too.

What the fuck? Who did that?

As if on cue, Zayne comes out with paint splatters on his white shirt and on his hands, and I nearly melt into a puddle. He did that for me?

I look at the paint first, a dark gray that goes well with the room because it gets a lot of natural light, even though I just got some dark burgundy curtains to keep the sunlight out and, therefore, the television glare away.

The beige-colored, cloud-sectional couch is actually a pit where all the modular pieces are put together and make what looks like a bed yet it's a couch. It's hard to explain, but it's fucking nice. And Damien let me get it. What I love the most is that everything is cohesive with the decor around the house. The colors I picked look like the ones downstairs. The rug is the same color as the couch with touches of burgundy, and the throw pillows on the sofa are burgundy as well. One charcoal gray throw blanket is draped over the side of it in a way I would do, and I know instantly that Damien did that. He pays attention to those details.

A tall plant is in the corner of the room next to the fireplace, with a Samsung Frame TV installed above it. I love it because you can set it up to where it can have a painting when it's not in use, and it makes the room feel prettier. I'm choosing Van Gogh's Skull of a Skeleton with Burning Cigarette. Feels fitting for me.

I also love that there's no coffee table because I told him I'd want to try to do game nights and blankets and pillow forts at some point. If we need a table, we will get the table trays and put them on the couch. I'm not too attached to material things at this point, but this feels like a dream. One that I thought would never come true, especially having both of my favorite people in the same house.

A pang goes straight to my heart as I think of my favorite people. Brittany comes to my mind, but I shake it off and smile. These intrusive thoughts will need to wait a few more hours until I'm alone again.

"This is amazing!" I scream, jumping up and down. Damien nods toward Zay, who doesn't even notice as he looks down at his hands and turns around. "Wait, Zay!"

I hear Damien retreating down the stairs, and I open Zayne's door right as he intends to shut it all the way. He's taking off his clothes, his abs pronounced as he stretches his arms over his head to take off his shirt.

My mouth waters at the very light, happy trail making its way down the front of his jeans, and suddenly I want his cock back in my mouth.

I drop to my knees right in front of him and begin to unbuckle his belt, then undo his zipper, and he looks at me with wide eyes. "What are you doing, Hals?"

"Whatever I want," I reply, yanking his pants down his legs and forcing him to step out of them. I guess he's not making this one easy, but I refuse to let him win. If he's pissed at me, he can tell me why and how to fix it. If not, I will keep living my life as I have been. "Now put your fucking cock in my mouth, Zayne."

A breathy chuckle comes from him, and he steps closer until his dick is nudging my lips. "What if this isn't what I want?"

"Then what do you want?" I lick my lips, grazing the head of his cock with my tongue. "Tell me so I can give it to you."

"I want you on my bed, on all fours, giving me that pretty ass of yours."

Liquid heat pools between my legs, and I rub my thighs together. He definitely noticed I did that if his smirk is any indication. "Only if you call me a good girl," I tell him.

"You're not, though."

I frown, moving to the bed and taking off my pants, getting in the position he just requested. "Why?"

"You're fucking bad, Hallie." He gets behind me and slathers cold lube on my ass, then on my clit. "Not one part of you is good for me."

The head of his cock lines up against me, and he pushes in slowly. I push back on him, needing more of him *now*. "You've never liked the things that are good for you."

Zayne pushes all the way inside me and plasters his front to my back, moving against me in shallow strokes. His fingers come to my clit, rubbing circles on it slowly before trailing lower and plunging two into my pussy. The way he's rubbing my clit with his thumb, fucking my pussy with two fingers, and thrusting into my ass has me seeing stars. My toes curl, and I moan, wanting to bite something yet unable to move.

"This is gonna be a quickie, baby," he breathes against my ear, then bites it softly, making me shudder. "Wouldn't want to make poor Damien feel left out."

"So, fuck me again later," I tell him. "With him."

"I'll do whatever the fuck you want me to."

His fingers curl inside me in a come here motion, rubbing a part of me that has me clenching all over, and his thumb moves faster as I begin to move against him.

Holy shit.

I feel the familiar tingling taking over, and he works harder, faster, rougher. He knows I'm getting close, it's like his sixth sense or something. I moan loudly, and he fucks me harder until my eyes water and I start talking incoherently.

"That's it, Hals," he groans from behind me. "Come for me. Be my good little fucking slut and come right *now*."

"God, yes!" My toes curl again when my legs start trembling, and the orgasm is so intense my knees buckle, making me face-plant on the mattress.

With my ass up now, he has better access though, and I have the advantage of the bed muffling my screams as he drags it out of me. I fist the sheets, seeking the friction even more as I climb and climb, and once at the peak, I stay very still while he takes control of my body, which I give to him freely.

Soft moans escape me as my body goes slack on the bed, and he takes this opportunity to pull his fingers out of me and fuck me faster. "Za—" I try to say his name, but right as I open my mouth, he sticks his fingers in it—the ones with my cum on them.

"Taste yourself, baby." I moan around his fingers, and he moans against my ear. "Fuck, you taste so good, don't you?"

"Hmmmmmm."

"You can never be my good girl again, Hallie." He breathes into my ear, "No, you're my *bad* fucking girl."

I suck on his fingers, then push them out with my tongue. "I'm your dirty little," I start, and Zayne grabs my neck, choking me with one hand.

"Fucking slut," he growls, finishing the sentence for me.

I feel him twitch inside me, his cock jerking as he empties himself. The most erotic groan comes from his throat right against my ear, and I know that even if nothing is right between us ever again, at least this moment was.

I go to the bathroom and clean up as he jumps in the shower, and once I'm satisfied with my appearance, I leave his room and walk down the stairs. It's as if Damien can always read me, though, because he smirks as soon as I make it to the kitchen.

"What?" I ask him, and he laughs.

"Do you want me to help you cook?"

"Sure, babe." I smile as he opens the pack of pork chops.

I heat up the pan with the gas stove and start giving Damien seasonings: garlic powder, black pepper, and flour.

"Okay, you have to mix them all in a small bowl and then rub them on the pork chops once mixed."

"Flour? On pork chops?"

"Yes."

He looks confused. "Is it fried?"

"No."

"Okay, Ms. I-only-answer-questions-with-one-word," Damien replies with a teasing tone.

He does what I said though, rubbing the seasonings on, and once he's done, I put a tablespoon of butter in the pan and spread it around until it melts. Once it does, I put the pork chops in and let them cook. Thankfully the oven has a timer setting, and I use it, knowing damn well if I don't, I'll get distracted by one of these handsome men.

As if on cue, Zayne descends the stairs and comes to stand on the other side of the kitchen island, playing music from an Amazon echo dot. Surprisingly it's early 2000s country music, which I love because, of course, I do. I'm from Texas.

The timer goes off, and I flip the pork chops, starting to prep the glaze so I can cook it when I take the pork chops out of the cast iron pan. The glaze contains honey, brown sugar, flour, and vegetable stock. Once the pork chops are done, I take them out and begin to cook the glaze.

The guys watch me cook as I determine if I'm satisfied enough to put the pork chops back in, and once I do, all we have to wait for is the rice, which I quickly put in the pot. When everything is cooking, I finally sit down at the island to relax. After a minute or two, one of my favorite songs comes on, and Zayne looks at me with hopeful eyes.

And now you're my whole life
Now you're my whole world
I just can't believe the way I feel about you, girl
Like a river meets the sea
Stronger than it's ever been
We've come so far since that day
And I thought I loved you then

Zayne gets up from the chair and offers me his hand, twirling me in a circle before bringing me close to his body, one arm around my waist while the other holds one of my hands up slightly. And just like that, we're two-stepping around the kitchen. I laugh loudly when he attempts to spin me again, but I trip while Damien snorts in the background.

Zayne kisses me deeply, then turns me around and hands me over to the man with the most gorgeous blue eyes I've ever seen. No matter what, I'll never get over those eyes or him.

Damien takes my hand and pulls me in just the way Zayne did, but our two-step is much slower until it turns to a sway with his hands on my ass and my arms around his neck. We look into each other's eyes until it feels like I'm going to drown in his blue depths, and I sigh when he brings his lips down to mine. They're soft at first, probing, and then he pulls back. I look up at him and smile through hooded eyes, and his mouth comes crashing down on mine once more. His tongue probes my lips until I open wide for him, then he thrusts it into my mouth. Our tongues dance to the rhythm of our sways, and the longer he kisses me, the more my panties stick to my skin.

He breaks the kiss first with a chuckle and goes to sit next to Zayne at the kitchen island. They look at each other briefly, and surprisingly, they both smirk—at each other. It feels like some kind of competition between them. I don't care, not right now, not when I finally got another piece of Damien to add to my puzzle.

I go back to cooking, stirring the rice as I think of how I'll get them both in my bed later tonight. Honestly, anywhere in this house will do as long as they're both inside of me at the same time. No sex will ever compare to that feeling ever again.

The pork chops smell so damn good they break me out of my erotic thoughts—more like memories—of them fucking me together. I flip them, making a mental note that they're almost done too, then turn to stir the rice.

Damien takes a bowl from a cabinet and begins to make our salad, which I'm thankful for because I'm starving. After a few minutes, everything is cooked and ready to be eaten. I serve us all our dinner, and we sit at the dining table for the first time. It feels like a family dinner while simultaneously I feel weird for feeling that way. Like we're a throuple or something when I know damn well that will never happen. In my dreams, maybe, but Damien is waiting and waiting… and waiting for me to make a choice. I'm afraid whatever choice I make, two people will be hurt by it: me and the person I don't choose.

The guys look at me with appreciation and tell me how good the food tastes, inflating my ego, because let's be serious, there's nothing better than being told something you did was incredible. We eat in comfortable silence, only talking a few times to decide on a movie to watch after dinner. I don't think we will ever all agree on anything considering how different both Damien and Zayne are from each other. Zayne and I have never truly had common ground on TV shows or movies. We just compromise and watch it together anyway for the sake of spending time together. Damien and I, on the other hand, like the same things. Movies, shows, books. We can bond over that. So, what the fuck do we watch tonight?

When we're done with dinner, they both work like a well-oiled machine together, washing and drying dishes while cleaning the kitchen. I go up to what is now the movie room and sit on the couch, beginning to browse for a movie, for anything we could find common ground on.

They come up the stairs, their footsteps loud and echoing, and they seem to be deep in conversation. What are they talking about in hushed tones? Not suspicious at all. When they come in the room though they look at each other and back at me. Zayne has a smirk that would make the devil himself fold for him, and Damien cocks an eyebrow. Something feels different right now, and my panties get damp just from looking at them. They're up to something, I know it.

"Strip," Damien says. "Then lie down on the carpet."

I do as he orders, laying down while rubbing my thighs together from how horny I am.

"Show us that pretty pussy, baby," Zayne groans when I spread my legs. "Goddamn, you're dripping for us already, and we haven't even touched you."

I whimper when they both start taking off their clothes, their glorious cocks fully erect, and they begin to make their way over to me.

Zayne sits on the carpet next to me, and Damien grabs my ankles, flipping me over and making me land on Zayne's hard body. He wastes no time grabbing me and making me straddle him.

His palms roam my body along with Damien's hands, making me dizzy with the sensations and the deep, primal need I feel for them both. Damien presses his chest against my back, rubbing his erection on my ass, and I groan at how bad I need them.

I'm trapped between them, like two walls closing in on me with no escape. But I don't want to escape—I want them to smother me.

Zayne lifts me up suddenly and lines up his cock against me, then slams me down on it. I scream as he stretches me, my entrance burning from the invasion. "God, that hurts so good," I tell him, looking down at him in awe. His face stretches into a full grin, and it makes my heart stutter in my chest.

"Ride me, baby." He grabs my hand and kisses the inside of my wrist right below my stitches, the same way he always has. "Do it like it's the last time."

I frown, trying to understand what he means.

"Don't overthink it," he tells me.

"I need you," I breathe, my voice hoarse with desperation. "I need *both* of you."

Damien pushes me down onto Zayne's chest, pushing us down to the ground until Zayne is lying on his back, and I press my cheek against him. "I thought you'd never say it."

His fingers probe at me where Zayne and I are connected, and he slowly inserts one *inside* of me. Wait, what the fuck? "What are you doing?"

"Trying something." His cock nudges my entrance too now, and I tense. "Relax, love. Let me in."

"Where?" I ask him, slightly panicked. There's no fucking way this is happening, no way he'll fit.

He nudges against my entrance again as if in answer to my question. "Here, babe."

"There's no way it's going to fit, Damien!"

Zayne's hands come to my back, rubbing it in slow circles, soothing me. It's working, and soon enough, I relax. Melting on top of his body, my limbs languid. Damien nudges my entrance again, and I feel myself stretch as he tries to fit inside me too. There's a bit of pain from how big he is, and my breath catches when he's halfway inside of me at how full I feel. Impossibly full.

He fills me up inch by inch, and I fist the plush rug under me with one hand, digging my fingernails into Zayne's arm with the other until he winces. "Fuck, fuck, fuck. I don't think I can take it, Damien."

"You will."

"I can't!"

With a chuckle, he tells me, "*You're going to.*"

Damien buries himself inside of me to the hilt, filling me up along with Zayne. "Goddamn," I whisper, holding on to Zayne for dear life when they begin to move inside me.

Zayne pushes up from the floor while Damien thrusts into me from behind, and the combination of both of their movements is enough to make my eyes roll to the back of my head. They move together, as one, so in sync that I can't tell where one ends and the other begins.

Damien moans, and Zayne groans, making little butterflies take flight in my stomach. There're hands on me everywhere. My neck is being squeezed while another hand digs into my shoulder blade painfully, a good kind of pain. Another hand gropes my ass, and another holds my waist. I don't know which hands belong to whom, and I don't fucking care right now, either.

The more they move, the more I curse and moan. And soon enough, I'm turning into a mess in their hands, on their cocks. There's a puddle under me. I can feel it as Zayne fucks me from the bottom, my wetness all over his pelvis and abdomen. It's messy; it's fucking amazing.

They begin to fuck me so hard we're scooting across the room, and if we were on a bed, the headboard would be broken. I close my eyes to feel everything more intensely, but then Zayne slaps me across the face to bring me back. "Don't close your eyes, Hals." He growls at me, "I want to see the look in your eyes when this threatens to stop your heart."

Suddenly, my legs start shaking just as I feel my body getting hotter. A feeling like I've never felt before takes over my body and makes me clench. Both of them moan loudly, Damien into my ear from behind. It makes it feel even better to know they're enjoying it too. I never thought this would happen in the first place.

"Fuck, Zay—" I moan, "Damien, yes! I'm about to come," My body tightens impossibly as I begin to shake, and I spread my legs even more so they can go deeper.

"Almost there…" Zayne moans.

I moan and scream and nearly cry from the sensations flooding my body as the most powerful orgasm of my entire life takes over. It feels like I'm being possessed by a force much stronger than me, and I'm just here for the ride, which wouldn't be a far stretch either way.

Two thrusts later, and I feel both of them emptying inside of me, their dicks twitching against each other. Fuck, that's so damn hot. I can't believe this is my life—the most important people to me giving me what I so selfishly need. Sometimes in life, one needs to be selfish to find our way. I won't apologize for it.

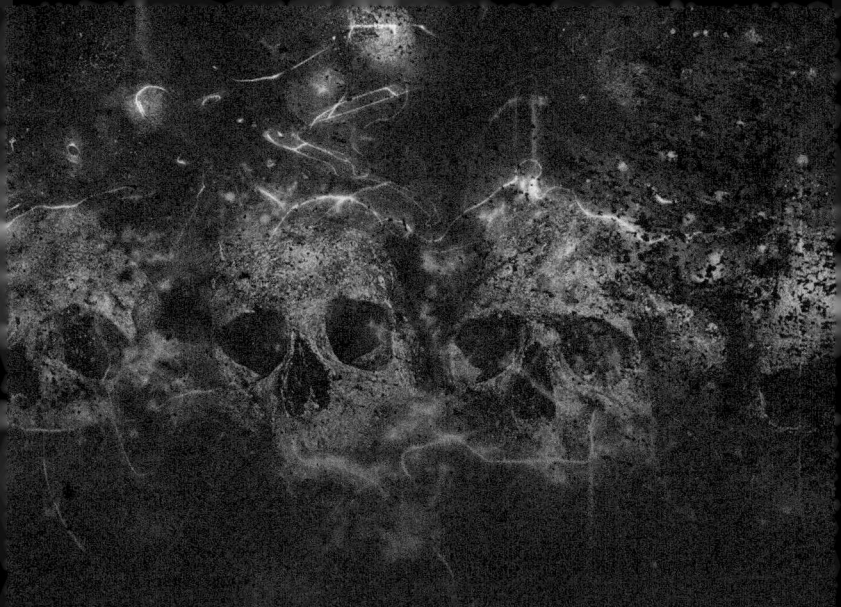

CHAPTER 31

Damien

When I told Hallie I'd take her snowboarding for the first time, I knew it would be bad. I just didn't expect it to be *this* damn bad.

The girl has no balance, goddamn, not even a little bit. I'm holding onto her waist, trying to show her how to brake if she needs to stop suddenly or slow down, but she just keeps falling backwards. She can't make it one foot without falling down the bunny hill, and now I'm chasing after her as she scoots on her ass down the hill, seemingly giving up on it. We reach the bottom, me with my board and her on her ass, and I begin to laugh.

"Shut up, Damien!" She pouts. "I'll get better, I swear." Doubtful, but I won't break her heart, yet.

"Yes, babe." I smirk at her, which only makes her narrow her eyes at me. I'm sure she's frustrated. I would be too, after all that scooting. "Let's start at the top."

"There's no way." I hold out my hand to lift her up, and she falls back on her ass when she's halfway to standing. "See? Fucking hopeless."

I hold back the urge to laugh and unstrap her feet from the board, helping her carry it to the top of the hill again. She looks positively pissed off, and I almost feel bad. *Almost.* It's too funny though, and I want her to do it again for my amusement.

"Okay, Hallie," I start, and she huffs again. "Remember what I said. You need to put your weight back a little and twist the board then shred slightly to stop."

"Yeah, I get that." She nods with pursed lips. "I just can't fucking do it."

I chuckle, and she smacks my arm. "One more run, love. You got this."

It's easy to help her strap her feet back in and help her stand this time. At least we have that going for us. I position her to go down the hill and say, "On the count of three, okay?"

"Yeah."

"One—" I push her down the hill so she doesn't have to think about it.

On the bright side, she makes it five feet before falling instead of two, so that's an improvement. I know I'm an asshole for that one, but she's too far in her head to make this happen. She needs to relax, and I think the unknown is really fucking with her. I get it, but this is supposed to be fun.

"What the fuck?!" she screams as she falls down the hill face-first, and I have to cover my mouth to keep her from hearing me laugh.

I meet her at the bottom again, and she smacks my arm again when I help her up after unstrapping her board. I tried to get her to walk with one foot strapped in, but she almost ate shit again, so we quickly gave up on that idea.

"This sucks, Damien."

"What would you rather do then?" I ask her, genuinely wanting to make her happy.

"How about tubing?"

I nod, smiling at her. "Let's return the snowboards to the car and change boots."

We go back to the car, and I strap the snowboards at the top while she changes into the black waterproof Sorel boots I got her, which look good as fuck on her. After admiring her for a moment longer, I change my own boots.

The walk up the mountain to the tubing area is steep, and I can tell Hallie is getting tired by the way she slows down halfway to the top. "Come here, babe, hop on my back."

"Hell no." She laughs, "How are you supposed to get all the way up there?"

"I think you underestimate me," She weighs less than my damn warmup weight, for fuck's sake.

Hallie reluctantly hops on my back, holding onto me for dear life, choking me the entire way up. Don't get me wrong, I may be into that shit sometimes, but there's definitely a time and place, and that shit did not feel good just now.

I let her down once we make it to the small cabin where the tickets are sold and get in line. She goes to a wooden bench and sits there until I'm done purchasing them. They give us tags with zip-ties that have our names on them and have to attach them to our winter coats in the most visible place.

The tubing line is long as fuck, Thankfully, there are enough tubes for a hundred people at least, and we get in line to be taken up.

"What would you like to do after this?" I ask her, looking at her brown eyes being illuminated by the sun, turning them a rich honey color. There are black flecks in them. I never thought brown eyes were pretty before meeting her, but hers… they're gorgeous.

It's like she sees me become mesmerized by her, always knowing when I'm fucking weak over her, and she breathes just a little faster as she gazes back into my eyes. "I'm kind of hungry."

I want to say I have something to give her, that she still hasn't taken my cock down her throat, and I want to make her mine in every way possible. Instead I tell her, "We can eat right after this, yeah?"

Hallie nods and turns around, pulling her tube up the hill to be attached to the rope that takes us all the way up. She's next in line, and the guy does a double-take when he sees her. It makes me want to claw his eyes out. Yeah, I know she's fucking hot, no need to have that reaction.

The man attaches her to the rope, and she goes up. I'm next, and I make sure to give him a side eye as he ties me too. The way up is smooth until we get all the way up the hill, then there's a significant drop that makes my stomach clench.

We both get out of the tubes and drag them to the fast lane. "You sure you don't want to go in the family lane?" I ask her with a grin. "It's slower."

"Shut up, Damien." She rolls her eyes and positions the tube in front of the drop.

She's competitive with me, and I actually love that. I never see that side of her come out with anyone else, with *him*. Then again, he's boring as fuck, and I wasn't wrong about it. Hallie and I can have fun. It seems all the fun they have together is fucking. To each their own, but it doesn't seem like it's enough.

"Just thought I'd offer."

"This isn't much different than sledding, right? And I did fine with that. Now let me be happy."

I laugh and get on my tube, then we both push off at the same time. I look over at her as we fly down the hill fast as fuck, and all I feel is an inner peace that I have her back. I've always been an adrenaline junkie. That's why I got the motorcycle to begin with, and this takes me back to the speed I love, though it's short-lived. A few seconds tops.

Hallie hits the yellow stoppers from how fast she's going, and I wait until she recovers to help her up. "Was that fun?"

"Fuck, yes!" she squeals. "Let's do it again."

She gives me heart eyes, making something deep in my chest stir, clench, hurt. I nod and grab my tube, letting her follow after me so she doesn't see my face. I'm supposed to be having fun, not being sad. *Get your shit together.*

We go up and down about ten more times before calling it quits almost an hour later. That's all I paid for anyway, but I would've gone back for more time if she wanted it.

The walk back to the car is easier than going uphill, and Hallie can walk back down on her own this time, thankfully. I can't wait for it to warm up a little so we can go on hikes again. We got lucky with a warmer day today since it's in the twenties. That's why I brought her here to get out of the house. We're a few hours away in a bigger town, and I've never felt better about having her all to myself. She actually was the one who told Zayne we were spending time together—*alone.*

"Do you want McDonald's?"

"Huh?" she asks, surprised. "You? Fake French fries? Who are you?"

"Someone who doesn't want to pay twenty dollars for real French fries." Easy enough. I really don't want to do that, plus the line is long as fuck, and now I'm actually starving.

She laughs at this like she can't believe the words coming out of my mouth. "Wow, I never thought I'd see the day, Mr. Health Freak."

The car is fucking freezing when we open the doors, and I quickly blast the heat to warm it up as fast as possible. Once buckled, I hand Hallie one of my jackets for her to use as a blanket, then pull out of our parking spot, heading to McDonald's. She's not wrong, any other time I'd refuse this, but I don't want to wait forever to eat. Plus, I saw one on the way here.

I drive carefully over the snow and ice, not wanting anything to happen to her, and then go through the drive-thru. She orders chicken nuggets and honey mustard, and I order the same but with ranch. The only difference in our order is that she gets a chocolate shake that contains *milk*, and I get a lemonade.

"Are you sure about that, love?"

"Never been more sure."

Lord, she's going to be so fucked up after this. "Babe, be reasonable."

"I'm not drinking it all!"

"So how much are you drinking, then?" I ask her, grabbing a parking spot so we can eat.

"A safe amount, obviously."

"Obviously," I repeat. "So, what's a safe amount?"

"I'll know when I get there."

We devour our food, and she only takes three sips of the shake and makes me drink the rest. I don't think she can handle being sick like the last time she drank the coffee with the milk in it, and I'd also rather not have her all messed up the rest of the night, either.

"Damien," Hallie says. "I'd like to ask you something."

Automatically, I tense. She never uses those words. Usually, when she wants to ask me something, she just does it. "What?"

"What happened in Mexico when you got Zayne out?"

I draw in a sharp breath, and Hallie's eyes never leave me. "I don't know what you mean."

"Something happened," she replies. "I know you. Please don't lie to my face this way."

I sigh, rubbing a hand down my face. "Okay, something did happen."

She looks at me expectantly, "So… what happened then?"

"Um." I don't know how to say this without crying, without looking pathetic as fuck. "Uh—" I breathe in deeply. "I can't say it," I say on a whisper.

Hallie gets closer and holds my face between her hands. "Tell me so I can be here for you."

A tear trails down my cheek out of nowhere, then another, and another. I guess if I'm crying already, I might as well tell her. "I found my mom."

"Huh?" Hallie asks, confused. "What do you mean? I thought she was dead."

"He told you, didn't he? Are you playing dumb right now, Hallie?" I pull away from her, moving my face out of her grasp.

"He said something, but I didn't believe him."

"I won't ask what he said." I don't give a fuck about the snitch. Motherfucker needs to learn how to keep his mouth shut. It wasn't his place to tell her about something so personal; it should've been my choice. "My mom didn't die, Hallie. The cartel took her."

"The same ones who took me?"

"No. There are many cartels, many *Capos*." It's hard to keep up sometimes. "This man was different. He was friends with Michael, and they came to an agreement. They'd share you, and if I delivered you, I'd get my mom back."

"You were going to trade me?"

A chill runs down my spine at her tone. She'll never forgive this. Maybe I don't deserve it. If she feels deceived, then it's rightfully so, although I couldn't divulge the truth about my mom, no matter how much I wanted to. My mother might as well have been dead all this time anyway, so I don't know why it hit me so hard to find her that way. I never actually thought I'd get her back, that's the funny part. Then when I finally find her, she's dead.

"I didn't, Hallie." I sigh and look at her. "I chose *you*. Over everything, everyone. Even my own mother."

"I didn't ask for—"

"You didn't have to…" I sniffle, looking away. "I couldn't hand you over because I love you." My voice breaks on the word *love*, and it makes me feel fucking pathetic.

Hallie's face is full of pity when I gaze back at her. "What happened in Mexico, Damien?" I look at her again, her eyes begging me to speak. "After you found her."

With a hoarse voice, I reply, "She was… dead." She gasps, putting her hand up to her mouth. "No need to act surprised, love. I know you knew before now."

"Like I said, I thought he was making shit up." I thought he'd be more fucking loyal. "That you were sad over something else. Maybe me."

"I wasn't sad about you, Hallie." I was over the fucking moon. "I was happy to find you again, even if you didn't want me back. I just wanted you safe."

There's a pregnant pause, one that you don't recover from with mere sweet words. Breathing is a little hard; my chest is tight from talking about all this. Been trying to ignore that it ever happened, convincing myself all over again that she was dead way before now. I would've never known it had happened if I hadn't found her dead. Even if I brought Hallie to them, I knew she wasn't going to come home with me. There's no way they would just hand her over. She knew too much, saw too much.

"I'm sorry."

"*Don't.*" My breath shudders. "Not you."

Hallie grabs my hand, pulling me toward her. I go, though not because I want to. "Yes, me. I want to be here for you. *Let me.*"

She climbs up the seat and sits on my lap, straddling me, holding my head to her shoulder until I'm lying my cheek on it. "I just thought…" Another sniffle. "I thought she was dead before all of this. I didn't expect for it to hit me this hard, finding her that way."

"Why?"

"Because that's what they do, Hallie." In case she hadn't noticed while being there. "They kill people."

"I know, babe." She shushes me when my shoulders shake, crying harder, sobbing louder. "I'm here, and this isn't okay. I'm sorry, so fucking sorry."

This is how we spend the next hour, with her holding me, me sobbing into her neck, and contemplating why I fuck everything up. Even though I knew my mom was never going to be handed over to me, I still was going to kidnap Hallie and give her to the cartel because a small part of me held onto hope. The little kid inside of me begged God for another chance. What I regret the most is knowing my true intentions when I first met Hallie. Yeah, it all changed as I got to truly know her, but it doesn't negate my character, who I am as a person.

Even if that's not me anymore.

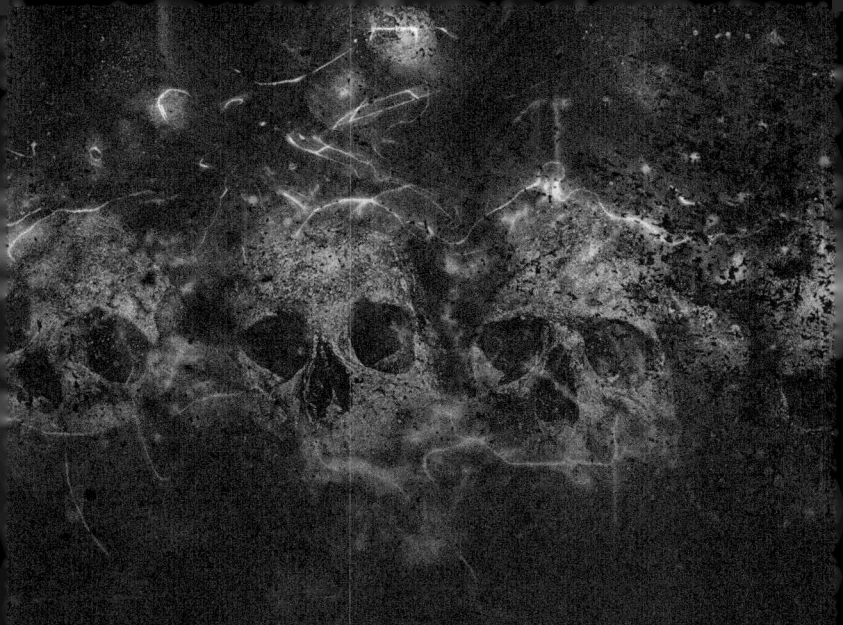

CHAPTER 32

Zayne

It's been a long time since I've been ice skating, but I guess it's like riding a bike. Hallie says she hasn't been in over a decade, but she's truly graceful as fuck right now, which I'm kind of jealous of. Yeah, I can skate but never like that.

Hallie does laps in this fancy ass backyard rink, and I wonder how Damien managed to get that done in time or if it really came with the house. Knowing him, it was a nice gesture for Hallie to love him a little more. I shouldn't care, it's for Hallie. So then, why am I jealous? Is it because he has enough money to do nice things for her? Or is it deeper?

They went snowboarding together five days ago and stayed out until very late at night, and I couldn't sleep in this empty ass house for so many reasons. One, I wanted to ensure she was okay and that she returned in one piece. Two, I was scared shitless the cartel was going to show up while I was here all alone. Either way, Damien asked me if I wanted to come with them, and Hallie shut it down really quickly, which pissed me the fuck off. So, tell me why last night Damien got 'Hallie' a piano. We all know she doesn't play that shit, and it's going to take time to teach her. Shit ain't easy. I'm willing to, but it'll probably be months before she understands what's happening. I have a feeling the piano is for me, but he doesn't want to say that. I think even Hallie knows it.

Hallie flies around the small rink while I just stand in the middle, trying to keep my balance. It's funny how life works, since this is exactly how I feel about ours. She usually has her shit together while I'm always hanging on by a thread. That's changed recently since I got her back. I'm the one who's had to have it together for her, especially with how she can't achieve that right now. I don't mind at all though. I think it's about damn fucking time. She's been there for me through so much; now it's my turn to be there for her. Not being on drugs has brought me a lot of clarity. It's given me time and space to think without tweaking the entire time I'm conscious, and all I want is her. There's nothing and no one else for me. All I know is that I'd never willingly let her go, and even if she wanted me to, I'd still put up a fight.

"Are you ready to go inside?" I ask Hals. "It's fucking cold out here, baby!"

"Fine!" She laughs, stepping off the ice and onto the snow. How the fuck does she walk in those damn skates? I can walk, but I'm wobbly in the snow. "What do you want to do then?"

I want to fuck you.

"Do you want to play piano? I can finally teach you."

"I'd love that."

"Let's make hot chocolate then do that?"

Hallie nods as she opens the back door, taking her skates off right before going into the house. I try to do the same and fall on my ass, which only causes her to laugh. I guess that's the only positive thing to come out of it, but it's something.

I go to the kitchen and make the vegan hot chocolate for her, then regular hot chocolate for me. She's already sitting at the table waiting for me, and the irony doesn't escape me. Hallie's always been the one waiting for me, and now I'm waiting for her. I'm here no matter what, whether she chooses me or both of us. It doesn't matter as long as I get a piece of her heart. I don't care how small it is.

The hot chocolate smell wafts through the house, and Damien comes downstairs when he smells it. I chuckle, "Do you want one?"

"Sure, just don't poison me."

"Don't tempt me," I mutter under my breath, and he laughs.

I hand over my hot chocolate, and he sits on one side of Hallie, leaving me to make another cup. I give Hallie her own hot chocolate and she has the decency to wait for me, thankfully.

The silence is a little weird when I join them, but I don't care. Truly. It's just awkward. No reason for me to act differently over it. Right? None of us speak until we're done, and Hallie is the one to break the silence.

"How about those piano lessons?" she asks me with a smile, and Damien and I make eye contact. It's as if he's trying to tell me something with his eyes, but he doesn't do it.

"Let's do it."

We go to the corner of the living room that is now taken up by the piano, leaving no more space for decor, and sit down next to each other on the bench. I begin to tell her about the notes for each key, which is clearly overwhelming to her. As if Damien knows she's stressed, he looks at her, and they make eye contact for a short moment before she pays attention again. I go through the notes and what everything sounds like, and her eyes cross at me. Okay, so maybe this shit is not for her. I laugh at her because I know it's not for everyone, this is hard.

Hallie looks at me with a pained face, and I frown. "Baby, it's okay if you don't want to do it anymore. I can just play it for you."

She smiles. "Okay, I think I'd like that better."

I begin to play the piano on my own, and she goes to the kitchen right across from us, getting more hot chocolate and making it for herself. Damien follows her, and I get lost in the music, still looking at her. They seem to be deep in conversation after a minute, and Hallie's hands go up as she clearly begins to argue with him.

I abruptly stop playing my song.

"Oh, because he's so amazing, right?"

"He can be!" Hallie says back. "I don't know why you care so fucking much, Damien!"

"Because I want you," Damien pushes her against the cabinets until she's trapped between his arms, his body flush with hers, "to *myself*."

"We don't always get what we want, do we?"

"Is that how it's going to be then?" Damien laughs. "You've made your choice?"

"That's not what I said—"

"Fuck this shit." He pushes away from her and grabs the car keys. "Congrats, man. She's all yours."

Hallie begins to sob as he walks away, headed for the front door of the house. "Wait, babe. Please," she cries after him, running a little to chase him. "Don't leave, *don't*."

"I need space, Hallie."

Not love.

Not babe.

Hallie.

Goddamn it, he has it all wrong. She doesn't want me. She wants us. He just doesn't want that for himself, but that doesn't mean she doesn't love him. He's being cold and cruel right now, and I won't stand for it.

"You need to stop being such a fucking asshole," I tell him, coming to her side. Damien narrows his eyes at me as he clenches his fists. "Yeah, take your space and do what you want, but she's told you what she wants from the beginning."

"She chose you. Aren't you happy?"

"She didn't choose shit, and you know it."

I go around and block the door.

"Get the fuck out of my way." Damien sneers.

"No."

"*Now*."

"I said *no*."

Damien punches me right in the temple, making my head spin, but I recover relatively quickly. I swing at him, my fist connecting with his jaw, and he looks shocked. Suddenly we're on each other, punching away, and all I can hear is Hallie's snivels getting louder, screaming at us to stop. I can't stop now, though; I'm too far in.

"Zayne!" she screams, and I halt, taking a hit to the face. I'm all bloodied up. "Cut it the fuck out. No one needs to be fighting over me. If he wants to leave," she tips her chin toward Damien, and he frowns, "then let him."

Hallie's face is sad as she walks away, going upstairs to retreat into herself. I take a step back and shake my head at him. "You're making a mistake, Damien."

"I know I am."

"Then why do it?"

"Because I love *me* too. And I deserve to be the one for her. If she doesn't see that, it's fine. I don't need her to understand it, but I don't want to live like this either."

"Just give her some more time," I essentially beg him. I don't know why, maybe due to knowing she's going to be devastated if he really leaves. "She deserves that much."

"What about what I deserve? It can't always be about her."

Yes. It can.

It is.

"Alright." I nod, "I hope you don't regret it."

"I already do." With that, I walk away, "But I'll be back in the morning." I hear him say before I go up the stairs, hearing the front door click shut, then lock.

While Hallie has gotten stronger, she still needs more time to heal the wounds inflicted by the person who's hurt her the most in this world, and no amount of time will truly get rid of the new and old scars. She doesn't need this shit on top of that, not from someone she cares about. *Loves*. Damien is selfish as fuck for this one. Although I know he's also right, if that's how he truly feels. I just don't want her hurting.

She's in bed, sobbing into her pillow, her shoulders shaking violently as she tries to calm herself down.

"Baby," I whisper, "Please don't…"

"I…" she sobs harder. "Can't," Another sob, "Do this."

I get in bed with her, pushing her to the side to cuddle her and line my body against hers. We do this well, this is where we excel. Loving each other has always been easy, but staying together hasn't. I'm determined now, though; I won't fuck this up ever again. I don't care what I have to do. Whatever it takes. I'm determined to live and die by her side.

"You can." I wipe her tears from her face. "You will."

"Make me forget."

"How?" I frown, knowing this can't be good. Unless she wants me to fuck her.

"Hurt me."

"No." I shake my head vehemently. "Absolutely not."

Hallie cries and sniffles, "If you don't, then I'll do it my fucking self."

"Over my dead body, Hals."

Hallie turns around until we're nose to nose, her tear-stained lips against mine in a not-so-there kiss. "I *need* you."

"You don't." I sigh, wrapping my arm around her back and pulling her into me. "You want to forget him, and I don't want to be the one to help you."

"No." She licks my lips like an ice cream cone. "I want *you*."

"What do you want, baby?"

"Make me feel something," she begs, grabbing my dick over my pants. "Anything."

I smile against her, dipping my head until I find her neck to lick, bite, and suck on it. "Be careful what you wish for, baby."

"Cut me."

I stiffen, pulling away to look at her. I remember the last time

I did that, my 'Z' is still on the inside of her thigh, just lighter now, more faded. The itch to renew it, to hurt her and lick the pain away, takes over my body, and I don't know how long I can restrain myself if she keeps begging me like this.

"Hals." I try again to convince her not to do this, no matter how much I want to. "We need to move past this."

"One more time and never again."

Little fucking liar.

Even though I know she's not being truthful, I nod anyway. I get up from the bed and stand next to it. "Where is it, Hallie? Because once I do this, it's going in the fucking trash, and you'll never touch one again." She looks pained, "Promise me."

"I promise."

"Swear on me."

"I—" Hallie looks at me with wide eyes, realizing the implications of this. "Swear," she says under her breath, barely audible. "Front pocket of my suitcase in the closet."

I open the mirrored closet door to find her suitcase in the back of it, hidden by some clothes. The front pocket calls my name, but it's dead weight, a sinking sensation in the pit of my stomach. I shouldn't do this. I know I shouldn't. So why am I still going to? Fuck my life.

When I grab the small razorblade and make my way back to the bed, Hallie's already completely naked, her legs wide open for me. I could feast on her right fucking now, and I will. But just this once, I'll do what she wants me to.

Getting between her legs, I spread them wider to see her dripping pussy. "Are you this wet from thinking of me cutting you, Hallie?" What the fuck?

"No." She shakes her head with a smile. "I'm wet from thinking of you licking the blood away and following it to my pussy."

"Is that so?"

"I need you to make me come, Zay."

"I always do."

"This is different," she replies. "I need to come harder."

I chuckle, but then I realize it's because she needs to forget. Forget her pain, her nightmares, and *him*. She's replacing me in all her thoughts; she wants him, hurts for him.

As if she can tell my thoughts, for maybe I've given myself away with my face, she wraps her legs around my waist and pulls me toward her. "It's always been you, Zay. You know that. I've been yours since the first day, and I always will be."

My heart squeezes in my chest as I remember the first time I saw her looking at the gallery wall with Brittany, then her eyes meeting mine from across the hallway. I felt sparks, a fucking lightning strike just from that look.

"You're my whole heart, Hals," I tell her. "If you don't beat for me, I can't go on."

"I want to be the one to pump blood into your veins, Zay," she replies, tears gathering in her eyes as she moves against me, soaking my sweatpants. "I'd live inside your rib cage if you let me."

God, I fucking love her.

"I'll do this for you one last time." I untangle her legs from me and lower myself between them, my elbows on the bed with her pussy right in my face. "Never again."

She nods like she doesn't believe me, but I'm fucking serious. Never again. I move her right leg, spreading it wider to see the 'Z' I engraved into her skin not that long ago. It pisses me off that it's so fucking light and faded. I wanted to brand her, and I wanted that to be forever.

"Ready?"

"Yes," she says with a breathy moan when I lick her from center to clit, needing a taste of her before I do anything else.

I take the razor blade to her thigh, poising it over my initial, and cut the first line. She hisses sharply, then relaxes as the blood trails down her leg and onto the sheets. I want to lick it away, I will, but it's not done. I continue with the next line, then the next.

Hallie stays very still for me, as if afraid to move, and her chest rises and falls quickly when I kiss her thigh, smearing my lips over the blood. I kiss her thigh all the way to her pussy, trailing the blood up to her center, then begin to eat her pussy. I alternate between licking my brand and her. She's fucking moaning for me, going crazy for me, clutching my shirt and holding on for dear life.

The sounds she's making will be my fucking undoing, and she has me rubbing my dick against the bed, trying to find relief. I go back to licking her clit, the taste of her and iron mixing, a perfect concoction. She's an aphrodisiac, the strongest and most potent drug I could ever ingest, and I never want to come down from the high.

I alternate between sucking her clit and swirling my tongue in circles. I can tell I'm driving her crazy as she clutches the sheets and tightens her thighs around my head, making the wetness of her blood get all over my face. I don't give a fuck though. I want her this way.

Coating my fingers with her wetness, I plunge them into her pussy, making sure they're entirely wet for me, then slowly insert them into her ass. She tenses immediately, her moans reaching new levels, and she presses her thighs together harder against me. I don't give up. I lick and suck and bite, and soon enough, she's pulling on my hair like a wild fucking animal. Just the way I want her.

She comes on my face while riding it, my fingers plunging in and out of her, and screams my name. "Zayne!"

I pull away from her, "That's it, baby. Call out to me. I'm the only one you'll worship tonight."

Going back for more, I lick and tease until she's too sensitive and pushing me away. "Fuck, that was amazing."

"Is that what you needed, baby?" I ask her.

"Fuck." Her chest heaves with her breaths. "Yes."

I smirk, "Bad girl."

I get on my side again, then pull her to me until we're flush with each other, her naked back to my clothed front, making me want to strip down and meet her in the middle. But I won't. Tonight wasn't about me, it was about her, and I want to make that very clear.

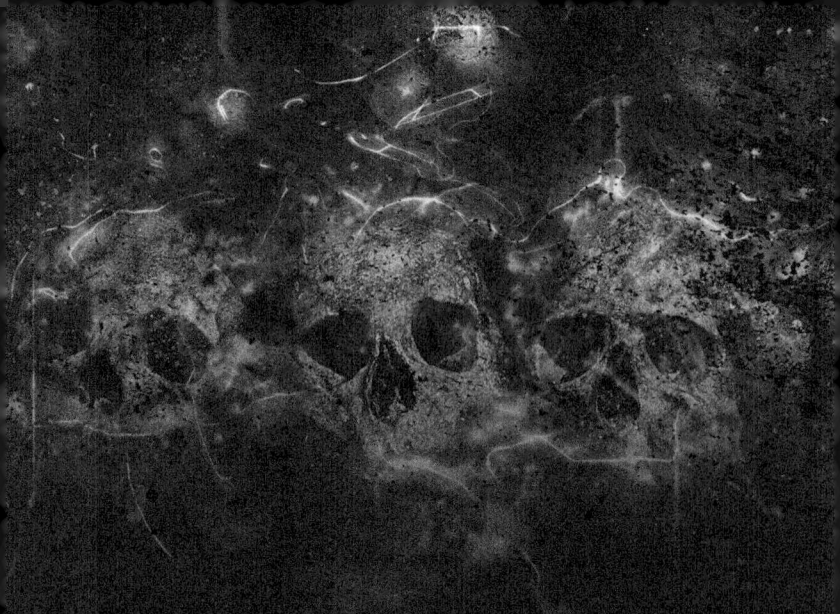

CHAPTER 33

Hallie

Damien actually came home last night, drunk as fuck, and headed straight to my room. Let's just say he didn't like what he found. What bothered him most was clearly the bloody sheets and my naked form being bloody as well. It didn't help that Zayne was sleeping beside me, seemingly oblivious to everything happening.

He went to his room, not wanting to see the scene before him anymore. And he still hasn't come out even though it's evening time now. I'm not even upset that he's still in his room. I can't believe the shit he pulled yesterday, with everything he said, and then still came back like nothing ever happened. As if he didn't just tell me he was leaving me.

Did he change his mind?

Is he too weak to do it?

Does he love me too much to walk away?

I don't know the answer to any of those questions. All I do

know is that I'm grateful to get another day with him. Regardless of last night's situation, he really is a kind, thoughtful, sensitive man. Everything I need in one package. Handsome, sexy as fuck, and has that bad-boy vibe. I can't get enough of it, of him.

I'm slightly glad he walked in on that last night. That way he knows I won't stop living my life over him. If he wants to be with me, he needs to get over his shit and love me as I am. Yeah, maybe I'm being selfish, but I won't settle anymore. I'll take what I want when I want it, and anyone who has a problem with that can move on.

Zayne puts chocolate chip pancakes and bacon on the table for me, having made breakfast for dinner, and I take a sip of my coffee, savoring the vanilla almond milk creamer. It actually tastes wonderful, the best one I've had yet. And I guess, of course, it had to be in Canada.

"Maple syrup?" he asks me, bringing the glass container to me.

"Yes, please." Another perk of living here is the syrup, which I will say is much better than the one sold at the grocery store in the United States.

Sitting next to me, Zayne drowns his pancakes in the liquid gold, then eats them like a freaking caveman. This guy has no manners at home.

I don't know if it's the smell of food or what, but Damien comes down the stairs, hair looking disheveled like he just had some good fucking sex, and he's shirtless. His perfect body, carved from stone, is on full display, and I have to pick up my jaw and put it back up. For fuck's sake, he knows what he's doing.

Damien obviously notices my reaction and smirks at me, moving to the coffee pot and making himself a cup. His back is turned to me, and his muscles ripple as he stirs in the creamer. The fucking man is way too hot for his own good. I can't look away even if I tried.

He comes over to sit right next to me, dragging his chair toward mine until they're touching, making our knees touch as well.

I look at Zayne briefly, and Damien's fingers connect with my chin, pulling my face roughly back to his.

"Don't look at him, love," Damien growls. "I'm right fucking here. Look at *me*."

I think Zayne takes his cue and leaves, taking the air in the room with him. I look at Damien, searching his eyes for a clue of what the fuck is going through his mind, and he grabs me by the back of the head, yanking me toward him by my hair. I fall on my knees in front of him, my head up toward his, and I wince.

"Okay," I whisper.

He gets up from his chair and one-handedly pulls down his sweatpants, still holding onto my hair tightly with his other one. "I changed my mind, Hallie." I stiffen, his tight grip on my hair somehow tightening even more. "I want you on your fucking knees for me, begging me to fuck you."

"I already want that."

"Oh yeah?" He fists his cock with his free hand, directing it to my mouth. "Open up then, love. I want those pretty lips wrapped around my cock tonight."

I open up just like he says, scared shitless because I know how much I can take, and I don't know if his size is feasible.

"Stick out your tongue." I follow his command again just as he slaps his cock against my tongue. "Now suck."

I swallow him down, sucking his cock like my life depends on it. My head bobs up and down, my nose hitting his pelvis as I gag on him, my jaw on fire from the pain of taking him, but I do it anyway.

My hands wrap around the back of his legs, nails digging in, and he begins to pull my hair back roughly then push me back down as he tries to control the pace now. It's fucking awful and amazing all at the same time.

Damien throws his head back in pleasure, his mouth wide open as I take him all the way to the back of my throat again. Then I twirl my tongue around the head of his cock. "*Fuck*," he hisses. "You feel so fucking good, babe."

The praise alone renews my strength, and I put in even more effort to take him all the way in, gagging on him until drool comes out of the corners of my mouth, drenching my chin and his pelvis. He loves the way it feels though, if his moans and both his hands on my head now are any indication. He lets go of my hair and uses both hands to push me down on his cock, impaling it down my throat until I gag on him again.

"Yes, love." He moans, picking up his pace until he's repeatedly slamming into the back of my throat. It feels like I'm going to fucking puke, but I breathe in through my nose and try to ignore it. "Look at you taking all of me like a good girl."

I moan against him, and he groans. He's losing control, and I can tell he's about to come. I know the signs. It happens when you've made someone come as many times as I have Damien.

My hands run up the length of his thighs until they reach his ass, and I claw at him, digging my nails into him again, marking him for myself. I want to see that he belongs to me. I want him to have the reminder when this is all said and done.

His hands tighten around my head, grabbing my hair again and pulling it, tilting my head up. "Take every drop of me." He tells me, and I close my eyes as tears begin to stream down my face when he fucks it harder, "Swallow every fucking drop, Hallie."

"Mhmm," I reply, and after two more thrusts, he's coming down my throat.

It's hard to keep it down when he keeps fucking my mouth, but I manage to swallow and not throw up, so that's an accomplishment. When he's done, rather than being sweet, he pushes me away, making me release him with a pop and fall on my ass.

He pulls his pants up and walks out, leaving me confused as fuck. "Oh no you fucking don't!" I yell after him, making him halt in his tracks. "What the hell was that? You're just using me now?"

"No more than you use me."

His sweatpants hang low off his hips, and I lick my lips, tasting the reminder of him from just a minute ago. There's no way he's walking away, not now.

"We should talk, Damien."

He shrugs, "Nothing to talk about."

"Don't be this way with me," I beg him, hurrying after him and grabbing his hand. "Please. Let's forget about everything for tonight."

"You want me to forget everything?" He smirks. "Do I forget I love you? Or that you're fucking him too?"

"I don't care!" I yell, surprising myself. He doesn't seem affected by my outburst. He stays still and breathes evenly. How I wish I could be that in control. I take a deep breath and say, "Just fuck me."

Damien raises an eyebrow.

"I don't care about anything right now, Damien." And I don't. "I just want you inside of me."

I walk closer to him until we're chest to chest, my face tilted up toward his, my lips parted. We make eye contact, his pupils dilating as he looks at me.

His hand connects with my throat, squeezing hard and pulling me toward him even closer. It slides from my throat to the back of my neck until our lips are centimeters apart, and we breathe the same air.

"Why do you do this to me?" He closes his eyes as if he's in pain. "Take me apart then put me back together?"

"Because I'm meant for you," I tell him. "In this lifetime and the next."

His fingers grip my hair while his hand stays cupping the back of my neck as he searches my eyes. He seems to have found what he was looking for because he yanks my head back, and his lips crash against mine.

I'm stunned for a moment at his violence. This isn't usually how he is with me, but I'll take him any way he will give. I open my lips for him. When his tongue slides into my mouth, I suck on it, hard. He groans against me, and I wrap my hands around him, clutching him like I'll lose him if I let go.

I pull away then drop my silk shorts and underwear, pulling

my tank top down my arms and waist instead of taking it off over my head. Grabbing his free hand, I bring it to where I need him most. His fingers slide up and down my slit, teasing me, and I spread my legs a little to allow him access. He plunges two fingers into my tight heat, then removes them, bringing them between us and licking them clean.

My insides heat up, my arousal drenching my thighs. I breathe just a little faster when he kisses me again, thrusting his tongue in my mouth, making me taste myself on him.

Damien turns me around and walks me to the couch, forcing me down onto the rug right in front of it. He kneels behind me, pushing one of my legs apart with his knee, and then lets me go. I peer back at him, his cock tenting his sweatpants, and he pulls them down while staring into my eyes.

His weight on top of me presses me down onto the rug, and even though it's plush, I can feel every bit of the hardwood underneath. His cock is hard as a rock and warm between my legs, and he doesn't even give me time to brace myself before entering me in one deep thrust. The savage thrust and force behind it have me feeling him all the way in my ribcage when he buries himself inside me.

Damien pulls his hips back, then slams them forward, pushing me even more toward the edge of the rug. My fingers dig into it, trying to keep myself in place, as he slams into me over and over. He pushes me down with his right hand on my upper back, restricting my movements, and grips my ass with his left hand, squeezing hard.

I moan when he hits the sweet spot inside of me, because even through the pain, it also feels amazing. "Harder," I cry out. When he smacks my ass, the sound of it vibrates through my whole body. "*More.*"

Damien's hips piston forward at a faster pace, fucking me harder. "Be careful, little love," he tells me. "I might just give you what you ask for."

My cheek meets the hardwood floor, my body still on the rug, and it feels like I'm scooting forward with every thrust. The wood scratches my face, but at this point the pleasure building inside me is too much to ignore. "Yes, just like that!"

"Just like that, huh?" His body envelops mine, one hand finding its way between my legs, his fingers on my clit. The other one comes around my face and covers my mouth. His fingers on my face pinch my nose, depriving me of air. "What about like *this*?" he asks against my ear, making me shiver.

I groan, then scream when he pounds into me with renewed strength. Only it's pointless, no sound is coming out. His fingers are doing something to me, and it feels like I'm going to fall off a precipice any second now. My pussy tightens around him, and he curses. My hips begin to meet him for each thrust, increasing the friction on my clit. He eases up on my nose so I can catch my breath for a moment.

"Damien," I cry out, "Goddamn it, *Damien*."

"What, love?"

His fingers speed up and my toes curl, my eyes rolling to the back of my head as I feel the orgasm within reach. It's right… there…

Damien's hand comes back to my face, his fingers pinching my nose while the rest of his hand covers my mouth. With a few more thrusts, I'm coming, squeezing him impossibly tight. I bite his hand as I scream, drawing blood, tasting the coppery substance on my tongue. It doesn't seem to faze him at all. In fact, he still hasn't let go. My chest is on fire, needing air. My eyes water as I claw at him to no avail, and he's not letting up.

He keeps fucking me into the floor, both of us completely off the rug now. His knees skidding on the hardwood are the only sound other than his moans in my ear. I'd do anything to hear those sounds. I don't even care if he kills me just like this.

A few thrusts later, my eyes become fuzzy, and I'm seeing double, fucking triple. Darkness begins to close in on me, little white dots bouncing and floating in my field of vision, and I know I'm close to fainting.

I'm on the edge, hovering with one foot toward the fall, then I feel him come inside me. He lets go of my face abruptly, making me choke and cough violently, making me feel like I might just die.

"I love you," I whisper when I stop coughing. "You're the love I've always needed." I lie down with my cheek on the freezing hardwood floor, closing my eyes as the tears escape, knowing he probably won't reply.

I don't know what kind of sex this was. Whether it was make-up sex or something else is unclear, but he's bitter. He hasn't recovered from our fight yesterday, and I have a bad feeling in my gut about it.

Still connected, he breathes into my ear softly, then smells my hair deeply. My lower lip trembles at the intimacy of it, and when he trails his lips down my jaw and to my neck, kissing me right below my ear, I sob. "And you're the love of my life," he whispers back.

"Please don't leave me," I beg him, scared as fuck that I know how this ends. "I can't live without you."

"You left me first, babe," he replies, and I sob harder. "But I won't."

Damien pulls out of me, getting up and fixing his pants. He extinguishes the moment between us, a short and weak flame blown by the wind. I begin to get up, flipping over but not wanting to get the rug dirty. He hands me my silk shorts, which I use to wipe myself, then he carries me bridal-style upstairs and lies me down on the bed.

He climbs in bed, cuddling up behind me, his chest to my back. His fingers trace me from my hips and up my arms, over the curve of my shoulder, then up to my jaw. It's like he's trying to memorize me, which makes me tremble in his hold. He trails his hands down my chest, cupping one breast, then down my stomach, cupping my most intimate parts.

"Why are you shaking, love?"

I cry silently, my tears soaking my pillow. "Stop memorizing me."

"I always do that."

I shake my head, "This is different."

"It is." He nods, "I want you to know that my walls will crumble without you," he says to me, making me sob. "I'll be nothing but a shell of myself. The version of me that comes after you."

"There's no after," I cry out, "Only before and during."

"You're right, my love."

I turn over in bed, tracing his forehead, the slope of his straight nose, and the curve of his full lips. He smiles under my fingers, but it's not a happy smile. More nostalgic, a tinge of sadness with it.

It feels like a lifetime has passed between us while simultaneously no time at all, as if we've been frozen in place the entire time we've loved each other. I want to be frozen again in the cold cocoon of his love, his safety.

That's how I fall asleep, thinking of ways to make him stay.

Time is a funny thing. Without a watch, you don't know how fast it goes by. Right now, it's still dark, and I don't know if I've been sleeping for three hours or five minutes. All I know is that he's kissing me softly, doing that thing again like he's trying to remember every detail. I want to cry again as he starts to get up, but I hold on to his wrist.

"I just have to pee, babe," he tells me softly. "I'll be right back."

I nod, relaxing back into the mattress, happily closing my eyes again.

I've never made a bigger mistake in my life.

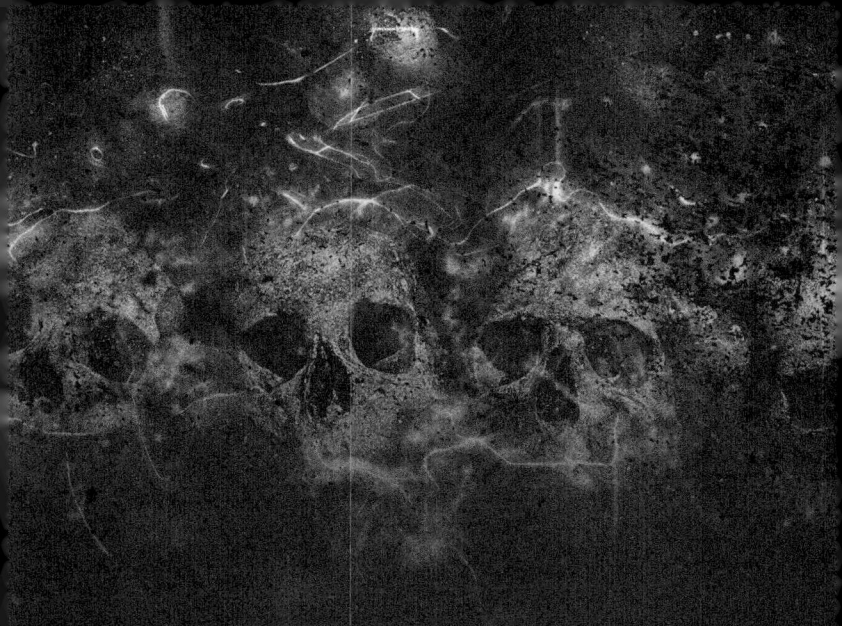

CHAPTER 34

Damien

Leaving her in that room, filled with my lies and the coldness of the night, is breaking my fucking heart. I have to be strong; I *need* to be. I'm doing this for myself because I deserve better. I trust that she's strong enough to handle this, that she learned her lesson last time. I doubt she can escape Zayne's watchful eyes anyway, he's on high alert now. The problem for me is that I want her for myself, and since I can no longer share her, I will not put myself and her through the pain anymore.

I grab all my bags and open my bedroom door, being quiet as a mouse as I make my way toward the stairs and to my Uber waiting for me outside.

"You're doing it then? You're leaving her?" Zayne chuckles. "Just like that, you fucking pussy?"

My nostrils flare as I take in his words, but he's trying to rile me up to start a fight again. I won't give him the satisfaction of making a sound and ruining my plans. "All the money from Mexico is in my room. There will be a letter on the dining table for her. Tell her I don't love her anymore."

"I refuse to lie to her that way." Zayne shakes his head, illuminated by the phone I just got him. "We both know it's not the truth."

"I don't care. It's the only way she'll survive."

"She'll survive," Zayne says, getting up from the couch, closing in on me. "Because of *me*. I'll be her shoulder to cry on, her dick to ride on, and she'll forget you sooner or later."

That hits me right in the chest as if I've been shot, the scar on my side burning and throbbing, reminding me of the pain I've already felt over her.

"I wish you both the best." Is all I say before turning my back on him.

"Don't do it." Zayne stops me in my tracks, and for a brief moment, I consider it. I even change my mind, wanting to stay.

But I don't.

I square my shoulders and remind myself I'm doing this for a reason, then descend the stairs. I pull out the heartfelt letter from the back pocket of the jeans I changed into and set it on the table, right in the middle.

Tears trail down my face as I turn the doorknob to the front door and look back. I could stop. It's not too late. I could set my bags back in my room and unpack them tomorrow. I could get back in bed with Hallie and forget about this stupid plan.

But I don't.

I never do what I should.

With a final look, I step over the threshold and lock the door behind me. My Uber is waiting for me at the curb of the driveway, and the negative temperature reminds me of my cold fucking heart. I can't believe I'm doing this to her, abandoning her, leaving her with no goodbye because I'm a coward. I'm not afraid to admit it, or that I'm scared she'd change my mind the way she knows just how to.

I get in the Uber, throwing my bags in the backseat and

climbing in right next to them. The cabin I bought is three towns over or something like that, so it's doubtful we will cross paths any time soon. I give the man directions and look out the window when he starts driving, craning my neck with my hand on the glass, yearning for Hallie. For any piece of her. I was dumb enough not to bring anything that reminded me of her, or maybe that's the smart thing to do. I don't know yet.

It feels like a lifetime before we get to the cabin, even though it's only been probably forty-five minutes. The man parks on the street since everything else is covered in snow, and I briefly remember I have no vehicle. I have to fix that. Even if I spend a lot of money, I will still be able to live for decades to come off what I have in my suitcase. Same for Hallie, if she plays her cards right. She'd never have to work again if that's what she wanted. I imagine it's not, though.

I grab my bags and open the door, handing the driver a tip then slamming it closed. The snow is deep, up to my thighs, and it's clear this house hasn't seen a shovel in months. I have to carry my bags on my back and front to push some snow away from the door, just so I can go in there.

Sadly for me, the house is entirely empty. This one didn't come furnished, and I'm going to have to figure it out. I'll probably get takeout for a few days. Hopefully someone delivers here, even if I have to meet them out front.

It's cold as fuck when I step through the doors, and I say a quick thanks to myself that I turned on utilities right as I made this decision yesterday. I couldn't leave yet though. I'm fucking selfish. I needed to get one last fix before never seeing her again.

The thermostat kicks in right as I set the heat to seventy-five, knowing I'll probably need to adjust it again, and I set my bags down in what's supposed to be the living room. I have a phone, a laptop, and my bags. That's it. But at least I have the internet to keep me occupied.

I sit on the floor, thinking about how much my ass is going to hurt when this is said and done, but I need to order some things for myself. This is kind of the middle of bum-fuck nowhere, and I need so much crap for this place. Everything a house needs to function.

Amazon Prime is my savior as I begin to add things to my cart. A snow shovel, mop, bucket, broom, dust pan. All the essentials. I even order all the kitchen and bathroom stuff I need and call it a night. I'm going to have to go to a store for at least the dining room, living room, and bedroom furniture. I don't know what I'll do for the spare room, probably turn it into a home gym, even if it's small. A cable machine, adjustable squat rack with a bench, and plates will do to start with. Then I'll have to look into dumbbells and mats. It sucks that I've been neglecting myself a little, but I'm going to prioritize my time to work on myself. Maybe in the future, I'll be functional once more.

In the morning I'll have to prioritize shoveling. This is a small yet beautiful log cabin in the middle of the woods right on a lake. No, truly. I have a deck with steps leading to a dock, but the lake is frozen now. I can still go ice skating if I want to, though.

I set my laptop aside and use my bags as a pillow, trying to close my eyes, but sleep never comes. I don't know that it ever will again. If it does, my dreams will be of her. Hallie's soft skin, pouty lips, upturned nose. The way she feels in my arms. Everything I committed to memory before coming here will haunt me. Leaving may have either been the best decision of my life, or the fucking worst one.

Three hours later, I still can't sleep, and it's seven in the morning. The nearest grocery shop opens at eight, so I take some layers out of one of my bags and begin to get dressed. There were not many Ubers for that time, but I still try. There's only one available to come to this side of town since it's secluded. It's about a ten-minute drive to civilization though, so it's not that bad. I like to be able to have everything I need accessible to me.

One thing I did for Hallie was get her a new nursing license with her fake identity. I put it with her letter. I'm hoping that it softens her heart a little bit, and she doesn't hate me as much. It's not realistic though, and I know that. I did the same for myself though, and my plan is to go back to work as soon as possible. I've already been looking for a job. I even have an interview next week. I need to move on and forget about Hallie, and staying busy is the best way to do it.

My Uber is finally here. I can't even believe I've had one twice in a span of hours, and I have to basically swim through the snow to get to the road. It's a fucking trek too, and my legs are burning by the time I'm done.

The woman takes me to a grocery store, and sadly I'll have to call her back to pick me back up. I begin to fill my cart with everything I need, all the healthy shit that I like, but it doesn't bring me joy. Instead, it only reminds me of Hallie and all our grocery shopping together. It especially reminds me of the first time we did when she was so sassy and full of life. I miss her already and haven't even been gone long at all. Just mere hours.

She'll probably be waking up soon, and I'm here grocery shopping for my new house, my new life. Not only will she be devastated, but she'll see me for the traitor I am. Although it felt like the right reason for myself, I can't help but feel guilty. I know I did the wrong thing by leaving in the middle of the night. I regret it already, not hearing her side, not letting her say her peace. We could've parted amicably, though I doubt that. I think she wouldn't have let me leave, mainly because I would've changed my mind no matter what I thought I'd end up doing.

I end up getting a snow shovel at the grocery store because it doesn't feel like I can wait for the one coming from Amazon tomorrow, and I go to the cashier to check out. Once I pay, I stay inside until the Uber gets here.

She's nice enough to wait for me outside the house while I put away my groceries, and once done, I go right back to her. I don't want to wait another minute to schedule my furniture to be delivered, but first, I must find a store. I don't need anything crazy, honestly. Just the most basic shit to get by.

Arianna, according to her, takes me to the most popular furniture store. "This is it, sir. I'll stay and wait for you."

"You don't have to do that," I reply, feeling bad for taking up all her time.

"This is the most money I've made in one day in this town for a long time."

Fuck. Now I feel like shit.

"Thank you for staying then."

I get out of the car and enter the store, smelling the new leather and the scent of a candle mixed together. It's soothing, and I'm ready to get what I need and get the fuck out of here. This reminds me of Hallie all over again, when we went shopping for our—*her*—house.

There's a tiny suede sectional couch in dark brown that I pick, a two-seater rustic dining table in white, just like Hallie's last apartment except with actual chairs, so basically everything reminds me of her. Fuck me and my life too.

Lastly, I order a king-sized bed that I definitely do not need, along with a dresser and nightstands, a rug for the living room, a coffee table, and two bedside table lamps. I also end up getting a floor lamp for the living room corner and calling it a day. Sadly, they don't sell televisions here.

They assure me they will be delivering everything in four hours, which means I need to get to shoveling as soon as possible. That will take a very long fucking time, and I know it can't wait now. The stairs need to be accessible, and so does the porch. Most importantly, there needs to be a free path to the house. Something tells me that not only will I be shoveling the entire four hours, but there will be mountains of snow on either side of the house. It kind of looks like something out of a Hallmark Christmas movie right now, a *very* white Christmas.

I go back to the car and head home—that fucking hurts—to shovel my life away. Tomorrow I will have to travel to get a vehicle, but I know that I want to get both a car and a motorcycle again. If I'm going to be miserable, at least I'll be miserable with the shit I like.

The tip I give the Uber lady when I get back to the house is more than she's ever been tipped probably, but I feel bad that she doesn't get a lot of clientele here. It's pretty noticeable that there are mostly elderly people in this little town, and the population is very small, to begin with.

"Thanks!" She yells after me with the window down as I try to huddle through the snow like a penguin. "Thank you so much!"

"You're welcome," I tell her, not even looking back, trying not to fall.

I go back in the house and grab the shovel, and I'm glad I bought the biggest one possible. I don't make quick work of it, but I am efficient, producing a wide enough path to the deck steps so that they can bring the furniture up. I also clean up the mountains of snow off the actual porch and steps as well.

My phone now says it's been three hours, and I have one to spare, so I order some lunch and have it delivered. All in all, it's been an eventful fucking day—which I didn't expect—and I just want to be done with it. I want to get my furniture and go to bed.

To dream of her.

Always of her.

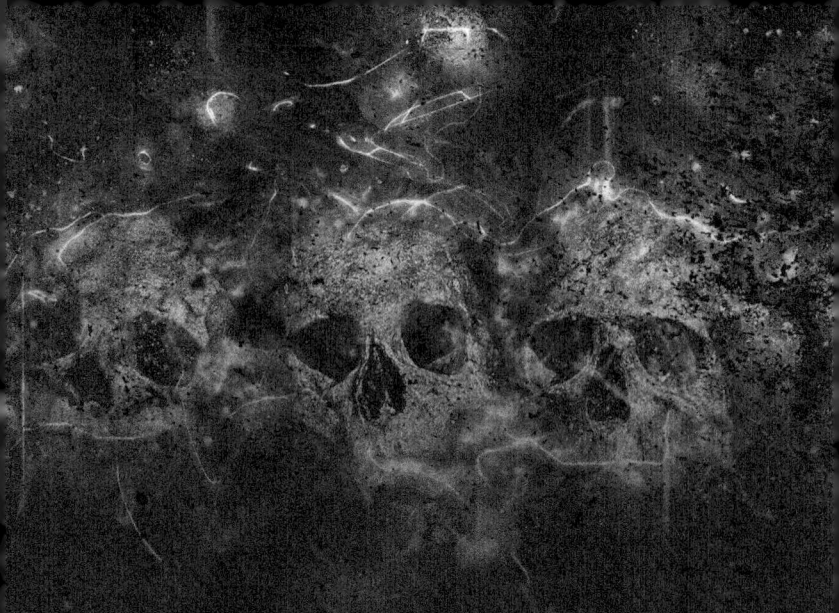

CHAPTER 35

Hallie

I roll over in bed with closed eyes to say good morning to Damien, but when I feel around his side of the bed is cold and empty. My eyes fly open, and I get out of bed to look for him. He's not in the bathroom, not in the movie room either. I knock on his door and it slowly opens, but it's not from him opening it. It does it on its own. He's not in there either, and when I go in his closet and drawers, they are all open and empty.

"Zayne!" I scream, "Zayne! Where the fuck are you?"

Did Damien leave? He left me? Did Zayne go with him too? Why is no one answering?

Oh, God.

I think I'm having a heart attack. My chest is tight, my fingers numb, and my heart on fucking fire. Even through my shallow, rapid breaths, I know I'm not going to die. That's what I hate the most. I fall to the floor, clutching my chest, my throat, my face. I can't live like this, I need help.

"Help!" I sob, "Zayne! Help me."

It hurts, it hurts so fucking bad.

I hear running up the stairs, and suddenly Zayne is by my side. "I'm sorry, Hals," he whispers, pulling my body toward his embrace. "I'm so sorry."

I rock back and forth on the floor, bumping into him with every movement, but he tries to hold me still anyway, "He left?" I whisper, as if saying it louder will make it true.

"Yes, baby," Zayne replies softly. "Last night."

"Why didn't you wake me?"

"This was his choice."

"*No*." I shake my head vehemently, turning around and pushing him away. "You could've stopped him! You could've told him not to go! You could've not let him leave." He grabs a hold of my arms, pulling me closer to straddle his lap, and I sob more.

"Shhhhh, baby," he says as he rubs my back, trying to soothe me. "It's going to be okay."

"No." I shake my head, "It hurts so fucking bad, Zay. Oh, God, it hurts." My body is shaking from my cries.

"I'll get you through it, baby."

"You can't," I reply, "No one can."

Only him.

He's the only one who can get me through it.

Damien.

I need him back. There's no way Zayne can help me get through anything, he's not the one who left me. I don't think he understands this is not something he can fix. He can't put me back together when I've been broken beyond repair.

What hurts the most is that Damien left me without saying goodbye. How fucking low is that? He can't get much lower. This is beyond fucking ridiculous. He lied to me so many times last night, telling me he wouldn't leave me, going back and forth yet saying he wouldn't do it. It was all a lie—more deception. I don't know how much more I can take of it, but I guess I dodged a bullet if he left this way.

I know for a fact he's not coming back.

"Come on, baby," Zayne says, getting up. He also picks me up to take me to my room. "I'll rub your back for a little while, and we can go back to bed."

"Okay," is all I say, because what the hell do I say to that? I have a feeling he doesn't know what to do right now, how to make it better. I can't blame him. I mean, I just shut him down with everything he offered to do.

Going to sleep doesn't sound half bad, though. In fact, it sounds like a great idea. Maybe then I can forget about this shit and pretend it never happened.

I wonder what he's doing, where he's staying, how the fuck he got where he is. I'm assuming he got a ride somehow. It's not that hard to figure it out, but is he still in town? Did he go somewhere else? Did he leave me here to never run into each other again? That thought makes me even more desperate to see him.

Of all the things I thought he'd do to me, leaving without a word was not one of them.

"He left you something, you know."

My heart almost stops beating. "What?"

"I thought I'd give this to you when you calmed down," Zayne replies, pulling out an envelope. "I can leave the room while you read it."

I grab it, then take out the folded paper. "Please, I need to be alone for this."

Zayne, surprisingly, doesn't fight me on it. He just goes without saying a word, closing the door softly behind him. I get on my side and open the letter, bracing myself for the emotional damage of it already.

Hallie,

My love.

I know no words can ever make up for what I've done, but before anything, I want to say how sorry I am. I've been a coward, and I know it, but it's because of my love for you that I couldn't say goodbye. I know that if I stuck around and told you my intentions, you would convince me to stay all over again. I've tried my best. I gave it my all, truly. Sharing you is not what I want. I did it for you, but now I'm doing this for me. I deserve to be loved for me, and only me. Not along with someone else. I hope one day you can forgive me, but if not, I get it. I just hope you understand why I did it. I love you more than words will ever express, and as you already know, you're the love of my life.

The house is yours, and so is the car. Everything is under your name now, and you will never need to contact me. There's money in a bank account for you and some cash on the table as well. I left you set up for life, you've always deserved that much, and I could never leave you unprepared. I hope you're happy with the house and car so you don't have to move. Feel free to sell everything if you need to. I will understand.

Again, I want to tell you that you're everything to me, which is why I couldn't stay. This had already been hurting for a while, but it now has become unbearable for me. I wish you and Zayne the very best and many years of happiness. I love you more than life.

Yours,

Damien.

My heart drops just as I let go of the letter, turning my head to sob into my pillow. It's soaked within a minute, sticking to my face along with my tears.

Damien loves me. He loves me so much he couldn't see me with another man. Have I made a mistake? Should I have picked? Zayne can see me with him; he can bear it. Does that mean Zayne loves me less?

Questions run through my mind in quick succession, and now I wonder where the fuck Damien is so I can go get him my damn self. I'll demand he comes home and forget this ever happened. But will I pick him? I don't know. I can't choose still. It pisses me off that he made the choice for me, that he forced Zayne on me.

What if it was never Zay? What if I was going to pick *him*? I can't believe this shit, to be honest. For some reason, I thought I'd have more time. More time with them without having to choose. It seemed to work so well for us, until a few days ago when Damien started acting weird. I thought it would pass, that it was just an outburst of jealousy, and he'd get over it and fuck me with Zayne again, share me with him.

No matter how much I keep telling myself I'm going to choose, I've liked the sharing more than I've cared to admit to myself, and I don't know that if it were up to me if I'd be able to pick between them. It doesn't matter anymore though; the choice was made for me.

I just need to find a way to live with it.

July

It's been six months since Damien left. Six months of pain, emptiness, and sadness. Yet also grateful for Zayne being the most gentle, loving soul. He's been here for me through everything. I can't imagine seeing your girlfriend crying over another man for months on end feels good, but he's been amazing through it all. I think he's playing the long game because he knows now that Damien is gone for good. Eventually, I will heal. That may not be entirely true, but I'll heal enough to live life and move on. Just not yet.

What's most surprising is that there's been no word from him, not a peep. At least not with me. I wonder every day what he's doing, where he is, how he's been. Is he working again or just living life off the money he has? Is he happy without me? Happier, even? Did he start dating again yet? Everything matters to me. *He* does.

I'm back to work now, loving the hospital, and I'm doing better. Even if it doesn't feel like I am. I'm on medication for depression, and Zayne is medicated for his condition as well. Therapy has benefited me, and I've needed that venting session more than I care to admit, even if I have to be careful about what I say. I mostly focus on my polyamorous relationship, how he left me, and learning to live without him. Her face is that of outrage half the time, but she's also very helpful, even though I imagine she's judging me.

Zayne is also working in construction a couple of towns away, and he looks more fulfilled than ever. He finally finished college online with my help, taking a *ton* of classes at a time. The drugs are but a distant memory, and he doesn't tell me of his struggles anymore. He's come such a long way. It feels like we finally have our lives together. Like we know how to live more healthily. I never thought we'd get here, having a strong relationship and loving each other the right way. Like partners.

We've been paying our bills with the money we earn from our jobs, saving the money in the savings account for things that are an emergency or even an impromptu little vacation. We've had one since Damien left, still staying within Canada, but it was much needed. I hope one day we can go to Europe or an island for vacation without drawing attention to ourselves, but these little stay-cations will do for now.

We never plan on returning to the United States, not for anything at all. As far as Zayne's family is concerned, he's dead. It's cruel in a way, however, we have to do what we have to do to survive. He told me his parents' relationship was changing right before all of this shit happened, before we got kidnapped. So we assume they're back together and at least have each other. It's not such a bad thing, after all.

I'm assuming the Mexican Cartel is still looking for us, and they probably will be for a long time. Not necessarily in an active way, but if they saw us, they would surely kill us. We're not taking any risks, though I'd be lying if I said I'm not paranoid that one day they will show up at my front door and end this life we've built. Out of everything, that scares us the most. Whenever someone knocks on the door or rings the doorbell, I'm scared shitless. So is Zayne. We've considered moving even further north, but I don't want to chance Damien never finding us again, if he ever chooses to return.

I shouldn't want him to. Moreover, I should want him to stay away forever. I can't help but think that he was right in leaving. Maybe not in the way he did, but if he felt that this was best for him, then I have to understand it was, no matter how much it fucking hurts.

And it hurts, *a lot.*

Zayne and I have agreed he won't be sharing me with anyone else. Damien was the exception, and he told me all about how they bonded. He rescued Zayne from a terrible fate, an awful situation to match my own. I never even thought it was a possibility that Zayne would go through such a similar situation. Now I wonder how the hell he has stayed sober. How we both have. It's insane and incredible at the same time how much we've grown as individuals as well as together.

"So, how does that make you feel?" my therapist asks, breaking me out of my thoughts. "The fact that everything has improved in your life."

"Guilty," I answer honestly. "Like I'm betraying him. Don't get me wrong, it's still hard to get out of bed most days. In fact, it's still hard to live my day to day without thinking of him. I don't know if I'll ever be able to do that."

"You will," She reassures me. "It will just take more time than we expected."

"But how long?"

"Only your heart knows that, Hallie. However, I will say this. You've come such a long way in the last six months you've been coming to see me. What about six more months from now? I bet you'll be feeling like a brand-new person."

I see her point, I genuinely do. It's just hard still. I can't imagine going one day without thinking of him. Of us. What could've and should've been.

"I just can't imagine never thinking of him again. How he's doing, where he is, if he misses me."

"Those are what-ifs that you will probably never stop thinking about. The difference is that maybe it will happen once every week or every few weeks instead of every day. Before you know it, it will be once a month. Then once every few months. It will get less and less until you can live a normal life."

"That's the only hope I have."

"Have you thought of something you'd like to do? A hobby? What do you truly enjoy?"

I think about that for a minute.

Zayne has been teaching me to play piano, which is hard as fuck, by the way. However, I am getting there little by *very* little. The one thing I enjoy the most though is sketching. I could do it for hours.

"Sketching."

"So find a class, get supplies, sketch your life away. Maybe it could be an outlet for your feelings. Draw what could've been, your what-ifs. Let it all out, and then let go of it. Ask the universe, as you said you believe in, to help you heal."

"I won't lie, I had never thought of doing anything like that."

It feels far-fetched, like I'm reaching. Yet, I won't deny that a sketching class sounds like something I could do and be happy with.

"That's what I'm here for. To make suggestions."

She's helped me a lot, and for the first time in my life, I have faith that someone can get me through this—with me putting in the work, of course. The first thing she asked me was, '*Are you home and in a safe place? Do you feel safe with the people in your home?*' And that made me feel cared for. Like she actually gave a shit, and it wasn't some farce to get through the session. She genuinely wants to help people, and it shows.

"Thank you," I say with honesty as the timer goes off. "I'll leave you to solve your puzzles, Doc."

She smiles. "Have fun at work."

"Oh, I will."

With that, I take my leave, rushing to the car to make the drive to the hospital, which is only ten minutes away. I usually go to therapy three times a week right before my shifts, which is amazing because I don't have to stay up during the day or wake up early before the night shift. I'm lucky enough that I only work three days a week now, not having to redo my residency. Even though I'm hurt over him leaving, Damien really did set me up for success.

The drive to the hospital is short and uneventful, and I say hello to the nurses on my floor as I clock in. I'm back in the ICU, doing what I love most, taking care of the patients I can save.

It's still a sad and gloomy atmosphere with the lights dimmed almost all the way, and the only sounds being the monitors beeping and the nurses charting on the computers. Yet it feels like home now, maybe because it reminds me of him; of all the times we worked together, and all the times I wish we still did. Every day that I come here, I remember him helping me with patients, telling me I was a good person and holding me during the honor walk. I'll never forget those moments; I don't know that I want to either way.

I get report on my patients and begin my tasks for them when I get a call on my work cell phone. "Hey, Hallie. You're getting an admission."

"When should I expect a report?"

"You'll have to go down to the emergency department for the Medevac. It's a nineteen-year-old patient, motor vehicle accident."

"Do I have to help in the trauma room?"

"Yes, they need all the hands they can get."

"Got it," I reply nervously.

The last time I had something similar happen, it ended with a brain herniation and eventual organ donation. I'll never forget the pain I felt during that honor walk; this time, I don't have anyone to hold my hand through it.

Once at the emergency department, I go to the nurse that is supposed to give me report. "What do you need help with?" I ask her.

"We need to go outside to get him and transport him into the trauma room."

I nod, running after her to the elevators to get to the roof where the helicopter pad is. We quickly get there, and once the helicopter lands, it's all hands on deck. More emergency nurses arrive, and the helicopter doors open. Out comes a blond, curly-haired, tall, blue-eyed man with the most gorgeous smile I've ever seen, and my heart stops. My knees fucking buckle.

Damien.

Our eyes connect, and it feels like time stops for me, for us. I see it in the way he briefly smiles, then remembers he doesn't have me anymore, and his eyes turn sad. He glances away first and goes on with his job, while I'm just left there, standing still as my heart breaks and everyone works around me. He gets back in the helicopter and closes the door, closing *our* door.

"Hallie, come on!" the nurse yells, making me snap out of it.

I go after her, running with the gurney to the elevator, headed for the trauma room. But even still, while I work on the poor guy, I can't help but be in another galaxy, far away from this place. I'm somewhere only Damien and I exist, where we love each other again, where we're together finally.

But it's not reality.

Instead, *this* is.

And I hate every fucking second of this pain.

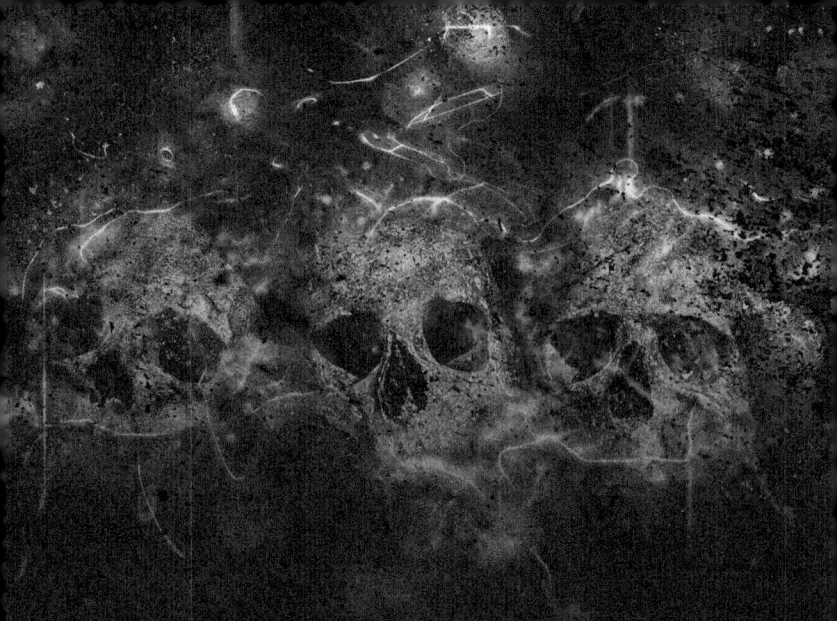

CHAPTER 36

Zayne
February

Hallie is beautiful in the gloom of Tadoussac as she watches the beluga whales at the beach. We sit on the rocky sand with only a towel under us and eat Uncrustables as we watch them. I finally convinced her to eat like shit occasionally, and she realized it's easier than making meals. She still cooks, but sometimes when she gets home from work and doesn't want to, she does this instead. She draws the line at the Hot Pockets, though. No amount of begging will get her to eat them.

We cuddle up since it's cold as fuck, but this brings her happiness, so I'm willing to do whatever it takes to make her smile. She does it more often and now looks happier than I've seen her in a very long time. I think therapy has helped her. She hasn't even done any self-harm in the last year, which is a massive step for her. There's been much growth on her end.

It's been a year since Damien left. That was a hard time for her, the anniversary of her broken heart. Although she seems better already after a few days.

She stares into the distance, clearly lost in thought. I grab her hand and kiss the inside of her wrist where the puckered scar begins, my favorite spot since the beginning. This rouses her, bringing her back from her mind, and she looks at me with love in her eyes. I can't believe it's been two years of loving her, and I do love her. More than anything in the entire world.

As if she knows, she softly says, "I love you, you know that? Always have."

"Always will," I finish.

"Promise?"

Forever. *I promise forever is how long I'll love you.* "Promise." We kiss on it, our little ritual we've always had, and we smile against each other's lips.

If someone had told me that this is where I'd be a year after escaping from the cartel, I would've laughed. Never in a million years could I have imagined we'd be living in fucking Canada with a dream life. A house, two cars, and jobs. *Sober*. It's hard to believe I've been this blessed, that I overcame and conquered my demons. Now here I am, living the best life I can with the love of my life by my side. I don't even know when I got this sappy, but goddamn. I can't help myself. I fucking love her.

My phone begins to ring, and I pull it out of my pocket. The name reads, 'Answer Me. "I'll be right back," I tell Hallie. "It'll be quick."

"Okay."

I walk away, looking behind me to see her staring out at the water, not even bothering to glance at me. Not one bit curious about who could be on the phone.

"Hey," I answer the phone while watching her.

"How is she?"

"She's fine now, but she wasn't a few days ago."

There's a sigh on the other end of the phone. "I wasn't either."

"So come back."

"You know I can't, Zayne."

"Have you even thought about it?" I know Hallie would take him back with open arms. Maybe it's stupid of her, maybe not. Either way, she would try because she loves him, and Hallie is the kind of person who loves hard.

"I don't want to." I bite my cheek, trying not to cuss him the fuck out for being this dumb. "Last time I saw her at the hospital… it broke me." His breath shudders on the other end. "I've been going back as much as possible to get a glimpse of her, but I never see her."

"That's because she always works in the ICU. That day, she was helping the emergency department. If you want to get a glimpse of her, try harder."

"I can't. It's selfish." Yeah, whatever, dude. We all do selfish things. "*I'm* selfish."

"Yeah," I reply. "You were selfish as fuck when you left."

"Why do I even call you? What the fuck?"

"Because you still care about her." Stupid ass fucker. "Have you even fucked anyone else in the last year?"

Damien's silent on the other end, debating how much to say. "Yeah, I have a girlfriend."

Girlfriend?

What?

"Shut the fuck up with that," I growl. "Never repeat those words, especially not to Hallie if you run into her. It'll break her. Why do you even call to check on her then?"

"Because I love her." He sniffles, and I roll my eyes. Fucking pathetic. He could have her if he wanted to, yet here he is crying over her like a dumbass. "I can't move on."

I turn around. "Either move on or come back. Stop dragging this shit out."

"You better keep answering the—"

"Who are you talking to?"

Click.

The line goes dead.

"Work, baby," I tell her. "But he just hung up."

Hallie narrows her eyes as if she can tell I'm full of shit, but then nods and holds my hand with her cold one to pull me toward the car. We get in, and I blast the heat as much as I can, then turn on the seat warmers.

"Do you think he lives nearby?" Hallie asks. "Damien?"

I know who she meant, but the fact that she has to clarify makes something stir inside me. Maybe jealousy. "I have no clue, Hals. I don't see why he'd stick around if he's going to leave you." I wince at the wording, and her head whips toward me, tears filling her eyes. "I'm sorry. That was harsh. It wasn't meant to come out that way."

"It's… okay," she says slowly.

I sigh, knowing I fucked up. "I don't know, baby, truly."

"I want to." She looks at me again. "I *need* to."

We pull up to the house, and I park in the driveway. It's almost evening time, which means she has to go to work, and I have to go get supplies for a new project. I want to make her a pergola for the summertime. Have it really pretty out back by the time it gets warmer outside, and I want it to be a surprise. I guess it's a good thing she never goes in the garage for any reason. I could be a damn serial killer, and she wouldn't know.

"I understand, baby," I reply to her. "But for now, you need to get ready for work."

She nods, taking her seatbelt off and opening the door to exit the car. I turn off the vehicle and go to the front door to unlock it, then spank Hallie's ass on the way in. She squeals and turns around, wrapping her arms around my neck briefly before undressing.

She has a lacy bra and thong under her baggy sweatshirt and matching sweatpants, and my mouth automatically waters. "How long do you have before you need to get ready?"

"An hour…" She winks, and I almost melt.

Hell. *Yes*.

"Let's go get in the bath."

I go up the stairs and into our room, yes, *ours* now, and turn the faucet to the hot water. If there's one thing I know about Hallie, it's that she likes her baths extra hot like she wants her skin to melt off, and I'm willing to suffer through it if it means I get that tight little pussy. It's a win-win, really, unless my skin does fall off. Then, maybe, not so much.

Once the tub is full, Hallie takes off her underwear and climbs in, and I immediately follow her. The water is hotter than I thought, and I wince on the way down while Hals lets out a contented sigh as she gets in and leans back, her hair getting a little wet at the bottom of her bun. She's about to get it all the way wet, she just doesn't know it yet.

"I need you, baby," I tell her, and her eyes turn dark. "Let me see that pretty pussy."

She spreads her legs for me, showing me all of her. I rub her clit with my thumb as I lean in to kiss her. Our lips meet frantically, desperate for each other. The kiss intensifies, our tongues clashing for dominance, our teeth biting each other's lips.

I thrust two fingers into her tight heat, my thumb still on her clit, and massage the inside of her pussy. At a slow torturous pace, I fuck her with my fingers, and I can already feel her walls tightening around them as I go faster on her clit. Hallie moans, biting her fist since she has nothing to grip but water. She's going to come soon, but there's something else I want to do.

"How close are you, baby?"

"Close!" She groans, then moans when I press my thumb into her clit with more pressure.

I get between her legs, lowering myself to the water's level, and look at her. Hallie's eyes widen, looking from me to the water, and she shakes her head. But I've already made up my mind. I'm fucking doing it.

"Come fast, okay?" I smirk. "Or I'll die between your legs, which honestly doesn't sound bad at all."

I breathe in through my nose and lower myself into the water, spreading her legs wider after I remove my fingers from her pussy. She's laid out for me like a fucking meal. So fucking beautiful. I know exactly how to make her come hard, and I wrap my lips around her clit and begin to suck. Automatically, Hallie's hands come to my hair, and she holds on to it, gripping it tightly between her fingers, making my eyes sting.

I suck on her clit hard, pulling it into my mouth roughly, until she's thrashing in the water, squirming so much it's difficult to keep her still. Her legs wrap around my neck, but I already can't breathe, so it is what it is. My chest feels like it's on fire though, the blood rushing to my head the longer I force myself to stay in the water. The only thing that keeps me going is the moans I can hear coming from those sweet lips, even under the water. It's fucking blissful to bring her pleasure. Better than I ever thought it would be.

With a light bite on her clit she comes, and I can tell how hard her orgasm hits from her scream and the way she pulls my hair like she wants to take it all with her. She's so fucking hot when she comes for me, and I'm almost regretful that I didn't get to see it. Then again, I really wanted to do this.

I come up for air, choking and coughing, my chest heaving. Hallie looks concerned until I shake my head and grin, proud of myself and the fact that I made her come with my mouth underwater. New level unlocked.

My dick is so hard it's painful, so I grab Hallie and flip her over abruptly until her face meets the porcelain of the tub. She braces herself with her hands, holding on to the edge of the tub, and she holds on for dear life as I thrust into her from behind. Her warm, tight heat envelops my dick perfectly, like we were meant to fit together all our lives.

I pull back and immediately thrust forward, moaning at her warmth. She grabs onto the edge of the tub as I fuck her, pounding into her over and over until water sloshes over the sides of the tub and onto the tiled floor.

Her neck arches back when I wrap her long hair around my fist once, twice, three times before pulling it hard. Hallie moans loudly, fucking me back, but I'm no longer concerned about her coming. She already did.

"Yes, baby." I push her back down until her face is almost in the water. "Give me that tight pussy."

"Oh, God," Hallie mumbles.

"Hold your breath, baby." I grab onto the back of her neck while I keep thrusting my hips forward. "It's your turn."

I hear her take a deep breath and push her head under the water, holding it down while I drive myself into her. She doesn't struggle yet, and the sight of this, her tight ass, and the knowledge that she'd even do this for me will make me come so fucking good—and soon.

The familiar tingling begins, all the way from my spine to my balls, and they tighten unbearably until it feels like I'm right on the edge. Hallie's arms begin to flail, clawing and grabbing onto whatever she can reach. I know if I don't come now, she'll probably drown. I thrust into her five more times before I find my release, fucking her so hard I'm afraid I'll either break her or she has swallowed water, for sure.

As soon as my dick stops jerking inside her, I yank her out of the water by the back of her neck and hold her to my chest. Our bodies are slick from the water, making us slide a bit, but I'm able to hold her up as she coughs and sputters.

"You good, baby?" More coughing, more sputtering. "Hals?"

"Fine," she squeaks out. "That was amazing."

"For real?"

"Hell yes, but now I really do have to go get ready."

Hallie and I both get out of the tub, and she gets ready for work while I get ready to go on a hunt for the best wood. The pergola is going to be a challenge, but I've always liked building things, so I'm up to it.

We say goodbye to each other with a kiss then get into our respective vehicles, and I let her pull out of the driveway first. The road is slick from snow and ice, so I go slow. When I get to where I need to be, I park near the entrance. There's a lot that's going in the bed of the truck.

Truck.

Who even am I? I never thought I'd be driving one of these. Yet here I am, driving it and using its back to carry wood. I'm stunned, clearly.

The store is pretty empty, and it's the equivalent to Lowe's. I get a cart and begin to browse for wood when I see a familiar man right in front of me. I could never mistake the build of his solid back and the blond hair. He's also looking for wood.

"Damien?" I ask, and he turns around abruptly, almost knocking everything over. This place is three towns over from where we live, so I guess he stuck around a little, even if it's nearly an hour away. "What are you doing here?"

"What are *you* doing here? Didn't take you for a man who knows how to build shit."

"I guess I just keep surprising you."

His face turns stony. "I guess so."

"What are you building?" I'm trying to make conversation so he doesn't leave yet. "I'm building a pergola for the backyard."

"Won't it rot?" he asks with a raised brow.

"Not if I buy something weather resistant. It's for the outdoors, it'll be fine." I roll my eyes, then turn serious. "You can come back, you know. She'd take you back in a heartbeat."

"I can't." He shakes his head vehemently.

"Why? Because of that girlfriend?" I ask with raised brows. Maybe he does care about her. "You love her?"

"No."

"Then what's the problem?"

"I fucked up, Zayne." Damien runs a hand down his face, and I can see the frustration in his posture. "I know you get that, but she will never forgive me."

"How would you know if you don't even try?" I know I have a point, and I think I'm getting through to him when his expression turns thoughtful. He's considering what I'm saying, but I don't know why he wouldn't come back.

"Why are you doing this?"

"Because I love her." His eyes meet mine, and they turn sad. I know he loves her too. "She's happy, just not as happy as she was before you left. Come back to her."

"I don't know, man."

"You do. In your heart, you do."

I nod at him, not waiting for a response before grabbing my wood and taking my leave. Maybe I shouldn't be begging him to come back. Maybe I should want to keep her to myself, but that's clearly not what she wants. Even though we *are* happy together, it still feels like something is missing. Something I can't give her, yet I suspect he can.

I just don't know what that is.

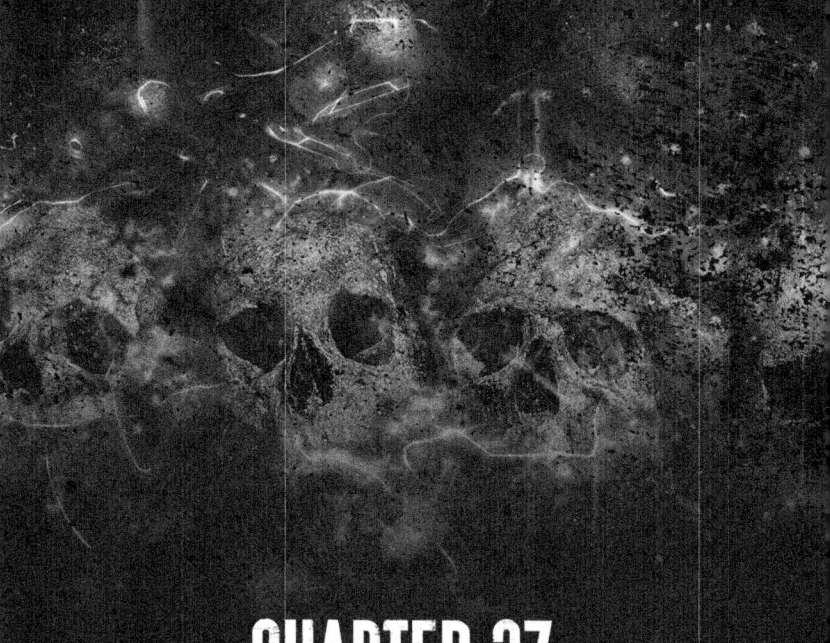

CHAPTER 37

Damien

Seeing Zayne at the store really fucked me up. When I left there, it was with a heavy weight on my shoulders, the kind that you can't shake off. I've been trying to forget her, losing myself in another woman. Cassie is an angel, except maybe that's the problem. I crave the things that aren't good for me. I never thought Hallie wasn't good for me until she didn't choose between Zayne and me.

Hearing that Hallie would take me back after all this time, that she misses me, hit the nail on the head of what I should do. What I should've done long ago. I've regretted not going back, begging for forgiveness on my fucking knees. Groveling until the end of time. But I've been weak, and rejection from her would be my undoing. I've suffered enough from my terrible choices, and I was depressed as fuck for at least the first six months. I'm talking about *couldn't get out of bed* kind of depressed.

I was lucky enough to be alive, to be honest. I couldn't

function. All I did was force myself to eat and work out. Finally, after six months, I decided it was time to have a life again, so I got a job as a flight nurse. Of course she'd be working where I dropped off a dead man. My heart stopped as my hands shook, yet I couldn't bear to keep staring at her, so I looked away.

I regret it every fucking day.

I wish I had looked at her face one more time. Her stunned reaction and the obvious pain on her face broke me that day, and I had to feign a stomach virus to get out of work for the rest of the night. I just couldn't keep going with thoughts of her in my head.

No matter how many times I fuck Cassie, she will never live up to Hallie, and that fucking bothers me. I can't love anyone the way I do Hallie, and that's what is driving me absolutely fucking insane. No matter how far I run away from her, I can't actually escape her. She's in all of my thoughts, all of my dreams. I still remember her hands on my body, her lips on mine. That's what makes me come every goddamn time, thoughts of her. The image of her. When I'm feeling low, I remember the way I traced her skin, trailed my hands down her body to memorize every crevice of hers, and yet it's not enough. It never will be. Of course, I have to have these thoughts when I'm down already, which only brings me even lower.

Which leads me to now. Between Cassie's legs, drunk as fuck, unable to come.

"Baby?" she asks me, her green eyes wide as she stares up at me. She cups my cheek, but it's too sweet for me. "What's wrong?"

I don't like it when she calls me baby, it feels wrong. It should be babe, but that would only sound right coming from Hallie's lips. So really... it should just be Damien. Maybe nothing at all. "I'm just... too drunk to finish."

Cassie's blonde hair—yeah, I can't date brunettes now—is splayed on my pillow, making it look like a halo. "It's okay," she whispers. "I got mine already. I just feel bad for you."

She's older than me by three years, making her almost thirty-one, and she has experience in the sex department, that's for damn sure. Maybe that's the reason I can come, other than the fact that I see Hallie when I fuck her. Different faces, different bodies. It doesn't matter. All I see is the love of my stupid life. And fuck, I'm so damn stupid.

"Are you sure?" I ask, "I can keep going?"

"No, I'm fine, really." She smiles, but it doesn't reach her eyes. "I should get going anyway."

Something doesn't feel right. It's strained. "Why? You're not staying?"

"No, I am not." Cassie sighs, "Listen, I know a man who doesn't love me when I see one. And you? You love someone else. I'm not dumb."

"I—"

"Be quiet. I need to get this off my chest." I nod, letting her talk. "I see it in your face. The way you look at me is not how I deserve to be looked at. You treat me like a queen but don't truly love me."

"I care for you." I nod, but I've never told her I love her. "But it's too soon to know about love for me. I think… I need to go back to her. You're right, I still love her. I'm sorry."

"How bad did she burn you?"

"I burned *her*."

Cassie contemplates that for a moment, and I grab her hands. She lets me. "I don't want to stick around to get burned too."

"I completely understand." I won't keep making her my second choice, living and loving the ghost of someone else. "I really am sorry."

She smiles sadly. "I know." Her eyes tear up. "You're a good person, Damien. I'm just not *your* person."

I look away, confirming what she has said even though it's not a conscious decision. "I wish it could be different."

Cassie pulls her hands away from mine gently. "Me too." She

picks up her clothes, puts them on, and then grabs her purse and car keys. "This is goodbye." Her lips meet mine for a short kiss, and I let her have it. I'm not a complete asshole.

When she goes to the door and opens it, I reply, "Goodbye."

She doesn't stop or look back, a decisive woman through and through. Her choices are permanent, and she doesn't falter. I'm left there, contemplating what the fuck I just did. I had someone to fall back on, to love me, to try to make me forget Hallie even if she never achieved it. Now for the first time in months, I have nothing to cushion my fall.

I sit on the bed with my head in my hands and think about what the hell to do. I know I need to get Hallie back, that's been on my mind since I left her, but I've never dared to go back to her. I'm afraid of her rejection. I don't think I can live through it. Though, I guess I'll never know unless I try.

I've given it a lot of thought and asked myself a million questions about this. Have I gotten over the fact that she didn't choose me? Am I okay with her not choosing me? What about sharing? Can I do it? Forever?

She's built a life with Zayne, around him. Do I even fit in there somewhere anymore? Or am I just a third wheel? An outsider? I can't imagine feeling that way after dreaming of going back for this long.

Either way, I'm still going to try.

I *have* to.

I owe it to both of us to go back.

After sobering up, I get in my car and make my way three towns over to the hospital she works at. I sit in the emergency department parking lot since I don't have a badge to go through the staff doors. Hours go by, and the sky gets dark before I go inside, my hands shaking uncontrollably from my nerves.

Is it because of how long it's been since I've last seen her?

Or the fear of rejection that comes with the knowledge that it's been a year?

I don't even care anymore as I get out of my car, walk

through the emergency department, and make my way to the ICU. It's dark and gloomy here, just as it is in every single one of these units, and the vibe that I get gives me chills. I considered going back to the ICU when I applied for my job, but I knew it would only make me think of Hallie. I needed to move on, not that it fucking worked.

Flight nursing is how I met Cassie, and now I hope it's not awkward between us when we work together. I don't think it will be though because she's a very kind person, forgiving. Unlike me.

I go to the nurse's station and wait for one of them to come to me. "What room number?"

"None," I reply with a smile. "I'm here to see Hailey Cordero." Also known as Hallie Cox. "Could you call her for me?"

The older nurse, probably with at least twenty years of experience, looks at me with pity. "Oh, sweetheart. It's her day off."

"Oh…" Fuck. My. Life.

Now she'll know I was here. I can't let that happen.

"What's your name?"

"Never mind," I say quickly. "I can surprise her at home. I just thought she worked today for some reason and wanted to eat with her on her lunch break."

She eyes me suspiciously, this Linda lady. "Alright, then. Have a good night." She's probably met Zayne or something, so this is suspicious as fuck.

"You as well."

I leave, returning to my car and feeling like I want to bang my head against a wall. What the fuck was I thinking? She will probably call Hallie and tell her someone came looking for her. I really hope she doesn't. I think I've lost my nerve.

Now I have to go home to my bottle of whiskey and consider what the fuck to do about this, with my life as well. How do I recover? Do I move on? Do I try again? Clearly, I haven't moved on yet, and it's been a year. Not if I'm contemplating talking to her again. Asking for her forgiveness.

She's the one who sets my soul on fire, that much I know. I want to marry her, love her forever. I can't believe I've missed so much—her twenty-fifth birthday. Now I'm twenty-eight and want to settle down and have someone by my side—*her*. I know she doesn't want children, but I've already established that I'd sacrifice a lot for her, everything, really. Can I share her? Do I want to? Do I have a choice? The answer to this is that it doesn't matter. I'll take her in any way I can have her.

If she'll even take me back.

I get back to my car and sit in it for a while, then dial Zayne's number. It goes to voicemail repeatedly, but I'm not one to give up. I should've called him before I even went to the hospital. Why the fuck didn't I do that?

"I'm a little busy." He answers the phone with those words, which honestly just pisses me off.

"I put my number in your phone as Answer Me, asshole. So fucking answer me!"

He's stunned into silence. "Okayyyyy, what do you need?"

I pause for a second. What *do* I need? What the fuck *do* I need? "Where is Hallie? I need to see her."

"Oh, man," he mutters, "She's at her sketching class."

"She takes a sketching class?" Of course, she does. She draws beautifully. "Where?"

Zayne gives me the address then says, "But hey, I've been sweetening her up a bit to take you back, by the way."

I don't know what to say to that. "Thank you?" I guess I could use all the help I can get. "I'll get going then. Thanks again."

Not waiting for him to hang up, I do it instead. The address in my GPS says the studio is about ten minutes away, and I speed the entire way there. I hope the class isn't over, but knowing my luck my chances aren't very high.

I pull up to the parking lot and run inside the building,

panting. Huffing and with a heaving chest. Catching my breath, I slap my hands on the counter. The lady looks a bit stunned, and I glance around to see that it's probably a classroom separate from the lobby, because I don't see anyone here.

"How can I help you, sir?"

"I need to pay for a class," I tell her, trying to figure out what exactly to say. "The sketching class that's going on right now."

"There's a few."

"Um… wherever Hailey Cordero is at the moment."

"Sir, I can't divulge that information."

"Listen…" I take a deep breath, trying to keep my composure and be nice. I have a nagging suspicion that if I'm an asshole, I won't get anywhere with—Amy. "I'm trying to get her back. She's the love of my life… consider this a grand gesture."

Amy looks at me like I've sprouted three extra heads and purses her lips. At least she begins to look at her computer, though.

"Sir, I'm sorry, but the class is full. Only one person was absent today, but I can't give you his spot."

"I don't need his spot. I'll pay the class fee to replace him for one day. *Please*. I'll pay double."

"Um." Her eyes almost bug out of her head. "I guess for one class you can have his spot."

"How much?"

"Free for a one-class trial."

It's my turn to be stunned. "Thank you for your kindness."

Amy hands me a sketchbook and pencils. Which I'll be honest I don't know what I'm fucking doing, and she takes me to a classroom with about thirty people. Once she closes the door behind me, I'm left to stand there and look for the only empty chair. The teacher comes to my side and points at the empty space. I still don't see Hallie. Where the fuck is she?

Making my way through the row, I finally spot her. She's right in front of me. Her dark brown hair falls in waves down her back, and her coat hangs from the back of the chair. She's still dainty as ever with her tiny waist, and I only know this because of the way she's leaning over the table, trying to reach something that's about to fall. Her round ass is basically in my face and I smirk, remembering everything I've done to that ass.

Fuck, I want her back so badly.

I miss her.

The way she smiles.

Her kindness.

Everything about her.

The way she loves Harry Potter, how we can spend all day sitting around and reading books, how we like the same shows and the same movies. Having outdoor adventures with her. The mind-blowing sex.

I fucking miss everything.

I keep my eyes trained on the back of her head, waiting to see how long it takes her to feel my stare. I'm surprised it's taken her this long, at least five minutes. I'm not paying attention to anything but her. Hell, my sketchbook isn't even fucking open. I don't give a damn about this class, I'm just here for her.

After about five more minutes of staring at her—almost unblinking—she finally looks back at me. It's as if time slows down, and her face turns leisurely. Without a care in the world, her eyes meet mine. At first, they widen. I see a lot of emotions going through them, and she forgets I can read her like a book.

Surprise is the first emotion that crosses her face, like she can't believe I'm here. Happiness is the second one, although brief. The third one is sadness, deep sadness that breaks my heart all over again. The fourth shatters me: betrayal.

Hallie turns around without a word and gathers her belongings, then practically sprints out of the room. She leaves her coat behind, which I grab. In her haste to get away from me, she's willing to go outside in negative temperatures without any outerwear.

I run out as well, after her, and she's unlucky because my

legs are longer and way faster than hers. "Hallie!" I yell, and she only runs faster toward the 4Runner. "Wait."

"Leave me alone, Damien!"

"No," I growl, catching up to her as she approaches the car. She opens it and practically throws her stuff in, then turns around with a red splotchy face. Tears gather in her eyes when I grab her hand and pull her toward me. "I won't leave you again."

"You already left, and you made it clear you wanted nothing to do with me when you left me in the middle of the night."

"I was wrong, and I'm sorry, I've regretted it every single day of the last year."

"Good." She grimaces, pushing away from me—hard. "Keep regretting it."

"I will—by your side."

"Fuck. You. Damien." I deserve that, *I deserve that*. "You have no business coming after me."

"I want you back, Hallie," I say as tears stream down my face, and her shock makes her rear back. I guess she thinks I'm heartless just because I left, that my heart wasn't as broken as hers, that it wasn't hard to get out of bed every day. "My life has been hell without you. I need you back."

"No, Damien." My stomach sinks at her words; this is exactly what I've been afraid of. Her rejection surprises me because instead of crushing pain, I feel a renewed sense of purpose. I am getting her back if it's the last thing I fucking do. "No."

"I'm willing to share," I blurt out, and her eyes widen. "I'll share with Zayne, babe."

Her eyes close, and more tears stream down her face. "Don't call me that," she whispers.

"*Love*," I reply. "You're everything to me. I don't want a life without you—I can't have it. I refuse to leave you again. Please take me back."

"Get away from me, Damien," she growls, and it's like I've been shot in the chest. Like she's stabbing me in my side all over again. "Leave me alone."

I step back as she gets in the SUV, driving away from me and leaving me standing in the middle of the parking space. With her coat heavy in my hand, I return to my car. I don't care what I have to do to achieve it. I'm getting her back.

I'm getting her back.

March

It's been a month since I approached Hallie and talked to her. I've been following her on her days off when she's going to places alone. Surprisingly, Zayne has also been helping me with it. I don't know if she suspects or thinks I just wait outside her house, but if he wasn't helping me, I'd be doing precisely that.

She doesn't run away anymore when she sees me. Instead she gets a spark of happiness in her eyes that's reassuring, for only just a moment before they turn blank. Mainly ignoring me, she goes about her life while I observe her.

Right now, she's sitting at a coffee shop reading a book, which takes me back to when I followed her to the bookstore, and she was doing the same thing. I see it's one of the books I got her when we got the new house, and my heart clenches in my chest.

I pay for my coffee order and wait for it before I go to the empty chair at Hallie's table. Which, again, takes me back to another day, another time when we did this exact thing. Maybe I'm feeling nostalgic, or maybe I'm a sucker for pain.

Hallie looks up at me and smiles, but it drops just as fast. "What are you doing here?"

"Begging for forgiveness... again," I tell her honestly. "Hallie, love, I'll do anything if you take me back. *Anything*."

"As appealing as that sounds, I'm going to have to pass."

Fuck.

She's so damn stubborn. I see how her eyes light up when she sees me, no matter how short-lived. She has to force herself to have an emotionless face, no feelings, and a cage around her heart when she's around me. I see it, I feel it. She's not over me and still loves me, just like I do her.

How the fuck am I going to get her back?

The last year of thinking of how to get her back still hasn't solved this predicament.

"What can I do, love?" I ask her with anguish, and her eyes snap up to mine. She's been trying to ignore me, but I know she can't. Not really. She's feeling the same pain I am.

"I don't know, Damien." She replies honestly, "You hurt me so bad. In here." She places a hand over her chest and tears gather in both of our eyes.

"I know, babe. I'm hurting right there too." I sniffle. I don't even care if I'm crying in public. *Again*. "I just want one chance. *Please*."

"I don't know."

"One," I beg. "I'll show you I can share."

"You should probably stop stalking me." She smirks while looking at the pages she's clearly not reading while refusing to look at me. "It's getting kind of creepy."

"Good." I smile, and our eyes meet again. I wipe my tears, and her expression turns sad, a frown taking over her features. "I don't give a fuck as long as you take me back."

Hallie purses her lips and gets up from the chair, grabbing her keys from the table and her purse from the back of her chair. Without a goodbye, she begins to walk away from me, passing right by me. I'm not letting her go that easily this time though, so I grab her wrist over her coat, lightly squeezing once so she turns toward me.

"Hallie, babe, please." I hug her waist, pulling her toward me, and she tenses. This is the first time I've embraced her in a year and more tears spring to my eyes. I bury my face in her open coat, nuzzling against her chest. "Please," I whisper.

I look up at her to see her shaking her head, and I get up from my chair to tuck a strand of hair behind her ear. My fingers find her chin and lift it, then I bend at the waist and brush my lips over her tears, kissing my way toward her lips. Her eyes close, and she opens up for me, letting me stroke her tongue with mine as I swallow her soft moan.

Hallie pulls away first, her lower lip trembling, but she shakes her head again. "I'll think about it."

I stand there while she walks away from me yet again, leaving me behind. But she kissed me back. Even if she didn't touch me, even if she stayed as still as a statue, she fucking let me.

And that's all it takes for me to be even more determined than ever.

CHAPTER 38

Hallie

The mailman knocks on the door, soft at first, then louder. What the fuck? Sometimes I wonder if I should slow down on my Amazon purchases. They get out of control, I will admit. It's a little bit of an addiction that I refuse to own up to, and don't even get me started on Zayne. Every time he needs to adjust the dosage of his medication, he starts spending like crazy. I guess it's a good thing he has a job and we don't have many bills. Just utilities, his car payment, and car insurance for both of us. It's really not bad for being twenty-five.

The knocking gets louder, incessant, and I open the door with attitude, turning to look at the person at the door. Except it's not the mailman.

My eyes water at the sight before me, my chest sinking, feeling like there's a thousand-pound weight sitting on it. His eyes are cast down to the floor like he can't look at me right now, and my knees buckle before I can catch myself. My knees hit the ground—hard, for fuck's sake—and he finally looks at me.

"Damien?" I cry, "What the fuck are you doing here?"

He drops to the ground to help me up, flinching at my question.

"Come on, let's get you up."

His attempt at nonchalance is laughable, especially when his voice gives him away.

"I asked you a question," I reply coldly, and his sad eyes snap up to mine. "You dare to show up here after everything you put me through? I don't care that you've been following me around, or the kiss, or anything. The house is off-limits."

"Babe—"

"Do not fucking call me that!" I get up on my own and take a step back, leaving him on the ground.

Damien crawls toward me, then grabs my legs, hugging me to him. My limbs are stiff, my heart guarded. What the fuck is he playing at? He doesn't want me; he never did. A month of following me around and begging for forgiveness doesn't mean shit.

"Hallie, *please*," he begs, looking up at me from his knees. A part of me wants to relax, to calm down. He's on his knees, for fuck's sake. "Hear me out."

"You should've talked to me before leaving me with no explanation."

"Hallie, I explained in a letter."

"A fucking letter, Damien? Is that all I deserved from you after everything we've been through?"

"I couldn't do it anymore!" Damien yells, and I look around to make sure he's not bothering the neighbors. We don't need the cops called on us.

"Then why are you here?" I ask him through gritted teeth.

"Because—" He licks his lips. "Now I can. And I've told you this a million times now."

I laugh, more like cackle, doubling over with the need to scream. "Oh, okay." I shake my head, stepping back into the house, shaking myself from his embrace. "*Now* you can. I'm glad you think you can just show up after a year, saying you're fucking ready to love me again."

"I never stopped, Hallie." Damien gets up from the ground, standing in front of me, imposing and intimidating as ever. "I was just hurt."

My eyes water, but I breathe through the tears. He seems to notice and pulls my chin up to gaze into his eyes. "What about me?" I whisper. "You don't think *I* was?"

Damien looks at his shoes, shame on his face. "I know you were." He shakes his head. "There's nothing I can do to make it better, Hallie. I just want to say I'm really fucking sorry. If there was a way I could take it all back, I would, but I can't. I want to work things out. I realized in the last year that I couldn't live without you. I've been thinking of you non-stop since I left. Asking myself if you're okay. If there's a chance you can forgive me, then say it now. If there's not… then say that too."

I'm stunned into silence. I don't think there's anything that can be said right now, except I really need to think about this and what he's saying. I already told him I needed to think about it. He's being impatient.

Why now? After all this time? I don't understand why he didn't come back before if he wasn't over me. Why did it take him this long to realize it?

"Why now?"

"I was trying to get over you, Hallie…" My lower lip trembles at that, knowing I was trying to do the same thing. "But there's no getting over you. You're everything… *everything* to me."

"No." I'm not his everything. He left me. He *left*. "I'm not. You should leave."

"I'm not leaving you again," he growls, stepping closer to me. "You won't get rid of me this easy."

"But you got rid of *me*, Damien."

Damien pushes me all the way into the house, coming in with me, then slamming the door behind him. He yanks me by my arm, shoving me against the door and blocking me in with his arms. "You look more beautiful than ever, love."

My stomach drops, butterflies somersaulting in it, like trying to escape a glass enclosure. I gasp as he presses his body against mine, his erection against me. "Damien—" I moan when he bites my earlobe. "I fucking hate you," I lie.

"So let me fuck it out of you."

I neither confirm nor deny, I just stand there. He kneels and pulls down my pajama pants all the way to my ankles, then buries his face between my legs. He's like an addict that's gone way too long without their fix as he moans into my pussy.

Damien licks a path over my underwear right on my slit, and I press my thighs together. "Keep them open for me, love," he whispers against me. Then he pulls my underwear down my thighs, all the way down to my ankles, until I step out of them. Standing up, he unbuttons his jeans and pulls them down. "Hold on to me, Hallie."

I grunt when Damien picks me up, pushing me against the entryway door as if I weigh nothing. Out of instinct—or at least that's what I'm going with—I wrap my legs around his waist. With one forceful thrust, he's inside me and doesn't let up.

My head meets the door when he begins to set a fast pace, fucking me into the wooden surface, literally. I almost wonder if it's going to break. There's clearly a lot of pent-up feelings between us, and we're laying it all out on the table. The longer he fucks me, the more I want him to go harder. Then the harder he goes, the more I feel like it will never be enough.

I claw at his back over his shirt, wanting to inflict pain upon him, demanding his fucking blood. He *left* me, he left me and came back like nothing ever happened. He needs to feel some pain.

Damien brings his lips to mine, and the kiss feels like our first kiss all over again. It's electrifying, heart-stopping perfection. I don't want to love it as much as I do, but fuck me, he's so good at this. His lips are soft against mine, his full ones sucking on my bottom one. His tongue is warm as it slips into my mouth and dances with mine, and my heart flutters in my chest as he pulls away and looks into my eyes.

"Tell me you're mine."

I narrow my eyes. "You wish."

"Lie to me, love," he begs, fucking me harder. "Lie to my face."

"No." My head falls back against the door, and my lips open on a gasp as he hits against my clit over and over, creating a friction that feels fucking incredible. My first traitorous moan escapes me, and I want to fist my mouth to stop myself.

Damien smiles knowingly. "I don't care what you say, we both know the truth."

I grab his face with my fingers, digging them into his cheeks, my nails piercing the skin. I dig harder when he winces. "You hurt me," I tell him, getting emotional. "Now I'll hurt you back."

"Hurt me good then, babe."

I shake my head and release his face, and then he turns around, walks us away from the door, and drops me on the couch. I bounce when my back hits the cushions and he immediately yanks me down by my legs, positioning me on the edge. He drops to his knees and thrusts into me again, this time going slower, putting more pressure on where I need it the most.

He puts his forehead against mine, nuzzling our noses together, slowly thrusting in and out of me. It feels too intimate to share with him right now, especially when I told him I didn't want to hear him out. I grab his neck with both hands and squeeze, but he doesn't falter. In fact, it's like he doesn't feel my hands at all.

I fucking hate him right now.

I slap at his shoulders and try to push him away. Turn my face away, only he's relentless. He doesn't budge and holds my face with an iron grip until he has me right where he wants me.

Damien's lips meet mine once more for yet another electrifying kiss, and when he pulls away, tears are trailing down both of our faces. My heart stirs in my chest, some unknown and unbidden part of me softening for him, and I melt a little into the couch.

"It's always been you, Hallie," Damien whispers against my

lips. "Every part of you fits every part of me, and I'm nothing without you."

"Liar…" I reply weakly, but I know he's getting through to my heart no matter how much I don't want him to. It's inevitable. I suffered so much because I loved him. I *love* him. "You left me…"

"I couldn't stand to see you with him, babe." He shakes his head, his tears spilling on my skin. "But now… I don't care anymore."

My breath hitches in my throat. What does this mean for us? Fuck, this is confusing me. "You don't?"

"I'll take whatever you'll give me." Another kiss, another thrust. I moan when he hits the spot inside me that makes my toes curl, and he smiles. "And if you don't give me anything at all, then I'll take this moment and keep it in my chest forever, right next to my heart. *Your* heart."

Damien's pelvis rubs against my clit torturously, and I moan again as he buries his face in the crook of my neck. He groans at the sound, keeping up his movements, not changing anything. I swear this man is top fucking tier when it comes to sex. No part of him is clueless, in fact, he pays attention to every little thing and makes it happen.

I reach my hands under his shirt when I feel the tingling sensation take over my body right before I begin to shake, and I throw my head back and close my eyes when I sense the most intense orgasm of my entire life take me under, trying to drown me in its wake.

My nails dig into his back, and I wrap my legs tightly around his waist, bucking my hips to get more of him, more of this feeling washing over me. He moans into my neck when I go slack in his arms, then he begins to thrust into me, more like pound. The sounds of skin slapping against skin fill the air, and I keep my eyes closed.

His hand wraps around my face, pulling my head down, "Look at how good you're about to make me come, love." He whispers, and I open my eyes. "Memorize it." He groans, his face with an expression of pure bliss. "Or don't. I'm not going anywhere."

Within the next three thrusts, he's coming inside me, scrunching his eyes closed and bracing himself on either side of me. I can tell he wants to collapse but won't because of me, so I pull him down on top of me.

We lie on the couch together for what feels like forever before he removes his shirt and pulls out of me quickly, using it to clean me up. I place the shirt between my legs, and he carries me upstairs to my room—Zayne's and my room—and takes me to the tub. If he has noticed the change, he doesn't mention it.

Damien turns the faucet to hot, knowing how I like my baths, and it makes me almost sad that he still remembers all the little details. Although I remember his, too. He says he's not going anywhere, that he loves me, that he wants to share. But what does this mean for me? For him? For us? For Zayne and me? Is he even willing to share me anymore? I can't choose now. Zayne and I have a great life together, better than I ever imagined we could.

"What is the meaning of this, Damien?" I ask him, then let out a deep breath when he begins to wash my back with the loofah. Why is he always so fucking thoughtful? "What do you want?"

"You." He doesn't hesitate. "Us."

"Us?"

"Everything."

I swallow at that. "You didn't want that before."

"I was scared, Hallie. I thought I deserved better... but what I realized is that there's no one better for me than you."

"So, what are you asking for? Be clear with me. I don't know what you're doing here other than fucking me and confusing me even more."

Damien takes off the rest of his clothes, then sits behind me in the tub, pulling me back toward his chest. I feel his heart beating wildly against my back.

"I want," he whispers, his voice cracking, "for you to take me back. To let me live here with you again. I want to see you wake up every morning and put you to bed every night. I want to kiss you whenever I want without wondering if you remember what it feels like. But most of all, I want *you* to be *mine*. From now until forever."

A tear trails down my cheek, falling into the water. "I've always been yours." His arms tighten around me as I cry, full-body sobs taking over me as I remember the last year filled with pain, sleepless nights, and thoughts of not being good enough. None of that will disappear overnight. "I will give you a chance, Damien. But you have to prove yourself. None of this is going away that easily. I'm still hurt."

"I understand, love. I wouldn't expect anything else. I don't want it or need it to be easy, I just need *you*."

"What about Zayne?"

"What about him?"

"Are you willing to share with him?" I ask tentatively. "Or will that still be a problem?"

"I think he wants you to share *him* with me."

"Shut upppp." I laugh, "I'm serious."

"Yes, Hallie, him. But no one else, not ever."

"You two are all I can handle, babe," I tell him, and it's true. There's no fucking way I can take on more than that. These men already give me headaches and heartache. "I don't want anyone else."

"Ever?"

I turn around and seal our lips together, then look into his eyes. "*Ever.*"

That's a promise I'll never break.

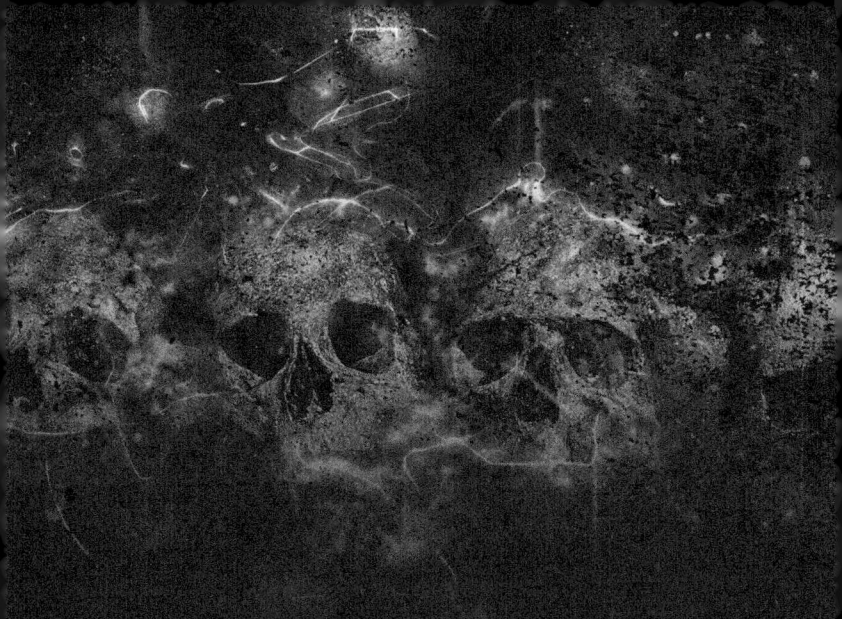

EPILOGUE

One year later

I just married the loves of my life.
 Both.
 On the same day.

Just when I thought my life couldn't get any better, Damien and Zayne both asked me if I'd marry them—at the same time. They proposed together. It was the sweetest fucking thing I've ever seen in my life.

Now a year later, I just married Damien in New York and Zayne in Ontario. Damien under my real name and Zayne under my new alias. It seemed a little backwards at first, but now it feels just right.

Hallie Carlisle.

Never in a million years did I think I would have a husband, much less two. Except here I am, on our wedding night, wearing a little white lace bodysuit that leaves nothing to the imagination.

My legs are spread open for them, and Damien is lying

between them, pushing the scrap of lace to the side to expose me to them as Zayne waits impatiently on his knees right next to him. I know they want to share this moment, but I'm not sure how they plan to do that.

Before I can even think of anything else, Damien tears the lace apart, baring me to them completely, and Zayne pushes my right thigh farther apart and up as he settles between my legs right next to Damien. They both lower themselves to me at the same time, licking me together.

It's fucking filthy, yet it feels so right.

Zayne grabs onto one thigh while Damien grabs onto the other, and their tongues are literally both on the same spot, working me, driving me fucking insane. This is the best it has ever felt, two tongues on me, so many sensations.

I moan loudly when one of them thrusts their tongue into my pussy, and the other stays on my clit, working together like they're fucking me. I hear Zayne moan into me the higher my own moans crescendo, and Damien groans when my back arches off the bed.

"Fuck," I cry out. "This is too fucking good!"

Neither one of them replies, too busy trying to push me over the edge of the tallest skyscraper to ever exist. For fuck's sake, their tongues are making me feel like I'm going to plummet to my death.

"I'm going to co—"

I don't get to finish the sentence as my body convulses, and I scream. It echoes in the hotel room walls. I'm almost sure someone's going to complain, but I don't give a fuck.

This is selfless of them, to work together on something this intimate. Fucking is one thing, but this? This is the best thing that's ever happened.

They let me come down from the orgasm enough to stop shaking before Zayne drags me to the edge of the bed with my head hanging off, "Open that pretty mouth for me, baby. Make me come, just like I did to you."

I open my mouth, wrapping my lips around his cock and sucking on the head of it. Damien spreads my legs and raises them to his shoulders, then kneels and pounds into me. There's nothing gentle about this. As Damien thrusts into me, I'm forced to take Zayne's cock all the way down my throat, and he keeps his pace fast.

It's awkward hanging upside down, taking Zayne's cock down my throat while trying to keep it together. I breathe in through my nose slowly as both their dicks pound into me, and the tears flow freely. I will give them their release one way or another, and I don't care how it happens.

"Look at you taking both of us like a dirty girl," Damien says to me, wiping my tears.

"You like when we both fill you up, don't you, baby?" I moan when Damien begins to rub my clit, and I see Zayne throwing his head back in pleasure from the vibrations. "Oh, God, Hals." I suck harder, faster, until my jaw is aching. "Yes, baby, just like that."

"Goddamn," Damien growls, and he goes faster. I can't tell if he's more turned on by the way I'm sucking Zayne's cock, or the way Zayne is going crazy over it, though honestly I don't give a damn. "That pussy looks too good, babe." Damien says, and I meet his eyes, "Is it all mine?"

"*Ours*," Zayne growls.

Damien smirks, then grins wider. "Take his cock down your throat, baby." Zayne moans when I gag on him. "Show us we're yours."

He rubs my clit harder, faster, until my chest rises and falls quickly, and it feels like I'm about to explode. I tighten my legs around his shoulders, trying to show him how I'm about to come apart.

"Oh, I'm gonna come soon." Zayne groans, holding on to my head and thrusting faster into me. Drool runs down my face, my tears mixing with it, and my jaw hurts so fucking much it feels like it's about to break. "I'm almost there—"

My spine tingles and my toes curl. I scream on his cock as I find my release, then feel Zayne's cock jerk in my mouth as he spills down my throat while Damien's thrusts become erratic. I'm shaking again, almost choking on Zayne's cum and cock, but I've never felt better.

"Fuck, fuck, *fuck*—" Damien moans, holding onto my hips tightly. "You look so fucking gorgeous when you come, love."

I swallow and more tears spill, then Zayne pulls out of my mouth, and I lick my lips. "Come for *me*, Damien." I tell him, looking at his face as his mouth opens on an 'O' as he moans, his dick deep inside of me. I feel him come, and when he looks back down at me, he bites his lip and lets my legs down.

Zayne goes to the bathroom for a second, then Damien follows when he comes back. After they're both done, I clean myself up as well. It's crazy what my life has come to, but I couldn't be more grateful.

We lie down together in a tangle of limbs, Zayne on my right and Damien on my left. One of them kisses my cheek, while the other runs his fingers down my arm, giving me a mix of feelings I can't explain.

Except maybe bliss.

It's quite possible I died, and now I'm in heaven. It feels like I'll never truly know. Having my dream life right in my grasp feels like it's not even happening, like none of it is real. How did I get here? And how did I ever get so lucky?

I used to think there was no hope for us, that our pieces were too scattered, the edges too fucked up. But God, was I ever wrong. Turns out you *can* fix the broken. They fixed me, put me back together, and made my jagged pieces fit again.

"You're ours, baby," Damien says.

"Yours," I reply.

"And we're *never* letting you go." Zayne chimes in.

I'm not sure what happens next or how this all will progress. All I know is that I love them, and they love me too.

Forevermore.

THE END

WHAT'S NEXT?

Thank you from the bottom of my heart for reading *Tattered Bodies*! Please don't forget to review if you enjoyed the book. Reviews are so important to indie authors like me. I am forever grateful for your support!

If you'd like to be part of the community and talk about the series, join the Facebook Group, Ruby's Darklings.

Lastly, there will be two more books published in 2023! I hope you stick around!

Stalk me:
My website is authorshaeruby.com
Sign up for my newsletter at authorshaeruby.com/newsletter
Follow me on Facebook at Facebook.com/authorshaeruby
Join my Reader Group at Facebook.com/groups/rubysdarkling

AFTERWORD

If you've read my books, you know how passionate I am when it comes to shedding light on mental health. A lot of you know by now that I've struggled with Bipolar 1 Disorder, anxiety, and PTSD. I want to bring awareness to this taboo subject, one that a lot of people are afraid to talk about. This book was very heavy, but it needed to be written. There's a beauty to healing from trauma, even though it's never linear, and doesn't always happen. Regardless, I want to say that it's okay to not be okay. Seek the help you need, and find your community, your people. *I can be one of them.*

So much love for you,
Shae Ruby

ACKNOWLEDGMENTS

Tattered Bodies was a journey filled with ups and downs, highs and lows. As you already know, it's a heavy fucking book. I am so excited to have finished this series, but also a bit sad that it's over. It feels oddly like a breakup, and I'm in mourning right now. Nevertheless, I'm thrilled about what's next this year!

First and foremost, I want to thank YOU, my readers. None of this would be possible without you. I can't begin to explain how grateful I am that you've taken a chance on me. I have no words, just happy tears, and love from the bottom of my heart. Thank you for not one, two, but THREE chances. WOW, I am stunned and so freaking grateful.

To my husband, Conner, thank you yet again for being my person. The one who will drop everything to give me a few hours of uninterrupted writing and not once complain. I know how difficult it is to be married to a writer. The hours are long and the time spent together is short. I love you.

To my mother, thank you as always for being here for me. I love you more than words can express and there's too much to say to fit in here, so I won't even try.

Michayla, Alyssa, Aliveah, Fay, Alice, CL, Danielle, Emily! You're literally the best of friends ever, and I can confidently say that. Thank you for putting up with me and always being here. I love you all!

Kylie! You're incredible and I appreciate you so much more than you'll ever know. The support I've found in you is UNMATCHED. I love you! Thank you for our friendship. I will cherish you forever.

To my amazing alpha and beta readers: Jay and Alyssa, I couldn't have done this without you. You went above and beyond the expectations for the role you played, you loved on my story, you poured so much of yourselves into it, THANK YOU! I love you both so much.

To my Street Team and TikTok team, you guys are AMAZING!! Thank you for all your help. My marketing would be terrible without you guys (we can laugh about this). No, but seriously. You're ALL incredible and I am so grateful. Here's to many more books together!! I love you!

I also want to thank my team!

Angie from Lunar Rose Editing Services, I literally could not have done this without you. You have been such a big influence in my life, a friend, and an amazing partner. Here's to many books, babe!

Quirky Circe, as always you're incredible and your talent is out of this world. I can't wait to keep working with you on all my covers to come!!

Stacey with Champagne Book Design, it's always a pleasure working with you! You have made my books even more gorgeous and I can't wait to see what else we come up with!

Lastly, I want to thank my social media followers both on Instagram and TikTok, my Facebook page, and my Readers Group. None of this would be possible without you spreading the word about my book!

All of you mean everything to me.
With love,
Shae Ruby

Printed in Dunstable, United Kingdom